Red
States

Red States

Anthony P. Jones

Brown Bag Books

Brown Bag Books Productions LLC.

408 Keithwood Ct.

N. Chesterfield, VA 23236

Library of Congress-in-Publication Data

Jones, Anthony P., 1958-

Red States / Anthony P. Jones

p. cm.

ISBN 978-0-9715899-4-0

1. CIA – Fiction. 2. Washington > (D.C.)— Fiction. 3. China – Fiction. I. Title

For Dad, Sybil, Vicki and Lee...there from the beginning!

Acknowledgments

As always, my first thank you, goes out to God for the creative ability, an undying perseverance towards success and for teaching me to trust that, He's got this! In 1994, my mother insisted that I write a story I shared with her— *Operation Smokeout* was the results. Parents see things in us, we have yet to discover— pay attention!

When I first shared this plot with three people charged with keeping this country safe, more than one set of eyebrows went up. One minute, we were sharing a cup of coffee at Starbucks at Virginia Center and a day later, I was emailing a CIA liaison, who made sure, I somewhat stayed on track.

I am nothing without my team! Releasing a book that can compete with any out there requires skilled professionals. I simply have the wild ideas, Vicki Moore (who believes in me and it's no easy task) makes sure the words fall in the proper order, things are spelled correctly, even when I invent words and makes sure I have some type of coherent flow (not always easy for a dyslexic A.D.D. mind). Any mistakes you find are entirely mine. If you're reading this then the cover caught your attention. That is due to the highly skilled, Scott F. Sherman, who has brought all my covers to life. My brother, Chris took the cover shot—that was an adventure. Ed Jones, my uncle, frat bro and all-around good guy covers my formatting. Sybil Scott continues to read every word I write. She praises me, yells at me and in the end, tells me if anyone will want to read what I've written.

My go-to information folks, Jim Clemente, Tim Clemente, Kevin Daly, Marie Daly, Paul, my CIA liaison and Dr. Raphael Joseph Wilson, my best friend since the day we met in 1979!

Where's a guy without family? Dad, Mike (you started this by sharing your story), Chris, Marty, Anne, Melissa, you guys are the best! My kids, Nick, Morgan, Alex and Cassidy— I am proud of you guys! Rowan, my grandson and running buddy— you're the best wing man a guy can have!

Stacy Young, Ken Mathis and James Curtis, your encouragement has kept the ball rolling! Le'Ander Nicholson came in to manage me, talk about a monumental task. Somehow, he was able to keep me on tasks to get this book in your hands. Dr. Ray (yes, another Dr. Ray), who keeps it real and constantly tells me to "Make it happen!" Your

friendship means the world to me. Meghan Avegno, who showed up to encourage me through the final process and, who has helped me to understand gratitude— she also got me hooked on Oprah's Super Soul Conversations. Kipling Wilson II a producer, who paid me one of the highest complements concerning my writing— I love OMEGA! To everyone, I failed to mention, please know that I am forever indebted. Finally, to my readers— without your gracious attention, my voice would be silent!

One last thing— reading the words any writer has placed on paper is akin to lifting the hood of a car to view the engine, you get the opportunity to see how things work in our heads. **PLEASE share your thoughts in the form of a review**. Reviews encourage others to read our works, which enables us to continue providing our readers with new material

Chapter
1

In a near-empty warehouse just south of Beijing, a slight man, shaken with fear, sat naked on the cold concrete floor. The stench of death, mingled with cigarette smoke, permeated the stagnant air. A single overhead light shone upon the man whose arms were bound at the elbows and his legs at his knees. In addition to discouraging any attempt to flee, this method of binding alleviated the need to explain the unsightly rope burns or bruises around the wrists or ankles.

Several well-armed men sat upon bales of heroin encircling the detainee and tossed ashes from their cigarettes towards him. In an attempt to avoid the hot ashes from hitting his face, he turned his head and caught sight of a pair of pasty legs protruding from a gap in the bales. Death was obvious and he shivered knowing what awaited him.

The men were unreceptive to his whimpers and promises of wealth in exchange for his freedom and yet they were amused by his attempts to persuade them.

A back entrance of the warehouse raised with the grinding sound of the garage door opener, that plunged the pleading prisoner into silence. A gleaming pearl-finish white Rolls Royce cut its lights and pulled into the warehouse, stopping in front of the men. The men seated on the bales of heroin stood and one of them approached the car, opening the back door. A pair of white alligator cowboy boots silently met the floor. Zhang Ju eased his six-foot two-inch frame from the car. His suit, shirt and tie matched his white boots; not a speck of dirt was anywhere near him. A white cattle prod dangled from Zhang's wrist, which he firmly clutched and pointed towards the associate who'd opened the door. Speaking in Mandarin, he gave the order. "Get the canes from the trunk."

Another of the associates grabbed the cowering man by the hair, forcing him to stand. The detainee watched as Zhang put on his white Stetson and stepped from the side of the car. The moment he saw the cattle prod a stream of urine flowed down his legs and puddled around his feet. He began to shake helplessly.

Zhang stabbed the prod into the man's behind giving him a shock. "I detest the smell of piss. One would think the Premier of State Council would have a little more dignity and self-control. Xie Yi, you are a disgrace! Did you expect because you're a ranking member of the government that you would be spared my wrath?"

Xie fell to his knees splashing the urine he'd deposited on the floor. "I just need a little more time. I can get your money."

Zhang prodded him once more. "It's no longer about the money— you have blatantly disrespected me, challenging my reputation. If I extend favoritism to you, every miscreant in the country will expect the same. Not to mention the fact that I will appear weak to my colleagues; every Triad boss would try to gain an advantage over me. We can't have that."

Xie didn't attempt to lift his face from the urine. "I'll do whatever you want. Please don't kill me."

"I have no doubt that you will." Zhang leaned to the associate that opened his car door and pointed to the canes. "Choose a man to help you and beat him like the dog that he is. Stay away from his face and hands. We don't want unnecessary questions raised."

Zhang reached into his jacket pocket, retrieved a white leather cigar case, opened it and pulled out a Cuban cigar. He pulled a lighter from his pocket and lit a bundle of Yuan that Xie brought in an attempt to buy additional time and used the burning notes to light the cigar. He arrogantly blew a stream of smoke in Xie's direction and watched his men savagely beat him. When he appeared lifeless, Zhang waved his hand for the men to stop. "Clean him up and bring him over here."

The associates poured a bottle of cheap vodka over Xie's open wounds to kill any germs and to inflict additional pain. He was far too exhausted to complain or twitch in response to the new throbbing.

The associates turned on a high-pressure hose and aimed it directly at Xie. The water's force rolled him over the floor washing away the blood, urine, and vomit that covered Xie's body. Another of the men drenched him with a bucket of soapy liquid and cut away his restraints. "Wash yourself!"

Xie cautiously moved his hands across his battered body as best he could and stood slowly. He tried to steady his stance before the hose blasted him again. With nothing to lean against, he held one hand out as if commanding the water to stop.

Dripping wet, Xie was plopped onto one of the bales of heroin and a table slid into place in front of him. Zhang took a seat on the opposite side of the table and unrolled a map. His hands caressed the paper, smoothing the map on the table. He looked over seven areas outlined in red, but never raised his eyes to meet Xie. "For years, I have provided you pleasures that you have doled out to your cronies so that you could advance within the ranks of government. I warned you when you began to gamble that only those with great control over their emotions should be involved in such a risky endeavor. But you did not listen."

Xie did not have the energy to raise his head to face Zhang. "Things were turning around for me. I was on a streak; I only needed a little more time."

"Spoken like a true addict. The only way for you to win is to stay away from all forms of gambling and pay me what you owe me." Zhang reached in his pocket and pulled out a switch-blade knife. He pressed the button and the blade shot forward. He used the tip of the blade to dig beneath his fingernails.

Xie raised his head to face Zhang. "I can do it; I can make your money back. I'm using a new system; I won't fail."

Zhang stabbed the blade of the knife into the center of the map. "You will no longer gamble. Is that clear? If I hear of you going to any of the other seven Triad families, I'll let you watch as I slowly kill your wife and daughter." He waved his hand around the room. "Of course, I will let my associates have their way with them first."

The weight of shame pushed Xie's head down again. "What can I do to pay you back? It will take me some time to raise four million Yuan."

Zhang rocked the knife back and forth to free the blade from the table. He used the tip of the blade to trace the red outlines on the map of China. "You will recognize each of these areas controlled by the other seven Triads. The Silent Dragon Triad has the smallest area, yet we have grown faster than any other. We are much more innovative. We were the first to recognize the billions that could be made transporting our citizens to the United States. I want to expand my business west." He slid the tip of the knife and tapped the center of the United States."

Xie gasped air as he tried to grasp the meaning of Zhang's words. "To understand how I might be of assistance, I would need to know more about your plan." His eyes darted to the knife blade resting in the United States. His predicament aside, he began to sense that there could be a solution to his problem as well as an opportunity for greater personal wealth.

Zhang noticed the look in Xie's eyes; it was the same one he got when placing a bet— excited, euphoric, uncontrollable greed. It was the reaction that Zhang expected to see. "Other than having to kill you and your family, there is only one way out of your predicament. To implement my plan, you will arrange several meetings, beginning with General Wen Gan."

The fire in Xie's eyes grew even stronger. "Arranging a meeting should not present a problem. Might I suggest that you bring me on as a consultant? My influence can smooth out the rough spots, pay you everything I owe and provide me with any left-over compensation."

Zhang looked at his associates. "Did anyone get a look at Xie's balls? They must be made of steel. He nearly loses his life because of his indiscretions and yet, he wants to place another bet." He lifted the knife and placed the tip of the blade under Xie's chin. "You will do as you're told. Then, I may take your usefulness into consideration. I am not a cruel master, yet even a cruel master occasionally tosses his dog a bone."

Chapter
2

In the Kowloon area of Hong Kong, two friends sat at a table at Felix, a restaurant and bar atop the Peninsula Hotel.

Just after finishing her music set, Jenna joined her friends at the table. She pulled out a chair and hurriedly sat down. "Has he been to the men's room yet?"

Cole tossed his hands in the air. "What's with the bathrooms here? Between the two of you, you've mentioned them at least four times. I haven't even had my first drink yet; I'll get there soon enough."

The two women looked at each other and laughed. "Whatever you say."

Zasha pointed behind Cole. "It looks like your first drink has arrived."

Cole turned to the waiter. "But, we haven't even ordered yet."

The waiter sat linen napkins in front of them. "Pardon me, sir, but the two gentlemen at the bar sent the drinks over. He said you look like a Scotch man, so he sent the Balvenie 40. If there is something else you prefer, I would be happy to provide it."

Cole took the glass never having tasted the Scotch. "No, this will be fine."

The waiter turned to Jenna. "As usual Miss Roulette, Crystal Head martini and the same for your friend." He set the last glass down. "Are the drinks to your liking?"

The three friends held their glasses up and nodded towards the men that sent the drinks from the bar.

A brilliant smile crossed Jenna's face. "Zasha, you're going to love this girl. The guys who sent the drinks are Russian, wait till they hear your name."

Cole took a drink of his Balvenie. "Do you think they're going to like 'Black Russians?' Or do you think they'll get that it's just a name?"

Jenna popped him on the hand. "Zasha, where did you find this guy? Black Russian, you mean Brown sugar, don't you?"

"Didn't I tell you when I called; he flew the 747 over here." She took a sip from her drink. "When I told him that I was meeting you here, he decided I needed protection."

Jenna stood and put her hand on Cole's back. "Sounds like bullshit to me. I'm going to get Vladimir and Borka."

"What kind of name is that? I mean, I recognize Vladimir, but Borka?" Cole tried not to stare at the men sitting at the bar.

"It means fighter. Borka is probably Vladimir's body guard; I don't know, I never asked." Jenna bounced over to the bar and kissed Vladimir on the cheek.

Cole took another drink and looked at Zasha. "Having a body guard can't be a good sign. What do you think he does?"

Zasha shrugged and sipped on her drink. "Oh, there's no telling— especially if they're friends with Jenna. But, I've never known her to do anything too outrageous."

Jenna returned to the table with Vladimir and Borka. They sat and she started the introductions. "Vladimir and Borka, this is, Zasha…"

Vladimir stood and took Zasha's hand and kissed it. "Your name means defender of mankind. I can tell by the simple touch of your hand that you are a special person. What is your last name?"

Zasha smiled broadly. "Davis."

Vladimir's face wrinkled. He observed her caramel-colored skin and long hair that was a mixture of blond, auburn and brown. Instantly, he could tell its color was not produced from a bottle. "Was your mother Russian?"

Zasha shook her head side to side. "No. She said that I was the end of the line so she found a name that started with 'Z' to drive the point home for my dad."

Cole worked hard not to roll his eyes during the exchange. He shook both the men's hands as they were introduced. "Thanks for the Scotch, it's great, probably the best I've ever had."

Borka nodded and smiled, but didn't try to speak. Vladimir touched Borka's back. "Sorry, but Borka doesn't speak very much English. He does understand quite a bit. I can act as translator for you." Vladimir turned to the bartender and swung his finger in a circular motion signaling him to bring another round.

Cole reached in his pocket for a credit card. "I'll take care of this round."

Vladimir grasped his arm tightly. "I wouldn't think of it. Tonight, everything is on me." Through the jacket Vladimir felt the strength in Cole's arm and spoke to Borka in Russian. *"He's a big son of a bitch."*

Borka laughed and pointed to Cole.

"What?" Cole observed the two men laughing at what appeared to be his expense.

Borka pointed to Cole's arm. "Big muscle." He put his arms in the air and flexed straining the fabric that contained his bulging biceps. He slapped Cole on the back nearly spilling the glass of Scotch and pointed to the women. "Good man."

Cole noticed that both men were in great shape, but Borka was without a doubt the larger and least refined. He turned his attention to Vladimir. "What do you guys do?"

Vladimir looked at Jenna. The smile never left his face. "I am a banker; Borka works for me. What about you and Zasha?"

Cole nodded to Zasha. She sat her glass on the table and folded her hands. "I am a journalist here on assignment. I'm studying how repatriating Hong Kong has affected China after so much time has passed."

Vladimir laughed and reached back taking the fresh drinks from the waiter, who'd just arrived. "That's easy; all of China has become capitalist-communists. They see the wealth that Hong Kong has achieved under British rule and they want to taste what has been the standard here for years." He handed the drinks out saving Cole's for last. "And you, sir?"

Cole polished off the first drink and exchanged the empty glass of the full one. "I'm a 747 Captain for United Airlines."

"That explains the musculature. Pilots must remain in great shape to control such a large plane." Vladimir raised his glass. "To new friends and the diversity, they bring to the world."

They clinked glasses and took drinks to seal Vladimir's toast. Zasha was the first to pull her drink down. "I'd like to go back to your comment about China."

Vladimir spoke to Borka, who produced a case from the floor. Vladimir opened the case presenting a host of Cuban cigars. "Ladies, do you mind?"

"Not as long as I can have one." Zasha reached for a cigar.

"I knew this lady was special." Vladimir held the travel humidor for Cole to make his selection. Vladimir then selected his favorite from the lot, pinched the end and put it to his lips to test the flow. Judging that it was perfect, he struck his Dunhill lighter and held the flame to the cigar before turning his attention to Zasha. "Please pardon the history lesson, but for thousands of years, China was one of the most advanced civilizations on Earth. Nearly a thousand years before the United States began drilling for oil, the Chinese had already begun. They also developed the first seismograph around the same time. Leaping forward, in 1921 Communism came to China and in 1949, Mao Tse-tung brought his brand of communism here. That single event plummeted China back to the dark ages. Of course, this did not affect Hong Kong, which was a British colony since 1841. When Hong Kong was returned to China in 1997 the change was inevitable. It would be easier to stop the incoming tide this afternoon than stopping Hong Kong's influence on the rest of China."

Cole swirled the Balvenie in his glass as he would a fine wine. "Don't you think that U.S. President Nixon had a hand in bringing China out of the dark ages?"

Vladimir put the cigar to his lips and drew deeply. The blue smoke rolled from his mouth as he spoke. "It is impossible to ignore his contribution; however, the overwhelming change has happened over the past ten or so years. Incorporating such a wealthy state into their fold did more to stimulate their growth than anything else. That event made it impossible for the government to hold back their citizenry from wanting or attempting to gain what Hong Kong has had for years. Believe me; people will always follow the money."

Zasha took a puff from her cigar. "So, it is your conviction that Hong Kong is responsible for the exponential growth China is experiencing."

"Simply examine the data for yourself. China is purchasing oil rights all over the world. They purchased a mega oil well just sixty miles off the coast of the United States from Cuba. How is it your geologists missed that one?" Vladimir took a long drink followed by a sustained puff from his cigar. "China is the largest acquirer of raw materials in the world. They have U.S. steel mills that are exclusively contracted to provide them with goods. I'm sure you had occasion to read the story about Nine Dragons Paper Company."

"Yes." Zasha pointed excitedly in Vladimir's direction. "Zhang Yin left China with her husband, who was a dentist. They went to the United States with only enough money to purchase a broken-down Dodge Caravan. She began going to trash dumps and asking for paper, which they gladly gave her. Now she's a billionaire. They say that in five years, she amassed a fortune greater than Oprah Winfrey or J. K. Rowling. And to top it off, the people of the U.S. get the paper back after it's been recycled and used to package the products we import from China."

"Precisely, the people here apply creativity to solve their shortcomings. There are nearly a billion and a half other Chinese looking to do something similar to what Zhang Yin has done; something they would never have dreamed possible ten years ago." Vladimir signaled the bartender to deliver another round.

The drinks continued to come. Vladimir ordered them faster than the table could drink them.

Beginning to feel the effects of the alcohol, Jenna reached for a menu. "I don't know about you guys, but I need something to eat."

Zasha touched Jenna's arm. "Why don't you show me to the lady's room?"

Vladimir took the menu. "Please, allow me to order for the table. They have exquisite dishes here. I'll order enough for us to share."

Zasha waited until they were out of earshot of the table. "How do you know these men?"

Jenna was a bit unsteady on her feet and took Zasha's arm. "What do you mean?"

Zasha looked back over her shoulder. "They don't seem to be your run-of-the-mill banker types, if you know what I mean."

"Vladimir was one of the first people I met when I got to Hong Kong. He's always been kind to me." Jenna pushed the bathroom door open.

"What are you doing for him?" Zasha took a tube of lipstick from her purse and freshened up her face.

"Are you getting all 'reporter' on me? We're not in college any more; I'm a big girl now." Jenna ran in a stall, gave a heaving moan and threw up.

Zasha shook her head listening to the retching sounds and the splash of the water. "Are you okay?"

"Yeah, I just haven't eaten in a while. I'll be fine after I eat." Jenna dry-heaved a couple more times ensuring that her stomach was empty.

"You shouldn't try to keep pace with the Russians; they're professionals when it comes to alcohol." Zasha put cold water on one of the cloth hand towels and handed it to Jenna. "We're not at

Georgetown and these guys aren't the type we used to deal with in school."

Jenna put the cold cloth against her face and then held it on the back of her neck. "Don't worry about Vladimir, I can handle him. At least I've known him longer than you've know Mr. United Airlines Captain. I think I should be giving you advice. That man is cocky…but you always did like them a bit self-assured."

Zasha smiled. "The word is confident. What else would you expect from a guy who used to fly E-2C Hawkeyes for the Navy?"

Jenna emerged from the stall. "You got all that from a short cab ride from the airport?"

"I'm a journalist. It's my job to get information and I'm good at it." She handed Jenna her purse. "Here, put some lipstick on; you look a little washed-out."

At the table, Cole was happy to have food on the way. Pilots have a notorious reputation for being drinkers, but he had no intention of pushing the envelope trying to keep pace with Vladimir, who didn't have to consider an FAA license. He watched the two men speaking in Russian without a clue as to what they were saying.

Vladimir set his drink on the table. "Pardon us for being rude. We didn't mean to remove you from the conversation."

Cole nodded and took a drink. "Don't worry about it; I've had lots of practice at being ignored. When I was married, my wife routinely ignored me. As soon as I got divorced, she wouldn't leave me alone."

Vladimir raised his glass. "Here's to the wisdom of living single."

Cole laughed heartily. "I'll drink to that. Love is like a parasite, you never feel the fangs sink in, but you have to deal with the aftereffects for ages."

Vladimir laughed so hard his head fell back and he slapped the table. "You can use your experience as an antidote whenever you begin to feel woozy around a woman. Speaking of that, Zasha is quite something don't you think?"

Cole hunched his shoulders. "She seems to be. We just met; I haven't really had a chance to get to know her."

Vladimir pointed to Cole. "What does that matter? If you like what you see, you should fuck her!"

Vladimir felt a hand on his shoulder. Jenna sensed the tone of the conversation. "Are you being boorish?"

He took her hand and kissed it. "I wouldn't dream of it. Cole was just displaying his phenomenal sense of humor. I'm glad you all gave me the opportunity to share the evening with you. I couldn't have asked for better company. This is considerably better than the client I'll be seeing in Beijing."

Zasha looked at Cole and quickly turned back towards Vladimir. "When are you going to Beijing?"

Vladimir sat his glass down. "I have to be there day after tomorrow."

"That's an interesting coincidence; Cole and I will be there as well." Zasha warmly clasped Cole's arm. "He's doing the hard work; he's flying the plane."

"Excellent! I'll make sure that we are on the same flight." Vladimir winked at Cole. "If he doesn't mind, maybe we can sit together."

Cole tossed his hand, holding his palm up. "I was about to say, 'it's a free country,' but then I remembered where I was. If Zasha wants the company, who am I to argue?"

Zasha gazed at each of the men. "This isn't getting ready to become a testosterone fueled battle is it?"

Vladimir's eyes remained fixed on Zasha. "Not in the least. I just appreciate good company."

"What about Borka here?" Zasha nodded towards the near-silent man.

"Borka, fine." He put his hands together and laid his head over as if he were sleeping.

"That settles it; I look forward to a flight filled with stimulating conversation." Vladimir noticed the waiter approaching with their food. "Ah, the food has arrived. Let's eat so that we can get back to our drinks."

Chapter
4

Zasha stood, leaving two untouched drinks on the table. "Cole, why don't you see me to my hotel room?"

Vladimir stood kissing Zasha's hand. "I can hardly wait to see you on the plane." He turned to Cole and slapped his back hard enough to make Cole take a step forward. He leaned close to his ear. "I'd give anything to trade places with you tonight."

Cole pointed to the table. "Have another drink, the feeling will pass."

Vladimir laughed and plopped back into his chair. "Have a lovely evening."

Zasha beckoned Jenna having her move a comfortable distance from the table. "Are you straight girl?"

Jenna waved the table off. "Yeah, I know he's got plans tonight and he's going to have to adjust them. All he did was talk about you; I'm not serving as a surrogate. He can pay somebody for that service."

Zasha took Jenna's shoulders in her hands. "You might want to cut off the drinks. I wouldn't want you to have a repeat session of what occurred in the bathroom. Plus, you know how you get when you've had too many. All Vladimir will have to do is breathe hard on your neck and he'll get whatever he wants."

Jenna's hands went to her hips. "Just as you said earlier tonight, we're not at Georgetown any more. You might be right about the drinks though; I am starting to feel horny as hell."

Zasha shook her read. "I knew it. Do you want to leave with us?"

Jenna looked towards the table. "I think I'm going to hang out here a while longer. I'll see you and Cole tomorrow."

Cole and Zasha left the restaurant arm-in-arm. The hotel was only a couple of blocks away, so they decided to walk.

Cole waited until the front door of the hotel was in sight. "I hope you warned Jenna. Those guys are Russian mafia; I guarantee it."

"I'd have to agree. He dumped money as if it were regenerating in his pocket. I've never known any banker to be that frivolous. Hell, that Scotch you were drinking cost nearly five-hundred and fifty dollars a glass and he ordered you at least six." Zasha sat on a bench facing Victoria Harbor.

Cole put one foot on the edge of the bench and leaned his arms on his knee. "Mob sources always have insight on information. The trip to Beijing may yield something of value."

Zasha crossed her legs and folded her arms across her chest. "I was thinking the same thing. He could have gone on a long time when he began to espouse conversion of the rest of China to be like Hong Kong. He touched on things we already know, debt, acquisitions of any oil field willing to be sold, and the phenomenal gathering of resources. I want to know what he knows that's below the surface."

Cole looked out across the water. "You're going to have to be careful around Jenna. You're sure she doesn't know what you really do?"

"Yeah, she was long gone before I got into the training program." Zasha leaned forward. "Jenna's a good person; she's got a heart of gold. But she could never handle her alcohol. She's been known to divulge things that were originally meant for her ears only. So, unless there's something we need to disseminate, it's best not to mention it to her."

Cole bent his head. "You mean like out real mission here?"

"Yeah, something like that." Zasha looked up sharply. "Hey, did you catch any of what they were saying at the table when we were in the lady's room?"

"My Russian is a little rusty; I thought this was a Chinese mission." Cole looked down and laughed. "Vladimir was telling Borka what he wanted to do with you. And just in case you were wondering, Borka was going to get to watch."

Zasha's face twisted. "Pig!"

"Yeah well, you're the one that has to sit with him on the way to Beijing. You may want to check with headquarters to find any details on him. He could be ex-KGB. If so, he'll have to be watched much closer." He pulled an iPhone from his jacket pocket. "Did you tell Jenna where you were staying?"

Zasha dropped her face in her hands. "Ugh, yes, I didn't expect to be hanging out with Russian mafia."

Cole pushed a button on his phone and began to scan Zasha's clothes and purse for any planted bugs. "You'd best check out the room as soon as you get there."

"Good idea. We're going to have to be extra vigilant. The briefing didn't include anything about the Russian mafia. During the flight to Beijing, you might consider getting both their pictures and check them out with Langley." Zasha pulled her iPhone out and checked for messages from CIA headquarters, which would have come in under a completely obscure ISP.

Cole cleared his throat. "I guess we're going to have to appear to be a lot closer once we get to Beijing, so that we can explain all the time we're spending together. I guess you'd better work on that *after-glow*. Or if you prefer, I can help you work on achieving a blissful state."

Zasha stood and patted her butt. "Kiss my ass, Cole."

Cole grinned. "Gladly, just pull up that dress and show me which cheek you want the hickey on; I'll make it in the shape of a heart.

Zasha shook her head. "You're a sick bastard."

Cole took her arm and interlocked it with his. "And you wouldn't have it any other way."

Zasha stabbed him in the ribs where she knew that he was ticklish. He jumped and grunted as they walked through the front door of the hotel. She ran her fingers through the back of his hair. "We'd better make this look good." She pulled his lips to hers and they kissed effortlessly. It lasted long enough so that there was no mistake of passion, yet short enough to make him want more.

Cole punched the elevator call button. "Sure, you don't want me to come up with you?"

"I think we both need the rest. Besides, if Vladimir has someone watching us, I don't want him to think I'm easy. We just met, remember?" She reached up and wiped the lipstick from his lips.

He held her gaze. "You're such a tease."

Zasha grabbed his belt at the buckle and pulled. "I think you'd better let some of that steam out."

The elevator door opened and Cole held it open for her to get in. He followed her in and punched the button for her floor. As he was stepping off, she pinched his butt. He spun around quickly. "I'm going to take a cold shower! No, no, I think an ice bath may be more in order."

Zasha looked away. "You could always call that singing group."

Cole's face wrinkled. "Who's that?"

The doors of the elevator began to close. "Rosey palm and the five fingers." Zasha giggled and waved letting her fingers fall one at a time into position.

Cole walked out of the hotel with a blank expression on his face, but he could do nothing about the uprising in the south.

Chapter
5

Xie Yi waited for General Gan at the Laoshe Teahouse. Xie's status allowed him to secure an area away from the common abstractions, such as music performances and plays which were commonplace. He sipped tea designed to soothe. In the short time that he'd been at the table, his shaking hands subsided enough to avoid questioning.

In his mind, the story was straight. All he had to do was present the facts, appeal to the General's vanity and seal the deal. If he needed reinforcement as to the importance of his task, he only needed to pull the pictures Zhang gave him. In the series of pictures, Zhang's associates bound a girl, took turns raping her, but the most frightening picture was saved for last. As the last two associates took their turn with the girl, a third slit her throat.

The image shook Xie all day. The pictures arrived at his office delivered by currier. Xie recognized the currier as one of the men that assaulted him at the warehouse.

General Gan arrived and acknowledged Xie's position by snapping a salute. "General Gan reporting as ordered, sir."

Xie stood, bowed and offered the general a cup of tea. "Please be at ease, General, this is not a formal meeting."

The general accepted the cup and took his seat. "You neglected to provide an agenda for today's meeting, Premier Yi. As such, I did not file this with my office. It will not appear on any official records. If your intent was different, inform me now so that I may contact my assistant to correct my oversight."

Xie sat his cup down. "That won't be necessary, General. I appreciate your discretion." He refilled his cup and offered the general a refill as well. "Recently, General Gan, I came into possession of a manifesto you wrote concerning the United States. I found it quite interesting considering we have worked closely with them for over thirty years."

"May I speak freely, sir?" General Gan placed his hands flat on the table. "I take it that you don't agree with my position. I drafted it at the request of the President. We were searching for solutions to the shortages plaguing our nation; this simply made the most sense."

Xie reached out and touched the general's arm. "I think it was brilliant!"

General Gan didn't move or speak right away. The acknowledgement was a first. He tried running different scenario through his head, but was having difficulty processing. His hands found their way back to the sides of his teacup. "It's an unusually simple plan. All the parts are already in place; very little training would be required for our soldiers."

"Simplicity is where the true genius of the plan lies." Xie refilled Gan's cup.

The general accepted the tea and bowed. "If you don't mind me asking, what is your interest in the plan? The President suggested that we would keep it secure until the timing was right."

"A man with a mind as great as yours must find it humbling to have such a perfect plan shelved. I think that an offer may present itself for you to test your plan. That is, if you're willing to sidestep protocol. Shall we call it product testing? By the time anyone is the wiser, they will be helpless to stop it. And you will go down as a great innovator." Xie bowed and raised his cup above his head.

Gan eyed Xie curiously. "What would be required of me to test my plan?"

Xie looked into his eyes. "Just your experience and your silence. No one can know what we're doing until our methods are proven. At that point, you will be handsomely rewarded. My benefactors are not without means."

"I welcome the opportunity to exchange ideas with your contacts. If we are to proceed a mutual understanding is essential. I wouldn't want discomfort on either side to cause any type of misunderstanding. Injury is far too prevalent when everyone's not on the same page." Gan nodded and finished his tea.

Xie spun the tea cup in his hand. "My people are anxious to meet with you. If you will, be here tomorrow at 5 p.m. I will send a driver for you."

Gan spun the tea cup with one finger. "This is most unusual."

Xie shook his head. "There is nothing to be concerned with. The meeting is nothing more than routine."

"Premier Yi, I do not enjoy surprises. It's in everyone's interest to be on the level concerning this engagement. I will expect to see you when I arrive with the driver. If I'm uncomfortable for any reason, I will see to it that no one leaves this establishment." Gan sat his cup down and stood. "Please forgive my assertiveness, but there's no reason to leave anything to chance...it's best for everyone involved."

"I quite agree. I look forward to seeing you tomorrow. It will be the beginning of a revolutionary and rewarding endeavor." Xie stood and bowed to the general before casually walking from the tea room.

General Gan drank his last bit of tea. Whatever Xie had planned it didn't involve anyone else within the power structure of China's government. As innocuous as this meeting appeared, it could be fatal under the wrong set of circumstances. Failing to notify the President could be one such incidence...informing him could be another. He decided it best to gather additional information that could be used to his benefit before sharing any details.

Chapter
6

Zasha and Cole decided they needed some one-on-one time before joining Jenna for the day. Vladimir had a way of forcing himself into situations. The plane ride to Beijing was an example. Zasha would have to keep him company rather than concentrate on the files she planned to review. Cole could not intervene. Even though computers controlled most of what the plane did, he was captain and was responsible for everyone on board. It was a hell of a CIA cover, albeit one that served him well in the past.

Cole met Zasha at the entrance of her hotel dressed in running clothes. They began a steady jog along the waterfront. It was a perfect way to sweat any remaining alcohol from the night before out of their systems.

Zasha set the pace taking a few strides to regulate her breathing. "Did you get a chance to review this morning's briefing?"

Cole nodded. "Yeah, they haven't picked up much chatter from Beijing. We've got a conference call this evening before dinner. I think we should mention Vladimir in case they have something on him. He may prove useful."

Zasha was breathing effortlessly despite the pace she'd set. "We've got to see what Jenna knows as well. She's definitely involved with Vladimir. She was always nosey. I expect there was a little bedroom talk passed around; especially with the amount of alcohol he consumes."

"We can't neglect the effect that Borka may have had on her. Intimidation can be a powerful motivator to keep your mouth shut. I don't see Borka as the type that ignores the potential for loose lips. If he is the bodyguard, his job is to avoid any slipups." Cole looked around as if he suspected to see Borka. "I can tell you, he wouldn't hesitate to kill any of us if he suspected that we would harm Vladimir"

Zasha glanced toward Cole. "I can see why you were assigned to this detail; you always suspect the 'stone-cold killer' on these cases. We're just here to look into exportation of Chinese citizens. The Triads have transformed human smuggling into a fifty-three billion dollar a year business."

Cole turned towards her. "And you think they wouldn't hesitate to kill you if you interfered with their enterprise? The question I have is why they have increased their shipments. China is becoming the largest economic force in the world. They are buying up oil rights and raw materials all over the globe. The kind of growth they're experiencing has got to translate to the people and yet, they are exporting their workforce in record numbers."

Zasha glistened with sweat. She looked over to Cole, who didn't seem to be quite as affected by the run. "Think about it for a second; people are an asset. The Chinese have bought up so much of Africa that parts of that country could soon resemble cities here. Look at the Northwest corridor of the US; the Chinese have a significant imprint there. As Little Italy shrinks to one block in New York, Chinatown continues to grow; not only there, but DC and every other large city in the US."

Cole watched his feet hit the pavement for a few steps. "The oil project in Cuba is going to require an enormous amount of manpower; you can bet the majority of them will be Chinese citizens, they don't typically trust outsiders. The proximity to our coast and the relationship with our government will most likely allow ease of entry. That would give the Triads another base for exporting citizens. They are already in Guatemala, the Dominican Republic, Jamaica, Puerto Rico and some studies suggest that the Taiwanese Triad has purchased the nation of Belize as bases for transporting citizens to the US. If their objective is to flood the US with their citizens, Cuba would be an excellent location."

"That's what we're here to find out." Zasha turned the corner and picked up the pace.

As they neared the hotel they spotted Borka sitting on a bench drinking a cup of coffee and eating a pastry. He waved and held out the pastry. "Breakfast."

They waved back but didn't slow their run. Cole observed Zasha curiously. "Do you believe me now? He's out here to check us out, or do you think I'm being paranoid?"

"Okay, I'll admit that it does seem to be a bit more than coincidence. Maybe Vladimir sent him to find out what we were doing." Zasha looked at Cole with a huge smile on her face. "He might want to know how close we've gotten."

Cole stopped running and grabbed Zasha's arm pulling her to his body and kissed her hard on the mouth. He looked past her head to make sure Borka was watching. "That ought to send a clear signal."

Zasha took a second to compose herself. Her eyes couldn't hide the surprise on her face. "Don't start anything you can't finish."

Cole took off. "I'll race you to the shower."

Zasha looked at her watch. "There's no need to run, we've got plenty of time before we have to meet Jenna. Besides, part of our assignment was to appear to be developing a relationship to explain the time we're spending together."

"I take my duty seriously." Cole grabbed Zasha's behind.

She jumped and returned the favor. "I guess it's okay as long as you realize it's work."

They didn't look back to see if Borka was following them, but they expected he was. They entered the glass elevator in the hotel and kissed long and passionately during the ride to Zasha's floor. The display would give Borka something to report to Vladimir if that was his intention.

Zasha opened her door and pulled Cole in. As soon as the door closed she turned to him and pulled his shirt over his head and ran her hands over his muscle-bound chest and arms.

Cole put his finger over her lips gesturing for quiet. He reached behind and freed his iPhone and signaled for her to do the same. Borka's appearance made him cautious and he wanted to scan the room for bugs. The scan didn't take long. There was only one placed behind the lamp on the nightstand.

Cole left it in place showing it to Zasha. He pulled her to the bathroom and turned on the shower. The momentary interruption did little to cool the passion rising in them. He pulled her close, kissing her deeply. "We'd better make this look good." He slid her top off and they pressed their bodies together.

Zasha slid her hands beneath his shorts freeing him with little effort. She saved him the trouble and did the same with her shorts before stepping into the steamy shower.

Cole followed, more excited than he could remember. The full-body shower sprayed them from the top and sides tantalizing their nerves that were already on edge.

Zasha pulled Cole's mouth to hers and resumed the kiss that brought them to her room. When his hands squeezed the most firm, round butt he'd ever held, she effortlessly wrapped her legs around his back. Their steady rocking provided waves in the water as rhythmic as the ocean, rising and swelling, growing in intensity.

Air rapidly escaped their noses because their mouths were locked. Cole's strong arms pulled Zasha's hips closer melting their bodies in the dance. Her arms shot around his back. They both could feel their muscles becoming ridged and they pulled tighter in anticipation for the release that was about to come. For the first time since entering the shower their mouths parted to release the groans of pleasure radiating over their bodies.

Despite a flash of weakness, their bodies remained fused savoring every second of pleasure. Zasha laid her head on his shoulder. "Did you save any for the show that they're expecting in the bedroom?"

Cole kissed her on the neck. "I thought this was just the appetizer. I can't wait for the main course."

Zasha looked into his eyes. "Are you telling me it's going to get better than this?"

Cole pulled her closer. "With someone as delectable as you, I can't see it getting anything but better."

Zasha nibbled the nerve plexus between Cole's neck and shoulder sending a wave of excitement throughout his body. "Then I guess we'd better get ready for round two."

Chapter
7

Jenna arrived at Zasha's hotel room ahead of schedule and just minutes after Cole left to change. Knowing that it would be considered crude to walk through the hotel lobby half naked, Cole left behind his boxers upon Zasha's suggestion. A bug wasn't the only thing Vladimir had at his disposal; Jenna would be expected to confirm what he'd heard.

Zasha answered the door making no attempt to hide the glowing smile on her face. "Come in, Cole should be here shortly."

Jenna stepped through the door and immediately began scanning the room and sniffing the air. "I know that look on your face. It's the same one you wore at Georgetown after you got some. Besides, it smells like sex in here."

Zasha sat in a chair and used her foot to push Cole's boxers further under the chair. "I don't know what you're talking about."

Jenna dove at Zasha's feet and grabbed the boxers. "Here's the evidence…you little slut."

"I am no slut." Zasha stood and reached for a bottle of Ralph Lauren's Safari for women. She dabbed a small amount on her wrist and let a single drop fall between her ample cleavage. "I am however extremely satisfied!"

"I don't believe this; I've never known you to sleep with a guy that you've known for less than six months. I used to think it took you that long to get horny." She threw the boxers across the bed. "Are you sure you want me along with you guys today? The last thing I want to do is get in the middle of fresh, ravenous sex. You know how territorial men can be after they've gotten a piece of ass."

"We'll be fine. Cole isn't the type to be possessive." Zasha slid on a pair of sunglasses and a straw hat. "What do you think?"

Jenna looked at the boxers on the bed. "I think that I was always the 'rainbow coalition' when it came to dating and you never added cream to your coffee; no matter who was asking. When did you start messing around with White guys?"

Zasha cocked her head to one side. "I've been a journalist for ten years now. During that time, I have learned to recognize people for what's in their hearts, not what they look like."

Jenna got a wicked smile on her face. "Yeah, but you said that all White guys had little winkies."

Zasha blushed. "Then I suggest that Cole look into his background...that man's packing."

Jenna grabbed Zasha's shoulders. "What have you done with my friend? This isn't the same person I went to college with. This one has changed beyond recognition."

Zasha raised her sunglasses and looked into Jenna's eyes. "A leopard never changes her spots...oh sure, we may use them to camouflage ourselves in the bushes, but when we come out, we're still leopards." She let her statement sink in for a second and then took Jenna's hand. "Come on, Cole will be waiting for us in the lobby.

Cole could tell the moment the ladies stepped off the elevator that Jenna knew about the deed. To drive the point home, he walked over to meet them and kissed Zasha deeply on the lips. What do you say we begin with a little lunch before venturing out into the city?"

Jenna looked at Zasha. "I think some of us could use the nourishment to rebuild our energy levels...lunch seems in order." She didn't try to hide the fact that she was staring at Cole's crotch after Zasha's 'packing' comment."

Cole watched Jenna for a second. "If you'd like, I can arrange for a private viewing."

Jenna didn't hesitate. "That's okay; I often find imagination much more appealing than reality."

"Ouch!" Zasha reached for Cole's hand. "What was that you said about lunch?"

Cole was unmoved. "I read about three food districts here on the main island. Lan Kwai Fong has the coolest-sounding name, but from what I can gather, it's just like the stuff we can get at home. Causeway Bay seems to be the most authentic of the island

and Stanley is said to be the most romantic, or should I say, it has the most unique ambiance." He turned to Jenna. "Why don't we defer to the local lady to point us in the right direction?"

Jenna's wryer grin returned to her face. "I'd say there's been enough romance already today, so why don't we go with authentic."

"Sounds good to me." Zasha started towards the taxi stand.

They arrived at the Zhi Wei Shanghai restaurant in the Causeway Bay food district of Hong Kong. The restaurant won numerous awards and promised to be a tantalizing selection for lunch.

Cole ordered a bottle of wine to get things started. The relaxed atmosphere of the restaurant allowed their conversation to flow and the menus to remain on the table untouched.

After accepting the wine as satisfactory, he held up his glass for a toast. "To good friends and good food." Their glasses clinked above the table. "Speaking of good friends, maybe we should have invited Vladimir to join us for lunch."

Jenna pulled the glass from her lips. "That's quite alright; I get to see plenty of him. I want to spend time with my old college roommate."

Zasha allowed the wine to slide down her throat. "That's very nice of you. I gathered from the body language last night that the two of you were close."

"A more accurate description would be 'fuck buddies,' it's complicated. Vladimir doesn't allow himself to get too close to anyone." Jenna's eyes darted between Zasha and Cole before taking a long drink from her glass.

Cole sat his glass on the table. "That's an interesting observation. I would have guessed that you were closer than that. He indicated how intrigued he is with you."

"I thought you were a bit sharper than that. Haven't you learned to identify a person pissing to mark their territory? Don't get me wrong, he is good to me, but he would be happy to have a taste of your brown sugar." Jenna looked into Zasha's eyes.

Zasha sat her glass down and folded her hands over it. "I told you earlier, I'm no slut. What makes you think that I would be interested in Vladimir?"

Jenna grinned. "You were always attracted to powerful people. You said yourself that a leopard never changes its spots."

"I stand by that statement and I'm dealing with all the power I can stand at the moment." Zasha looked over at Cole.

His face was nearly scarlet both embarrassed and pleased by her comment. "If you don't mind me asking, what is the nature of your relationship with Vladimir; other than being complicated 'fuck buddies' as you stated?"

Jenna laughed and took another drink from her glass before holding it towards Cole for a refill. "Vladimir is not the type of guy anyone wants to cross. As I've said, he's been good to me. He's made sure that I have been comfortable here in Hong Kong. I have steady singing gigs; he's fronted the money for my CDs and arranged for distribution and airplay so that they sold. Jazz is big here in Hong Kong, but the support doesn't hurt."

Zasha involuntarily frowned. "So, he provided you with a loan from his bank to record your CDs and made sure that they would be successful?"

Jenna stopped in mid-drink and kept her lips near the rim of the glass. "He's never loaned me a penny. I guess you could say that he produced the CDs. I wouldn't want to be a borrower of Vladimir's; he's not very kind to people who don't pay him back on time."

Cole swirled his wine. "What do you mean by that?"

"Let's just say that Vladimir is not your traditional banker." Jenna took a drink from her glass and let her gaze fall to the table.

Zasha and Cole looked at each other. The look on her face expressed the fear she felt for Jenna. She placed her hand on Jenna's. "Honey, do you think that you should be involved with someone like that?"

"Too late for that. I told you, it's complicated, you know that I always liked the bad boys." She took a drink. "Or they like me; I'm not really sure which."

Cole signaled the waiter to bring another bottle of wine and distributed what was left of the first bottle among the three glasses. "Do you have any reason to fear what Vladimir may do to you?"

"I can handle him. He's a pussycat as long as he gets what he wants. I don't plan to ruin my good thing." Jenna drained her glass as the waiter arrived with a fresh bottle.

Zasha lifted her menu and opened it. "Let's see what this place has that makes them so famous."

Cole joined her. "That sounds like a great idea. What do you recommend, Jenna?"

Jenna's eyes were distant. She spoke as if in a fog. "Just about everything on the menu is good." She looked at Zasha. "Order for me; I'm going to the little girl's room." She left the table without another word.

Zasha watched her leave. "I'm more worried about her than I was last night. She all but confirmed what you expected, Vladimir must be Russian mafia."

Cole put the menu down and shifted his attention to Zasha. "It would seem so. Jenna was right about one thing; she doesn't have anything to fear as long as she does what he wants. Talking to us about his business probably doesn't fit into his wish list."

Zasha tapped the rim of her glass. "Hopefully, we'll learn a bit more about him this evening during the conference call."

Cole reached out for Zasha's hand. "You're not going to be able to take him too lightly during the flight to Beijing tomorrow. Maybe Jenna can shed some light on what he's going to be doing there."

Zasha looked towards the area of the restaurant where Jenna walked. "I'd better go check on her; she really seemed out of it."

Jenna was blotting tears when Zasha walked in. She continued facing the mirror when she began to speak. "I always seem to mess things up when men are concerned."

Zasha pulled her close and hugged her tightly. "You'll be fine; you've just got to change your outlook when deciding who to get involved with."

Jenna's tears flowed again. "I don't know what to do. It's not like I had a career singing jazz in the US. At least here, I have a following. My CDs sell really well. I don't know what else to do."

"If you want to get out of here, I've got contacts back home. A friend of mine is the head of the music department at Xavier University in New Orleans. He's friends with the Marsalis family. Once he hears you sing, you won't have a problem making it back home."

Jenna's tears subsided and she smiled. "You always were little miss sunshine. How do you propose I tell Vladimir? He's not going to sit by and let me leave. I've actually made him a lot of money."

Zasha waved a finger back and forth. "Don't worry about him. If you want to get out, Cole can get you a plane ticket and we can set you up in New Orleans."

Jenna's face slid into a frown. "What are you going to do; write a story that gets me free? Vladimir's not going to let anyone stand in his way if he wants me back here."

"We've got connections. He won't be a problem!" Zasha wiped away the remaining tears on Jenna's face. "You let me worry about the details. All you need to do is give me the word that you want to get out of here."

Puzzlement was pasted on Jenna's face. "What is it that you're not telling me? Did journalism turn you into some kind of superhero? I can't just waltz out of here, that would be putting you in harm's way."

"You'll just have to trust me; I can make it happen if that's what you want." Zasha leaned on the sink. "Do you know why Vladimir is going to Beijing tomorrow?"

Jenna shrugged. "He's got some big financing deal he's looking into. I really don't know the details, but he's really excited about it. He said if the deal works out that it could make him one of the wealthiest men on the globe. Whoever he's meeting must be powerful. The only people in China that wield that kind of power are the Triads and the government."

Zasha looked at the floor and slid her hand over her head. "Why don't we forget about Vladimir? I just want you to give some serious consideration about my offer."

Jenna put her hand under Zasha's chin and lifted her head. "Are you going to tell me how you are able to guarantee my safety if I decide to take you up on your offer?"

Zasha looked deep into Jenna's eyes. "Have I ever let you down when I made you a promise?"

Jenna shook her head side to side. "No, but this is my life we're talking about and yours as well."

"All the more reason I'll make good on my offer." Zasha hugged Jenna again. "I'm so worried about you."

Jenna laughed. "Yeah, this is about the biggest mess I've ever gotten myself into. I'll think about your offer."

Chapter
8

At the completion of their outing, Cole arranged a separate taxi to take Jenna home. He knew Borka was not able to follow him thus his hotel room was bug free. Rather than chance prying ears in the open, he and Zasha would hold the conference call in his room.

The call went through without a problem and they expected to hear the voice of their handler on the other end. Instead of the familiar voice, they were surprised with another. "Do you two ever do anything the easy way? You're supposed to be in China to gather information about the Silent Dragon Triad. How in the hell did you get involved with Vladimir Nikitin and Borka Petrov?"

"Director Carson?" They answered in unison. Cole held out his hand giving Zasha the floor. "Well, sir, it was quite by accident. We met an old college roommate of mine, who's here in Hong Kong and she's involved with Nikitin."

"Goddam! You two are playing soccer with a hornets' nest. Petrov is a stone-cold killer. He's the muscle and Nikitin is something of a mega loan shark. He provides funding for all types of questionable projects worldwide. He's ex KGB and is involved with the illegal arms trade, drugs and anything else he can exploit to make a buck. Our estimates put his net worth somewhere north of a billion and a half. You'll do well to steer clear of him."

Cole cleared his throat. "Well, sir, that's going to be a bit difficult. He's on my flight to Beijing tomorrow. He's become smitten with agent Davis and has arranged to sit next to her during the flight."

Director Jessie James Carson often said that his name reflected his 'white trash' upbringing. When excited, he occasionally slipped backwards. "Ain't this just fucking great? I've got two agents not content to deal with the fastest growing Triad in China; they've got to play in the biggest festering shit-pile they can find."

Zasha remained as assertive as ever. "Sir, based on a conversation between Miss Roulette and me, Vladimir Nikitin is headed to Beijing for a deal that promises to make him one of the world's wealthiest men. If it's not a deal with the Chinese government, it's bound to involve one of the Triads. It could very well be related. Regardless, anything this big has to be something we need to know about."

Director Carson blew a long airy whistle. "What else does your friend know?"

"I'm not certain she has details, but she is aware of what he does and the power he wields." Zasha looked at Cole, who seemed to be taking it all in.

"Agent Davis, let me be clear; if Nikitin finds out she's been talking to you, she is as good as dead. Petrov enjoys making messy examples of anyone who crosses Nikitin."

Zasha didn't wait for any additional comment. "Which brings me to another point: Jenna, Miss Roulette, is open for extraction. I've told her we can help her start over in New Orleans. She's a jazz singer..."

"Jenna Roulette sounds more like a porn star." Carson caught himself. "Sorry, that wasn't fair. Go on."

Zasha shot Cole, who was working hard not to laugh out loud, a dirty look. "Thank you, sir. Jenna may have additional information that she would be happy to share in return for her safety."

"What time is your flight in the morning?" Carson reached for a pen and pad.

Cole took the question. "We're leaving at oh-eight hundred."

Carson readied his pen. "Is Petrov on the flight?"

Cole nodded. "According to Nikitin, that's affirmative."

"Agent Davis, give me your friend's address. I'll have a couple of Marines from the Embassy pick her up as soon as you confirm that both Nikitin and Petrov are on the plane." Director Carson wrote the information on the pad and handed the sheet to an assistant. "We'll discuss your plans for her when you return."

Chapter
9

At 8:15 a.m. a black Range Rover rolled down the street and stopped two doors from Jenna's house. Two burly men wearing Timberland boots, jeans, baggy shirts hanging outside of their pants, sunglasses and baseball caps worn backwards, exited the car. They lingered on the sidewalk, pretending to talk while they took in the neighborhood.

Inside the car, a third man scanned everything in sight using a binocular-like device designed to pick up heat signatures. Once he completed his scan, the two men on the sidewalk heard a crackle in their ears. "It's clear, proceed to the house."

The two men walked at a brisk pace towards Jenna's front door. When they arrived, one pushed the doorbell and the other stood with his back facing the door.

Jenna cautiously approached the door. She'd not expected company and she knew Vladimir and Borka were at the airport; they left her house earlier that morning. She peered through the peephole on the door and was alarmed to see one of the men with his back towards the door and his hand resting beneath his un-tucked shirt. "What do you want?"

The man facing the door reached in his shirt and pulled out an ID and held it in front of the peephole. "Miss Roulette, we're from the American Embassy. Zasha Davis sent us."

Jenna's heart was racing and she found it hard to concentrate. The men had not spoken with Russian accents, but that really didn't mean a thing. Vladimir had all types of people on his payroll.

Sensing her apprehension, the man produced a hand-written note and slid it under the door. "Ma'am, this may help. It's a note from Miss Davis."

Jenna reached down and got the note unfolding it, immediately recognizing Zasha's handwriting.

Jenna, these men are Marines from the American Embassy. They are here to safely get you out of Hong Kong. Do whatever they tell you. They are your friends. See, I always keep my promises.

Zasha

The Marine at the door looked around. "Ma'am, it would help if we could get moving. Are you comfortable enough to open the door?"

Jenna was more frightened than she'd ever been. From the handwriting she could tell the note was Zasha's and if these men were not who they said they were, Zasha was probably already dead. "Okay." She said, but still hesitated with the lock.

When the door opened the two men hurried inside and the one who had his back to the door pulled an Uzi from beneath his shirt. He put a finger over his lips signaling Jenna to remain quiet. "Are you alone?"

Jenna squeaked and nodded. "Did Vladimir send you?"

The Marine who rang the doorbell gently took Jenna's arm. "No ma'am. We're here to save you from him. Agent Davis sent us."

"Agent?" Jenna looked at the Marine with her face knotted. "Did you say Agent Davis?"

The Marine nodded. "Yes, ma'am and we don't have a lot of time. Get a couple of changes of clothes. We'll send someone back for anything else you need. We've got to get you to the Embassy as quickly as possible."

Jenna jumped into action grabbing a couple of pairs of jeans and three blouses. "Let's get out of here. I don't want to be anywhere around here if Vladimir finds out."

The black Range Rover pulled as close to the door as possible and the first Marine hustled Jenna to the car. The second Marine followed bearing the Uzi for anyone who may be paying attention. If Vladimir questioned the neighbors, the Marines wanted this to appear to be an abduction, which undeniably, it was.

Chapter
10

Cole's voice came over the plane's loudspeaker. "Ladies and gentlemen, we'll be at our cruising altitude in just a few minutes and then I will turn off the seatbelt sign. Until then, please let a flight attendant know if they can be of assistance. Flights are on time today and we should be touching down in Beijing in just under four hours. Thank you for flying United Airlines. We look forward to serving your travel needs in the future.

Vladimir bumped Zasha's ticket to first class so that they could sit together. He called the flight attendant that was just a few feet from his seat. "I'd like three Bloody Mary's; make two of them double."

Zasha turned from the window. "Getting started a little early this morning, aren't you?"

Vladimir laughed and slapped his leg. "It's never too early to drink vodka, especially if you're a Russian. Vodka is mother's milk. It's good for the heart."

"I bet you consider the tomato juice as a serving of vegetables for the day."

Vladimir slapped Zasha's leg and let his hand lay there. "I knew I liked you, you're a thinking woman."

"I'm also a lady." She moved his hand to his seat. "Do you come to China often?"

"Yes, I have several business ventures here. I'd say I spend fifteen to twenty days a month here. China has the fastest growing economy in the world. I provide financing for several areas. They have a relentless need for raw materials to meet their demands." The drinks arrived and Vladimir handed the single to Zasha and the second double behind him to Borka.

She took a sip of her drink and sat the glass on the tray. "So, you provide financing to acquire the raw materials?"

"Not exactly. In many cases, I broker the deals that provide what they need. My financing is concentrated in the shipping arena. I've helped acquire ships they need to deliver products to their buyers, such as the United States." He drank nearly half of the Bloody Mary in one gulp.

Zasha suspected the alcohol was necessary to stabilize Vladimir's blood alcohol level: 'hair of the dog.' In most cases, she knew that it would also loosen lips, but Vladimir was a seasoned pro. The drink would probably just settle his nerves. "I assume you find your work very rewarding?"

Vladimir polished off the drink. "In more ways than one. Since I've been involved with China, I have not had to consider losses. My clients here always pay on time and they never balk at the interest rates. At the end of the day, everyone is pleased."

Zasha took a sip of her drink giving her time to shift her approach. "I bet since you spend so much time here that you've noticed the great changes the country has undergone since Hong Kong came back into the fold."

"Since 1997, the growth here has been exponential. Hong Kong became somewhat of a template of the potential the entire country could expect. In truth, the greatest effect has been in the large cities. Most of the countryside is as poor as ever." Vladimir ordered another drink. "Eventually, wealth will begin to spread across the country, which is great for me."

"Would you say that most of the people leaving China to go to the United States are from the poorer areas? I mean if they are aware of the vast growth, why leave?" Zasha lifted her drink and held it against her lips without drinking. "The other night, you said that the people always follow the money. Considering China's phenomenal growth, I would think the money is here or at least on its way."

"Wealth here is not as widespread. In the rural areas of China farmers don't make twenty-two hundred yuan a year. In the urban areas it's about 5300 yuan per year. That's not even eight hundred American dollars a year. They can make that in one a month in the U.S. Wouldn't you leave?" Vladimir took a large gulp of his second drink.

Zasha shook her head considering the question. "Everything they know is here, their families and friends. The U.S. is unknown territory, it can't be an easy transition. I can't imagine leaving everything I know to go to a foreign land."

Vladimir pulled the glass from his lips. "Zasha, you are far too innocent. Money trumps everything! Without it, you are nothing and so, the people will do whatever it takes to acquire it. A new land is a means to an end."

"Following the money, not waiting for change; even if it means losing their lives or ending up in perpetual servitude. Where is the freedom in that?" Zasha turned to the window.

Vladimir sighed. "It's not like anyone's holding a gun to their heads...unless of course, they can't pay. Freedom lies in their ability to choose the life they want. With success stories such as Mrs. Yin at Nine Dragons, people believe the risk is well worth it. As long as there is a disparity and chance for great reward, the Chinese will continue to leave and there will be people standing by to help them."

Zasha cocked her body to one side. "You can't be serious, helping? Am I supposed to believe that the people helping do this completely altruistically? From what I've gathered, the people leaving are packed onto boats like sardines. That is no different than the slave ships transporting, what they considered cargo to people waiting for free labor."

Vladimir allowed his eyes drift to, Zasha's arms noting their brown color. He took a gulp of his drink and exhaled an extended sigh. "Given your heritage, I understand why you feel that way. The difference is, these people are making a choice. The people piloting the ships are providing a service that helps them reach their goal."

"As long as 'helping' is exorbitantly lucrative, there will be people willing to send these people to an uncertain fate." Zasha was genuinely irritated, but tried to keep her voice neutral.

Vladimir shrugged. "As I said, no one is making them do anything. I've heard that hundreds of people are turned away because there is a lack of space on the transportation vessels. You can imagine how little value is placed on the lives of the people leaving, so you can guess how over-crowded things are. An industrious entrepreneur could guarantee a safe comfortable trip and charge three times the money. I can assure you, people would be knocking his door down."

Zasha turned to Vladimir. "Sounds to me like you've already calculated the risk-return ratio. Is there no room for humanity in this situation?"

Vladimir smiled. "Any banker worth his salt knows all potential competition, legal and illegal. As far as humanity goes, comfortable safe passage fills that bill."

Zasha shook her head. "If it is illegal, then the trip is anything but safe. I don't view you as a callous person, I hope you're not involved."

Vladimir's eyebrows rose and her pulled his drink to his lips. Without a word, he drained the glass.

Chapter
11

Vladimir waited on the plane with Zasha until everyone else left and Cole appeared from the cockpit. "Thank you for the pleasure of your company during the flight. I wish that I could join you two for dinner later, but I'm afraid that duty calls." He kissed Zasha's hand and turned to face Cole.

Cole extended his hand and shook Vladimir's. "Next time we get together, the drinks are on me." He leaned over the seat reaching for Borka's hand as well.

Zasha's purse toppled over spilling its contents on the floor. She reached down rapidly gathering the contents. She stood moving to the center isle of the plane. "Thank you for the information. Your insight will be helpful during my interviews."

"How long will you be working here in Beijing?" Vladimir's question was meant for Zasha, but he looked at Cole.

Cole touched his chest. "Were you asking me? I'll only be here for the next couple of days." He touched the door leading to the cockpit. "I've got to get this bird back across the pond."

Zasha felt all eyes on her. "I will be here in Beijing for a couple of days and the next week or so, I'll be visiting several other areas of China."

"You'll have to let Jenna know when you'll be back in Hong Kong. We should get together again." Vladimir motioned to Borka, who grabbed their bags.

Zasha didn't flinch at the mention of Jenna's name. She hoped that Vladimir didn't try to call Jenna for the next few days. Instincts told her that Vladimir wasn't that type of guy. He would probably be meeting some other woman he kept in this area. Jenna was convenience not love. "I'll do that."

Cole held his hand out giving Vladimir and Borka the jet bridge. He held Zasha back. "I've got one more thing to do in the cockpit before we leave. It was nice meeting you gentlemen. I look forward to doing it again."

As soon as they were down the jet bridge, Zasha plopped in a chair. "We're going to have to contact Langley right away. He's here for something big. He said that his concentration here is shipping. Based on what Jenna said, it could involve one of the Triads. The Chinese government wouldn't need him to broker any type of deal; they have all the resources they could possibly need."

Cole looked down the jet bridge. I don't think we should risk making a call from here. We're also going to have to keep a watchful eye out that he doesn't have us followed. You didn't tell him where we are staying did you?"

Zasha shot Cole an incredulous look. "I'm not a rookie. Of course, I didn't."

"I'd like to know what he's up to." Cole grabbed his flight bag and held his hand out for Zasha."

She grinned. "That shouldn't be too hard. I slipped a tracking dot into the cuff of his pants."

"So that's what the toppled purse was all about. Damn, you're good." Cole started down the jet bridge and stopped. "You'd better send a text to HQ so that we can get another team on them."

Zasha pulled out her iPhone and pressed send. "I'm a step ahead of you." She switched to a different screen and the blinking red dot placed Vladimir at the entrance of the airport near the cab stand. "They're about to leave the airport. Are there any private areas in the pilot's waiting area where we can make a call?"

Cole cocked his head towards Zasha. "I think we can make it work. Let's get moving. The sooner we contact Langley the better I'll feel."

Chapter
12

Zasha and Cole waited for the call to go through. They heard Director Carson speaking with Oscar Fenton, who the Director sent for as soon as he'd been made aware of the text message.

Carson sat behind his desk tapping a pen against it pushing it through his fingers, flipping it and repeating the nervous procedure. "Are you two in a secure location?"

Cole closed the door of the pilot's lounge and walked to a chair next to Zasha. "For the moment, we're in the pilot's lounge, alone."

"Then, let's not waste time." Carson stopped tapping the pen and sat forward resting his elbows on the desk. "Why are you tracking the Russians?"

Zasha uncrossed her legs and leaned towards the phone. "Sir, Nikitin is here on business. He indicated that he brokers deals involving shipping. During the flight to Beijing, he talked about the numbers of people willing to give up everything for a chance to come to the U.S. Based on the conversation with Miss Roulette, Nikitin is here for a deal that will bring him a considerable fortune. The Chinese government doesn't need his assistance for ships. The Triads are another story. They are raking in billions illegally transporting Chinese citizens to the U.S. It's the only scenario that makes sense."

Oscar Fenton looked to the Director for permission to speak. "If what you're saying is correct, you two need to back off. Nikitin and Petrov know you. Showing up where they happen to be would be a disaster."

"Which is why I sent the text for an additional team." Zasha was on the edge of her seat.

"Good work, Agent Davis." Carson resumed tapping the pen. "We had a chance to debrief Miss Roulette at the Embassy in Hong Kong. She confirmed that Nikitin was into some heavy shit.

She mentioned someone that Nikitin referred to as the 'man in white.' That's who she believes he is in Beijing to meet."

Zasha cleared her throat. "Is Jenna okay?"

Oscar took the question. "As we speak, she's on a military transport en route to Washington. We may have some further questions for her before she makes any additional moves. I think it's best we change her identity before she embarks upon any new endeavors."

"Good idea." Cole reached for Zasha's hand. "The last thing we need is for Nikitin to come looking for her."

Oscar continued. "It's against my better judgment to keep you two there in Beijing, especially if Nikitin is involved with transporting illegals to the U.S."

"But, sir, we have a head start. It would take too long to get another team up to speed." Zasha looked at Cole. "We can handle this and steer clear of Nikitin. Besides, he is convinced that I am here to gather information related to change in China."

Carson stopped tapping the pen. "She's right. We're going to have to leave them in place for the moment. I don't want to hear of you two having dinner with Nikitin. Steer clear of him at all cost. It's going to be difficult enough to get Chinese citizens to talk about how they're leaving the country, but that is the only thing you are to do. Do we have an understanding?"

"Yes, sir." Zasha and Cole answered in unison.

"Agent Peterson, I'll arrange for someone else to take your flights for the next couple of weeks. I want you right by Agent Davis' side for the duration. Get the information and get out. I'll expect continuous updates."

"Consider it done, sir." Cole looked at Zasha as the line went dead. "It seems like this thing is bigger than we expected."

Zasha dropped back in the chair. "The Triads have been responsible for bringing nearly one hundred thousand illegals a year to the U.S. for some time. If they're looking to get whole ships for the same purpose then we're facing an enormous escalation. There's something we're not seeing here. I intend to find out what it is."

Chapter
13

Vladimir and Borka kept a watchful eye to see if they were being followed. KGB training made them paranoid of all situations. At the first opportunity, Vladimir would contact his sources to see what information could be found on Zasha Davis and Cole Peterson. The timing of their appearance didn't feel like coincidence to him.

Vladimir had the taxi drop them off at a Tea House. They walked in and straight through to a back door, where a car was waiting for them.

An excessively large man stepped from the white Rolls Royce and used an electronic wand to scan Vladimir and Borka for bugs. Carefully, he moved the wand over their bodies. Pronouncing them clean, he opened the door, motioned them into the car.

Zhang Ju sat in the back seat with a glass of Balvenie Scotch in one hand and a cigar in the other. "Gentlemen, I trust your flight was uneventful?"

"It was as quiet as ever." Vladimir relaxed in his seat.

Borka rubbed his hand across his mouth, attempting not to speak.

Zhang sat his glass down and handed one to each of the men. He filled them with Scotch and lifted his glass to meet theirs. "We are about to embark on the most important venture of our lives."

The two Russians took a hefty drink from their glasses. Vladimir sat his down. "I don't mean to be rude, but this is business."

Zhang signaled to the giant next to him, who lifted a suitcase and unzipped it. The case was filled with American hundred-dollar bills. Zhang lifted several stacks out placing them in a briefcase and handed it to Vladimir. "This is the down payment, ten million American dollars."

Vladimir caressed the case. "Excellent, when do we learn the details of your plan?"

Zhang pulled out a humidor and offered the men a Cuban Trinidad cigar. "These were once only available from heads of state of Cuba. I secured a large amount before they disappeared." He grabbed the bottle of Scotch and refilled their glasses. "We have some minor details to complete here in Beijing then we'll take a short trip for the conference. There, the details will become clear. I can assure you, you have done nothing as grand or important as what we are about to do." He tapped the glass separating them from the driver and the car pulled into the streets of Beijing.

A BMW motorcycle pulled next to a Mini Cooper and the man inside the Mini Cooper lowered the window. The motorcyclist pulled a GPS device from his leather jacket. The screen lit up revealing a map of the Beijing area where they were. A blinking red dot indicated the direction the Rolls Royce was traveling.

"How long will the transmitter be active?"

Agent Julie Hu sat the GPS on the seat and took off her helmet letting her long black hair fall free. "It's good for at least seventy-two hours. According to Langley, Davis put it in the cuff of Nikitin's pants. It's new technology, which is why it wasn't detected. When a detection wand is activated the tracking, device emits a jamming signal canceling its presence. We should be able to find out where he's headed and who he's with."

Agent Chin looked at the screen in his car. "Let's hope they stop for lunch somewhere. If we're lucky, we can plant a secondary device."

Julie tucked her hair and put the helmet back on. "They're only about two miles away. I'm going to head back in the direction they're coming from and try to get a look. You get ready to pick them up and see where they're headed. Give them plenty of room. Fenton said that both Nikitin and Petrov are ex KGB. They'll be looking for company."

Chin put the window up and spoke into the mike against his face. "If you get confirmation, let me know what we're dealing with."

Julie gunned the bike, speeding off. She intercepted the oncoming car a couple of minutes later. The dark visor on her helmet shielded her eyes and she slowed passing the car. She went a block past before contacting Chin. "Holy shit, you're not going to believe this. They're in a white Rolls Royce."

Chin cranked the car and readied to pull out. "Did you see who they were with?"

Julie turned at the end of the block and pulled over. "There's only one person in Beijing who rides in a white Rolls Royce with white rims…Zhang Ju, head of the Silent Dragon Triad. Whatever's up, it's going to be big."

Chapter
14

Agent Chin knew that there was no reason to follow Zhang's car too closely as long as the transmitter was working. The white Rolls stopped a mile ahead of where Chin was positioned. He causally pulled past their location and parked on the opposite side of the street. "Julie, they've stopped at the Laoshe Teahouse on Qianmen Western Street."

Julie pulled the GPS from her jacket and noted the blinking dot. "You haven't made any attempt to make closer contact, have you?"

"Not yet, but we're going to have a hell of a time getting ears on their location." Chin looked in his case to see what might work.

"I've got a plan. Don't do anything yet, I'll be there in a few minutes." Julie turned her bike around and sped off in the direction of the teahouse. "Chin, turn around and meet me. I'll be five blocks south of their location."

Chin cranked the car and turned around to meet Julie. When he saw her bike, he made a 'U' turn in the middle of the street and pulled behind her bike. He rolled down the window and peered at Julie over his sunglasses. "I'm almost afraid to ask what you're planning."

Julie slid her gloves off and jumped in the passenger seat of the Mini Cooper. "What have you got in the case?"

Chin looked at her and reached in the back seat for the case. He unzipped it revealing his tools. "You can't go in there with a directional dish; everyone in the place would know what you're up to. The only small devices would require that you place them at the table."

She gathered five bugs. "I'll see to it that one of these makes it to the table. You fire up your end and don't miss any of their conversation. We need to know what they're up to."

Chin flipped a switch activating the listening device. "You'd better watch your ass; the big son of a bitch that's with

Zhang got out of the car with a scanning device in his hand. My guess is that he plans to examine anyone who comes close to them."

Julie held one of the bugs in front of her face. "That probably means that they're expecting additional company. Stay back a couple of blocks. I don't want them getting suspicious."

Chin waved his hand. "I can handle my end. You just make sure that you don't run into the giant. He's not likely to overlook anyone spying on his boss."

Julie took the bugs and jumped on the bike. She parked just across from the teahouse, pulled her helmet off and shook her hair loose, letting it fall her shoulders and back. She walked into the Laoshe Teahouse and began looking around for Zhang and Vladimir. They were seated in a private area that allowed them to see the show on the main stage, yet remain isolated from the general crowd.

She sat at the bar and ordered green tea. The giant guarded the door to the private room and the people inside seemed uninvolved with conversation. Through a mirror at the bar, she noticed Xie Yi and General Gan come through the front door. It took only a matter of seconds for them to spot Zhang and they hurried to join him.

Julie watched a waiter take their order and head back to the bar area. She stopped waiter. "Is this order for the Comrade General?"

The waiter hesitated and looked back towards the men seated in the private room. They didn't appear secretive or concerned with who may see them. "Yes, among others."

"Please allow me to pay for their order." Julie reached in her pocket and handed the waiter enough to cover the order along with a generous tip. "Do you have blank note paper that I may use?"

The waiter placed the order and handed Julie a blank piece of paper. "Please be discreet."

"Of course," Julie said and took the paper. She wrote a quick note. *Comrade General, thank you for your efforts for China.*

The waiter returned with the order and reached for Julie's note. "I must examine it first."

Julie held the note open for the waiter to read and waited for a nod of approval. She slipped the note between two of the ornate tea pots. "Please make sure that the Comrade General sees this note." While the waiter listened to Julie, she slipped two bugs beneath two of the teapots.

"I will see to it." The waiter took the tray of teapots and cups to the private room. "Excuse me Comrade General, the young lady at the bar asked that I give this to you. She has paid for the order."

He read the note and looked towards the bar, holding the note up and slightly bowing in Julie's direction.

Julie stood and walked to an empty table. Seeing his gesture, she bowed and took her seat facing away from the group in the private room.

Zhang couldn't help but notice the young woman in black leather that appeared to be a second layer of skin. "It would seem that the Comrade General has a lovely fan."

General Gan tucked the note into his pocket. "She simply appreciates my work."

Vladimir drained his cup of tea. "I wouldn't mind having a fan like that. I hope she's still here when we're done, I'd like to get to know her better."

Chin broke the silence in Julie's ear. It seems that you're developing quite a fan base. I'm going to link you in to hear the conversation."

"Roger that," Julie said and finished her tea.

General Gan scribbled a number on the note paper and summoned the giant. "Take this to the young lady in the black leather outfit. Inform her that I would relish getting to know her better."

The giant reached her table just as she was standing to leave. He grabbed her shoulder with one of his massive hands. "The general asked that I give you this and tell you that he would like to get to know you better."

Julie looked towards the private room and bowed to the General before tucking the number into her back pocket and sashaying from the tea house without another word.

Chapter
15

Zasha paced the floor of her hotel room. "We should be out there doing something. Who knows what Nikitin is up to."

"You need to calm down. You heard what the Director said and he's right. Nikitin knows us; if we show up where he is don't you think he'll know that something isn't right?"

"Yeah, yeah, I know, but sitting around here doesn't make me feel any better." Zasha grabbed a bottle of water and took a swig.

"Agents Hu and Chin are on the case. They'll take care of things now." Cole laid back on the bed and blew an exhausted sigh.

Zasha pulled out her iPhone and pulled up the grid where Vladimir's dot broadcast its signal. The son of a bitch isn't far from here. Maybe we should take a walk."

"Not on your life." Cole sat up. "What's got you so spazzed out about this guy?"

She stopped pacing the floor and turned to Cole. "He's a worthless piece of crap. If we hadn't gotten Jenna out of Hong Kong who knows what he would have done to her?"

"So, this is about Jenna? True, she could have picked her company better. However, if she had not been with Vladimir we never would have known about him. At least how he may be involved with our case." Cole stood and massaged her shoulders. "Take it easy, we can check in with Hu and Chin if it will make you feel better."

Zasha turned abruptly and poked her finger in Cole's chest. "Damn good idea." She put her gun in her belt and grabbed a jacket.

"Where the hell are you going?" Cole tried to keep up.

"I'm heading to the safe-house. Hu and Chin have to come back there at some point. I intend to be waiting." Zasha shot out of the door, closely followed by Cole.

Taking a taxi to a safe-house was forbidden, so they walked the twenty blocks. Using a provided key, Zasha unlocked the door and stepped in. Her hands went up noticing the laser sighted Uzis pointed at her chest. "Is this the house of hope?"

The words were code for any agents that may be in the area. Chin lowered his weapon. "What the fuck? I almost blew you guys away. Ever heard of letting someone know that you're coming?"

Cole stepped through the door still half holding his hands up. "I tried to tell her. We're not even supposed to be concerned with Vladimir and his friends."

Julie finally lowered her gun and stepped towards the door. "Why don't you come in and close the door. We've just began monitoring five men at Laoshe Teahouse. It's starting to get interesting. By the way, Oscar Fenton said that you wouldn't stay away. It seems he knows you well."

Chin set up two pairs of headphones and set the digital recorder to start at the beginning. "If you guys can shed any light on what's going on, we'd appreciate the help."

Zasha and Cole listened to the earlier recordings while Julie and Chin continued to monitor the live conversations. Both pair scribbled notes of things they thought were significant. Julie recorded times when the group talked to women in the tea house. This allowed Zasha to fast forward past the babble and catch up to the live broadcast. On a notepad, Julie distinguished the speakers so that it would be easy to know who was speaking.

Zhang: *Gentlemen, I would like to welcome each of you to what will one day be viewed as the greatest event of the twenty first century. Much has been written about the future of China. Views of how we should proceed are as varied as the colors in a box of crayons. In each opinion, there may be an element of truth. I believe we can ascertain these elements, assemble and institute a plan that will be both beneficial and rewarding.*

You may recall a manifesto prepared by Comrade Chi Haotian. In it, he states that the twenty first century belongs to the Chinese. He believes that we must begin to rejuvenate China and expand throughout the world. Unlike the balance of the world, he believes that the Chinese people did not derive their heritage from Africa. According to him, we possess a unique heritage.

Vladimir: *I'm not sure I like the tone of this conversation.*

Zhang: *Bear with me for a moment. If I didn't think that you were an integral part of our plan you would not be here. As I was saying; Chi believes that we are now at a period in history similar to Germany when Hitler came to power. Unlike the Germans, he believes that we must eliminate our enemies one at a time to become successful. He states that we will be the victors because we are the only nation on earth that is one hundred percent atheists. Since we do not worship a god, we will follow man— a Chinese communist man to be exact. And because we are a ruthless people, we are willing to kill all of our enemies. He has even suggested that ongoing development will produce biological weapons that will kill everyone that is not yellow and the Israelis, who are assisting in the development of the weapons.*

Vladimir: *Where does that leave the Russians?*

Zhang: *A moment longer if you please. Chi says that the root of all wars is in response to basic sustenance and resources. We all are aware that our resources here in China are nearly depleted. We are actively acquiring resources wherever we can find them. Africa, Cuba and even in America. The one resource that we have been unable to acquire is additional lands for our people. We are the only dominant country that has not bothered to colonize other lands. Either we find other lands or he believes eight hundred million of our people must die. If we are to accept his position, we must accept that the Western countries will oppose China's colonizing of other countries. Since the United States is the most powerful Western country, or should I say the world, they are China's greatest impediment.*

General Gan: *He has also stated that Chinese people were the first to arrive in the United States. Therefore, they should relinquish half of their lands for our people.*

Zhang: *Quite right, however, he does not believe that China and the United States can coexist. In his mind, war is the only answer. However, before going to war, we should continue to develop China with a concentration on economic development. Yet, we should maintain a low profile until the time is right and put up with the United States for the time being. Then he wishes to issue a warning to the American people to vacate the United States or face total destruction. In addition, he believes that we should take Canada and Australia as well, on our way to having the Communist Party rule the world. He ended by saying that Marxism pointed out that violence is the midwife of a new society. Therefore, war is the midwife of the birth of the Chinese Century. General Gan, would you enlighten us about your writings?*

General Gan: *My view is much more simplistic. China is facing annihilation if we do not provide the necessary commodities, we need to sustain our people; including the necessary living space for our people. Of course, we have begun to search out other lands. There are parts of Africa that China owns for all practical purposes. It would be impossible to ignore, as comrade Haotian has stated, that the United States holds an abundance of resources. It makes sense that we should look there as a source. Unlike, Chi, I do not believe that we must completely destroy the American people to become their rulers. They have provided us with the methodology by which we can conquer them. Their government willingly accepts immigrants, who easily gain citizenship with full voting rights. All we need do is to continue to flood their cities with our people; their democratic process will do the rest.*

Zhang: *I propose that we institute the movement. By controlling the process, we will become the most powerful men in the world. What's the matter Xie Yi? You appear as if someone has drained all the blood from your body?*

Xie: *Your proposal neglects the Party. If we begin operating without them and they find out, our deaths are certain.*

Zhang: *By the time they become aware of anything, General Gan will have assumed the role of leader and we will be free to claim all the wealth we desire.*

Vladimir: *When are you going to get to the part that makes me comfortable with this plan? I don't intend to be one of the people you aim to conquer.*

Zhang: *You have nothing to worry about my friend. Take a look at the computer screen. This is a live broadcast from the United States. In a matter of weeks, they will have a new leader. Listening to them, they are discussing which states are 'blue states' and which ones are 'red states.' The frontrunner had as a part of his campaign making immigrants who have been in the United States for five years, full citizens. Using his platform, we can make all their states 'red states,' China red. My company transports more people from China to the United States than any other. By providing us with ships and cargo containers, we will be able to quadruple the number of people we carry to the United States. We will also provide them with documentation that has put them there the required five years, giving them full citizenship. I also believe we will be able to formulate a relationship with Mexico that will help to increase their numbers in the U.S. with full citizenship. In return, these people will be instructed to vote for candidates that we choose. Within eight years, we will control their Congress, Senate and very possibly the Presidential office as well. The five of us are flying to Mexico tomorrow to meet with like-minded members of their government. This plan will allow us to take over the most powerful country in the world without firing a single shot.*

Chapter
16

The conversation at the teahouse ended and Zasha took her headphones off. She looked at the others in the room. "Is anyone else having an 'oh shit' moment?"

Cole tossed his headphones on the table. "So much for our work here. They've just answered all our questions. Not only are they escalating the shipment of illegals, they plan to use them to take over the country. We'd better get Oscar on the phone."

Julie stood from the table. "How are we going to get a listening device on the plane with them?"

Cole eyed her. "That shouldn't be too hard. All we need to know is what flight they'll be taking. I can find out what seats they'll be in."

Chin shook his head side to side. "It's not that easy. Zhang has a private jet for all his travels. You can bet it's constantly guarded. Getting access to it will be nearly impossible."

Julie crossed her arms. "Then, I guess I'll have to do it." She reached in her back pocket and pulled out General Gan's number. "The General will be on the flight. I'll bet he wouldn't mind some company during the flight."

Zasha pushed back from the table. "That's insane! There's no way that we can cover you and you can bet that none of the men on that plane will have honorable intentions."

"This is a tough job; it requires tough decisions." Julie turned her back sighing with the weight of her decision.

Cole was already dialing his phone. "We need to talk to Oscar. Most likely, he'll want the Director in on this call as well." He sat the phone on the table and initiated the speaker function.

Oscar dispensed with any pleasantries. "Let me guess, you just had to get involved and you two showed up at the safe house."

There was a pregnant silence before Cole sat up and relayed the information they'd just heard. "Agent Hu believes that she may have a way onto Zhang Ju's private jet. The problem is she'll be there with at least six men and no backup."

"Hang on a minute. The Director wanted to hear about any developments. He's going to shit bricks after hearing this." Oscar put them on hold and called Carson.

"What a shit storm!" Director Carson's voice was an octave higher than usual. "The President's going to have a cow when I fill him in on this. It hasn't been enough that we've had to deal with tainted food and poisoned toys coming from China, now this shit. Things have been icy between our countries because China felt our accusations of their safety practices sucked. They've been going tit for tat banning our products in response to us putting a moratorium on theirs."

"Sir, I believe the greater problem is that we're dealing with more than the Chinese government. True, it may be their hidden ideology, but these are freelancers, albeit with government ties." Chin stuttered as if unsure what to say next.

"The Chairman will sure as hell get bent out of shape if the President implicates his top general and the Premier of State Council. The only choice we have is to follow Zhang and his crew. If the Mexicans buy into his plan, we're going to be facing more that icy relations. This could be the beginning of a much greater problem." Julie sat back in her chair and let her head fall back.

Director Carson's fist hit his desk. "Fenton, map out a strategy for the flight. I'll get a team in Mexico to dig in to this meeting they have planned. If we're lucky, we can get a man inside. We've got to know everything we're dealing with here. Zhang just didn't come up with this plan; he's had to have been working on it for some time. I want to know everything. As soon as we do, I want to smash these motherfuckers into oblivion! Get on it! In a few days, I'll have to convince two administrations what we need to do. If you believe the polls, I'll have to convince the very man that believes we should open our borders to anyone who wants to come here." Carson disconnected, cursing as he hit the button.

Zasha pressed her hands against the table. "Maybe it's time I accidentally stumbled into Vladimir."

Chapter
17

Zasha and Julie retreated to a separate room to talk. The guys watched them helplessly, hoping to be brought into the conversation.

"The first thing we have to worry about is giving the impression that we know each other. Someone may get suspicious when you contact General Gan and I look up Vladimir. I'm sure he's checked into my background by now. Vladimir is former KGB, he's distrustful by nature. He won't find out anything, there's nothing that can connect me to the CIA." Zasha leaned back in the chair.

Julie did the same. "General Gan doesn't even know my name. If one of his cohorts managed to get the plates from the bike, they will find that they are registered to a fictitious company." She put her feet on the table and leaned her head back letting her hair fall behind the chair nearly touching the floor. "To get on that plane, we've got to get by Zhang. He may be the most difficult critic; he hasn't reached his level by being loose."

"Then we'd better formulate a backup plan. If we show up and are not allowed on the plane, we've got to plant a listening device on them. We need to know what they're up to. You can bet that the giant with his ever-present wand will scan everyone before they get on the plane." Zasha pulled a case from the floor and opened it. She scanned the various bugs provided by Oscar. She pulled out the smallest one and held it on the tip of her finger. It was so small that breathing hard would have sent it aloft. Yet, placed correctly, it would broadcast the entire conversation.

Julie looked down her nose without moving her head. "That's the one I'd use. Have you given any thought to the fact that if they let anyone on the plane, it may only be one of us?"

Zasha sighed. "I hadn't thought of that and I wish I didn't have to think of it now. It's going to be really hard to control that much testosterone in a confined space. Once we're in the air, there's no one to rush to our aid. I don't like the idea of being used as a sperm bank for a group that large."

Julie laughed, though it was contemptuous. "The life of a dedicated spy; I always knew that I could be tested, but I didn't expect anything like this."

Zasha put the device back in the case. "Hopefully, this is all useless conjecture. I seriously doubt if either of us will get on the plane."

Julie sat up and rested her elbows on the table. "That sounds like wishful thinking. These men are used to having their entertainment. We will be considered as nothing more. You'd best start thinking that way. It will make reality less painful."

Cole softly knocked on the door and came in. "Things seem a little intense in here. Maybe we can add something to the discussion."

Zasha looked at him intensely. "What would you think if two women joined a private flight with six men? Do you think we'd be expected to put out?"

Cole sat and turned to look at Chin, who was standing in the doorway. "You two can't be seriously thinking about trying to get on the plane with them."

Zasha looked at Julie. "Question answered."

Chin moved to the table. "There's probably another way. As long as the tracking device is active on Vladimir, we can tell where he is. Since he believes you and Cole are a couple, you two can intercept him before the flight tomorrow and plant a bug on him. Julie, don't call General Gan before tomorrow morning. If you meet him for breakfast, you can give him the illusion that you'd like to get to know him better when he returns. Then, you can plant a listening device on him as well. It's got to be a better alternative than what you all were suggesting."

Zasha kept Julie in her gaze. "I like the way he thinks. Do you think we can make it happen?"

Julie dropped her feet to the floor and sat up. "If we don't, we've fucked up in grand style."

Chin waved off the comment. "Don't worry about it, I'll be your backup and Cole will be with Zasha. It should be a cinch to pull it off."

Chapter
18

The following morning, Zasha pulled her iPhone out and shared the screen with Cole. "If nothing else, Vladimir is predictable— he's having breakfast." She pointed to the screen that showed the restaurant where Vladimir stopped.

Cole nodded. "He's just a couple of blocks over, let's make our move."

Vladimir chose an outside table near the front of the restaurant— it made him feel more European. He caught sight of Zasha and Cole walking in his direction laughing and talking like new lovers. He stood and waved his arms. "Of all the people I could run into...please, you will join me for breakfast?" He looked into their faces. "I insist."

Zasha wrapped her arm around Cole's. "Well, we were just headed out to find something to eat." She looked at Cole. "Do you mind?"

"It's okay with me. Vladimir knows his way around, I'm sure the food is good here." Cole stepped towards Vladimir's table and held a chair for Zasha.

Borka stood and pointed to Cole. "Gentleman...good man."

Cole smiled and reached for Borka's hand. "My daddy wouldn't have it any other way."

Vladimir turned to the waiter and put two fingers in the air. "Two more!"

Zasha hit Cole with her elbow. "Vladimir likes Bloody Marys. What do you want to bet that's what he was just talking about?"

Vladimir bowed. "Have I become that predictable?"

Zasha lifted her menu. "We all are creatures of habit— you like Bloody Marys with breakfast, double if I remember correctly."

Vladimir sat his menu down and looked at Zasha. "Just like a reporter to remember details. Have you two been enjoying yourselves here in Beijing?"

Zasha's face blushed. "We haven't seen much of the city; we didn't venture too far from the room yesterday."

Vladimir looked at Cole. "Well it seems that someone was enjoying himself."

"Hey, don't look at me. I flew a plane all day; I needed to catch up on my sleep." Cole ducked behind his menu unable to blush on demand as Zasha had.

She attempted to change the subject. "What looks good on the menu?"

"I think we should order a variety of things so that you may try several items." Vladimir looked up at the waiter, who was arriving with the Bloody Marys. He pointed to several selections and the waiter ran off to fill the order.

Zasha folded her hands and rested her chin on them. "What do you say you and Borka show us around Beijing today?"

Vladimir looked at Borka and spoke in Russian. He turned back to Zasha's direction. "Sadly, for me, that is impossible. We have business meetings that may carry over for the next few days. There's going to be very little time. Perhaps, you will allow me to make it up to you some other time."

"I guess our paths may cross again in the future. I'm wrapping up here in the next day or so and headed to see the Great Wall of China. After that, it's back to the States." Zasha worked to display her disappointment.

Vladimir nodded in both their directions and rose from the table without eating a bite. "Well, if either of you find yourselves back in this part of the world, let Jenna know so that we may get together."

Zasha's focus fell back to the menu. "That, we can do."

The food arrived and Borka again spoke in Russian. Vladimir glanced at his watch. "Please forgive me, but Borka and I must prepare to leave. Please stay and enjoy yourselves. Anything that you want, please don't hesitate to inform our waiter. I have taken care of everything."

Zasha and Cole stood when the other men did. She walked around to Vladimir. "Thank you for a wonderful time. Jenna is lucky to have such a wonderful man to look out for her." She leaned and kissed Vladimir on the lips.

Cole kept Borka busy and his attention focused away from Vladimir. The kiss lasted long enough to surprise Vladimir and give Zasha time to slip a listening device beneath his lapel.

Zasha looked into Vladimir's surprised eyes and let her hand rest against his chest. "If I swing an assignment in Russia, maybe you can be there to show me around."

"I will make sure of it." Vladimir shook Cole's hand but never let his eyes leave Zasha.

Cole was the first to sit and watch the men leave the restaurant. "You handled that effortlessly."

Zasha reached in her purse for her iPhone. "Yeah, now we'd better let Julie know so that she doesn't try to get on the plane. Vladimir never opened that opportunity for me, Julie can't be there alone."

Cole hunched his shoulders. "It all seems a bit overdone to me. All we need is his cell phone number and we can hear everything that's going on."

Zasha dialed Julie and looked at Cole with disbelief. "Why didn't you say something earlier?"

Chin didn't feel right leaving Julie by herself with General Gan. He beat them both to the restaurant and presented official Chinese Government documents, which allowed him to take the place of the waiter handling the table where they would be placed.

Julie nearly choked seeing Chin approach their table. She wanted to wave him off, but knew she couldn't without drawing unwanted attention. With the general's trip being subversive, she hoped that he was alone and that no one was watching them.

Chin handed a menu to each of them, opening Julie's and using a finger to point to the bottom of the page. There a coded note was written on the bottom of the page: *No one tells a salmon how to find a breeding ground, they know by instinct.*

Julie handed the menu back to Chin, having read the message. She recognized it as the prearranged message not to follow General Gan. "I'll have the eggs Benedict."

General Gan looked over his menu. "That didn't take you long. I like a woman who makes up her mind quickly."

Julie nodded. "Comrade General, you stated that your time this morning was short. I thought it prudent to make a quick decision."

General Gan handed the menu back to Chin. "I'll have the same with the salt fish."

Chin took the menu. "Can I bring you anything to drink?"

"Tea." General Gan looked at Julie, who nodded her approval. "Tea for the table."

Chin left to place their orders. He prepared their tea away from the other staff. He slid a hair-thin transmitter from his pocket and attached a charge that would deliver a sharp blast of air, which would send a dart into his victim. It would feel like an insect bite and leave no visible sign.

The receiver in his ear crackled. Zasha's voice was the next thing he heard. "Chin, I don't know what you're planning, but eighty-six it. Cole says all we need is a cell phone number. Julie, if you can hear me nod to Chin."

Chin watched for the signal. "Okay, she's nodding."

Zasha came back on. "Julie if this is General Gan's cell phone number on the paper you left on your desk at the safe house, tug at your ear."

Chin waited. "That's the one, she's tugging her ear."

"Good, then we have all we need to follow him. Chin, whatever you were planning, back off and get out of there. As long as the battery is in his phone, we've got him and anyone in the area."

Chin slid the metal tube in his pocket. "What if he decides to turn it off, will we lose our connection?"

Cole took over the call. "That's the beauty of the cell phone; as long as he leaves the battery in it, we can hear everyone near the phone."

Chin shook his head. "Kind of makes this shit I'm carrying around obsolete. I bet the phone companies had a shit-fit when this news got out. No wonder the drug dealers change phones so often."

"This isn't the type of thing that will remain quiet. By then, we'll have something else that works even better." Cole disconnected.

Chin returned to the table with the tea. "Is there anything else that you will need? I will be leaving for the day momentarily."

Julie nodded in Chin's direction dismissing him as she reached for the general's hand. "I had hoped that we would have been able to spend a little time together before you had to leave—duty comes first."

"There will be time when I return. Then we will have time for proper introductions." Gan sat back to allow Chin to set the tea on the table.

Chin went back to the waiter's station and checked the listening device in his ear. The general's voice was clear. *Some men don't appreciate an assertive woman. I am different, I find it stimulating.* Chin stepped out far enough for Julie to see him. He winked and moved to the back of the teahouse to leave. Cole worked his magic and the General's phone was transmitting beautifully.

Julie smiled at the general. "I trust that your mission isn't dangerous."

General Gan pushed his chest out. "Not at all. I am just investigating ways to spread China's influence. The future of our country depends on all of us doing everything we can to spread our message. It's time we take our rightful place in the world. No country has done that by sitting back and waiting for conversion to come to them."

Julie let her hands fall to her lap and set back in her chair. "Most countries have taken what they need by using war as their pretext. Should China be any different?"

General Gan's brow furrowed. "War can be waged in other ways than the conventional bullets and bombs. Traditional methods open us up for far too much destruction. Much more power and influence can be gained by flexing our financial might and revolutionary ideas. Enemies are much more malleable when there is only one place they can turn to have their needs met. Why do you think the United States has been so powerful for so long?"

Julie leaned on her elbows. "China meets a lot of the worldwide needs now. How can we become a single source for what the world needs? Our resources are already strained."

General Gan also leaned forward, stimulated by the conversation. "Simple, the most sought-after commodity in the world is oil. China is now the second largest consumer of oil just behind the United States. Yet, unlike the United States, China is not burdened by policy that prevents them from searching in some of the most oil-rich areas of the world. We are actively purchasing oil rights in places like the Sudan, Venezuela, Iran and we've just purchased the rights to one of the largest finds in the Gulf just miles from the U.S. border in Cuba's waters. Our purchases represent billions upon billions of barrels of oil, while the United States remains crushed by their own policy. They are perfectly at ease with China. Soon, they will have nowhere else to turn for oil; we will own the majority of the world's supply."

"Comrade General, your shrewdness is unmatched— the United States will never know what hit them." Julie smiled.

"Until it's too late. A simple feat that they've overlooked is that China owns forty percent of the U.S. mortgage debt. The interest rate crisis has foreclosures at an all-time high. We could care less about the money— we want the real-estate. Who said the U.S. could prevent China from annexing the land we need?" The General smiled and raised his tea cup. "To China."

"To China." Julie responded and touched his cup.

Chin left the restaurant and called Zasha. "Did you just hear what he told Julie? Meet me at the safe house. Text Julie, just say that San Francisco is lovely; she'll know what it means."

Zasha tugged Cole. "Come on, we've got to go, we've got to contact Langley."

Cole stepped out of the restaurant and slid on his sunglasses looking in all directions. He wasn't comfortable since seeing Borka on a bench during their run in Hong Kong. "I've got an uneasy feeling. You know that we can't trust Vladimir and Borka— once KGB always KGB. With a meeting this big looming, they will be extra careful. Keep your eyes out, someone may be watching us. Why else would they leave early? Julie's still with Gan."

Zasha took Cole's arm, kissed the side of his face and whispered in his ear. "I think we'd best walk for a while. Smile and let's look like tourists."

Cole complied and led the way. About three blocks away, he posed Zasha beside a temple lion outside of a tea house and pulled a digital camera from his pocket. He snapped several shots then turned the camera facing the other side of the street and snapped several additional shots. "No one made a move that could be considered evasive. I think we're in the clear." He saw a lone taxi coming down the street and hailed it. They hurriedly jumped in and looked to see if anyone was following their ride.

Zasha pulled a mirror from her purse and used it to look behind them. The streets were filled with people in cars, none of whom seemed to care about who they were. "So far, so good."

"I'll be a lot more comfortable once they're on the plane." Cole leaned to the driver and gave him the hotel address. Then he took his iPhone out and dialed a number that allowed him to receive the transmission from Vladimir's bug.

Zasha looked at him. "Anything?"

Cole shook his head. "I told you my Russian is rusty...seems he wants to have a discussion with Jenna about you when they return."

"Fat fucking chance!" Zasha sent the text to Julie.

Chin's head nearly did a one-eighty when the white Rolls Royce passed him going in the opposite direction. He pulled over and waited for it to get out of sight before turning around and following. He reached for the GPS to see Gan's location. He stopped two blocks from the restaurant and waited.

General Gan Stepped from the front door just as the Rolls pulled up. He got in and the car pulled off.

The signal was strong, so Chin waited before following. He called Julie. "You okay?"

"Yeah, I'm just getting ready to leave the restaurant. Where the hell did you disappear?"

"I'm a couple of blocks away. Zhang's white Rolls just stopped and picked up the general and there's someone else in the car. I'm going to follow to make sure they all get on the plane and find out, who the mystery man is. Meet Zasha and Cole at the safe house. I'll be in touch."

Julie stopped in mid stride. "Why risk following them, don't you have a signal?"

"Yeah, but what if this is someone we need to know." He cranked the car and pulled off.

Julie put a hand on her hip. "Chin, don't do anything stupid. There's no need to approach these men, we have everything we need."

"Hey, it's just in case. If this guy doesn't get on the plane with them, it could be important. I might get a few pictures of the group before they leave. I'll call you in a few minutes." Chin disconnected the phone and threw it in the seat.

Chin followed the car to a back lot at the Beijing airport. He remained a safe distance away and pointed a flexible digital camera lens out the window and began snapping pictures. He watched a screen that slid up from the console that let him see what the camera lens saw.

Vladimir pointed towards Chin's car. "Who the hell is that over there?" He tapped Zhang. "Is that one of your men?"

Zhang motioned to the giant. "Go through the hangar and approach his car from the back." He turned to Vladimir. "Have your man approach from the front. Let's see what he is up to."

Chin saw the men move and loaded his phone, the GPS and camera into an opening behind the viewing screen. He pressed a button and everything went in, molding itself into the console completely hidden. He reached for his keys and the giant slapped the back of his car with such force, his hands fell off the keys.

Borka jerked the door open and the giant reached in for Chin. "Get the fuck out of the car." He slammed Chin into the side of the car. "What are you doing here?"

Chin swung his arms. "I like to come here to watch planes take off and land, I find it relaxing."

The giant's massive hand crashed against the side of Chin's head and he went down. Blood gushed from his mouth. He spat on the ground but didn't look up. "What did I do? I'm only here to watch the planes."

Borka jerked Chin from the ground and pushed him towards the men waiting near the Lear.

Chin stumbled forward. He knew that he was in trouble if General Gan recognized him. He wiped the blood from his face and noticed that one of his teeth was loose.

Zhang motioned for the other men to get on the jet while he dealt with the problem. The white cattle prod dangled from his wrist. He grabbed it when Chin reached him. He held it against Chin's chest. "What are you doing in a restricted area?"

Chin kept his eyes averted. "There's usually no one in this area. I come here to watch planes land and take off. I find it relaxing."

Zhang pushed the prod into Chin's chest activating the shock. Chin shook violently and fell to the ground. Zhang kicked him in the groin with his pointed-toe cowboy boots. "Restricted area means that. You don't ever come into this area!"

Chin heaved and gagged rolling in pain. "I understand. It won't happen again."

Zhang drove the cattle prod into Chin again the looked at the giant. "Did you find anything in the car?"

The giant shook his head side to side. "No, it was clean."

Zhang waved the cattle prod. "Take him back over there and teach him what restricted means. Hurry back, we're on a schedule."

The Giant dragged Chin back to the car. He and Borka beat Chin until he stopped moving. They threw him in the car and slammed the door.

From her vantage point nearly a half mile away, Julie watched helplessly. Chin was lifeless, very possibly dead. All she could do was wait until the plane took off. She pulled her phone from her jacket and called Zasha. "We've got a major problem. Chin followed the group to the airport. They made him and kicked the shit out of him. I'm not sure he's alive. I can't safely approach until the plane leaves."

Zasha grabbed Cole's arm and squeezed. "Why would he do something like that? We tagged two of them, we had all we needed."

Cole was still monitoring Vladimir's transmission. He could hear Zhang speaking to the group. *I'm sorry for the delay; someone was snooping where he shouldn't have been. I'll call my men and have them deal with him.* Cole spoke towards Zasha's phone. "We'd better get him quickly; Zhang is sending some of his men to finish the job."

"Meet me here at the airport. I'm going to call for an ambulance as soon as the plane's engines come on. That's right about now. I'll see you shortly." Julie disconnected and called the emergency number.

Xie looked out the plane's window towards the car where Chin laid back in the car, most likely dead. "If that man was a government official none of us will have a welcomed return to China. General Gan and I are not on a sanctioned trip. He may have been sent to see where we are going."

Zhang dialed his phone. "Don't concern yourself with him. He will be bait for the fish before anyone is aware he's missing."

The plane taxied down the runway and lifted into the air. At the same time, an ambulance zipped down an access road towards Chin.

Chapter
21

Zasha and Cole arrived separately at the airport joining Julie. They moved closer to where the EMTs worked to stabilize Chin but they made no move to approach the site.

Julie's eyes didn't leave her binoculars even though they couldn't prevent the tears that leaked from the sides. "We've got to get to that car before Zhang's men arrive. We can't risk having them take the car apart. It's loaded with equipment."

Cole used a monocular to scan the area. "We're going to need a key unless either of you knows how to hot-wire a car."

Julie reached in her pocket and retrieved a key. "I'll take you down on the bike as soon as the ambulance leaves."

Cole took the key and reached into his hip pack pulling out two Glock 40s. He cocked both guns, placed one in his belt and the other back in his hip pack. "Just in case we encounter any unfriendly types."

"Pure cowboy style, guns a-blazing." Julie reached in her jacket for her gun and cocked it as well. "It's in and out; we don't want to draw any attention."

Zasha walked around to the trunk of the car she came in. She popped it and reached for a case. She walked around and popped the latches of the case. She assembled the M14, 7.62mm sniper's rifle and attached a scope. "You guys don't think that I'm going to leave all the fun up to you, do you?"

Julie looked at the rifle. "Damn, you've had sniper training? Shit, I've been waiting to get into that school for months."

"Somebody's got to watch out for your asses. I won't miss if I'm needed." Zasha took her position in a thicket.

Cole looked at Julie. "A woman with a big gun always turns me on."

Julie became more serious. "The ambulance is leaving. Let's get going." She jumped on the bike and cranked it.

Cole jumped on and put his arms snugly around Julie. One of the Glock 40s was in his hand. She looked at the gun. He tapped her leg. "Don't worry; I've got complete control of my trigger finger."

Zasha shook her head from her place in the thicket. "Would you two get going?"

Julie maneuvered the bike back to the street and sped down the access road towards the Mini Cooper. They arrived and Cole jumped from the bike and into the car.

Julie saw a car approaching rapidly. "Get your ass in gear, we've got company."

Cole burned rubber heading in the opposite direction of the approaching car. Julie popped a wheelie matching Cole's speed. Behind them a man hung out the side of the car and began firing his gun at them.

Zasha locked the car in her sights as soon as they hit the access road. When the firing began, she moved the cross hairs to the driver. With a simple squeeze of her finger, the driver's head disintegrated and the car swerved sideways launching into a nasty roll.

Bits of metal and body parts flew over the access road. The car landed on its roof sliding across the pavement with the top half of the passenger's side pinned between the pavement and the roof of the car.

A fresh streak of blood, hair and skin lined the pavement. Zasha knew that it was useless to check for survivors, neither man had any remnants of a head left.

Zasha called Cole. "The problem's over for the moment. Those guys lost their heads trying to get to you. You guys head back to the safe house, I'll meet you there. Slow down, we don't want you to get stopped and have to explain what just happened. I'll get in touch with Oscar and have him check on Chin. We're going to have to have him moved if he made it."

Cole rolled down his window and put his arm out signaling for Julie to slow down. She pulled next to him and he yelled into the earpiece above the whipping sound of the wind. "Head back to the safe house, Zasha took care of the problem."

Julie nodded and darted in front of the car, still moving fast, but not fast enough to draw unwanted attention.

They reached the safe house and Julie led Cole around to the back of the house. She pulled her helmet off. "We're going to have to get the equipment out of this car and ditch it. It's going to have to be cleaned; we don't want anyone looking for us."

Cole jumped from the car. "We're going to have to get in touch with Oscar. After this last incident, I doubt he's going to want any of us to stay in-country."

Julie shook her hair loose. "We have to check on Chin. We just can't leave him behind. Zhang will surely have his men looking for him, especially when the two that showed up don't report in."

Zasha pulled in front of the house and hurried to meet Cole and Julie. "Let's get moving boys and girls. We've got to gather our equipment from the car and house. Oscar is monitoring the wires. A cleaning crew is on their way to get the car and anything else we leave behind. We've got to get to the Embassy, pronto!"

Julie reached in the car and lowered the hidden compartment and gathered the equipment. "Is there a report on Chin? Zhang's men will be looking for him soon. If Oscar alerts the government, there'll be another fly in the ointment and that's something we don't need."

Zasha took both Julie's shoulders. "We've got to go! Chin is critical. They can't risk moving him right now. We have people working to alter the records. They'll have his pick-up location changed. Even his identity won't match what they brought him in with. As soon as possible, our people will retrieve him. You're going to have to trust Oscar at this point. He'll take care of Chin."

Julie threw her helmet to the ground. "I told that stupid bastard not to go near those men. He just had to play hero. He wanted to get pictures."

Zasha picked the helmet up and tossed it in the car. "His pictures may prove invaluable if we need to put heat on the Chinese government. They have no idea what two of their top people are up to. The pictures may prove to be Chin's lifesaver."

Zasha heard the truck pull up. "They're here— we have to go." She turned to Cole. "Get the things out of the house. The truck's here for us. When the other one arrives, we don't want to be here."

Chapter
22

The truck carrying the three agents reached the American Embassy and immediately turned away from the front gates. Sitting in the back of the windowless truck, they couldn't see anything that was happening. Seconds before the turn, the driver announced their arrival. But the truck did not slow to allow the gates to open and they were picking up speed.

Cole slapped the wall separating them from the driver and a small window opened. "What's going on? I thought we'd arrived at the Embassy."

"There's been a change of orders." The heavily armed man in the passenger's seat said and closed the window.

Cole looked at Zasha and Julie, unsure of what to say, or what he felt. He sat back in his seat and touched the Glock 40 beneath his left arm. "Do you guys still have your weapons?"

Julie nodded and Zasha pulled hers out. "Yeah, and I've got all my extra clips."

Julie laid her head back against the side of the bouncing truck. "They wouldn't have left us armed if they planned to harm us. Something else must be up."

Cole slid in a fresh clip. "I'd like to think that way too, but just in case, we should be ready."

The truck began to slow and pulled to a stop. Two Marines holding M-16s opened the back doors wide. The three agents were spread out with their hands behind their backs. One of the Marines lowered his M-16 and tried to hide the smirk on his face. "Put the guns away guys. We're just here to make sure you make it to the plane safely."

Cole let his weapon slide to his leg. "Where are we?"

The Marine pushed the door back against the side of the truck so that Cole could see. "We're at a private airstrip. There's a Lear 28 gassed and ready to take you home. Director Carson wants you there as soon as possible."

Zasha stepped down from the truck and holstered her Glock. "Don't you think you could have warned us of the change of plans?"

The Marine smiled. "Ma'am, what fun would that have been? Besides, if anyone was following us to the Embassy, they would have had to stay on our tails here then we would have adjusted our protocol accordingly."

The jet's engines were humming loudly letting them know it was time to go. Julie patted one of the Marines in the middle of his chest. "Thanks for the efficiency."

They picked up their pace towards the plane and Cole turned to Julie. "What was that all about?"

Julie, who had not holstered her Glock, slid the gun in her holster. "I wanted to see if they were wearing bulletproof vests. It could have been a statement of their intentions."

Zasha looked back at the Marines. "Getting shot at tends to make everyone overly cautious. There's no reason to want us dead unless, those men were working for Zhang."

They heard the truck pull off as they were boarding the Lear. Three other Marines were waiting for them on the plane. Cole listened to the familiar sound of the Lear's engine's whine lifting the plane despite the earth's gravitational pull. Seconds later, the landing gear retracted and they were blazing away from Beijing.

Julie looked out the window. "My parents were born not far from here. When I was growing up in San Francisco, my mom used to talk about home. She longed to see China again. Dad had grown fond of an American saying, something which he decided to live by, *you can't go home again*. This time, I believe him."

Chapter
23

Zhang's Lear touched down on a private government landing strip in Puerto Vallarta, Mexico. Taxiing down the runway the image of the fifty thousand square foot villa filled the jet's small windows.

Xie took in the full scope of the villa and turned his attention to Zhang. "I thought you said these people were poor."

Zhang seemed unimpressed with the grandeur. "Even poor countries have their share of wealth. Just as in China, it is concentrated among those of us willing to do what others will not." The jet pulled to a stop and Zhang stood. "Gentlemen, welcome to your future."

Vladimir repeated Zhang's statement to Borka in Russian—adding a warning to be aware at all times. He was still uncomfortable after hearing Zhang's speech the day before. "If this place is any indication of what's to come, I trust we shall all be pleased with the venture."

Zhang pointed towards the villa. "Comrade Nikitin, this place will be considered a shack compared to what you will be able to afford once we launch our plan. Refreshments are waiting on the veranda. Let's not keep our hosts waiting."

The giant lowered the steps to the tarmac and the group deplaned lead by Zhang and General Wen. They were met by several servants, who came to gather their luggage. The older of the servants escorted the group to the veranda.

The five-man Mexican delegation stood as their guest approached. Carlos Acosta stepped forward to greet the men. "Welcome to Puerto Vallarta." He embraced Zhang. "Good to see you again my friend."

Carlos stepped aside to introduce the other four men. "This is Rafael Calderon, my second in command, next to him is, Alejandro Javier, a government representative, Armando Ramirez is Tamaulipas' Director of the MFJP and Pablo Juarez is your contemporary here in Mexico."

Vladimir nodded towards Armando and spoke to Borka again in Russian. "That man there is the Commander of the Mexican Federal Judicial Police. Keep an eye on him."

One-by-one, the men all shook hands and were led to a large table filled with food. They took their seats; only Carlos was left standing. He held his hands out, waving towards the food. "Please enjoy. For simplicity's sake, I believe the only common language between us is English, so we should use it for our meeting...agreed?"

Everyone nodded except Borka. Vladimir looked at Carlos, who was waiting for complete agreement. "Don't worry about Borka. If there's anything that he needs to know, I will make sure he understands; likewise, if there is something he wishes to add, I will translate."

"Very well then, shall we begin?" Carlos took his seat and signaled to one of the servants. "What may I get each of you to drink?"

"Vodka," Borka said in near perfect English.

Carlos looked at the man. "It seems he doesn't have a problem with that question."

The others at the table laughed and placed their drink orders.

Zhang laced his fingers and leaned forward on the table. "Gentlemen, this is a remarkable moment for us all. We are preparing to embark upon an event that history will prove is greater than anything before it. Through our corporative efforts, we will gain control over the most powerful country in the world. Greater still is the fact that we will do it without firing a shot. This phenomenon will be carried out using the very laws the United States has setup in the name of democracy."

This was the first moment the Mexican delegation had any clue to the course of their meeting. Hearing the words, the weight of the conversation pushed each of them to the backs of their seats.

Alejandro swirled the wine in his glass and observed it with little regard to the others at the table. The red wine ran around the sides of the glass. "Do any of you recall what was said after the 9/11 attack against the United States?" He moved his eyes from the glass to the others in the room. "It was said that Al Qaeda should not have awakened a sleeping dragon. Once the sleeping dragon has been awakened, anyone in his path is in danger and it is very hard for anyone to ease the dragon back to sleep. If word of this plan gets out the world best hang on. Destruction will surely be the new world order."

Zhang downed a double Balvenie Scotch and roughly pounded the glass against the table. Even very powerful dragons grow fatigued straining to maintain dominance."

"That is true." Vladimir held his glass in the air for a refill. The Middle East has taken a lot of the fight out of the United States— even their people have grown tired of their efforts abroad. This may be the perfect time to strike."

"Then, I suggest that we begin right away." Zhang looked at the giant, who brought over his white buffalo hide briefcase. Zhang carefully unfolded a poster-sized paper, which he had the giant hold so that everyone could see. "Vladimir will deliver ships so that we can increase the numbers of our citizens delivered to the U.S. In addition, we will relocate additional citizens in areas where I have business interest. Like the Chinese government, I have gained substantial interests in oil wells, especially in Cuba. There, we have negotiated with the Cuban government to provide citizenship papers to a large number of our people planted there."

Pablo smiled and slapped the side of his leg. "You're a sneaky bastard. I see where you're going with this already. Because of the 'wet foot-dry foot' laws that once existed in the United States, they will not turn back any Cuban citizen that reaches their soil. Recently, I have provided pathways for many Cuban citizens that come to Mexico en route to the U.S. They cross the borders with our citizens. If they are caught, the Cubans are allowed to stay while my fellow Mexicans are sent back."

Zhang tapped the paper with his finger. "I'm happy to see that you recognize the potential. Silent Dragon Enterprises has set up Spanish classes across China. Anyone seeking passage on our ships must be proficient with the language. It will surely be one of the tests that the Americans will require before allowing an Asian with Cuban citizenship papers to enter the country."

Vladimir slapped the table. "In that case, I would suggest that you acquire speed boats as well to make the run from Cuba to

Mexico. I have boats that can outrun anything the American Coast Guard has. After a while, you can bet that they will try to intercept boats carrying human cargo from Cuba."

"Excellent suggestion; build it into your cost and have the boats delivered here." Zhang pointed to Pablo. "Begin funneling people to the U.S. as soon as they arrive in Mexico. I will leave it up to you to control the boats."

"And my fee?" Pablo stabbed the table top with his finger.

"You may charge the Cubans whatever you like, but my people will settle with me and they have priority." Zhang pointed to another area of the paper. "Once in the U.S., we have centers setup in several medium-sized cities that will receive our citizens. There, they will receive documents that will prove they have been in the U.S. for the required five years. Bound by their own laws, the U.S. will be required to grant full citizenship to our people. We have even gone to the trouble of hacking into each of these cities' utilities computer systems to document service for over five years. It will serve as a clear record that will be hard to dispute."

Carlos tilted his glass towards Zhang. "Are you prepared to do the same for our citizens?"

"Yes…with one caveat." Zhang hit the center of the paper. "Just as our citizens, they will be required to register to vote. We will provide each area with a list of candidates for each election. They must vote for our candidates and confirm their vote by cell phone pictures. If they fail to follow these instructions, we will deal with their indiscretion. Putting our candidates into office is key to the success of our plan to rule the United States. We will make their democratic process our own. Within six years, we will control cities across the U.S. The more citizens we can put in place, the faster we will gain total control of their Congress, Senate and even the Presidency."

Armando finished his drink and set the glass down and pulled out a cigar. He bit off the end and spit it on the floor. "We can see to it that our citizens are compliant. That won't be a problem. However, in addition to the fees we collect during this operation, I have one additional demand. Once this project is successful, Texas and California will be returned to Mexico. China is not the only country that has suffered at the hands of the United States."

At CIA headquarters in Langley, VA a small group was gathered listening to the cell phone transmissions from the meeting in Puerto Vallarta.

Zasha, Julie and Cole entered the room wearing earpieces that they used to monitor the conversation. Zasha looked at the stunned faces of the people in the room. Director Carson placed a hand to his mouth and leaned back in the chair. She pulled the earpiece from her ear. "Does the President know what's going on?"

Carson's eyes shot in her direction, but his head remained still. It took a few seconds before his hand came down. He punched an intercom. "Get my helicopter ready and alert the White House that I'm on the way. Have them inform the President that I will be there with a Code Red report." He pointed to the empty chairs. "Take a seat. What in the hell have you all stumbled into?"

Cole slid into his chair. "We're going to have to handle this situation carefully. If the President approaches the Chinese and Mexican governments this could escalate into an international incident— not to mention, they might like the idea and use it themselves bypassing the others."

"That's not our call; the President will have to make that decision. We just have to make damn sure that we get all the information. We have the upper hand knowing their plan. Nevertheless, we're about to have to deal with a whole new administration and the idiot that seems to be leading the charge built his platform on making the United States the 'melting pot' of the world by accepting anyone who wants to come here." Carson stood and shoved his chair into place. "Goddamned candidates don't know their asses from a hole in the ground and they want to be in charge of the most powerful country on earth. It's surprising we've lasted this long."

Zasha stepped behind the Director. "Sir, why don't we just take out the players? It's got to be simpler than letting them attempt to go through with their plan."

Carson kept moving towards the door. "Yeah, take out China's top Generals. The fucking Chinese have a two million-man army. Talk about an international incident, shit, we'd end up destroying the world trying to fight those bastards. This job never gets any easier."

The door closed behind the Director and Oscar took the floor. "Okay, let's get down to work. We know the players on the Chinese side. We've already pulled their profiles. We have the names of the Mexican delegation, let's get their profiles pulled. The way I see it, there are only four sensitive players. Nobody's going to blink if the other seven disappear. So, let's put it all on the table."

Julie took her hair loose and shook it out. "Sir, I don't mean to delay our proceedings, but is there any news about Chin?"

Oscar's eyes diverted to the table before finding Julie's. "I'm afraid his wounds were too severe. He died while you were in the air. I'm sorry; I wish there was something else we could have done."

She fought back the tears. "I'll personally take Zhang out if given the opportunity."

"Duly noted, but first things first. Let's get these other profiles pulled and reviewed. Go wherever you'd like to, but let's meet back here in an hour."

Zasha sat next to Julie and touched her arm. "I can only imagine how you feel. Losing a partner can really put you on edge. Are you sure that you're up to this?"

Julie turned; her face was knotted and strained. "It's not what you think— I feel badly because I'm not experiencing enough emotion. I didn't even know Chin that well. He could have been anybody."

"Yes, but he wasn't. He was your partner and no one likes losing someone they feel responsible for." Zasha touched Julie's back and returned her stare. "If you're not going to be thinking clearly, I would rather see you take it easy for a while. This case is too important."

Julie bristled a little. "I'm as clearheaded as anyone here. Let's get started. We're probably down to fifty-five minutes."

"I like your spunk." Zasha rose from the chair. "Oscar took Armando Ramirez; I'll take Carlos Acosta and Rafael Calderon since they are interconnected. Cole can handle Pablo Juarez and that leaves you with Alejandro Javier. I'll see you back here in fifty minutes. I want to compare notes before the rest of the group returns."

Chapter
25

On the Mexican Riviera the group of men broke their meeting so that each of them could have time to freshen up and rest before returning for lunch.

Alejandro reached into his shirt pocket and retrieved a slip of paper. *Jesus Camarena's* name and the word *bartender* was written on the paper. He went to the bathroom and washed his face, patting it dry before returning to the door of his room. He peered out of the door to make sure that no one was in the hallway. Stepping out, he hurried to the veranda and found Jesus. "Would you be so kind and deliver a glass of single malt Scotch to my room?" Alejandro handed Jesus a folded bill and left for his room.

Jesus stuffed the bill into his pants pocket and walked to the bar. There, he took the bill out and unfolded it. *Eagle I* was scrawled across the face of the Aztec warrior on the hundred peso note. He put the bill beneath a napkin and wrote a short note then positioned the glass directly over the note.

Alejandro answered the knock at his door. Jesus handed him the glass of Balvenie Scotch on a small tray and left the way he'd come. Alejandro noticed the note through the amber liquid. The vibrations of the Scotch made it difficult to read the note. He took the tray into the bathroom and placed it on the sink, while he turned on the shower. Through the calmed Scotch, he read the note. *The rooms are bugged, complete with cameras. Only the bathrooms are safe.*

Alejandro pulled a lighter from his pocket and burned the note and the hundred-peso bill. He held each of them by the smallest tip and let the ashes fall into the toilet before flushing. He closed the toilet, sat down and drank the glass of Scotch. He pulled one of two cell phones from his jacket pocket and dialed his daughter. "Marianna, I will be sending you a text message later this evening. Do exactly as it instructs and tell no one what you are doing…it is a matter of life and death."

She excitedly questioned him. "Father, are you okay? What is going on?"

"Not now Marianna. Just follow my instructions to the letter and be certain that you do not discuss this conversation with anyone. You hold my life in your hands. Do you understand?"

She nodded, though she could not be seen. "Yes, father."

"Good, expect to hear from me later." Alejandro closed the phone and sighed. He looked at the empty glass of Scotch and wished it was refilled. Sliding the phone open, he revealed a miniature keyboard and began typing a message:

Marianna, I want you to take a vacation. Your mother was always proud of saying that she was 'Black Irish.' I'm sorry you two couldn't have made this trip together. Take one hundred thousand pesos from the safe. Convert them to Euros today. Take only one carry-on bag, you can get anything else you need in Ireland. Tonight, I want you to take a flight to Waterford, Ireland. It's a late-night flight, so you will arrive tomorrow morning. One of your 'Black Irish' relatives will be there to meet you. Tell them the Aztec Warrior has risen. They will present you with a picture of the most feared warrior; you will recall our history lesson. Go with them and do as they say. Marianna, TELL NO ONE! Call a cab to pick you up from the complex— use cash to purchase your ticket and for God's sake, TELL NO ONE! I will see you in a few days.

Alejandro set the message to arrive in Marianna's text center at 4 p.m. It would be enough time to exchange the money and pack.

Chapter
26

Jessie James Carson's helicopter circled the White House as his name sake would have circled a bank. Clearance was given and the chopper sat down on the lawn. The phone on his side giggled rapidly— this was an unexpected call.

Carson pulled the phone from his waist and looked at the screen. The sender's I.D. kept him in his seat...*Eagle I.* Quickly, he pulled the message to his screen; it was a copy of what was planned for Marianna. "Oh, shit," audibly escaped Carson's lips.

Carson punched the direct number for the Langley conference room where he expected to find Oscar and his team.

Zasha answered the call as Oscar Fenton was entering the room. "Conference room B, Agent Davis."

Carson ran his hand over his brow. "Zasha, is Oscar there?"

Zasha looked at Oscar. "He just walked in, sir. Should I put you on speaker?"

Carson thought for a second. "Yeah, this will involve all of you."

Zasha looked at the others in the room and punched the speaker option on the base. "We're all here, sir."

Carson waved everyone from the chopper and listened as the whine of the blades ground to a stop. "Which one of you pulled the profile on Alejandro Javier?"

Julie looked at the profile in her hand. "That would be me, sir, Julie Hu. From what I've read, he really doesn't seem to fit with this group."

"There's a good reason for that." Carson stood and paced in the limited space of the helicopter. "Javier is a friendly. He has worked for some time with the Company. As a matter of fact, I recruited him personally. We've worked together for years."

Oscar rapidly moved to his chair. "Sir, does that mean that you knew about this meeting ahead of time?"

Carson stopped pacing. "I found out as soon as he did. Since everything was developing on our end, I wanted to see what played out…something has come up. Javier's daughter, Mariana is carrying a message for us. She's going to be in Waterford, Ireland first thing tomorrow morning. I want Davis and Peterson to be there when she arrives at seven and get her on American soil immediately. If Alejandro is sending her away, she is in grave danger."

"Based on the profiles I read, I'd say she is." Zasha tossed her files on the table. "This is a nasty group of boys that wouldn't hesitate to kill anyone in their way. They're not the type we watch passively."

"Indeed! When you arrive, have a picture of an Aztec Eagle Warrior. That will allow Mariana to know who you are." Carson sat and rubbed his temples. "In the meantime, I've got to get to the Oval Office. The President is waiting."

Zasha disconnected the speaker phone after hearing the line go dead. "Should we pass copies all around? It looks as if Cole and I will have to finish this via teleconference."

Cole looked at his watch. "To get there by seven in the morning, we're going to have to be in the air within the next couple of hours." He turned to Oscar. "Who's going to be co-pilot on the flight?"

Oscar lifted the receiver and punched in a number. "I know just the guy; since we're not sure if anyone will be tailing Marianna, I'm bringing in the best."

When the call went through, the response was short. "Yeah?"

"This is Oscar Fenton, Paramilitary Operations Officer, CIA. I need a couple of men to ride shotgun with my team to retrieve a friendly." He looked at Cole and winked. "One of the men needs to be certified on birds. He'll be co-pilot on the mission."

The voice on the other end was emotionless. "What are you putting in the air?"

Oscar's eyes again diverted to Cole. "A Lear 28; our destination is Waterford, Ireland. Your men need to be ready for any situation. We're not sure what may be waiting for us on the other end."

The voice continued. "Will your office be notifying the Irish authorities, or are we going in under the radar?"

Oscar rubbed his temples. "I think we'll wait until your plane hits the tarmac before giving them a call. We don't want too many anxious people on the ground. If things do become confrontational, handle everything as quietly and quickly as possible. Retrieve the package and get her in the air."

"Your agents can brief us on the package in the air. We'll be prepared for any surprises."

"Get your men in 'civies' and on a chopper. We need to get this bird in the air immediately. We'll be leaving from the Langley airfield." Oscar put the phone back in the cradle and turned to Cole and Zasha. "Saddle up. They should be here within the next twenty minutes. Make sure you've got that damn picture of that warrior guy."

Chapter
27

Director Carson stepped from the chopper and was met by two Marine sentries, who were there to escort him directly to the Oval Office. In his brief case, he carried a copy of the recording made during Zhang's meeting in Mexico. Also, he had several hand-written notes with possible strategies to counter Zhang's plans. It wasn't as well thought out as Carson would have liked, because his time to prepare was so limited.

The President rose from his desk as the Director walked in. "Jessie, what's so important that it couldn't wait until tomorrow's briefing?"

Director Carson shook the President's hand and reached into his briefcase for the recording. "Mr. President, as you are aware the volume of tainted products coming from China has been a major concern of ours for some time. This coupled with Haotion's manifesto I shared with you recently required that we take a closer look into what the Chinese are up to. What we didn't expect to find was a conspiracy, led by a Chinese national to overthrow our government."

The President remained standing looking at Carson without speaking for some time. "And I thought, 'lame duck' meant I coast into retirement. When I took this office eight years ago, I inherited a war that no one wanted to claim. Now you're telling me that my legacy is being besieged by something else outside of my control. What's next? Do I have to declare war against the Chinese?"

Carson sat the digital player down and rested a hand on top of it. "If it's any consolation sir, we haven't detected any direct Chinese government involvement per se, but I'm afraid that's where the good news ends. This group has involved a faction from Mexico as well. Both groups contain elements of powerful criminal underworld figures and members of their respective governments. However, the government personnel do not appear to be functioning in an official capacity, at least, that is what the tapes suggest."

For the next hour and a half, the President sat and listened to the recordings from Zhang's meeting. On occasion, he paused the playback to gain clarification as to who was speaking and how they were involved. When the playback was finished, the President folded his hands in front of his face and sighed. "The easy thing here would be to allow the fellow following me to inherit this problem. But, if the current polls are correct, he would be content to let everyone who wanted to enter the country to come in with a free pass playing right into the hands of their plot."

Carson held the eyes across the desk from him feeling the stress that they conveyed. "Sir, we both know that if we leave this alone it will only fester. Unfortunately, if we go public with what we've gathered, we face all kinds of backlash. You would be accused of trying to influence the election and you can bet that Mexico and China will threaten retaliation. If we round up all the suspects, we run the risk of being accused of an act of war. Even with the irrefutable evidence, the two governments won't remain idle if we take their high-ranking officials into custody."

The President's hands fell from his face. "We can't just sit by and do nothing." He fell back in his chair. "The way things have been going, I sincerely believed that the Chinese people would correct a large part of our problem with their country. Faster than we can speak, China is forming a middle class, which is a curse to communism. All we have to do was sit back and wait…and now this."

"Since waiting is not an option, we have to handle the domestic politics. I think bringing in the nominees from both parties and breaking down the situation is the best way to reach consensus."

The President waved his hand cutting Carson off. "Yeah, but what's to stop either of them from using this information to bolster their position in the weeks leading up to the election?" That's like tossing a grenade into a room full of people. There's going to be a lot of collateral damage. They're not likely to sit on the information."

Carson tugged at his ear. "Well, there goes the international politics. The situation isn't leaving us many options. We're going to have to start somewhere."

The President eased forward on his elbows. "What do you suggest?"

Carson cut his eyes to a Remington statue of Geronimo on a table behind the President. "Well, they're still meeting in Puerto Vallarta. We could send a team in and detain the group. Then, we could bring in their perspective presidents and share our findings. Of course, we would have to inform Mexico first, which could muddy the waters. We suspect these drug lords of providing the Mexican government with substantial kickbacks. Depending on who's involved, they might not let us in."

The President folded his hands where they lay on his desk. "I have always found Nestor Suarez to be a reasonable man. With this evidence, he has no reason to object."

Carson's eyebrows rose slowly as if lifted by heat. "Reaching into a man's wallet tends to negate reason. There's also the possibility that word of our plan will leak to the group prior to our arrival and these men will scatter in the wind. If we go in without permission, at some point we'll have to explain what we've done with the four government officials. Unless, we chose to have them completely disappear."

"That's not an acceptable option!" The President slid his hand over his mouth and dragged it across the stubble that was quickly returning. "Didn't you say that you had a man on the inside?"

Carson's eyes diverted as he debated how much to reveal. "Two actually; one agent and a friend of the Agency's; Alejandro Javier has been a loyal confidant for years."

The President sat the paper in his hand down. "Then, why don't we simply plant a tracking device on these men? We have access to them. It shouldn't be that difficult."

Carson tapped his finger on the President's desk. "It's not that simple. Zhang is a very cautious man; he routinely has everyone around him scanned for tracking bugs. Fortunately, he is not as careful with cell phones. That is how we were able to monitor the conversations. Pablo Juarez and his crew are quite different. It wouldn't surprise me if he didn't suggest that everyone present dispenses with their cell phones. Sometimes, he changes his five or six times a day. Going in now may be our best opportunity."

The President folded his hands. "I'm sure you have some idea of how you would proceed. Let's hear it."

Carson opened a folder. "We know that the compound is heavily guarded. I would suspect a minimum of a five-mile radius, which includes the ocean front. We could send in a Delta team that will hit all sides of the compound simultaneously. Using silent weapons, striking when they are at dinner will provide us the element of surprise and we'll have all the major players in the same room. Once we're in the compound, we can switch to narcotic darts to incapacitate our main targets. The Delta team can get them loaded and out to sea in a matter of minutes. A cleanup crew will come behind them and make any evidence of this meeting an enigma."

The President lifted his phone. "Assemble the Joint Chiefs in the War Room; I'll be there in fifteen." He sat the phone in its cradle still holding the receiver as he turned his attention to Carson. "Let's see what the military has to say. If there are any fuck-ups with a mission like this, they're going to have to pick up the ball. You and I both know screwing up something like this is just the 'wet dream' China has been hoping for."

Chapter
28

The Joint Chiefs waited in the Situation Room anticipating the President's arrival. No handouts waited on the table for the men increasing the moment of mystery for them.

The President entered followed by Director Carson and the room rose to greet them. As the salutes dropped, focus shifted to the folder in Carson's hand.

"Please take your seats." The President slid into his chair and pulled it close to the table. "Gentlemen, Director Carson has briefed me of an extremely tenuous situation rising just south of our border. A Chinese national has convened a delegation of Chinese and Mexican crime and government figures with the intent of overthrowing our government."

The Joint Chiefs exchanged looks that eventually fell back to Carson. The CIA Director opened his folder and delivered a synopsis of the brewing event. When he finished, he closed the folder and began tapping his pen against it. "As you can see, this situation is complicated because of the government officials involved. We could let these men return to their lives and clamp down on our borders and hope to intercept the illegals, but that hasn't worked in the past. We could impose more stringent regulations in order to gain citizenship and the election could undo that effort based on who we suspect will inherit the office. Our other option is to hit the meeting, which is still in progress and deal with the political fallout at a later date. What we can't do is treat this as a bogus threat.

The Marine General addressed the President. "Sir, since the incidents concerning tainted Chinese products, the Chinese military has used the media to promote their buildup. The rhetoric they have spewed in cooperation with their media blitz is intended to serve as a threat to us. I believe they would welcome the opportunity to engage our military. In large part, they are responsible for fanning the flames of discontent around the world. They have concentrated their effort in the Middle East, North Korea, Africa, Cuba and Russia. If word gets out that we have taken their top military official into custody, we might as well get ready; they'll have the excuse that they've wanted."

"I can't say that I disagree with you." The President leaned forward. "Even with the overwhelming evidence there's no guarantee that anyone will listen. Despite the uncertainty, one thing is for sure, we can't sit by and wait."

The Army General reached for Carson's folder. "May I take a look at the location of their meeting?"

Director Carson handed him the page containing the satellite photograph. "We are running additional heat-signature shots of the area to get an estimate of the number of people we're dealing with. Considering who's involved, I've ordered a five-mile radius of the compound. As you can see from the shot, they are isolated."

The Army General scanned the photo. "In addition to the known participants, have you received any indication of staff on hand?"

Carson opened his folder. "The bartender is ours; the other staff varies. During the day, housekeepers are there along with the kitchen staff. Immediately after dinner, the kitchen staff leaves and our bartender is there until they retire for the evening."

The General continued looking at the photo. "How much longer will they be attending the meeting?"

"We don't know for sure. To date, the staff has been alerted each evening if they are needed further. Of course, this is only day two." Carson closed his folder. "If we agree to hit the compound it better be soon."

The Army General handed the photo back to Carson. "How soon will you have the additional shots?"

Carson looked at his watch. "They may be ready I can check with my team if you would like."

The General pointed to the folder Carson was holding. "That would be good. Puerto Vallarta is what, three hours behind Eastern Time? It's 13:30 now; I could dispatch a Delta team from the West Coast and have them in place before dark. As soon as the sun ducks for the day, we can hit them from all sides. I'll need a constant intelligence feed so that we can secure the perimeter as quickly as possible. That could limit any firefight."

The President placed both hands flat against the table. "Director Carson has suggested that we use narcotic darts inside the house. We don't want to unnecessarily kill anyone involved with the group."

Carson tapped the folder on the table to level its contents. "It would be safe to assume that the criminal element among the group will be armed. For that matter, I would suspect General Gan to be armed as well. You're going to have to secure the room as quickly as possible." He reached in the folder and produced several photographs. "These are the most current photographs we have of each man. These two, Jesus Camarena and Alejandro Javier should be considered the lowest priority; they are ours. The others, I will leave to your discretion. I'll see to it that you're immediately linked into the intel feed."

The President stood followed by the others in the room. We will meet back here as soon as the Delta team is in place. Place the feed on the screen. I want to see this operation from beginning to end."

Chapter
29

The giant walked across the moonlit sand in search of his boss. Zhang was seated on a chaise lounge. Blue smoke curled from the tip of his cigar and the waves in his glass of Scotch were just beginning to calm. "There haven't been any additional transmissions. The phone that was used must have contained some type of jamming device that prevented us from locating the precise signal. A search of the rooms proved useless. Nothing new turned up."

Zhang brought the cigar to his lips and took a long slow pull. A small stream of smoke blew from his lips as if under pressure. The smoke trailed off and Scotch filled the empty space in his mouth. "Did you review the video to see who may have used a phone, or even pulled one from their bags?"

"We can account for everything that we saw, including staff." The giant noticed that the Scotch in the glass was low and lifted the bottle of Balvenie for a refill. "What would you like me to do next?"

Zhang took another drink of the Scotch. "Is there anything to suggest that someone on the staff could have been involved?"

The Giant hunched. "Not likely. We monitor them much too closely."

"Then how do you explain the disappearance of the phone?" Zhang put the cigar in his mouth and stood. "No one else has been allowed to leave the premises. Make sure the guards are extra vigilant. We don't want any unexpected guests. If someone should arrive, see to it that our escape plans are flawless."

The giant walked away without another word. He knew that Zhang was planning something and knew not to ask; he would know in time.

Zhang finished his Scotch and tossed the cigar into the ocean and watched the waves carry it out. It was time for another plan. One he knew the members of the gathering wouldn't like, but one that was necessary to insure the future safety of the entire group.

The crackle in the Giant's ear alerted him that a call was coming in. He moved out of sight and waited.

"Tell the men to hold their posts at all cost, but stay out of the house. Given the hour, we must move quickly. Meet me back at the house. We've got to get everyone moved." Zhang disconnected and walked to the house. Once inside, he grabbed a pad and wrote something in large Chinese characters. He sat at a console and looked at each monitor broadcasting the goings-on in each of his guest's rooms.

Vladimir only settled in a few minutes earlier. As usual, the abundance of vodka made his entry into sleep quite sudden. Engaging several levers, a silent rubber seal formed around each of the bedroom doors. Windows that were opened closed and every exit locked.

The giant walked into the control room and started to speak. Zhang thrust the paper in the air slashing the words forming in the giant's mouth. He read the sign. *Total silence! I suspect someone may be listening. As soon as the gas has taken effect, we'll leave via the underground tunnels. Is the crew prepared on the yacht?*

The giant nodded and Zhang pressed a button releasing a gas that quickly filled the bedrooms of each of his guests.

After nearly ten minutes, the giant entered the rooms dressed in a space-like suit with its own oxygen supply and proceeded to strip each of the nine men. He looked for any sign of hidden transmission devices on each of the men and injected the contents of a syringe in each of their arms. The propofol would keep them out well into the next portion of their trip. Any protest at that point would be futile; they would be hopelessly lost.

The giant put the men on a gurney two at a time and took them to an elevator. Inside, he placed his hand on a hidden panel that was nearly nine feet up on the back wall of the elevator. A hiss escaped what appeared to be a solid metal wall and revealed a floor choice that didn't exist on the front panel. The elevator carried them to a subterranean tunnel containing a waiting van. The giant positioned the naked men side by side on the floor of the van as if he were stacking slaughtered meat.

On the last trip, he went to the control room for Zhang and found him recording something on a camera. He transferred the recording to the control panel and pressed a few more buttons. Once he was finished, he slapped the giant on the back and motioned for him to lead the way.

They road in silence until they reached the mouth of the tunnel; Zhang placed his hand on a panel and a keypad slid out. He punched a series of numbers and letters thirty characters long and pushed the red button on the bottom of the keypad. "In the event that whoever was listening to us discovers our escape route, they'll receive a roaring welcome. Did you collect all their electronic devices?"

"They're sealed in a container in the van. Once we're on board and under way, I'll send them on their own cruise in a totally different direction." The giant opened the door of the van and waited for Zhang to get in. Thirty minutes later, they transferred the men from the van onto one of Zhang's yachts and the ship steamed into the dark waters.

Zasha and Cole waited hidden in the security office of the Waterford, Ireland airport. They monitored movement around the gate where Marianna was scheduled to arrive. They watched for anyone who may be carrying a picture or acting overly nervous.

One person repeatedly walked over to view the arrivals board. At this viewing, the few flights scheduled to arrive all were marked 'on time.'

Zasha looked at her watch. Marianna's plane was scheduled to touch down in five minutes. She walked to the director of security. "Call the tower; have them change the gate for this flight." She handed him a slip of paper. "Also have them list it as late and tell the pilot to keep everyone in their seats until we get on board. Make sure no one is allowed to use a cell phone until we're off the plane."

The security director looked at the MI5 agent for approval. "Do it. I'll go with them. Divert the plane to the other side of the airport. What's the girl's seat number?"

The director looked at the manifesto. "She's in 2-A."

Cole nodded to the MI5 agent. "We couldn't have caught a better break. Let's get her off that plane and on ours."

"My car is just outside the door. Let's get moving." The MI5 agent held the door for Zasha and Cole. A few seconds into their trip, a message appeared in Gaelic on the agent's cell phone. *They'll be at Gate 4 in two minutes.* The agent glanced at the message and pushed the gas.

The guide man signaling the plane to the gate nearly jumped from the tarmac as the car squealed its tires sliding to a stop.

The MI5 agent, quickly followed by Zasha and Cole ran to the guideman. Zasha shouted into the man's ear protection. "Stop the plane short of the docking station. We've got to get on board as quickly as possible."

The guide man placed his cones in the shape of an 'X' and the pilot cut the engines. He radioed the pilot. "You need to let these guys from MI5 on the plane before coming all the way to the gate. They're in a hurry!"

Cole jumped into a bucket truck and the driver raised him to the plane's opening door. He jumped from the bucket onto the plane and took the mike. "Ladies and gentlemen, thank you for your cooperation. In just a few seconds, we will have you at the gate and allow you to deplane. In the meantime, I must ask you to refrain from using any electronic equipment."

A man two seats from him ignored the request. Cole pulled the mike from his mouth. "Sir, do you speak English?"

The man nodded affirmatively. Cole stepped next to the man. "Sir, please put the cell phone down."
The man continued to ignore the request. Cole slid his Glock from his holster and put it in the middle of the man's head. "Give me the phone, now!" Cole took the phone and looked over the other people on the plane. "Does everyone understand that I need each of you to remain off all electronic devices until you are deplaned?'

Behind Cole, the MI5 agent entered the plane waving his creds. He lifted the noncompliant man from his seat and walked him to the back of the plane. "You can keep me company for a while. During that time maybe, you can explain your malfunction."

Cole dropped the picture of the Aztec warrior in Marianna's lap when he first entered the plane. Her heart was racing because she knew that he was here for her. Cole holstered his gun and leaned close to her ear. "We must hurry."

Cole and Marianna stepped into the bucket and were lowered to the ground. Zasha kicked the car door open. "Come on, I've got the plane's engine running."

Cole put Marianna in the front next to Zasha and jumped in the back seat.

Marianna hid her nervousness well, but soon turned to Cole. "What's this all about?"

"Your father asked that we meet you here. He had reason to believe that you were in danger." Cole slid the Glock from its holster and watched for any unwanted company.

Zasha spoke into the wireless mike on the side of her face. "We're almost there. Stand ready just in case."

Several well-armed men took positions around the waiting jet and watched as the car neared. The leader of the team scanned the area through binoculars. Jerking them from his face, he yelled to his men. "Get them on board; it looks like we're going to have some company."

The team members grabbed the doors of the car and flung them open. "There's no time; we've got to hurry! Zhang's reach is much further than we anticipated. The approaching car has to be his cohorts."

Shots rang out just as they reached the plane's steps. Zasha stumbled and was lifted and nearly tossed on the jet by one of the team members. Cole was the second to last to get on the jet. He pointed to the last member of the team. "Secure that door or we'll all have a bad flight." He dashed to the cockpit and shouted to the co-pilot. "Get this thing moving; we've got to get in the air now."

The MI5 agent's voice came over the radio in the cockpit. "You've got priority— get her in the air. We'll mop up here on the ground."

The ground force had not yet caught up to the car rapidly approaching the jet. The driver pushed down hard on the accelerator attempting to ram the jet from behind.

The excited voice of the MI5 agent broke in again. "Do something quickly, he's about to ram the back of the plane."

Cole jammed the throttle forward bathing the car in jet wash. The windshield immediately blew out and the force of the thrusting air violently flipped the car in the air. Static caused by the tremendous friction ignited gas spilling from the car and a fireball engulfed the airborne vehicle. As the whine of the engine climbed, the jet pulled further from the burning car.

The jet lifted in the air and began to level off at thirty thousand feet. Cole eased back in the seat taking a second to relax for the first time since they'd boarded Marianna's plane.

The team leader ducked in the cockpit. "She doesn't look too bad. We've got the bleeding stopped. Luckily, the bullet went right through."

Cole spun in the chair. The tension he'd tried to blow off seized him harder than before. "What in hell are you talking about?"

The team leader pulled at the Velcro holding his vest around his torso. "Agent Davis— she was hit when we were running to the plane. I thought you knew."

Cole looked at the co-pilot. "I'll be back in a few." He left the cockpit and went to Zasha. The bloody clothes were just being gathered by a member of the team.

Zasha flashed a weak smile. "I wish I'd had a chance to shoot first."

"How bad is it?" His eyes alternated between the team member who attended to her wound and Zasha's face.

She looked at the team member and could tell that he wanted no part of coming between them. Zasha tossed a hand in his direction. "Since he's such a pussy, I guess I'll have to tell you. I'm fine; it's a through and through. The blood makes things look worse than they are."

Cole pulled his iPhone from his jacket and dialed. "Oscar, Agent Davis took a round in the shoulder. We didn't take time to find out who was shooting. I'm going to set down in Frankfurt to have a military doc take a look at her."

"That's an excellent idea. I'll call ahead. By the way, you didn't leave us much to work with in Waterford. You toasted the guy, literally. So much for any information he may have had."

"He didn't leave me much choice, he was about to ram the back of the jet." Cole cut his eyes to the team leader. He knew what Oscar was about to say next.

Oscar didn't disappoint. "You've got a Delta team on the plane; they could have taken out everyone at the airport in a matter of seconds. They could have handled the situation."

Cole placed the phone on speaker and Oscar received a rally cry from the team leader. Cole shook his head. "There was no need to start a firefight on the ground, we had the target secure. Besides, the Delta team would in effect achieve the same thing. Agent Davis usually walks on water— who knew she couldn't dodge bullets."

Zasha flashed Cole a bloody 'bird' and turned her attention to Oscar. "I'm fine Oscar, though I can't say that I'd mind if we stopped to get a little pain relief."

Oscar changed directions. "Have either of you taken the time to debrief Miss Javier?"

Cole and Zasha looked at each other and Marianna took the question. "Between getting shot and roasting our attackers in jet-wash, they haven't had the time just yet. My father wanted me to tell you, 'There's no moment better than the present.' Does that make any sense?"

"Indeed, it does. Was there anything else?" Oscar jotted a note on his iPhone and forwarded a copy to Director Carson.

Marianna looked at the text message on her cell phone. "That was all. Is he in danger?"

"Not if I can help it." Oscar read an incoming message from Carson. "Marianna, I have to leave you in the capable hands of Agent Peterson. I'm needed for a meeting. As soon as we can, I'll put you in touch with your father."

Marianna could hear Oscar's attempt to convey hope, but knew that he was unconvinced of her father's fate. "Thank you." She gazed out the window hoping that she had not seen her father for the last time.

Alejandro patted the sheets before sliding his hand beneath them. He was shocked feeling his bare skin. He had not slept naked since before his wife had died. He sat up straight in the bed and blinked to get his eyes to focus. This was not the room he remembered.

Outside his window, he could hear water, but it was not the sound of waves lapping against the shoreline. The unmistakable swaying brought him to the realization that they were on the water. A quick look out the window and a feeling of despondency washed over him…there was no chance of escape. They were surrounded by water.

Alejandro looked around the room for anything familiar. There were no suitcases, no clothes, no shoes and no electronic devices. In short, there would not be any outside contact. A soft knock at the cabin door sent him quickly back beneath the covers.

The giant stepped through the door. "You don't have to be modest with me; I've already seen everything you have." He tossed a package on the bed. "Here are some clothes and shoes."

Alejandro reached for the package. "What is the meaning of this? You can't just snatch people up and take them where you please. I want to see Zhang right away."

"First of all, the fact that you're here suggests that I can snatch you up and take you wherever I please. Breakfast is in an hour. Zhang expects you there. At that time, he will offer any necessary explanation."

Alejandro tore open the package. "Am I confined to the room until then?"

The giant stepped through the door. "You are not a prisoner— you may come and go as you please." He closed the door quietly. "You're also free to leave if you can swim for days without taking a break."

The giant returned to the control room where Zhang was waiting. "The others are starting to stir; we'd better get some clothes to them. Be careful with Carlos and Rafael; they're not going to be happy about their current situation." Zhang pointed to a box on a table containing all his guests' phones and other electronic devices. "You might as well toss those overboard."

The giant placed the box under his arm and left to deliver the other clothes. On deck, he tossed the phones overboard one at a time. In the bottom of the box were the batteries that he'd removed before they left the mainland. He dumped them all at once. He then silently delivered clothes to the remaining guests, saving Carlos and Rafael for last.

Carlos took the pillowcase from his pillow and wrapped it around his right hand. If it worked as he'd planned, it would give him extra punching power and he planned to knock out the first person who walked through his door.

The giant punched a code on the wall beside Carlos' door and a lock slid open. He opened the door and instantaneously noticed that Carlos was not in the bed. With cat-like quickness, he stepped to the clear side of the room and held up the package of clothing.

The motion was just in time to catch the hardest straight ahead punch that Carlos had ever thrown. It ripped through the package containing the clothes. The giant caught both legs on the pants in the package and with amazing speed, looped them around Carlos's wrist. He stepped to Carlos' right side, where the punch came from and jerked pants down and towards his left ankle.

Unable to conquer physics, Carlos flipped, landing near the giant's feet; one of which pressed so hard on Carlos' chest that he found it difficult to breathe.

Zhang sharply yelled into the speaker at the control room. "Carlos, that's enough! My giant is a master in Kung Fu. He would kill you before you could so much as scratch him." Zhang turned the speakers on over the entire yacht. "Gentlemen, I realize that you are all confused right now. You have been brought to my yacht for your own safety and protection. Please forgive what you may consider deception, this was the only way to bring you out safely and determine who among us is a traitor. Please join me for breakfast where I will explain everything."

They arrived in the dining room pissed off to various degrees. Carlos, by far possessed the most anger. "You'd best start explaining this shit right now. I don't like this one goddamned bit!"

Zhang sat at the head of the table. "Please sit-down gentlemen. Carlos, if it's any consolation, I don't suspect you in the least." He waited for them to take their seats. "Yesterday, one of you communicated with someone outside the compound with an unapproved device. Here is a list of all your phone and device IDs that you arrived with. The digital signature we picked up doesn't match any of these."

"Now you understand why I change phones every day." Carlos took the list from Zhang. "Cell phone technology originated from the American military. Anything that they created, they can manipulate— you can't trust those bastards."

"Did you change phones after you arrived in Puerto Vallarta? That would allow us to clear up this little misunderstanding and get back to the mainland quicker." Zhang took the papers back from Carlos.

"You know damn well that we didn't. You explained your reasoning before we arrived. Did you share that concept with the others?" Carlos sat next to Zhang.

"Everyone was told that they must register each electronic device with us. I don't see how this could have been mistaken." Zhang looked at the giant. "You did double check, didn't you?"

The giant, who was standing in front of the door with his massive arms folded nodded.

Zhang waved one hand. "There you have it, he doesn't make mistakes." He pointed a remote to the wall in front of him and a one-hundred-and-twenty-inch screen deployed from the ceiling. He pressed another button and a picture appeared on the screen. "This is a live broadcast of the complex. The guards have been instructed not to let anyone in or out of the building. They have no idea that we are not there."

On the outside of the building, they could see guards moving about in the sunshine. Armando took his seat and turned to Zhang. "Do you have any other views of the property?"

Zhang slowly let a smile burn across his face. "Of course." He pointed the remote and pushed a button in a steady rhythm.

Each of their bedrooms from the complex flashed onto the screen. The last three pictures were of the kitchen, laundry room and the bar. Each of those rooms also contained the bodies of the people who had once worked there; three dead in the kitchen, two in the laundry room and Jesus at the bar. There were no signs of a struggle in any of the rooms even though each of the bodies had a knife jammed into their hearts.

Alejandro knew that he could not express the pain he felt— Zhang would be looking for that. He pointed to the screen. "Judging from the way each of these people was killed, I'd say you were trying to leave a message. Since we are here with you, who are you suspecting?"

"Excellent question— I think we should watch the screen to see if anyone else appears. However, I feel it is pointless during the day. There would be no chance of surprise." Zhang clicked another button and the screen went dark. He rose from his chair. "Enjoy your breakfast. If anything of interest should occur, I will bring you together. Please feel free to roam as you please. The ship is yours."

Carlos stood. "Unlike the rest of your guests, I have a business to run. I can't do that without being able to reach my people."

Zhang leaned until his lips nearly touched Carlos' ear. "I will send for you. For now, sit as if I have scolded you. It will make it easier to locate the conspirator."

Carlos plopped in his chair and hung his head. Zhang scanned the group. "Does anyone else have anything to say?"

They all took their seats without another word.

Chapter
32

Oscar walked in Director Carson's office and took a seat while Carson finished a call. His leg bounced up and down rapidly flashing a sign of his anxiousness.

Carson looked at Oscar's bouncing leg and pointed to it as he hung up the phone. "You should have that looked at."

"What, oh the leg." Oscar put his hand on it and stopped bouncing. "We've got to mobilize a team right away. The message from Javier is our code to come in."

Carson nodded. "I recognized it the second I saw it. I've had the team on stand-by. I was just on the phone with the President." He turned his computer monitor so that Oscar could see it. "The satellite images are loaded with people around the complex right now. We'll provide the Delta team with heat images at nightfall. Hopefully that will enable them to pinpoint their strike. You'll be coming with me to the White House this evening to observe the offensive."

"Agent Hu has asked if she can be part of the strike force. She feels that she owes it to Agent Chin." Oscar's leg resumed its bouncing.

Carson pointed to the leg again and Oscar calmed it. "Is she completely clear that we want these men alive? This is not a revenge mission. One bullet in the wrong person and we will be in one hell of a mess."

"Absolutely sir; I'll spell it out. There won't be any mistakes." Oscar crossed his legs so that they wouldn't start bouncing again.

"Is she going to be able to keep up with the Delta team? We can't have anything slowing them down. If she falls back, I'll have them leave her." Carson jammed his finger on the top of his desk.

Oscar continuously nodded. "Completely understood, sir—I believe they will find her in top shape. She'll be right in the mix."

Carson rose from his chair. "Get her in the air. She'll have to rendezvous with the team before they leave the base in San Diego. She may actually prove helpful. She has seen at least half of these men face-to-face. I'll give the team leader a heads-up. Get yourself in gear; we have to be at the White House by twenty hundred. The strike will commence at twenty-three hundred."

The War Room in the White House was set up to watch the progress of the Delta team. Five minutes ten seconds was left on the countdown clock and the twenty-man team was in position surrounding the complex in Puerto Vallarta. From the heat tracking and the live satellite broadcasts, there were eighteen guards that needed to be dealt with before they could gain entry to the building.

Most troubling was the lack of heat signatures inside the complex. From the command post at the White House, the Joint Chief's suggested that something in the roof of the building was most likely causing interference with the equipment. Regardless, the mission would move forward.

The last few seconds ticked from the clock and the order to commence was given. Near silent shots flew through the air ending all potential opposition from the guards. The team leader touched the mike on the side of his face. Cupping the end, he spoke softly. One by one, he asked the other three flanker groups for a status report.

Eighteen shots— eighteen kills. The team leader waited for the men in the boats to make it to his location. The decision was made to hit the complex from all sides. With no confirmation of internal movement, stun grenades would go in ahead of the team. Disoriented people were a lot easier to handle, especially since everyone inside was to be kept alive.

The team positioned themselves around the exterior of the complex structure in four groups of five. The team leader spoke into his mouthpiece. "Prepare two grenades at each location. We're set for a non-lethal assault. Get them to the ground quickly; the whole operation shouldn't take more than twenty-five seconds."

Julie Hu was in the team leader's group. She reached for his shoulder. "If we're fired upon inside, what then?"

The team leader never turned around. "Make sure that the shooter doesn't get you with a head shot; your vest will take care of the rest. Agent Hu, for the record, I was against you coming on this mission. Emotion doesn't mesh well with the type of work we do here."

Julie wanted to snatch his head around to face her, but she remained calm. "Did I show any emotion during our extensive run-throughs?" She didn't wait for an answer. "I didn't think so. I'll do my job, as I'm sure you will yours."

The team leader looked back just as Julie pulled the pin from her grenade. He turned back to the front door. "On my mark in three; three…two…one."

The front and back doors along with two windows on opposite sides of the house all blew at the same time. Stun grenades rolled in and exploded shaking the entire complex. Laser sights sliced through the fog of confusion searching for targets.

Six figures seated in various rooms were located at nearly the same time. Tranquilizing darts sailed towards their marks; the force pushing each of the victims to the floor.

Julie rushed to identify anyone she recognized. She grabbed the man at the bar pulling him back. In the background she could hear yells of 'clear' confirming their safety. "We're too late."

The team leader, still shouldering his weapon, lowered it and turned to look at the man slumping in the chair. The first thing he noticed was the knife handle protruding from the victim's chest. "Do you realize how much strength it took to push a knife straight through someone's chest?"

Julie looked at the other victims. Each had a knife blade sticking out of their backs. The killer has pushed the knives completely through their torsos. "Whoever did him had the strength to do it five more times." She captured each of their faces for the broadcast transmitting at the White House.

The team leader scanned the ceiling and walls. "I've got a bad feeling about this place."

A crackle in her ear caused Julie to pause. "Agent Hu, the deceased at the bar is one of ours."

Director Carson made a note on the pad in front of him. "Tell the cleaning team to take him home, they can deal with the other five as prescribed."

The team leader noticed Julie preparing to remove her face cover. "Maintain cover!" He then turned his attention to his mike. "General, we've got a problem. At the very least, this part of our operation seems to be on film; I spotted one camera."

The general slid forward in his chair in the War Room. "Have the *cleaners* deal with it. In the meantime, have your men look for any secret rooms or hiding places. We've had that complex under constant surveillance for the past two days and no one has come or gone. They have to be there somewhere."

A sensor on the team leader's epaulette alarmed. "Masks! I'm getting a reading of some type of gas." The team quickly donned their gas masks. "Let's find the source of this. That's where we'll find the others."

They moved room to room, but found nothing. The control room door was bolted shut. Julie took a device designed to listen through walls from her pack. She placed the earphones in and positioned the microphone against the door. She waved the team leader over. "I'm getting some mechanical noises but I don't hear anything human."

The team leader put the earphones on and listened. "Set a charge, we're going in."

The charge blew ripping the door from its frame. The Delta team rushed into the room. It too was empty. The second they entered a camera mounted in a corner of the ceiling flashed four times in half second increments before rapidly flashing without any breaks. When the control panel went dark the team leader shouted. "Everyone out!"

An angry hiss came from the sprinklers in the control room. They began to spray covering everything. The last team member to exit the room was hit by the liquid on the back of his bullet-proof vest.

In the hallway, the team leader waved his men by. He noticed that the last man in the group had smoke rising from the spot the liquid had hit him. The team leader grabbed his arm. "Get your vest off quickly, but don't stop moving. Keep it away from your body."

The team burst from the front door into the grass. Everyone was accounted for except Julie. Director Carson punched a button so that he could be heard by the team. "Where's my agent?"

The team leader looked around. "She was near the front of the group. Did anybody see where she went?"

Heads shook and the leader walked near the house. "Sir, this is not good. When we entered the control room the sprinklers released some type of acid. One of my men was hit leaving the room. If I hadn't gotten him out of his vest, he'd be in a world of hurt." He put his finger on his earpiece. "Agent Hu, this is Alpha Wolf do you read?"

Three agonizing seconds passed without a word. Carson jammed his finger on the button. "Where's my agent? How is it none of you saw her?"

The team leader cautiously stepped through the front door. The sprinklers in the front rooms were quiet. He heard a grunt and spun in its direction with his rifle shouldered. "Why the hell didn't you respond?"

"My earpiece must have fallen out of my ear when we were clearing the room." Julie looked at the leader watching her struggle. "Are you going to just stand there watching or are you going to give me a hand?"

The leader spoke into his mike. "Agent Hu is safe. She went back to retrieve the agent who was killed. We're on our way out now."

Julie and the team leader laid Jesus in the grass and they turned with the rest of the team as they heard a minor explosion coming from the complex. Black smoke crawled its way from the open windows and doors.

All of the team heard the crackle at the same time. Oscar had his finger on the button allowing him to speak to the Delta team. "Get out of there now. If this place goes up, you're going to have a lot of company. You'll have to remove the dead guards. I've got the cleanup team en route they'll meet you at the beach."

The team leader signaled to four of his team. "Get the spent grenades from the house. Haul ass, we've got to get moving."

The men ducked in the house disappearing in the intensifying black smoke. The rest of the team grabbed dead guards and began dragging them towards the beach. Julie was struggling with Jesus until the team leader reached out with one hand and slung the dead man across his shoulders without losing one step.

Julie sighed with relief. "Thanks."

The team leader set their pace. "Don't think for a minute you're getting out of this. There's a skinny guy on the sand— he's yours."

Julie trotted ahead. "You're too kind."

They reached the sand and saw a group of Zodiac rubber rafts speeding towards shore. Both groups reached the beach at the same time. The team leader dropped Jesus in the sand and met the commander of the cleanup team. He pointed to Jesus. "This is an agent, he gets brought home. There are five more bodies in the house. My men have gathered the others. We removed traces of us, however, they may have filmed our invasion. That plus the fact that the house is about to go up in flames."

The commander turned to his men. "Bring two flamethrowers; we've got to put this place down quickly." Without another word, his group headed towards the house. When they left the house, any arriving fire department would only have to cool the ashes.

The President watched the screen as the Delta team jumped into their Zodiacs and headed back to their waiting ship. "Is anyone else feeling as unsettled as I do?"

Director Carson was tapping his pen against a folder and sliding his finger down its length. "I hate to say it, but it does seem that they expected us."

Everyone in the room could feel the President's glare on Carson. "Just how in the hell is that possible— we didn't even know that we were going in until a few hours ago?"

Carson put the pen down and folded his hands over it. "It's impossible to say exactly. I guess they could have gotten to Javier, but he would never have admitted to anything. Doing so would have meant giving up his daughter and she is the only family he has left."

The President lifted his briefing folder. "Might I remind you that two of Zhang's group are former KGB and the highest-ranking Chinese general is there as well. Do you think they're inept when it comes to techniques necessary to break a man?"

Director Carson briefly looked at the table. "It's possible, however; Zhang doesn't seem to trust anyone based on the chatter we picked up earlier."

The President's gaze oscillated between Carson and Oscar. "And what does the latest chatter tell you?"

Oscar looked at Carson, who nodded. "Mr. President, the chatter ended before we arrived here at the White House. Carlos Acosta suggested that cell phones were not safe. It would seem that Zhang took his warning to heart."

The President turned his attention to his generals. "Pull satellite photos from their location for the past twenty-four hours. I want to know where these men are. They caught us tripping over our own dicks. That's not going to happen again! Find these sonsofbitches and get them in custody!"

Director Carson and Oscar left the White House and headed back to Langley. Carson flipped on an overhead light and looked through file for anything he might have missed, or paid little attention to. "It's going to be impossible to get back on the site of the complex. There's got to be something there we didn't have time to locate— an underground bunker or some way out of there that allowed them to escape."

Oscar kept his eyes on the road. "My guess is they went underground. We'll have to use a GPR, or ground penetrating radar to see if we can locate any evidence of underground activity and trace the satellite reconnaissance to that point. That ought to give us all we need."

Carson scratched his head and turned out the light. "Let's just hope shit doesn't blow up in our faces before we find out anything."

They drove in silence for the duration of their trip to Langley.

Chapter
34

Zhang's yacht steamed through Bahía De Banderas at forty knots on its way to the Pacific Ocean. The four thousand one hundred nautical miles would take nearly four and a half days to complete. At that time, they would be in the waters off the coast of Rio de Janeiro, Brazil.

It would be impossible to keep the men from seeing the shore, but it would be too far away for any of them to swim. Zhang knew that once he carefully explained the situation, no one would want to leave the yacht for any length of time. Even though the hour was late, he called everyone to the dining room for a briefing.

When they were seated at the table, Zhang pressed a remote control and a recording began to play on the screen behind his head. "This is what I'd been waiting for. If we had not removed you from the complex when we did, your fate would have rested in the hands of these men."

Everyone watched as a group wearing all black moved around the complex waving automatic weapons. Guards, who also wielded automatic weapons, fell to the ground as silent bursts erupted from the group in black. The grenades on the screen blew with the same intensity as when they blew live at the complex and the men in the room responded accordingly.

Zhang observed each of the men. "So, you think we still should have left you in Puerto Vallarta? Carlos, haven't the Americans put a multi-million-dollar price on your head? You and your men would have been a nice seven-figure payday. Instead, you are free to enjoy yourself as you see fit. As I see it, those facing the greatest scrutiny are the members of government. The Americans surely won't leave this alone. If they were willing to send in commandos, their next step will most likely be approaching the Mexican and Chinese governments."

General Gan appeared pale. "Did you determine if our sessions were recorded? That would present enormous difficulties."

Zhang looked towards the giant, who was shaking his head side to side. "We didn't detect any type of listening devices at the complex."

Rafael snorted and mumbled. "Look at how long it took you to take my advice concerning the cell phones."

Vladimir slapped the table. "Have any of you given your cell number to anyone that you didn't know recently? Because Rafael is correct, if anyone had your number, they could have listened to conversation via your cell. One thing is for sure, these commandos didn't happen upon our meeting place by accident. At least one of us is responsible."

Zhang held up one finger. "Which brings me to another point. I thought we made it clear that we had the significant people in your lives under surveillance in case there was a problem. Only two of you have one person that you consider significant." He nodded towards Vladimir and Javier. "And in both cases, that person has gone missing."

Vladimir's stair was nearly lethal. "You're full of shit. Jenna is right at home where I left her."

Zhang shook his head. "You may be shocked to learn that three rather large men arrived at her home and took her away before your plane taxied down the runway on its way to Beijing."

Vladimir came to his feet and the giant stepped beside Zhang. "Why the hell didn't you say something? I could have had my men rescue her."

"From the reports I received, a rescue is exactly what appeared to be going on at her house." Zhang tossed several photographs in front to Vladimir. He turned his attention to Javier as Vladimir sank into his seat. "Why is it you don't seem surprised Alejandro?"

Alejandro looked down at the single picture that was tossed in front of him. "I knew that she had planned a vacation. I have no reason to suspect anything was extraordinary. Who are the people in the picture with her?"

"I was hoping that you could tell me." Zhang's hand fondled the white cattle prod hanging from his wrist.

"I have never seen them before." Alejandro sat the picture back on the table. "Your men should be protecting my daughter. She is all I have left?"

Zhang gripped the prod. "The man sent to watch over her was killed trying to rescue her from a private jet she'd been carried aboard. I was counting on you identifying the people in this photograph so that we could safely bring her home."

"My daughter represents all that is good in my life. Since I have no clue who these people are and you have confiscated our freedom, there is nothing I can do to alter the outcome." Alejandro pulled the picture closer to his face and saw the picture of the Aztec warrior, putting him at ease. "What would you suggest?"

Zhang didn't answer, but took his seat. "This invasion has left us few options. We have to initiate our plans. Vladimir, how soon can you have a ship at our disposal?"

Vladimir rubbed his chin. "You want to begin exporting people to the US even before you know whether they have intelligence? That may prove to be unnecessarily expensive."

Zhang held his hands out to his sides. "Who cares, it's not my money."

Vladimir looked at Borka then back to Zhang. "In that case, I already have the ship in international waters just outside of Shanghai. They're not going to be too pleased that they haven't heard from me in a couple of days. Once I can confirm the funds have arrived in my account, they will bring the ship in and turn it over without further questions."

"Gentlemen, by tomorrow morning, we will be in business. People are lining up for a spot on the ship. Our first shipment will be about nine thousand people. The ship will make stops in Mexicali and Merida, Mexico before stopping in Havana and Belize. Once on land, Pablo, your people will begin immediate plans to get them to the United States. Armando, Carlos, Rafael and Alejandro will support your efforts in any way you need. Once they are safely in the US, we have papers ready establishing their residency. A second ship will be on the way arriving days later. They will make stops in the Bahamas, Puerto Rico, the Dominican Republic and Jamaica. In six months, we will be able to double the number of people that arrive in the US from China."

Pablo nodded toward the table in general. "What function will you have the Chinese delegation performing?"

Zhang smiled broadly. "They have a most important function. In addition to providing us with a steady stream of paying customers that want to come to the United States, they must see to it that healthcare is received by everyone on the ships and any others we choose to protect."

Alejandro's eyes fell on Zhang's. "What do you mean by that?"

"Phase two of our plan. That's why we tried so hard to reach your daughter." Zhang pressed the remote. Premier Yi will see to it that my company purchases the largest fireworks company in China. As you might imagine, one of their largest customers is the United States, especially for their Independence Day pyrotechnics display. We will provide them a little extra bang. With such a widespread distribution across the US our fireworks are the perfect delivery system."

Chapter
35

Two weeks later...

Director Carson dropped the file on the conference room table. "The more I look at this picture, the uglier it gets! I don't like being fucked with and right now, Zhang and his people have me holding my ankles with both hands." He clicked a remote and a live-action sequence of the raid at Zhang's compound came on.

Julie tilted her head trying to change the angle of the picture. "This is not the film we shot; it's from a totally different perspective."

"Bingo!" Carson whipped his finger in Julie's direction. "Just keep watching, it gets worse."

From killing the guards, tossing grenades which exploded causing the fire to carrying out the naked bodies of Zhang's consortium, the events on the screen were completely different from the film that the Delta team shot. The sequence ended with Jesus and the housing staff begging for their lives before one of the Delta team mercilessly stabbed each of them.

Zasha looked at Cole and turned towards Carson. "I'm a bit confused. Didn't we forward our recordings to both the Mexican and Chinese governments? Where did this version originate?"

"We sent our recordings just before the change of administration two weeks ago. The new Commander In Chief ripped me a new one this morning during the morning briefing." Carson turned the recording off and sat in his chair. "The President knows that this tape does not represent what really happened. However, that didn't stop the leaders of Mexico and China from demanding an explanation when they received their copies yesterday. China even began making serious threats accusing us of illegally holding two of their top officials— no one has heard from General Gan or Premier Yi in over two weeks."

Zasha brushed the satellite photos aside. "I've viewed and reviewed these damn things for weeks and it hasn't brought us any closer to finding them. I've expanded the grid each time I go over the photos. It's possible that they ducked out during a window while the satellite was dark, but that doesn't explain why we didn't spot them; they're not dark that long."

Julie leaned forward on the table. "There had to be some type of escape area or bunker that they hid in when we were there. The only area that we didn't fully examine was the room that sprayed acid through the sprinkler system."

Cole seemed to be studying what everyone was saying. He leaned back in the chair looking as if he might put his feet on the table. "Anybody ever watch *Myth Busters*? They were looking for Jimmy Hoffa at Giant's Stadium. They used this machine that set off a charge sending back images of what was below. If we did the same thing, we could find out if there was anything below the complex. That could help us to narrow the search."

Oscar shook his head. "Have you been listening? Mexico is a bit pissed at us right now, asking them permission to conduct this type of operation is a bit far-fetched."

Zasha chuckled. "That's never stopped us before. If they're done investigating the cause of the explosion, or even if they haven't, we can show up with a work order that allows us to complete the test."

"The only possible complication I see is Zhang's men overseeing the site." Carson took the wrapper off of a miniature *Sugar Daddy* candy bar and popped it into his mouth.

Zasha held her hand out. "I know that's not the only one of those you have."

Carson reached into his brief case and tossed some of the candy on the table. "Bring your own damn candy next time." He pulled his candy out of his mouth and pointed it at Oscar. "Let's see who we have in the area and get them by to see what they find. Zhang's not fucking Bin Laden and we got him. If his ass is in a cave drag it out and bring him in."

The sound of an approaching helicopter brought several of Zhang's group to the yacht's upper deck. Zhang gathered General Gan, Carlos, Rafael and Vladimir leading them to the heliport.

"Gentlemen, I have put my trust in you four because you, better than the rest, understand the intricate details needed to pull off our plan. In a few minutes, you will witness the only weapon we need."

Vladimir pulled close to Zhang's side. "Zhang, we would be fools to attack the United States. Even in the depleted state their military finds themselves, they could still destroy the world."

"What if I told you that I could wipe out one to three quarters of the US population in twelve hours without firing a single shot?" Zhang looked past Vladimir to the other three men for their reaction. "Let's board the helicopter. We can reach the farm in thirty minutes."

The flight was uneventful and arrived within the time Zhang promised. General Gan spoke into his mouthpiece. "This doesn't resemble any farm I've ever seen— jungle would be a more accurate description."

"The human eye is far too deceptive to trust." Zhang slid the door of the Sikorsky S-92 open. "Shall we take a look, gentlemen?"

Carlos laughed as soon as his feet hit the ground. "Someone has deceived you— this is nothing more than a weed."

Zhang waited for everyone to clear the helicopter. He reached for one of the bushy plants. The bright green leaves were in pairs of five to fifteen emanating from a single woody stem. Oval pods were bunched together topped by purple flowers. "What else do you know about this plant, Carlos?"

Carlos pointed to one of the pods, which seemed to have exploded revealing a group of hard, round scarlet seeds with black bottoms. "Never eat those seeds unless you're ready to leave this world."

Zhang clapped his hands. "Very good, the Rosary Pea was brought to Europe and America by the Dutch during the sixteenth century. It got its name because the Catholics began using them for their Rosary beads. Buddhists also began to use them for their prayer beads." He pulled two of the seeds, pointing the black bottoms towards the men, moving them back and forth. "The plant is also called Crab's eye, looks just like their eyes don't you think?"

Vladimir reached for one of the seeds. "If these seeds are poisonous, how do you plan to get half the people in the United States to eat them? Since the other bad food from China has come into question, their government is checking your products far too closely."

Zhang tossed a seed to General Gan and wiped his hands. "That's the beauty of this plant. It is completely legal, even plentiful in the warm regions of the US where they are used to landscape homes. Inside that seed is Abrin. If you didn't realize it, Abrin is considered the most toxic plant poison known. It can be ingested, inhaled or it can even get into your body through broken skin. Once inside, it's lethal within eight hours."

Rafael took a seed from the plant. "That still doesn't explain how you plan to deploy the Abrin."

Zhang grabbed General Gan's shoulder. "The good general here is going to convince the US to do it for us, we'll simply sit back and wait."

"I think you've been holding these seeds a little too close to your face." General Gan dropped the seed and rubbed his hands across his pants.

"You give the Americans too much credit. There is one holiday that all Americans come out for en masse. They spend all day celebrating then they cap off the night looking up to the sky to watch the lovely fireworks…fireworks in great measure provided by China. Recently, I made significant investments in these fireworks companies. It is summer here in Brazil; the Rosary Peas are fruiting prolifically. My people will begin harvesting the peas. The top third of each of the shipping crates will be covered by Buddhists' prayer beads; the bottom two thirds raw seeds. Once in China, all the seeds will be ground into a fine powder and placed as a payload in all of the fireworks headed to the United States for their Independence Day celebration. Eight hours later, their citizens will begin dropping like flies."

Vladimir's face drew tightly into a prolonged frown. "Why are you sending thousands of people to the US from China that you plan on slaughtering in five months?"

"Do you recall having to set up a hospital quarters in each of the ships that will transport our people?" Vladimir nodded that he did and Zhang turned and beckoned everyone to return to the helicopter. "A simple inoculation will prevent our people from being affected by the Abrin…so deadly and yet so simple to prevent its lethal intentions."

Chapter
36

Zhang, General Gan and Xie flew to Linyang, China to oversee the purchase of China's largest fireworks company. In days, the Rosary Peas would arrive by the hundreds of cases. Prior to this, additional grinders needed to be installed and all the workers would have to be inoculated to prevent any unwarranted deaths.

The helicopter approached the plant and the Giant took hold of General Gan and Xie's arms. "This is strictly business gentlemen. We are not here on a permanent basis. Any attempt to alter our immediate plans will be met with certain tragedy. Am I clear?"

Both men nodded then General Gan turned towards Zhang. "It's going to be impossible to keep our identities a secret. We can't be responsible for what the workers may do."

Zhang used his white cattle prod to touch the General's knee without shocking him. "I've taken everything into consideration. We will be met away from the main facilities. The motivation of the men we are meeting is clear. They have no interest in you two."

Xie chimed in. "Aren't you concerned that they may use our presence as a means for blackmail?"

The Giant's laugh punctuated his disdain for the question. "That would be even stupider than anything that you've done so far. If they dare try it, I'll roast their balls for your dinner tonight."

General Gan didn't seem phased by the threat, but Xie sank into his seat. Zhang waved his prod. "Let's not keep them waiting."

They entered a two-room shack that was barely large enough to hold the Giant. A man, who never revealed his face, looked over at General Gan and Premier Xie and nodded. He handed a group of papers to Zhang offering him a seat at a small table. "Everything is in order. Once you sign the papers, it will be done."

Zhang took the papers and sat opening the file. He didn't bother reading them— if anything was not to his liking, he would eliminate the instigator. With a few swift motions of his wrist, his name rested on the document. "The shipment will be arriving next week. It is imperative that the workers be vaccinated before then; inhaling even a little of this dust will be fatal."

Zhang nodded and pointed the prod towards the plant. "I understand." The man answered taking the file from Zhang.

"Additionally, you will need to have manufacturing running day and night. The US orders must be ready for their Independence Day celebration. I will accept nothing less!"

The man bowed. "I understand the urgency. We will not let China down, we will be ready."

General Gan and Premier Xie's eyes met. The Giant slapped them both on the back. It was a threat against speaking as much as the enthusiasm he would exemplify killing the entire room if they happened to say the wrong thing.

General Gan looked around the room. "This will represent a new century, one where China takes our rightful place...world supremacy."

"I couldn't have said it better." Zhang rose from the table and swung the prod towards the door. "My representatives will be here to oversee the production. They will not be here to interfere; rather, they will insure that daily quotas are met. See to it that they are well received."

Walking back to the helicopter General Gan moved close to Zhang. "Have you given any thought to what may happen with US customs? They are still on edge because of a few less than safe products coming from China that passed them before. Once they're paying attention, it's harder to slip things by."

"General Gan, allow me to share a universal truth. Everybody wants something. To be successful at any quest, you need only to find out what the person who can help you wants and provide it." Zhang looked at Xie. "For instance, the weasel next to you wants to be free of my debt, but it doesn't end there. He has the balls to want me to make him rich. His greed makes him resourceful. He realized that I wanted to ensure that my plan would work. Then he found out something that you wanted and delivered you to my table. As long as he remains true to his greed and forsakes ambition, there's no reason that he won't be pleased with the results. Those who want money make my job easier. Idealists on the other hand, require a bit more care. What is it that you want?"

The general shrugged. "I've not really given it much thought?"

"Come now, General, this is no time for modesty— everyone wants something." Zhang rested his hand on Gan's shoulder.

General Gan glanced at the Giant before speaking. "One should take care with such a decision. You have just warned against ambition."

"Ambition is only dangerous in the wrong hands. Well placed, it can be a thing of beauty." Zhang stepped onto the helicopter and beckoned the general to sit next to him. "It would be unrealistic to believe that our fireworks plan will eliminate everyone in the United States. Yet, they will be facing massive devastation. We will take out some of their leaders, who will need to be replaced quickly. Our people will be in place with full citizenship, completely free to vote. A well-placed candidate will be a shoe-in with our backing. You can assume your place; begin healing America bringing them on the road back, letting them witness your leadership. Then in four years, you will run for president on a platform of healing and proven leadership."

General Gan raised his head, more than just a little interested in the tone of the conversation. "Have you forgotten that the president of the United States must be born in the United States?"

Zhang reached for a satchel at his feet and retrieved several papers. "General Gan, you were born in San Francisco, California, educated at Stanford before attending Harvard Law. Since then, you have been teaching at University of Richmond Law." He handed Gan the papers, which included a picture.

General Gan positioned the picture before his eyes. "Who is this?"

Zhang tapped the picture. "Don't you recognize him? He is you after a bit of plastic surgery."

Gan stared intensely at the photograph. "How can I possibly pull this off? I don't know anything about this man?"

"We know everything about him including the fact that he is an expert on Chinese/American relations. He has just received a letter from the president requesting his services as an advisor concerning China." Zhang took the photograph. "Everybody wants something; George Wei is no different. His...your great-grandfather worked on the Transcontinental Railroad in the late 1800's. One night after work, alcohol was passed liberally as was often the case. The white men used to give it to the Chinese workers and have them make fools of themselves. Of course, they too drank heavily. Once the white men were drunk, they began to slap your great-grandfather around because he dared to have a white lover." Zhang lifted the photo. "George's great-grandfather was killed that night by the drunken white men. George wants revenge. You will become George and have your revenge by being elected to the highest office in America. Americans love a story of triumph over prejudicial odds."

Chapter
37

Zasha and Cole touched down in Puerto Vallarta with a plan to rent a jeep to drive to the burned-out site that was once Zhang's Mexican villa. Just as they cleared the jet bridge, a clean-cut, twenty-something young man wearing shorts, a baggy shirt and sandals approached them holding a sign.

Cole pointed him out to Zasha. "Did Oscar mention anything about having someone meet us here?"

"No, but you know how things can change...give him a chance before you kill him." Zasha reached for the sign with their last names on it and folded it in half. "Is there a reason you're broadcasting that we're here?"

The young man looked at them twisting his face with puzzlement before relaxing. "I heard Jessie James never made it to Mexico."

Zasha nearly laughed out loud. "Did you come up with that yourself, or did someone else tell you to use it?"

The young man hunched his shoulders. "I just wanted you to know that I'm legit. *He* said you would recognize the reference."

"The next thing this guy's going to do is give us the 'secret handshake.' Why are you talking in code? *He* said...please! Which *he,* are you talking about?" Cole took Zasha's arm. "Come on, let's get out of here."

The young man shrugged. "Mr. Fenton told me to meet you guys. I wanted to be professional; I didn't want to seem like a rookie."

Zasha stopped and turned facing the young man. "Let me ask you a question. Did Oscar send you our photos?" She waited for his head to nod. "Then why did you approach us with a sign, why not just walk up and say, 'Oscar asked me to meet you.' If we're here in secret, do you think broadcasting our names is professional? At least you didn't show up in a black suit and white shirt. You did, however bring your 'company issued' sunglasses."

The young man's eyes held a sadness that indicated that he was sufficiently chastised. "I see what you mean."

"You obviously know who we are." Zasha held her hand out. "What's your name?"

"Agent Arturo Mendez. I've got a car waiting out front. Where would you like to go first?"

Cole decided to save Arturo before Zasha really started to slash him to bits. "I think we need to see the site. I want to get a feel for the area and see if there's anything that we may have missed from the photo surveillance."

They reached the car and Arturo popped the locks on the Range Rover. "I thought it might be a good idea to be familiar with the site, so I checked it out yesterday. It's four hundred feet from the oceanfront. The fire destroyed the building, but left the metal elevator shaft in tact. If Zhang's interested in the place, he hasn't left any of his men to monitor the site— no one has been there for at least the past week. There are no physical signs of any tunnel entrance near the place. For the past week, I have kept an eye on the gas exchange signature around the site. There has been nothing to indicate the presence of a tunnel. My thought is we should attempt to use the passive acoustic, seismic electromagnetic ground sensor program that uses low altitude airborne sensor systems to detect the presence of tunnels and caves. It's still in development but it may work."

Cole, who was sitting in the front passenger seat, turned to see Zasha. "A Range Rover, how in the hell did he swing that?"

Zasha turned her attention to Arturo. "What area of engineering is your degree in?"

"I've got a PhD in geological engineering from MIT. I wanted to use my skills to help my country." Arturo pulled from the airport onto the highway, never turning to look at either of his passengers.

Zasha's brow wrinkled. "You can't be more than twenty-three and you're a PhD. Hell, we should be calling you Dr. Mendez."

"No ma'am, that's not necessary. I'm here to learn from you. I've heard that you and Agent Peterson are two of the best." Arturo offered a quick glance towards Cole.

Cole ran his hand across the dashboard of the car. "A Range Rover…how did you swing a Range Rover?"

Arturo edged out his first smile. "At MIT I developed a portion of the technology that we will be using at the site if that's what you want to do. The royalties are fairly substantial. That's how I got the car. I'm glad you like it."

Zasha pulled out her iPhone. "Agent, Dr. Mendez, why haven't you already run the test?"

He shook his head. "Please just call me Arturo, ma'am."

"So be it." She pulled Oscar's info up and prepared to send him a message.

Arturo's grip tightened on the stirring wheal. "I wasn't authorized. Mr. Fenton said that it would be your call."

"Are you always a *by-the-book* type of guy?" She finished her message to Oscar and sent it off.

Arturo nodded. "I'm an engineer ma'am, I follow procedure. It usually gets the best results."

Zasha touched the back of his seat. "Then here's another *law* to commit to memory. Dealing with all that we have to do, there are no rules. Making things up as you go can save your life, so loosen up your asshole just a bit."

Arturo seemed nearly afraid to breathe. "Yes, ma'am."

Cole touched his shoulder. "What she's trying to say is that you have to think on your feet. The training we all went through is just a guideline. You're obviously smart as hell; you've got your PhD at twenty-three. Pay attention to how we work— street smarts can save your life."

Arturo exhaled releasing a sigh that was screaming to get out. "Sorry, I just wanted to make a good impression. Sometimes, I'm a little tight."

Chapter
38

Zasha and Cole found the site just as Arturo described. Ash and soot were all around the site. No one's made any attempt to clean anything since the fire nearly two weeks ago. Protruding from the bowels of the hole was the metal shaft, now rusting from the combination of salt and moisture surrounding the area.

Cole picked up a stone and threw it into the pit. "Have you tried to get down into the hole?"

Arturo shook his head. "I was told not to do anything until you two arrived. We don't think that anyone is watching the site, but then again, we didn't think that anyone knew that we were sending in a Delta Team to bring anyone out of here."

"Good point." Zasha seemed to be studying the pit more intensely than her colleagues. "Let's talk a little more about the electromagnetic thingamajig you were talking about earlier. How fast can we get what we need on location to run your test?"

Arturo pointed to the car. "Part of what we need is in the car. Once we put them in place all we need is a flyover. To minimize attention, we probably should wait until late night; the test can be a little noisy. I can set up a direct feed and we can take a look at what's below the ground."

Cole started back to the car. "Let's have a look at what you have. Tell us a bit about how it works and we can decide what to do."

Zasha followed a few seconds later. "What he's going to do is to set off a charge which will bounce off of things in the ground. If there's a tunnel or cave, we'll see the empty space. It's something like a sonogram, right Arturo?"

He nodded. "That's a fairly accurate description. If it works as planned, we should be able to get a team in here and explore whatever is below." Arturo turned to Zasha. "By the way, how did you know about the procedure?"

Zasha pulled her iPhone from her pocket. "I'm very good at research."

Arturo smiled and let his shoulders relax. "I can tell that we're going to get along very well."

Just after 2 a.m. the three agents emerged from the Range Rover dressed in all black. Arturo handed Zasha and Cole a grid map showing the position where he wanted the equipment placed. He opened the hatch of the Range Rover and pointed to a group of metal boxes that was about a foot square. "Each of these boxes contains a charge; it's important that each of them is placed just as they are on the grid map. Once in place, flip the slave to the 'on' position. It's set for a specific radio signal that the helicopter will generate when it flies over. The charges will fire simultaneously and if all is well, we will receive an image. We've got ten minutes to get these twenty-four boxes in place before they arrive— they're a little heavy, so we might have to make a couple of trips."

Zasha tossed eight of the boxes into a duffle bag and tossed it across her shoulder without changing her breathing pattern. She winced a little due to the wound she'd sustained earlier, but refused to bow. "Don't be pussy's boys, let's get this done."

Cole looked at Arturo. "You just had to challenge her manhood, didn't you? Get ready to have your ass kicked the rest of the night."

Zasha set out across the field. Arturo pulled up the rear. "I didn't mean any harm; I was just trying to be considerate."

Zasha yelled to both of them. "Arturo, you take sector one since it's closer. I'll take sector three. See if you can finish before I do. If you don't, you buy breakfast!"

"You're on!" Arturo tried to speed up, but Zasha was nearly in place.

Zasha and Cole arrived back at the Range Rover with time to sit before Arturo got there. She slapped Cole's shoulder. "Did you pull a list of restaurants in the area?"

Cole waved his iPhone back and forth. "Yeah, and I listed them by price. What do you have a taste for?"

Arturo hung his head conceding defeat. "My grandfather used to say, 'you can't tell an old person anything, the old person has been here longer than you.' I can see I have a lot to learn."

"Who is he calling old? I'm fine as hell— I'm not even old enough to be his aunt." Zasha folded her arms and dropped her chin in Arturo's direction.

"Boy, you're digging a deep hole." Cole heard a crackle in his earpiece and placed his finger against the ear bud. "Saved by the bell, the chopper's ETA is three minutes."

Arturo flipped his laptop open and booted it up. A graphic of the area they'd just seeded filled the screen. "The charges are designed to focus their blast directly into the ground. We have been working on ways to minimize the sound. It's not perfected yet. Just in case, be ready for a bit of noise."

Cole was the first to hear the helicopter and pointed in the direction it was approaching. "That's an HH60 coming."

Zasha looked towards the sky. "How can you tell? I don't even see anything yet."

"You can tell by the way the blades cut through the air. Every chopper has a unique sound." Cole slid ear protection over his ears and looked at the field.

Arturo clicked the mouse activating his screen. Seconds later the blast shook the ground beneath their feet. The computer screen lit up painting an image on the screen. He listened intently to the voice coming across his ear piece. *"Rain dancer, this is thunder cloud. Do you see what I see?"*

He pointed to a long red line running across the blast zone indicated by the grid on the computer. "This worked beautifully. It's exactly what we needed." Arturo punched a series of keystrokes and watched as the red line expanded across the screen.

The unmistakable voice of Oscar Fenton filled their ears. "Give me some good news, I see the picture, now what does it mean?"

Arturo watched the red line spread. "Sir, we've definitely got something. It begins at the elevator shaft and goes beyond our vibrations."

"What does that mean?" Director Carson blurted out.

Arturo stiffened and looked at Zasha and Cole. "Umm, Director Carson, it's big, I mean…"

Zasha touched Arturo's hand. "What he's trying to say, sir is it's one long ass tunnel. We're going to need a team to help us gain entry if we can't determine where it ends. From what I can gather, we're going to have to go in near the elevator shaft."

Carson started tapping his pen. "What are you going to need, Davis?"

Zasha slowly shook her head. "We don't know what we're dealing with here, so I like having guys that are ready."

"Delta?" Carson asked quickly.

"That's probably a good idea." Zasha looked at Cole for his input.

Cole's eyebrows rose and collapsed to a frown. "Sir, considering that we're dealing with this pit, I think the Seabees are probably a better choice."

"I've got the perfect solution. I have a couple of Navy SEALs that have worked with the Seabees before. In the event things get hairy, they could take out half that town without batting an eye." Carson scribbled something on a note pad and handed it to Oscar. "We'll be ready tomorrow evening. I'll have the team meet you at twenty-three hundred. If you need anything else, let Oscar know before twelve hundred. Good work!"

Chapter
39

The Puerto Vallarta Beachfront folded into mountainous forestation. Zhang's villa sat all alone in the middle of a one mile stretch of land that he owned. Zasha and Arturo waited near the access road hidden by palm trees and other dense vegetation.

Cole sat between two large boulders on the beach looking through a pair of night-vision binoculars for the SEAL and Seabee teams. It didn't take long for him to spot the inflatable black Zodiacs skimming across the water. He was sure there was a SEAL in each of the two rafts— one was holding a M4A1 carbine, standard Navy SEAL issue and the other held a MK11 SWS, or Sniper Weapon System. Without moving the binoculars, he spoke into his mouthpiece. "Carson wasn't kidding. Two of these guys have enough firepower to take out a herd of elephants."

The SEAL with the SWS cheeked his rifle taking only seconds to bead Cole. "Agent Peterson I presume?"

"I can see we're all linked in. You want to point that thing somewhere else? Cole knew that he wasn't in any real danger even though the man pointing the rifle at him was one of the deadliest people on the earth.

"I thought you fly-boys possessed nerves of steel." The SEAL raised the rifle.

A few seconds later, the rafts flew onto the beach. The eight men jumped from the rafts and carried them to the dense brush to conceal them. The Seabee team leader approached Cole. "I hear you guys want to go down an elevator shaft to have a look around. Do you have any idea how far down it goes?"

Cole turned sideways and pointed towards the metal protruding from the ground. "Let's get the engineer over here. He may have some idea."

Arturo and Zasha were nearing the structure. "Judging from the file pictures of the place, I'd guess it's about three to four floors in all. In this satellite photo, you can see the top of the elevator." He handed the photo to the team leader.

The Seabee team leader shined his flashlight onto the photo and then onto the steel girders. "Alright gentlemen, let's see what type of integrity this structure has."

One of the team members secured a climbing rope and tossed it down the shaft. After a few quick tugs, he repelled into the bowels of the shaft. Reaching into his backpack, he pulled out several high intensity glow sticks, shook and snapped each of them before placing them over the girders. He tugged on the elevator hatch, which didn't open. "Sir, the heat must have welded the hatch shut. Send me down a hammer and a crowbar. I'll see if I can get it open."

The team leader shined his light down the shaft. "What does it look like down there?"

The Seabee jumped up and down. "The elevator is on the base, which is grounded. I don't think we'll have any problem here."

The team leader reached into the equipment bag and took out a huge mallet and a crowbar. He attached them to a tool belt and repelled to the elevator. Several loud bangs resonated from the hole. Then the rusty creek of reluctant hinges moaned as the hatch moved. "Wait a second. We don't want any surprises. Let's put a scope in and have a look at what we're dealing with."

Using the crowbar, the junior Seabee slightly propped the hatch open and the team leader eased the flexible scope through the opening. A light source at the tip of the scope illuminated the inside of the elevator. "The intense heat should have destroyed any explosives that may have been here to ward off intruders." He maneuvered the scope scanning the entire elevator car before opening the hatch. "It looks clean down here. We're in."

Zasha slid a halogen Maglite into her utility belt and made her way to the rope. One of the Seabees reached for her arm. "Ma'am, don't you think we should go in first?"

The sternness streaming from her face was all the answer the Seabee needed and he backed away. Beneath the form-fitting black bodysuit, it was clear that Zasha was capable of taking care of herself. "This is a walk in the park, boys. My boss is going to want a blow-by-blow description of what we find."

Several other loud bangs came from the hole as Zasha descended. She reached the top of the elevator just as the team leader nearly shouted. "Holy shit!"

Zasha jumped into the elevator car bending her knees to cushion the shock. She straightened up and pulled her Maglite out turning it on. "Cole, you need to get down here!"

Oscar broke in. "What the hell is going on?"

Zasha shined her light around the tunnel opening. "This is one big fucking tunnel! You could drive a dump truck in this place."

One-by-one, the Seabees repelled down the shaft. Cole followed. Arturo seemed a bit hesitant as he grabbed the rope. As soon as he took hold of the rope, a shot rang out striking him and he fell down the shaft.

The SEALs hit the ground searching desperately for the source of the shot. The SEAL holding the SWS squeezed off a single silenced round and they heard a thud about a hundred yards away followed by the sound of running through the underbrush. "I hit that sonofabitch; there must have been more than one of them."

Director Carson was on his feet yelling into the conference room speaker. "What the fuck was that?"

The SEALs ran through the brush. "We're taking gunfire! One of the bastards is down; we're in pursuit of the other."

Less than ten yards in front of them, the second gunman dove into a truck and struggled to get it cranked. The SEAL carrying the M4A1 dropped to one knee and released a burst of gunfire blowing out the trucks rear tires. The gunman jumped from the truck with his rifle swinging wildly.

"Put that fucking gun down!" The second SEAL yelled in English.

"Take him alive!" Carson yelled over the speaker.

Another shot rang out and the gunman fell to the ground screaming and clutching his knee.

The SEAL holding the SWS stood over the gunman with the rifle against his head. "He'll live, but he's going to have a terrible limp from now on."

Carson was still yelling. "What the fuck is going on? Who the hell is shooting at you? You didn't kill the second one, did you?"

Cole climbed to the top of the elevator to attend to Arturo, who was lying lifeless and crumpled on top of the elevator. "Oh shit, this doesn't look good! Mendez was hit. He fell down the shaft."

Cole stretched out Arturo's legs and rolled him over. His head was bloody and Cole looked for signs of a gunshot wound. He found the hole in the center of Arturo's chest. He ripped the shirt open. "Fuck!"

Zasha was coming through the hatch. "Is he going to be okay?"

Cole's face was drawn tightly. "The rooky was wearing a flak jacket."

Arturo's body heaved and he coughed several times as he reached for his head. His second hand reached the spot where the bullet hit him. "It's dragon skin and I'm damn glad my girlfriend insisted I put it on. Does anyone have an aspirin?"

Cole rose to his feet. "Mendez is going to be okay. He's a little banged up from the fall; at least he knows how to stop bullets."

"What's going on at the surface?" Carson demanded.

The SEALs were returning to the shaft area. "We've got one in custody and one casualty. We're going to set up a perimeter in case anyone else decides to join the party. What do you want us to do with these two?"

Carson paced in front of the speaker. "How bad is he?"

"We've stopped the bleeding somewhat, but he's going to need a doctor."

"Take them both back to the ship." Carson dropped into a chair. "Cole, you and Zasha will need to fly to the ship as soon as you finish there. I want to know what's going on. They had to be working for Zhang."

The Seabee team leader broke in. "Sir, we've found signs of motor oil and tire tracks down here. This may take a while. This tunnel goes on much further them we can see."

"Shit!" Carson began tapping his pen sliding it through his fingers. "Cole, can you get Mendez to the surface?"

Arturo stood, but was wobbly. "I'm fine, sir."

"Bullshit! I'll get him up, sir." Cole took Arturo's arm. What would you like me to do then?"

Carson cupped his hands over his mouth giving him a second to think. "Take one of the SEALs, one member of the Seabee team and get Mendez and the two perps to the ship. Have a doctor attend to Mendez and the dumb fuck then put the dead guy on ice. Find out what the other one knows. Zasha, stay with the other Seabees and see what you can find out about the tunnel, but get out of there before sunrise and keep me apprised of everything!"

Cole was the last to reach the surface. He found the SEALs with the wounded gunman stripped down to his underwear protesting loudly. He thrust his finger nearly stabbing the man in the chest. "Have you got anything that will put him out? I'm tired of listening to him bitch."

One of the SEALs reached into a field pack and pulled out a syringe. "This should do the trick." The gunman screamed and kicked with his one good leg. The flailing stopped as soon as the SEAL jammed the needle into the man's butt cheek and depressed the plunger of the syringe.

"Okay, let's get one of the rafts to the water and get back to the ship." Cole looked at one of the SEALs. "Give Arturo your sidearm until we get back. If anybody comes near you don't ask questions, shoot them."

Cole, the SEALs and the Seabee carried the raft to the water's edge. The three military men went back to get the gunmen and Arturo. Once everyone was in the raft, Cole addressed the SEAL, who was staying behind. "Make sure everyone is out of here before sunrise. Make sure there's no sign of us ever being here."

Arturo leaned towards the SEAL standing in the water. "Give these to Agent Davis. She's going to need them for the car." He handed his car keys to the SEAL.

Cole leaned against the side of the raft. "Damn, she gets to drive the Range Rover?"

In the tunnel shaft, the Seabee team leader pulled several high-powered lights from an equipment bag and flipped them on thrusting daylight against the darkness of the tunnel. He handed one to Zasha. "If we're going to get through this tunnel before daylight, we're going to have to make up some time. Are you up for a little PT?"

"Good for you, good for me!" Zasha held her light up. "Lead the way."

The SEAL guarding the entrance to the shaft looked at his watch. "It's oh one thirty. We need to be on the water by oh five hundred. I'll be in touch in an hour and a half. If you haven't made it to the end by then, you're going to need to get back."

"Damn right!" Carson's voice broke in. "Zasha, I don't want any fucking around. Make sure that raft is in the water and everyone's out of there. There's been enough action for one night."

Zasha looked over her shoulder at the Seabees pulling out M-16s. "We'll be fine, sir. These guys are ready for anything we might encounter."

The team leader handed her an M-16. "And so are you." He started out in a steady jog making sure he maintained the lead. "Stay close. We don't know what to expect down here."

An hour into the run, Zasha was fairly certain that the end of the tunnel was nowhere near, so she stopped the team. "Oscar, do you still have us on the GPS tracking screen?"

"As if I were right on top of you." Oscar looked at Carson. "Have you reached the end?"

"Not even close if you ask me." Zasha looked at her watch. "How far have we gone?"

Oscar checked the screen. "Looks like about nine and a half miles. You're running out of time."

"Yeah, I noticed." She glanced at the watch a second time. "Here's what I'm thinking. We haven't seen anything down here that could be viewed as suspicious. Three of us can continue the trip and the others can return. Arturo has a laptop in the car. You can patch our GPS transmission into it and one of the team can use the car to follow our progress and meet us at the end of the tunnel. We've got to find out where this thing ends. It's our only chance to get a lead as to where Zhang has gone."

Director Carson blew a sustained sigh through his teeth and looked at the speaker sitting on the conference table. "Shit…she's right. Zasha, I don't want you taking any unnecessary risks. If you guys run into some type of underground base, stay out of sight and call for backup. I'll have a team on standby just in case."

Zasha turned to the team leader. "Okay, who gets to drive the car?" He pointed a man out and she slapped the side of her head. "I don't have the fucking keys."

"Fine time to think of that." The SEAL stationed at the entrance pulled the keys from his pocket and jingled them near his mouthpiece. "Agent Mendez gave them to me before he headed to the ship."

Carson recognized the SEAL's voice. "Then, I want you driving the car. If extra firepower is needed, you're just the man."

The SEAL put the keys back into his pocket. "I hear it's a Range Rover, I'm in."

The Seabees began their jog back. Zasha and her two escorts continued down the tunnel. She addressed the team leader. "I've been listening for anything that would indicate that we're nearing the end. Have you heard anything?"

The leader shook his head. "The only thing I've heard is the sound of our boots hitting the dirt. This type of run almost makes me want to sing some 'Jody's.' Given the circumstances, I don't think that's such a good idea."

Oscar projected a map of the area onto a screen and with a few clicks of his mouse, superimposed three blinking dots indicating the team's path. "At least we can keep an eye on where they are. It could help directing the SEAL to their location."

Carson leaned back in his chair and put his feet on the table. He studied the map intently, but had nothing to add. He stared at the clock occasionally…everything seemed to move in slow-motion. Three and a half hours into the run, the dots stopped moving. He dropped his feet to the floor and moved nearly on top of the speaker.

Zasha ended his angst. "We can see light up ahead."

Oscar quickly triangulated their location and zoomed in on a live satellite feed. "Give me a few seconds; I want to make sure there's no one near your area."

The SEAL driving the Range Rover pulled off the dirt road into a thicket less than a hundred yards from their location. "I've got a visual, but I don't see an opening." He pulled a pair of binoculars from his bag and scanned the area checking both the ground and the trees. "There doesn't appear to be anyone around. Director Carson, have you located any heat signatures?"

Oscar clicked the mouse again finding nothing on the satellite feed. "It looks clear."

Zasha tapped the Seabee leader's shoulder. "Let's be extra careful as we approach the opening. Just because we don't see any people doesn't mean that they haven't left anything behind."

The Seabee leader stayed on point. They rounded a slight bend and he dropped to the ground pulling Zasha with him. In a very hushed voice, he spoke into the mike. "Kill the lights. I've got a large van twenty yards ahead."

The SEAL left the Range Rover and moved slow and low towards the area he'd seen the dots on the computer. "I'm nearly on top of you guys. There's heavy brush all over the area." He pulled the rifle scope to his eyes. The ocean is less than fifty yards away, but it's not a beach area."

There was the unmistakable *thwack* of a bullet leaving a silenced gun barrel and striking the ground. Zasha reacted first. "What was that?"

"Breakfast." The SEAL used his rifle barrel to toss a large snake off to the side.

The Seabee leader raised his M-16 towards the opening of the tunnel. "Something just fell up ahead. Let's move in slowly, we may have company."

Zasha and the Seabees moved to the sides of the paneled van. She reached up and grabbed the back-door handle and put three fingers in the air, dropping them one at a time. When her third finger fell, she jerked the door open. The Seabees lunged forward with their M-16s sweeping them side-to-side. Zasha lowered her rifle and stepped to the front of the van and immediately jumped back. "Whoa, a big fucking snake."

The Seabee leader scurried to the front of the van training his rifle on the snake before noticing it was missing its head. "Did you throw a fucking snake down here?"

The SEAL pulled his scope to his eye again. "So that's where you guys are. Do you see any booby traps or explosives around the mouth of the tunnel?"

The Seabee leader turned his light on and held it up examining the mouth of the tunnel. "Good call. There's a wad of C-4 right over the top lip of the tunnel."

The SEAL tried in vain to see inside the tunnel. "Do you see any wires coming from it?"

"Calm down. You SEALs don't have a corner on the explosives market. I'm a Seabee remember? We use this shit all the time." The leader climbed on top of the van and pulled the ignition wire from the C-4. "There's probably a trip wire somewhere near the entrance. Whoever left it had the C4 ignition wire tied into the van's battery. We're going to check things out a little closer and then we'll be right out."

Zasha leaned against the side of the van drained. "Oscar, how far did we come?"

Oscar clicked his mouse. "Shit, you're not going to believe this— that was a twenty-five-mile hike."

"That may explain why we didn't find anything on the satellite images we pulled. We didn't look that far out." She rubbed the sides of her thighs. Even as much in shape as she was, twenty-five miles was a hump and she couldn't wait to sit in a steaming tub of water. "You should probably have Julie begin pulling the satellite archives. There's got to be something on them."

The SEAL walked to the edge of the water looking for any additional clues. "The best bet is to focus in the water. This is a deep-water area; they most likely had a boat waiting for them when they left the tunnel.

Chapter
41

Once again, the CIA jet was in the air. Julie established a reward tip line when General Gan and Premier Xie disappeared. For weeks, it was silent until a single call came in a day earlier. The caller only identified himself as a worker in a fireworks company in Linyang, China.

Oscar suggested that they meet in Hong Kong, a city that was much friendlier toward westerners and the democratic process. Hong Kong was also much further from Beijing, providing an extra layer of protection from prying eyes.

On the tip line, the man left specific instructions regarding the only acceptable time to reach him via his cell phone. Julie timed her flight and refueling stop in San Francisco to coincide with a calling time.

Julie dialed the number and waited for the man to answer and spoke to him using the Mandarin dialect. "Hi, this is Julie Hu. I'm anxious to meet you tomorrow."

The man spoke immediately. "There has been a new development. I will need additional tickets for my wife and daughter as well."

Julie didn't hesitate. "One of the reasons I was calling was to find out where to have your ticket delivered. Now, I guess it will be tickets."

He continued. "I have a better idea. Place funds in a locker at the Linyang airport and have a key to the locker delivered to me overnight."

"That won't be a problem." Julie lifted her pen. "What address should I use?"

The man paused. "I have more questions first. What division of the government are you from?"

Julie paused too long and knew that she had to come up with something quickly. "I am not from the government; I am simply an interested party."

He grunted. "In China, no one is merely an interested party. If you are not Chinese government then I suspect you are with some other government entity. Although your Mandarin is flawless, your accent gives you away, you are not a native."

"Maybe, I'm the one who should be cautious. You sound as if you could be part of the Chinese government." Julie noticed an e-mail coming from Oscar, who was monitoring the call. "Asking to have your wife and daughter join you could be cover designed to put me at ease."

The man switched languages and spoke in English. "I assure you it is not. We will have to leave this country after assisting you. I have family in the United States. We would like to join them without complication. If my information is useful, this should not be a problem."

Julie glanced at the e-mail before returning to the call. "In order to convince my superiors to grant your request, I need you to answer a few preliminary questions. First, where did you see General Gan?"

He shook his head. "I am no fool. The last thing I will do is release all my leverage before we have an agreement. So, this is all you will get for now. General Gan was at the fireworks company I work for and he was not alone. Being considered insignificant has served me well— I also know the intentions of the people who were at the plant." He paused giving his words time to resonate. "Have sufficient funds for my family to travel. We will not be bringing anything with us, so that we do not raise any suspicion. I will tell you everything as soon as we are safely on our way to the United States, not a second before."

Julie heard the dial tone before she could open her mouth to respond. Instead, she turned her attention to Oscar, who was waiting for the call to end. "What do you think?"

His labored breathing was evidence of his concern. "I think, we're going to have to give him what he wants and see how things play out. I'm going to have several of our people in place in case something goes wrong. Those tapes Zhang sent to the Chinese government still has us kissing political ass. They don't need much of a reason to turn the tables on us."

"I wouldn't want to be on the receiving end of their attention." Julie leaned back in her seat. "I don't know, something about this guy just feels legit."

Oscar reached for his notes. "Have you already set up a meeting location?"

"Yeah, after our initial call selecting Hong Kong, he selected a very public restaurant. The guy's not stupid." Julie reached for her note pad.

"Here's what we're going to do." Oscar pulled up the location of the restaurant and searched for another one on the opposite side of town. "In the locker with the money, we will leave a new meeting place. Just to be sure, we will instruct him to have the cab drive by the first location. His wife will object and he will give the new location. If anyone is following them, we'll be able to detect them and take the appropriate action. In the meantime, I will dig through Chinese records and find out where the owner of the cell phone lives. If we have time, I'll get a pair of eyes on their location. I want this to be as fluid as possible."

"I appreciate the added caution and detail." Julie looked out the window and noticed the fuel truck leaving. "We're about to go 'wheels up.' I'll be waiting for whatever you find. If I don't hear from you before, I'll call once we're on the ground."

Julie's plane touched down with a three-hour window before she was to meet her informant and his family. Logistics would be unfolding quickly, so her first order of business was to contact Oscar. "How did the phone information search go?"

"About as expected." Oscar grabbed the pad with his notes. "Ling Cao lives in a small house just outside of Linyang. As you may have gathered listening to him speak yesterday, he is college educated and was once a rising star in the Chinese government. Something landed him in a factory job as one of the lowest paid workers there. Maybe you can find out what when you two meet. I have a team headed to the home, but the Cao family should already be on their way to the airport."

"The intel won't hurt. Send me a link so that I can get in touch with the agent headed over there, I'd like to know what they find." Julie drew a line through the initial meeting location on her notes. "Where did you decide we should meet?"

"Instead of taking you all the way across town, I decided on a restaurant in the central region of the city, *2 Sardines*." Oscar tossed the note pad on his desk and leaned back putting his feet near them. "In case your guests want to leave quickly, you won't have as far to travel to reach the airport. We don't want them exposed any longer than necessary."

"Good thinking. I'll plan to get there early because I do plan to eat on your dime. I hear 2 Sardines is excellent." Julie glanced at her watch. "I need to check in with our folks on the ground. I'll be in touch."

The CIA team covering the airport received a message on their iPhones. A photo of the Cao family was attached to the message, making it easier to identify who they were looking for. Waiting to see who opened the locker was not as easy; they knew Ling could be using a surrogate.

Julie slid an earpiece into her ear and activated it linking her with all the teams on the ground and Oscar back at Langley. "This is Agent Hu. By now each of you should have received the Cao family photograph. Alpha team, have you spotted them at the airport?"

"Negative, there hasn't been anyone near these lockers. They'd better hurry; the plane begins boarding in one hour and fifteen minutes."

Julie checked her watch making a quick note of the time. "Zulu team, have you arrived on location at their home?"

A voice came back. "We got here about two minutes ago. We should be set up in a couple of minutes. I hope to have a visual of the interior by then. I'll check back as soon as I can."

Julie turned her attention to the next team. "Romeo, is there any activity at our original meeting location?"

The team member sitting on a bench near the restaurant responded. "We've been watching a couple of guys hanging around. They're not tourists. Generally, the Chinese military enjoys a show of force if the government is involved, but I haven't seen any signs of uniforms."

"Keep your eyes peeled. I once saw a wasp fly up to a spider web, turn and intentionally land in the web violently beating its wings. Of course, this drew the attention of the spider, who hurried to her catch. The wasp waited patiently before clutching the much bigger spider, stinging him and flying away with his prize. Just because they may not be wearing uniforms doesn't mean that they're not dangerous." Julie was part of the Whiskey team and was still on site with the Tango team, who would be waiting to fly everyone out of China. "As soon as any of you has confirmed contact, we need to ensure that this goes as smoothly as possible."

The wounded gunman on the ship outside of Mexican waters lost a considerable amount of blood during the ride and needed immediate surgery. Cole waited just outside the operating room for the surgeon to appear. He'd seen worse wounds when he'd been in Kuwait and assumed the gunman would retain his leg. The future limp was assured; the shot disintegrated the gunman's kneecap.

The surgeon approached Cole. "He'll live. I gave him a minimal amount of pain killer. I figured you'd want it that way."

Cole nearly grinned. "You've been binge watching too many episodes of *24*. I don't want to torture the guy. On the other hand, it won't hurt to dangle a carrot in front of him. He can have a full dose as soon as he gives us the information we need."

The surgeon held either side of the stethoscope around his neck. "Don't go in there undoing my work. I don't want to have to replace a single stitch or dressing. Do we have an understanding?"

Any hint of amusement melted from Cole's face. "Despite the CIA garb, I am still a member of the United States Navy— it's Commander Peterson, which means, I outrank you. I am here on orders from the President. The prisoner has information we need. I intend to get it. If you have an issue with that then I suggest you contact the White House."

The surgeon stepped back. "I'm sorry, sir. I didn't..."

Cole grabbed the doctor's shoulder disarming him. "Didn't know... how could you have known. Listen doc, I respect your work and the fact that you're a doctor first...do no harm, I get it. We all have jobs to do— I'll try not to get in your way."

"Thanks. If there's anything you need please let me know." The surgeon returned to the safety of his operating room.

Cole stationed two Marine sentries at the door of the recovery room and went in to wait for the prisoner to open his eyes and for the meager amount of pain killer to wear off. The anesthesiologist administered a drug to counter the effects of those used to keep the prisoner under. It didn't take but a few minutes for him to begin moaning and begging for something to ease his pain.

Cole eased his iPhone from his pocket and connected to Langley. The prisoner's hands and feet were secured to the sides of the bed so, he laid the phone on the center of his chest. "Do you speak English?"

The prisoner squeezed his eyes together tightly. "Give me something for this fucking pain! Does that answer you fucking question?"

Cole waited for the man to look at him before he pulled a pad and pen from his pocket. The gesture was meant to show his willingness to trade. "I'll be glad to help you with the pain, but I need your help first."

The prisoner strained at the bindings holding his wrist. "Help with what? I'm not the one who tried to blow your fucking leg off. You shot me, I'm the one, who needs help!"

Cole lowered the pad. "You're quite right— all you did was put a hole in the center of a man's chest."

The man smirked. "He was trespassing; you all were. That's what I was supposed to do."

Cole brought the pen to the pad. "Supposed to do for whom?"

The man looked away. "Fuck you!"

Cole took the head of the pen and pressed it against the side of the man's injured knee. The loud scream let Cole know that the anesthesia had worn off. "You're in no position to negotiate. This shit has got to hurt more than the original bullet. The good doctor has reattached all those severed nerves and has returned your blood flow, which means every time you're a smart ass; your knee is going to hurt like hell. Do you understand what I'm trying to tell you?"

The man jerked his eyes toward Cole and worked to moderate the contemptuous look on his face. "Look man, my job was to watch the hole. Been there nearly three weeks and not even so much as a curious kid came by. But he told me to stay, that you would be there before it was over."

"Who told you we'd be there?" Again, Cole touched the pad with his pen.

He looked Cole in the eyes. "Alright, look, I ain't trying to be a smart ass, but all you're going to do is hurt me a little; he'll kill me."

Cole placed the pen back against the man's knee until he winced. "You have no fucking idea who I am. This is going to get a lot worse for you if you don't cooperate."

He closed his eyes. "Do what you got to do. I can take the pain."

Cole pulled the pen away and reached in his pants and pulled out a *Buck* Alpha Dorado pocket knife. He effortlessly cut away all the fabric surrounding the man's groin area. "Here's the deal, I'm going to cut your balls out one at a time. If you still haven't told me what I want to know, I'm going to slice your dick away one inch at a time." Cole jerked the man's scrotum and let the blade prick the skin.

The man's head jerked back into the pillow. "Fuck! Okay, just move the fucking knife, shit! This shit ain't right man; you're with the US Navy. I saw the boat when we pulled up."

Cole didn't move the knife. "Ship."

The man looked puzzled. "What?"

"It's not a boat, it's a ship and you only assume that I'm with the Navy. That's where you're wrong— I'm much, much worse." Cole tightened his grip causing more pain. "This is your last chance; no more stalling."

The man swallowed hard. "I'm working for the Badger. That's what they call him."

"That's not going to do it." Cole slid the knife just enough to split the skin. "The next time I move this knife, I'll be setting your left nut on your chest."

His eyes moved to the knife in Cole's hand. "Pablo Juarez, they call him the Badger because he digs tunnels to move product from Mexico to the United States."

Cole loosened his grip and let the man see the blood on the blade. "That was close. Now that you got that out, what was he using the tunnel in Puerto Vallarta for?"

"I don't know!" He tried to adjust his position in the bed. "That's the truth! He only told me to get rid of you guys when you came there."

Cole heard Oscar in his earpiece. *Find out where he is.* "How do you stay in touch with Pablo?"

"Every week, money is delivered to my house. One week, my payment was short and there was a note with it saying that I was late one night. He docked me a whole day's pay for being five minutes late."

Cole stood and turned towards the door. "Oscar, we missed a camera, they were watching us the whole time."

Chapter
43

On the way in to Langley, Zasha called the satellite archive office. "I land in thirty minutes. I'll need satellite photos in three-minute increments of the coordinates I submitted earlier. Begin the time one hour before the Delta Team raid commenced and expand the range five miles with each photo."

Oscar held his hand up even though Zasha couldn't see it. "I've already got things underway. There was a yacht waiting at the mouth of the tunnel. From the pictures, we could see this big son of a bitch putting naked men on the deck. Get this, he carried them upside-down and laid them face down on the deck so they couldn't be identified."

"So, we're not dealing with first-timers." Zasha looked out the plane's window as if she might see the yacht. "Any idea of where they're headed since it's been a while?"

"Not yet; I'll upload the photos to you. Hopefully, one of us will have something by the time you land." Oscar looked at his iPhone; a call was coming in. "I've got to take this call. Julie has been waiting in Hong Kong all day to meet with a person who called in a tip. Something must be up. Let's talk when you get here."

Zasha logged onto her laptop. She used a program designed to isolate her target, Zhang's yacht. Using a series of logarithms, the software quickly triangulated possible routes tracking the yacht in time-lapse fashion until it stopped about a mile off the beaches of Rio de Janeiro, Brazil.

Zasha continued with her analysis using additional software to zoom in allowing her to identify faces on the yacht. The arduous task of identifying all movement on and off the yacht was taking much longer. What amazed her was the complete freedom the men seemed to have. They moved freely, engaged in conversation and didn't appear to be in distress. The sight of Vladimir and Borka gave her pause, realizing how they'd treated Jenna. As usual, they were drinking enough for the entire yacht.

Javier spent most of his time away from groupings in favor of solitude. He was pleasant enough when others were around, but spent as little time as possible with them. Zasha jotted a note about the behavior and hoped it did not cause Zhang to single him out making him the subject of potential harm.

By the time she reached a point where Zhang was about to leave the yacht, the plane was about to touch down. She closed the laptop and called Cole. "I heard you ended up having to interrogate the prisoner. Did you find out anything interesting?"

Cole ran his hand across his face. "I may have identified a potential problem. We may have missed a camera planted at or near the villa, or should I say, what's left of it. Pablo Juarez was responsible for the shooters and the tunnel. Whatever they've been planning, it has to have been for some time. You don't just throw up a tunnel that size."

Zasha's eyebrows rose. "Did you hear how long it was?"

Cole shook his head. "I didn't think to ask."

"Let's just say, I hadn't planned on a twenty-five-mile run." Zasha leaned back and rubbed her legs. "My feet still hurt like shit. I've just started going over the satellite reconnaissance. Zhang's yacht dropped anchor about a mile off the coast of Rio. Just before I shut the computer down, he was on his way to shore with General Gan, Carlos Acosta, Raphael Calderon and your buddy, Vladimir Nikitin."

"You shut it down without finding out where they were going?" Cole's voice rose with excitement. "Send me the upload, I'll find them."

Zasha smiled and looked out the window. "Cool your jets, mister. We just touched down at Langley; I'll be inside in a minute. Oscar may have already found out. If not, I'll shoot you a link."

Cole's sigh held the pressure of someone who was about to explode. "This is a big operation; I've got a bad feeling some really nasty shit is about to go down. We can't waste a lot of time."

Oscar met Zasha at the door leading from the landing strip. "Director Carson is waiting for us in the conference room. I had a tech piggyback on what you were doing. When you shut down, I had her keep going. You've got to see this shit."

"There's no way you're going to spring that on me and not tell me what's going on." Zasha handed him one of her bags along with a contemptuous look.

Oscar countered her look with a smirk. "The five of them jumped into a helicopter and flew to this humungous field of…some plant with red shit popping out all over them. We haven't identified what they are just yet."

Zasha didn't hesitate. "Did you shoot a picture over to the Smithsonian?"

"Duh, I didn't think of some shit like that…of course I did. We're waiting for the results now." Oscar opened the door to the conference room.

Zasha turned her back to the room and flipped him the bird. "Smart ass."

"If you two are finished insult fucking each other, come in." Carson depressed the flashing red light on the phone. "We've got Dr. Saul Zimmerman on the phone with us. Dr. Zimmerman, what have you found out?"

Dr. Zimmerman paused as if he were expecting the Director to list his resume and he responded accordingly. "Thank you, Director Carson. What you have here is a very common plant, *Abrus Precatorius*. It originated in India and has been transported to any number of warmer climates across the globe. In the U.S. it is commonly used as an ornamental plant." He clicked his mouse transmitting a picture to Langley. "Notice the seed. It is often called the jequirty bean, precatory bean, for obvious reasons, crab's eye. When I rotate the picture, you can see the resemblance. However, it is most often called the Rosary Pea because it was often used to make rosaries by monks. Interestingly enough, it was also used to make Buddhist prayer beads…"

Carson was growing impatient listening to the lecture. "Dr. Zimmerman, what else can you tell me about this, rosary pea?"

"To the average person, it is simply a plant that is appealing to the eye." Dr. Zimmerman licked his lips. "But, it has a dark side. The seed contains Abrin, which is a potent lectin."

Zasha dropped a pad against the table top. "Doc, do you think you could give us that in English?"

"Certainly." He cleared his throat. "Abrin is a very toxic poison. As little as point zero, zero, zero, one five percent of a person's body weight is enough to kill anyone."

"Whoa, whoa, whoa." Carson slapped the table. "How is it administered? Do you have to swallow one of those seeds?"

Dr. Zimmerman's tick started. He twisted one side of his mouth up and twitched his neck to the same side. No one ever knew if it was a nervous tick, or if he was expressing some great pleasure in delivering his knowledge. "Yes, swallowing it will work...but that's not all. The seeds can be ground into a fine dust, converted to a gas and if inhaled, injected, or if it simply touches any moist area of the body, death looms. Several hours after contact the victim may develop excess salivation, colic, vomiting, diarrhea and dehydration. You may also see lesions of the mucosa of the digestive tract and urinary bladder may have splotchy hemorrhages and ulcerations. Ultimately, pulmonary edema, congestion of various organs, and retinal hemorrhage may occur and, in some cases, mild to moderate hepatic and renal tubular degeneration has been observed."

"Shit!" Director Carson sucked in several short blasts of air. "Can this be treated?"

The doctor didn't hesitate. "If it's caught in time."

Carson rubbed his temples. "What are we talking about?"

Zimmerman's tick became more pronounced. "Well, Abrin inactivates ribosomes inhibiting protein synthesis, so I'd guess if you caught it within a few hours; you'd stand a good chance of recovery. But you may be able to last as long as a few days after exposure. You might want to check that out with the CDC. I know that they've done some work with it."

"Thank you, Dr. Zimmerman, we will." Carson disconnected the call. "Holy fuck!"

Zasha was typing furiously on her laptop and projected the developing document onto the screen. "Here's what we've got so far. Zhang brings together a group and discusses a plan to move massive amounts of illegals into our country to establish instant citizenship to vote their people into office. He suspects correctly that we'll foil his plan and moves his crew off the coast of Rio, where he reveals a shit-load of this Abrin stuff. From what Dr. Zimmerman said, I don't see how Abrin could be used to gain citizenship, although, it could be used to significantly reduce our population. If they put this shit in all the food headed here and the good doctor is right about how long a person could last, thousands of people could die before anyone noticed what was going on."

Director Carson shot his finger towards Oscar. "Get on the phone to the CDC and find out everything there is to know about this stuff. I want to know if there is anything that can prevent the effects of this shit." He turned to Zasha. "And you…"

"Just a second, sir." She projected another document onto the screen. "This is the CDC web page about Abrin. It's real similar to Ricin, only seventy-five times more potent. It also says that no vaccine has been fully developed, but there are some promising results in mice."

"Good work." Carson rose from his chair. "Now get Cole. The two of you have seen some of these guys up close. I want you to travel with a Delta Team; get to that boat and get those motherfuckers in custody now! Fuck everything else. I want them at Gitmo under lock and key. Oscar, get with the CDC and get the vaccine development in high gear. Have the FDA approve human trials— we can't wait. If they baulk, find some death-row guys, who are out of appeals. Cut them a deal. If they live, we'll commute their sentences. Explain to the AG that this can save lives— I'll fill the President in. Get on it!"

Chapter
44

Pablo came up from the hold of the yacht looking for Zhang. "There's something you need to take a look at below." Zhang followed immediately. "What is it?"

"I was going through the footage from the camera you set up to monitor the tunnel. We've had visitors." Pablo swung the door open.

Zhang watched the footage long enough to know that the people on it were not just curious onlookers. "Make a copy of this and meet me in the galley. I want everyone to take a look at this."

The Giant was sent to round up everyone to the galley. They'd grown accustomed to following Zhang's orders and chose not to protest having to attend another meeting.

Pablo was the last to arrive and put the DVD he'd just made into the computer. The first image was of a young Mexican man, who simply appeared interested in the hole. Time-lapse was used to bring the others to the screen.

"What the fuck?" Vladimir's heavy hands slapped the galley table. "Those two right there; they are Jenna's friends. What are they doing in this scene?"

Zhang stroked the length of his cattle prod. "Perhaps you should enlighten us."

Vladimir pointed to the image on the screen. "I told you, they are Jenna's friends. The girl, Zasha is a reporter and the man next to her is a pilot. He's the one who flew the plane that brought me to Beijing."

Satisfied, Zhang lowered the prod. "It would seem that they were not completely truthful with you. Why would a reporter be standing next to men with the arsenal we see? It's not likely that these are the same people who raided the villa, but just in case, Pablo, compare the pictures." He pointed the prod towards Vladimir. "When was the last time you spoke with Jenna?"

Vladimir cocked his head to one side. "And just how am I supposed to contact her?"

"Quite right." Zhang swung the prod in the Giant's direction and a phone came from his pocket. "Why don't you call her now."

Vladimir dialed the number and his face contorted. "It says the number has been disconnected."

"I see." Zhang nodded to the Giant. "Take the phone and dispose of it." He waited until the battery was removed. "Gentlemen, it would seem that our safety has been compromised once again. I would prefer if you willingly chose to follow me rather than having to repeat our retreat from the villa."

Javier looked around the table. "Aren't we going to take the boat?"

Zhang smiled. "I don't think that would be such an intelligent idea. I'm not sure how just yet, but these people have managed to find us in China and again in Mexico. With the available technology, they will find us once again."

Vladimir took a swig from his glass. "Won't they find us again if we go somewhere else?"

Zhang tapped the prod against the palm of his hand. "Not if they don't see us leave. Gentlemen, you came here with nothing and you shall leave with the same. I will give you instructions shortly. Follow them to the letter."

The men stood and drifted from the galley. Vladimir remained in his seat and poured another drink. Borka walked back in his direction and Vladimir waved him away. He tilted the glass and drank until everyone left the room. "The Giant told me you wanted me to wait. What do you need?"

Zhang tossed a file on the table. "From your KGB file, I can see that you've always been around water. As a matter of fact, you are an expert diver. I have a pressurized area in the aft portion of the hold below that will allow us to escape the ship unseen. There are also four two-man water sleds anchored to the bottom of the yacht. We are all going for a swim later this evening."

"Okay, but that doesn't tell me a damn thing." Vladimir sat the glass on the table.

"I need you to lead us out of here." Zhang sat a nautical chart on the table and pointed to a location. "We've got to reach this point, which is about ten miles out. We've got one hundred and twenty cubic foot diving tanks. Can we make it?"

Vladimir looked at the charts and began making calculations in his head. "If the damn sleds can carry two men at just over five knots, we've got a chance. If I remember correctly, you said you had four two-man sleds and we've got eleven people."

Zhang looked deeply into Vladimir's eyes. "Xie, Javier and Armando are dead weight; they're expendable. Once we're far enough out, we'll slash their hoses and kick them from the sleds—they won't survive."

Vladimir lifted his glass and took another drink. "I suggest we forgo drawing any blood. When I think we're far enough out, I will dive the lead sled. When we're deep enough, Borka can take care of one of them, I'll handle the second and you have the Giant take care of the third. Panic will take care of everything else. They'll never make it up alive."

The Giant entered the galley as soon as Vladimir left. "The two-man crew will be here as you requested. Would you like me to program the destination into the ship's computers?"

"I've been giving that a lot of thought my friend." A wicked grin crossed Zhang's face. "Since the Americans are spending so much time trying to find us, I think I'll send them somewhere that their president can appreciate and is a significant goal of our mission, Casablanca."

The giant couldn't contain his laughter.

Chapter
45

At the ninety-minute mark, Julie's team in Hong Kong saw their first hint of action. A man, not matching Cao's description, appeared at the airport locker and removed the contents. Instead of purchasing any tickets, he left the lobby stopping just long enough to read the note that was left in the bag.

"Whiskey one, this is Alpha one. I think now would be an excellent time to leave the restaurant. Someone just retrieved the contents of the locker and the only thing they cared about was the note."

Julie made a whirling motion with her finger and the Whiskey team moved quickly to wrap things up. "We need to get to an alternative location now." Her eyes darted around the room finding exactly what she'd hoped for. She pointed to a member of the team. "Put the camera there."

The team member walked to a plant near the front of the restaurant and took a five-millimeter camera with a pin-like anchor on the bottom and pushed the pin into the bark of the bamboo plant. An extremely fine hair-sized antenna hung from the camera allowing the picture to transmit to their mobile location.

Julie pulled her iPhone from her pocket and activated the camera. The high definition picture made it seem that they'd never left the restaurant. A program on the phone allowed her to adjust the view of the camera, zoom in or view nearly a three-hundred-degree angle. She pulled a second phone from her backpack and handed it to a team member. "Take the battery out of this. If someone has intercepted the Cao family, they may have this contact number. Since we're going to be hiding out right under their noses, I don't want them drawing a bead on the signal."

Julie and her two-man team joined an older man grooming the sand in the middle of a park containing a Zen garden. They sat on rocks and watched as the old man methodically rippled the sand with the wooden rake. One of the team members pointed to the man's work. "I bet if there was more of this at home, we could reduce all kinds of stress related illnesses."

"Yes, but then where would the pharmaceutical industry be?" Julie glanced at the iPhone screen just as six men burst into the front doors of 2 Sardines and vehemently approached the hostess. Julie touched the *Plantronics* listening device on the side of her face to hear the transmission. "These guys don't usually come out of their shells."

One of the team members turned his attention to the screen. "Who's that?"

Julie pointed to the man doing the talking on the screen. "The Chinese Secret Police. What I want to know is how and why they're involved. Let's get moving, I think it's time we checked in with Langley."

"Chinese Secret Police, how the hell did they get involved?" Oscar grabbed the back of his neck. "What the hell is going on? Julie, get to Linyang. On your way, have the Romeo team get a visual inside the house. We need to know if the Cao family is still there...in one piece. We've got to be careful with this one; we are not there in an official capacity. In other words, we don't have permission to be conducting this type of operation."

Julie shrugged her shoulders. "I understand. I also know that they're still pissed about the video and probably wouldn't give us permission if we asked."

"All the more reason to take extra precautions. Call me if you get a listening device close enough to hear what's going on."

The outskirt of Linyang was not as populated as Hong Kong or the city itself. The Romeo team was deployed to Ling's house, when he failed to show at the airport. For hours, they watched different men rotated in and out of the house driven by the necessity for a nicotine break.

Obtaining an interior visual was impossible, especially since Julie confirmed that they were dealing with the Chinese Secret Police. Civil rights were a scarce commodity in their presence.

Attracting attention in this area was far too easy and the last thing that Julie wanted to do. The Cao's house was in a farming community and backed up to an orange grove. She knew that the Romeo team had their hands full remaining in the shadows and she decided not to offer any additional attention. "Romeo one, this is Whisky one, we're going to stop in town to avoid drawing unwanted attention. Have you got anything that can get our ears in the house?"

"Whiskey one, I've got something that I've been dying to try out. It's a micro power impulse radar sensor. This thing will let you hear right through the walls, but we've got to get it a bit closer. It's nearly dark here; I think I know how to get it there." The Romeo team member donned a ghillie suit and entered the orange grove.

A car pulled up to the house and several men got out and entered the house. One of the men walked over to Ling Cao and jerked his head back. "You continue to be a disappointment, Ling. How could a man ruin a career as one of the top officers among our ranks and end up assembling fireworks, it's stupid?"

One of Ling's eyes was nearly swollen shut, yet he managed to look at the man standing over him. "I had to do what was right."

"Look where that's gotten you." The man spit in Ling's lap. "You and your family are sitting in the middle of your house tied to chairs. If you don't tell me what I need to know, I begin by killing your daughter. Where is your sense of patriotism?"

Ling contorted the last working muscles in his face to express his contempt. "I have always been a patriot to my country."

"And yet, you contacted the Americans to help you leave this country." The man sat backwards in a chair in front of Ling. "What did you tell them?"

Ling's head drooped. "We have been going over this all day. I have not told them anything. We were supposed to meet in Hong Kong this afternoon at a restaurant near the airport."

The man shoved the note towards Ling. "2 Sardines is not near the airport, it's in central Hong Kong."

Ling looked at the note. "That is not where we were supposed to meet."

He touched Ling on the shoulder. "I believe you. We've had people on both restaurants since we located the note. Tell me again, what did they want?"

Ling's head flopped to one side as he made eye contact. "I used to be in your position. At some point you have to accept the fact that the answers are not going to change. I went on line after General Gan disappeared and stumbled across a number to call if he had been sighted. The reward that was offered was substantial; I viewed it as a chance to start over for my family, so I called."

The Secret Policeman waved the comment off. "Yes, yes, you've said. You've also said that you saw General Gan at the fireworks plant. How is it you've seen him and we've been looking for him for weeks and we can't seem to locate him?"

Ling tilted his head to view the man with his one good eye. "You're probably looking in the wrong place. But that's not your only problem." Ling's head fell back and with all the energy he could gather, he released a hoarse laugh.

The man kicked Ling in the shin. "Look at me! I am sick of you mentioning Zhang Ju. He is a fool, pulling the Americans into our affairs. We've spent the last thirty-five years planning for the Americans. Their country will belong to us; it's only a matter of time." He signaled to two of his men to come over.

Ling looked at the man. "We both know what happens now. Please allow me to take my prayer beads from my pocket and take one last look at the orange grove."

The man roughly pulled the beads from Ling's pocket and put them in Ling's hand. He cut the rope binding Ling's hands and allowed him to walk. "These were a big part of your problem, Ling. True patriots have no need for religious stupidity."

Ling walked to his wife and daughter, who were both crying and kissed them. He reached the window and inhaled deeply. He held the beads out as if he were praying. "This is what it's about, Julie; here in my hands." He saw a van pull up and returned to the middle of the floor kneeling.

One of the team members spoke into his mike. "Whiskey one, did you hear that? How did he know your name?"

Julie was still trying to catch her breath at hearing her name called. They'd underestimated Ling and not planned for the Chinese Secret Police. "If he knows about me, it won't be long before they figure it out."

The team members' eyes moved to the van. "Oh shit, this isn't good."

Julie snapped back. "What's going on?"

The team leader shook his head. "It's the van that just pulled up. Six people in white lab jackets just got out of it. The side of the van says *Organ Donation Recovery*."

Three gunshots exploded flashing through the darkness of the house. Immediately, the six people wearing the lab jackets and carrying large coolers entered the house.

Chapter
46

Zasha adjusted in her seat yet again having no idea how many times she'd moved. The flight to the ship on the C-2A Greyhound was considerably less comfortable than the Lear 28 she'd grown accustomed to. She harbored a bit of contempt for Cole and the Delta team, who didn't seem to notice or care about the flight. "How long before we land?"

Cole looked at his Breitling Navitimer sensing her discomfort. "We should be there shortly." "You should check with the cockpit to see if they'll let you see the ship on approach. Of course, you'll have to be back in your seat when he slams this baby on the deck."

"I'm uncomfortable; I don't have a reason to be scared as well." Zasha leaned her head back settling as much as possible. "You said that we missed a camera at the scene."

Cole's head rocked to one side. "Yeah, what about it?"

"Since we missed it, isn't it possible that Zhang suspects that we're on the way?" Zasha closed her eyes. "He's been ahead of us at every turn. This is starting to feel like a snipe hunt."

One of the Greyhound crewmen handed Cole a headset. "Agent Fenton would like a word with you."

Cole took the headset and glanced at Zasha before putting it on. "Oscar, que pasa?"

Oscar grunted. "He's up to his tricks again. Zhang's yacht sat just off the coast of Rio for nearly one and a half weeks without moving an inch. As soon as we find him and decide to pay him a visit, he weighs anchor and takes off."

Cole cut his eyes to Zasha and covered the mike. "He's on the move." He dropped his hand from the mike. "What do you want us to do?"

Oscar gazed at the live satellite feed of Zhang's yacht. "Land on the ship, we've got Zhang in sight. We've also arranged for an underwater escort; they won't let him slip past us again. The sub will rendezvous in an hour."

Zasha slid on a headset and joined the conversation. "Oscar, have we seen anyone on deck?"

Oscar thumbed through several still photos. "Just a few crew members. It's early afternoon; they may be having a late lunch."

"Has anyone compared the crew on these pictures to the earlier photos?" Zasha opened her laptop. "Shoot me the pictures; I'll take a look at them. You can't trust this guy. Until we can confirm that no one left the yacht, I won't be comfortable."

"We've had the yacht under twenty-four-hour surveillance; no one has left the boat." Oscar flipped over several other photos. "As a matter of fact, we haven't seen much movement at all since Zhang got back from China."

"I would say that's suspect. He's operated right out in the open; what's different now?" Zasha looked over the satellite images. "What's our next move?"

"The sub isn't going to lose the yacht. I'd like you and your team to check out the Rosary Pea field." Oscar clicked a few keys and sent the coordinates to them. "Take a chopper from the ship; there's been a lot of activity in that area."

Cole pointed to the image Zasha had on the screen. "We could take a MH-53E Sea Dragon or an SH-60 Sea Hawk. Either will give us whatever we need and can handle most situations. Oscar, are you seeing anything on the ground that should cause concern?"

"Just a bunch of people in the fields gathering those damn peas." Oscar tossed the file on his desk. "The numbers have trailed off in the past couple of days. You might not even find anyone there today."

Zasha slid on her sunglasses and took a quick peek out of the window. "Oscar, I assume we haven't cleared our visit with the Brazilian government…so, what are we supposed to do with any workers we find in the fields? We don't have any jurisdiction even if they start shooting at us. And if we find any of Zhang's group, there's no extradition treaty in place with Brazil. It's not like there won't be witnesses."

"Why are we having this conversation?" Oscar paused seeing his door open. "You guys have a fucking Delta team at your disposal— do what has to be done."

Cole nodded to the Delta team commander. "I think she just wanted to hear it come out of your mouth. We've got it covered."

☯

The Sea Hawk flew past the field and Cole kept an eye on a screen transmitting heat signatures from the ground. There were a few scattered people in the field and three others near a large truck. He pointed to the screen getting the pilot's attention. "These three people by the truck may be a source of concern. Set us down just behind the truck and let's see how they react. I want to avoid a gun battle if possible."

The pilot made a tight turn and quickly landed the Sea Hawk. The three men standing near the truck pulled AK-47s from their shoulders and carefully held them with the barrels pointing towards the ground.

The Delta Team leader slid open the door opposite the approaching men and readied his men. "On my mark, clear the chopper covering either side. If any of them raises a weapon, put them down, but don't harm the civilians."

Seeing that the men were Chinese, Zasha grabbed the mike and spoke in both English and Mandarin. "Shoulder your weapons!"

The Delta Team deployed from the Sea Hawk with cat-like quickness and landed in shooting position. Each of the approaching men had multiple rifles trained on them prepared to inflict a life-ending wound.

Zasha repeated her demand more forcefully. The men stopped in place but their intentions weren't clear. "Shit, they're going to try something." She tapped the pilot on the shoulder. "Rotate the machinegun and train it on that guy on the left; he seems the jitterier."

The sound of the M-60D machinegun moving was imposing even to the Delta Team, but the approaching man on the left was not deterred. He slowly raised the AK-47.

"Take him!" Zasha yelled to the pilot.

One quick blast from the M-60D cut the man into pieces. The workers abandoned their harvesting and ran from the fields searching for cover in the forestation. The other two men tossed their rifles to the ground and thrust their hands into the air.

Zasha handed the mike back to the pilot. "There's always one stupid son of a bitch who thinks he can stop bullets."

The Giant waited near the pressurized hatch for the others to arrive. With one twist of his massive hands, the valve turned and the hatch opened. The water lapped the sides of the tube keeping the sea at bay.

Vladimir stepped to the tube holding two large pair of bolt cutters. He handed one pair to Borka and slid on his diving tank. He sat on the edge of the tube and dipped his mask in the water. "Borka and I will go in first and free the water sleds. Make sure that you stay on the sled; it's too dark to be looking for any of you down there. These tanks have enough air for us to make it to our destination; if you fall behind, you're on your own. I'm not wasting time."

Zhang walked to the hatch and turned to face the other men. "Only about half of us have ever done any diving. It is imperative that all of you remain calm. If you start hyperventilating, you'll run out of air before we reach our rendezvous point." He pointed to the Giant, Borka and Vladimir, who were all behind him. "The four of us will pilot the water sleds. Carlos, you ride with me. The rest of you will be on the other three." The Giant pointed to Xie and Rafael and Borka gathered Alejandro and Pablo. Zhang looked to the last two. "General Gan and Armando you will be with Vladimir."

Vladimir and Borka slid through the hatch and went to work on freeing the water sleds. As a sled was freed, the engine was turned and the lights switched on. In less than a minute, all the sleds were awaiting riders. Vladimir shined his flashlight through the hatch to let them know it was time to begin.

Zhang waived to the men. "Put your masks on and clear your regulators, it's time. Get with your partners immediately. We don't have any time to waste."

The Giant tapped the men sending them down the hatch to the waiting sleds. He leaned close to Zhang. "I bled the tanks of the three we're losing. They won't make it regardless." He followed Zhang in the water closing the hatch and swimming to his sled.

Vladimir punched in coordinates on his sled's control panel and pulled the gear. The propellers engaged and he dove the sled to a depth that would help to keep them hidden from anyone on the surface.

Alejandro paid close attention to each of the sleds when he'd entered the water. Zhang's was the only sled with spear guns on both sides. The other three had a spear gun next to the pilot's hands. Riding on the last sled enabled him to see other disparities. Each of the men piloting the sleds had knives on their legs. Carlos was the only non-pilot, who also wore a knife. Suddenly, he wasn't feeling comfortable with this trip. When asked about diving experience, he'd lied and said it was his first time. Now he hoped the lie would serve him.

Vladimir constantly watched the control panel to see how far they had traveled. He was careful not to dive too deeply in order to reserve their air supply. When it came time to eliminate the deadweight, they would have to have enough air for any possible struggle with the three they would leave behind.

Twenty minutes into their dive, Zhang began constantly looking at his watch. He knew that they were approaching the halfway point and soon Vladimir would begin diving deeper.

The sled lights occasionally lit a passing fish, which captivated the men; especially the ones who were new to diving. Any care that they may have exhibited seemed to pass with the wonderment of their underwater surroundings.

The lone exception was Alejandro. The pit of his stomach continued to churn. He knew that Zhang could not be trusted. He noticed before they left that the pressure in his tank was less than the others he'd been able to see. Even more concerning was the fact that most of the men wearing knives were superior in strength to the ones without. He began making plans to escape if things turned bad as he anticipated they would.

Zhang was now looking at his watch every few seconds. He was riding in second position just behind Vladimir. He began turning around to see the other sleds behind him.

Without warning, Vladimir began diving his sled. Each increased inch of depth darkened their surroundings. A large school of fish suddenly darted in their path swerving in what seemed to be a large ball. Something was driving the school of fish and it was not the sleds.

The school of fish jumped in tandem leading them directly in the path of the sleds. Alejandro pointed to one side to the culprits; two sharks were feeding. He released his hand from the side of the sled and watched as they dove under the fish.

Vladimir pushed his gear forward stopping the sled. The other sleds stopped and he, Borka and the Giant pulled their knives from their legs.

The fish had already panicked Xie, who had bubbles rapidly flowing from his regulator. Trying to watch, the confusion, he didn't notice Vladimir slide his knife through the hose providing him with the air he needed to live. His eyes grew wide realizing that he couldn't breathe and he grabbed Vladimir with both hands praying for life.

Armando suffered a similar fate and tried to rip the Giant's regulator free as his lungs felt as if they would explode. He darted man to man begging for a breath of their air. He rushed towards Rafael, who pulled the spear gun and shot him in the middle of his chest.

Noticing that Alejandro was missing, Borka spun his sled around searching for him. He took the spear gun from the side of the sled and positioned it just over his controls. He'd moved about fifty yards from the group and hadn't noticed the blood rushing from the wound in Armando's chest.

Pablo looked towards the other three sleds and noticed that they were beginning to move forward. He tapped Borka and pointed to the others.

Borka swung the lights of the sled covering as much area as possible in a final attempt to find Alejandro. Without the coordinates to their destination, he gave up the search and headed towards the lights of the other sleds, which were fading fast. He signaled to Pablo to kick his feet so that they could make up ground faster.

Alejandro was just inches from them. He held his breath to prevent bubbles from escaping and giving up his location. He was grateful when Borka turned the sled leaving the area. He took a deep breath and held one hand above his eyes and the other beneath his chin to determine which direction the bubbles flowed. When they hit the hand beneath his chin, he knew that he was upside-down and righted himself. In complete darkness, he had to follow the bubbles to reach the surface.

The climb to the surface was slow. His tank began to sputter and he realized it was nearly out of air. He swam the last thirty seconds holding his breath. When his head broke the surface, he gulped for air. Alejandro felt relief and was instantly overcome with grief. He couldn't prevent the tears which streamed from his eyes. In all directions there was nothing but darkness and endless ocean. He had no sense of direction. He looked up at the stars locating the North Star, but without knowing where he was, he didn't know what direction he should swim. Floating on his back he wondered if he would be found and if his daughter would ever receive his body for a proper burial.

Chapter
48

The Romeo team member in the guille suit inched from the house after the organ recovery group entered. From the conversation coming from the house, the Romeo team knew that they had not imagined what was going on. One of the lab-coat group entered the house and relayed to a nearby hospital which organs the rest of the team was harvesting.

Once safe in the orange grove, he sat back concentrating on isolating the conversations inside the house.

A car pulled up and an excited man ran into the house. He approached one of the Secret Police agents with his back to the harvesting operations. "There have been a couple of people spotted in a nearby tea house. The proprietor called us after hearing these two speaking English." He held out a photo.

The Secret Policeman asked. "Are they still there?"

He nodded vigorously. "Yes, I left one man to watch them until we returned."

"Whiskey one, you've got company. Leave your position right now. You're going to have a tail. I suggest you take him out, you're about to have additional company." The Romeo team member peered through binoculars gauging the movement at the house. "Agent Hu, they're on the move, I suggest you do the same before they send the organ recovery team for you."

The Whiskey team left the tea house walking rapidly. Julie used a mirror from her purse to look behind them. "He's right on our heels. We're going to have to duck in this alley way. It's our best chance of taking him out without being noticed."

"I'll take care of it." One of the team members slid a Glock 22 .40 caliber pistol from his jacket and attached a silencer. He grabbed Julie by the arm and sped up their pace. He heard the man behind them begin to jog. In one swift move, he turned and fired two shots striking the man in the head and chest.

The dead man barely hit the ground before the sound of cars speeding to the area could be heard. The Glock went back into the team member's jacket and the silencer remained in place. "We've got to get out of here as quickly as possible. When they find the dead guy, they're going to tear this place apart looking for us."

Moving quickly alley to alley, they knew that running would draw too much attention. A farm truck idling in one of the alley ways garnered Julie's attention. "That truck over there is covered in crates. Since it's running, my guess is he'll be going to some market soon. That's our ticket out."

Reaching the truck, it was clear that there was only room for two riders in the back. "You two get in. Since I was waiting outside of the tea house, no one saw me. I can handle things here."

Julie hesitated. "Do you think you can make it to the Romeo team's location?"

The agent's head jerked around and his hand slid back around the Glock. "Someone's coming, get in the truck quickly." He pulled a canvas tarp over Julie and her partner. "I'll handle this."

The truck driver approached quickly. "Hey, what are you doing near my truck?"

The agent kept the gun low hidden just behind his leg. "Where are you taking this crop?"

The driver cocked his head to one side. "What concern of yours is where I'm going?"

The agent moved closer. "I don't mean to intrude, I could use a ride. I'm willing to pay." He reached in his pocket and pulled out a wad of yuan. "I've got about two thousand yuan."

The man visibly stepped back. "What have you done that you are willing to pay such a sum in exchange for a ride to Hong Kong?"

The agent smiled, Hong Kong was perfect. He flipped the money clip holding the yuan revealing a badge resembling one used by the Chinese police. "It is official business."

The driver wiped his mouth eyeing the money. It was more than the entire truck load would bring him. "Let me see your badge closer."

The agent raised his hand with the gun. "We're wasting time. We need to get underway now. Get in the truck."

They got in the truck and the driver placed it in gear and moved onto the road. "So much for the offer of generosity."

The agent pulled the yuan from the clip and sat them next to the driver. "I'm sorry for the gun, I'm in a hurry. The money is yours— just get me to Hong Kong quickly without additional questions."

The driver eyed the money for some time before lifting it and placing it in his shirt pocket. He pointed to a neatly folded bag sitting between them. "My wife packed me food for the road. It's always more than I need if you're hungry."

"Maybe later." The gun rested in the agent's lap for nearly fifteen minutes before he slid it back into his holster. "You can see that I mean you no harm, relax; we'll be fine."

The agent slid back in the seat and heard a click in his ear. *"This is Romeo one, activate your phone long enough to get a fix on your location."* He pulled his cell phone out and typed in a text giving the road they were on and which direction they were headed. *"We've got you. It's an overnight ride to Hong Kong. Give it a couple of hours and then look for a place to stop. We'll pull in and scoop you guys up. Make sure that he gets out of the truck and goes inside. I don't want him to be able to identify us."*

Three hours into the trip the agent sent a text to the Romeo team and to Julie letting them know that they were about to make the switch. He pointed to a sign of an upcoming rest stop. "Pull off here for a quick break."

The driver slowed the truck. "Now may be a good time to have a snack."

"I'll take a look when we stop." The agent turned in the driver's direction. "You can go first; I'll hold the keys until I'm done. I also want your cell phone. We don't need any mistakes."

The truck pulled to a stop and the driver got out and leaned through the window. "You're not going to take my truck, are you?"

"I thought we'd gotten past that. Your truck will be right here when you get back." The agent pointed to the building. Hurry along, I've got to go too."

The Romeo team waited just out of sight until the driver got in the building. They pulled behind the truck. Julie and her team jumped into the car and they pulled from the stop.

The driver came out of the building and the closer he came to the truck the faster he walked. When he didn't see his rider, he broke into a jog cursing himself for trusting the man. He jerked his door open and saw his keys and cell phone on the seat. He lifted the items from the seat noticing an additional one hundred yuan where his cell phone battery used to be.

Nearly an hour further down the road, a police statement announcing they were looking for two people that had been seen in a tea house in Linyang, broke on all radio stations. The broadcast further said the pair was responsible for killing a member of the Chinese Secret Police. The statement ended by saying anyone assisting in the escape of these fugitives would be prosecuted to the fullest extent of the law.

The driver pulled off the road and found a phone to call the police. After sharing a description of his rider, he blew a sigh of relief that it did not match the people the police were looking for.

The call prompted the Secret Police to set up a dragnet for all traffic entering Hong Kong from Linyang. The description the truck driver provided, even without the mention of the money, suggested the rider he'd had was connected.

Chapter
49

The blast of gunfire from the Sea Hawk sent the field workers running for the cover of the dense vegetation at the edge of the mountains surrounding the Rosary Pea field.

Zasha and Cole followed the Delta team from the protection of the helicopter. The two men who'd thrust their rifles in the air, were on the ground encircled by the Delta team binding their hands. She kneeled next to one of the men. "Where is Zhang?"

The man's face was mashed into the ground under the weight of one of the Delta team members. His eyes were the only thing he could move and he used them to gaze at Zasha. "I don't speak English."

Zasha repeated her question in Mandarin much to the surprise of the man. "I don't have time for games. I won't ask you again."

The man smiled and spoke in perfect English. "Fuck you bitch!"

A swift blow to his kidneys ripped the smile from his face. The Delta team member delivering the punch grabbed the man's hair and jerked his head to one side. "Watch your damn mouth!"

The man coughed and vainly attempted to move. "I have nothing to say to any of you."

Zasha stood. "Get them to the chopper. We'll see what he has to say once we get them back to the ship."

Cole led several other members of the Delta team over to the crates containing the Rosary Peas. "We don't have time to burn this shit. From the looks of it, this is the last of the crop. We'll have to take the crates and get them to the lab at Langley."

The Delta team leader looked towards the mountains where the workers fled. "What do we do about the others?"

Cole shook his head. "There's not a lot we can do. We're not even supposed to be here. We'd best get this stuff loaded and leave before some of them decide to return with the local authorities. I don't want to be tied up in political controversy."

They gathered the crates and loaded them onto the Sea Hawk. In less than eight minutes, they were back in the air on their way to the ship.

Zasha slid a headset on and was immediately connected to Oscar. "Zhang had three men there. They're on board, one in a body bag, at least what's left of him. The other two are being much less than cooperative."

Oscar ran his hand over his head. "I wouldn't have expected anything less. Did you torch the fields?"

"No, there wasn't time. Several workers were still there. They ran for cover when the shooting started. We didn't want to stay around to see if they returned with reinforcements. We did get five or six crates of the peas they'd harvested. We'll bring them along with Zhang's men as soon as we return to the ship."

"I'll have things set up here." Oscar checked the time. "I've got to meet Director Carson. Let me know when you're underway."

Zasha sat up quickly. "Before you go, have the satellites turned anything up?"

Oscar shook his head. "Nothing new— we're still on the yacht, there's nothing to worry about."

The pilot kept the Sea Hawk just over the water leaving the Rio area. It was the easiest way to avoid questions from the Brazilian government, who had not given them permission to be there. Nearly twelve miles from shore, he eased the helicopter higher.

Something in the water caught the copilot's eyes and he signaled for the Sea Hawk to make another pass over the water.

Alejandro had nearly given up being found alive. He struggled to reach a flare he'd secretly stashed in his wetsuit. Seeing the helicopter turn, tears leaked over his parched face. It took all his strength to punch the bottom sending the flare aloft.

"Commander Peterson, there's a man in the water. He looks pretty bad off, but he's alive. What should we do?"

Cole looked at Zasha for support. "If we don't get him out of the water, he'll probably die. What do you think?"

Zasha turned her head away. "Why do you want me to be the heartless bitch?"

Cole shrugged his shoulders. "Because you're so good at it?"

She flipped Cole the bird. "We're not supposed to deviate from this mission, especially since we've got prisoners. How in the hell did he get this far out without help?" She took a pair of binoculars and pulled the man into view. "Shit, it's an old guy. Who's going in to get him?"

The Delta team leader sat his rifle down and stripped off his excess clothing. "Get me close." He slid the door open and waited until they hovered over the man before jumping in.

"Thank you, thank you, thank you." Alejandro's voice trailed off as he continued his mantra.

The Delta team leader waived for the winch to be lowered. "You're going to be fine, sir. What are you doing out here all alone?"

Alejandro struggled to get past the dryness of his mouth. "Are you an American?"

The team leader watched as the cable dipped into the water. He hooked the harness around Alejandro. "Yes, I am an American." He gave a 'thumbs up' to the men above and the winch pulled them towards the helicopter.

Alejandro grabbed the team leader's arm. "I need to speak to the director of the CIA." His hand dropped away and he passed out.

As the harness came closer to the open door of the helicopter, Zasha recognized that the rescued man was Alejandro Javier. She reached for the team leader. "Is he okay?"

"He's had a rough time in the water." The team leader stepped in and moved Zasha away from the others. "He said that he wants to speak with the Director."

Zasha looked towards Alejandro, who showed no sign of coming around. "Did he say what he wanted?"

The team leader shook his head. "I'm afraid not. Right after making his request, he passed out."

Zasha motioned to Cole, who joined them. "We've got to get him to Langley as soon as he comes to. He asked to speak to the Director."

Cole watched as the Corpsman started an IV. "How did he get out here?"

The team leader shook his head. "He didn't say, but the wetsuit and diving tank suggest it was planned."

"That would also imply that he was not out here alone." Cole looked at Zasha. "Now the question is, where are the others? Chances are they're not on Zhang's yacht."

The water sleds began ascending and the area surrounding the men seemed darker than when their trek began. Breaking through the surface of the water the deafening silence unsettled most of the men traveling with Zhang. The lights from the water sleds did little to ease the darkness or their discontent.

Vladimir and Zhang banked their sleds. Seconds later, the sound of sand scrapping the bottoms of their craft could be heard. The others quickly followed the maneuver bringing their sleds to rest. Powerful flashlights hung on the sides each sled. Zhang and Vladimir used theirs to light the area to help the others find their flashlights.

"Welcome, gentlemen. This cave was once used by pirates to hide their loot. We'll use it as a quick stopover before getting back to work." Zhang began walking down a path. "In the next few days, each of you will return home and implement our plan."

General Gan rushed Zhang slamming into him. "What the fuck were you thinking? You killed the Premier of State Council. How am I supposed to explain that?"

Zhang put his hand up keeping the Giant at bay. "That fucking weasel got exactly what he deserved and you know as well as I do that the Mexican government can't be trusted. We had to get rid of them. Our remaining crew is strong; strength is needed to complete our task."

General Gan spat at Zhang's feet. "We'd better come up with a good story, or I might not be around to help. You of all people know how China operates. Killing all of us wouldn't even raise their heart rate one beat."

Zhang stepped past General Gan. "We'll be ready for them. I suggest you keep yourself together; acting irrationally won't serve any of us."

General Gan followed. He reached for Zhang's shoulder and decided against it dropping his hand. "Was it absolutely necessary to kill Xie? He was a sniffling punk, but his cunning could be useful."

Zhang spun and General Gan nearly ran into him. Practically nose-to-nose, Zhang spoke softly. "That fool owed me a fortune. He involved himself in this undertaking thinking it would settle his debt. Seeing the look on his face when he lost his air supply settled his debt. I am prepared to make you one of the most powerful men in the world, please don't have me reconsider my decision."

General Gan didn't flinch. "Xie's unfortunate run-in with the Americans will require intervention by the Chinese government."

"Excellent." Zhang resumed walking down the path. "Once we arrive at our base, we'll have to release a statement."

Julie and her team pulled from the highway to an isolated wooded area. They sighed in unison and Julie turned to face the two men. "Based on what they're saying on the radio, we're not going to be able to make it into Hong Kong. I'm going to call Oscar to see what he knows." She took her iPhone out and selected the 'sat-phone' option and scrambled the call.

Oscar answered and scrambled the call on his end as well. "Where are you guys?"

"We're a hundred kilometers outside of Hong Kong. From what we're hearing on the radio, we're not going to be able to get to the jet."

"That's a correct assumption. They've had the jet under surveillance since the bulletin went out earlier." Oscar clicked his mouse bringing up their location. "I'm transmitting you coordinates to an underground Catholic church in Nanning. We've supported the congregation there. I'll contact the priest and arrange for them to get you to Tibet. As you know, several of the monasteries there have been voicing their opposition to Chinese rule. The subsequent chaos will help in getting you out of the country."

Julie's eyes darted between the men seated with her. "What about Zhang?"

Oscar tapped his finger beside his mouse. "We'll have to leave him to others. We're not even sure where he is right now. Just get to Tibet and get out of there."

The portable GPS lit up with Oscar's instructions to Nanning and the team member driving the car pulled back onto the highway and headed to the city.

Julie reached for a bag in the back seat and pulled it to her lap. She opened it and looked at the contents before looking out the window at the setting sun. "As soon as it's dark, we should stop and change our identities."

As the sun retreated and the lights of any nearby city were a dim memory, Julie began looking for any quiet area. Just off the road, she spotted a small creek. "Pull over here and keep a lookout for anyone in the area."

The driver eased off the road and turned the car's lights off. "I'll keep an eye out while you two make your changes."

Julie grabbed the duffle bag at her feet. Slinging the bag over her shoulder, she stepped from the car and pulled a bottle from the bag and poured the contents into her hair. Her long dark hair instantly began turning white. She tossed the bottle to the agent with her and he began where she left off. They both knelt at the edge of the creek and scooped water over their heads.

Nearing the car, the buzzing sound of the electric razor was unmistakable. The team member in the driver's seat moved the electric razor back and forth across his head. He let the hair fall into a towel on his lap; satisfied that the job was done; he folded the towel over and placed it in a bag. Pulling off his shirt and pants, he added them to the bag as well and stepped from the car. He opened the trunk and pulled out traditional Buddhist robes and stepped into them. A second later, he tossed Julie Buddhist nun's garb.

The team member with the white hair dressed in black loose-fitting pajama-like clothing and pulled a hat made of sea grass onto his head. He then moved behind the wheel and adjusted the seat so that he could drive.

Julie pulled two small boxes from the duffle and handed one to her head-shaven partner. Each of them pulled fitted dental prosthetics from the boxes and affixed them to their teeth. She then took the duffle to the back of the car and pulled two IMI, Israel

Military Industries made .50 caliber Desert Eagle and slid them into holsters beneath the Nun outfit. Finally, she stuffed the duffel into a hidden panel in the trunk of the car and slammed the lid.

Traveling what seemed to be an unending road that consumed hour after hour, they arrived in Nanning without being stopped or for that matter, questioned. Julie found this at the very least odd, since the unrest among the Buddhists was growing and the Chinese military struggled to squelch their efforts…nevertheless, they had arrived safely.

Chapter
51

The Chinese president anxiously rocked in his chair listening to his party members addressing potential solutions as they related to General Gan's return to China. His hand came down hard on the table. "The fact is, gentlemen, that we are not certain of what we are dealing with. Each of us has seen the tapes of the abduction and heard repeated denials of involvement by the Americans. General Gan's trip to Puerto Vallarta was not state sanctioned and we have no knowledge of what the trip involved."

One of the men spoke. "Yes, Comrade President, but the Americans have suggested the general's involvement in a plot to flood the US with our citizens, which if true, could work in our favor."

The president shot a glance in his underling's direction. "If the Americans are aware of this scheme, how could it possibly benefit us? They will adopt a position of vigilance towards any of our ships coming into their ports. This, in addition to their posture on our products, could have a devastating effect on any plans we've made to position our people in their country."

Heads nodded around the table; one spoke up. "Another question exists: if the Americans were not involved in kidnapping the delegation in Puerto Vallarta, how did they come by this information?"

The president looked at a clock over the entrance door. "Gan will be home shortly. To benefit the country, we will greet him with a hero's welcome. Then, we will take him to the *dragon's tomb* to ensure that he is forthcoming. Since the tomb is his creation, he is aware of the consequences of being less than candid."

Another official chimed in. "But sir, shouldn't he be afforded the benefit of doubt? General Gan has faithfully served the state."

"Need I remind you whom he was with?" The President stood. "We have tolerated Zhang's exploits here in China simply because his actions have been mutually beneficial. It is clear to see this time that he has involved himself in affairs concerning our greatest adversary. We've spent years planting our investigators in the United States. If it were time to act, we would know. Zhang has brought superfluous attention to China. General Gan has long thought that we should invade the US— joining forces with Zhang can't be positive for our cause. It is never intelligent to stir a sleeping dragon if your intention is to behead him. General Gan and Zhang Ju may have brought the dragon to his feet."

General Gan leaned back in the over-stuffed goose down white leather recliner aboard Zhang's plane. Facing him, or at least the transmitted digital image of Zhang, General Gan put his feet up appearing very relaxed. "If I were the one in Beijing awaiting my return, I know what I would do."

Zhang pulled the cigar from his mouth and blue smoke surrounded his head. "Won't the president give credence to your position and accept what you have to say?"

General Gan lifted the drink from the holder on the chair and drained the glass. "Paranoia is what has kept our president in office so long. I guess that it is my karma that I will face the techniques of the tomb— but, I did develop them. I even trained the men to carry out their procedures without regard to whom they were interrogating."

Zhang moved the cigar near his lips and held it just short of them. "Maybe in the back of their minds they will suspect that you are innocent and carry out their duty in a less efficient manner."

General Gan held his glass out for a refill of Scotch. "You don't understand the degree of training these men have— if the president were brought to the tomb, he would receive the same treatment as anyone else."

Zhang puffed the cigar and reached for the snifter resting on the tray next to his chair. "It doesn't seem that I would enjoy the president's hospitality. It seems wise that I decided to remain here in Buenos Aires. When you assume command of the country, make sure the president receives his just desserts."

"Maybe we should go over things again to insure consistency." General Gan lifted his notes and took another drink of Scotch.

Zhang took a methodical pull from the cigar. "Don't you trust me General?"

General Gan sat forward in his chair. "Of course I do. However, I also know our president and he will be looking for discrepancies in our accounts of the situation. You sent him the doctored account of what happened in Puerto Vallarta. But, we still have to deal with what happened to Xie. He was akin to the president's lap dog. He may accept that the Americans were responsible for his death, but he will still want the body."

"Fuck Xie!" Zhang's voice rose uncharacteristically loud. "He was a weasel and received exactly what he deserved!"

"Yes, but the Americans will deny any involvement. Surely, they also have a recorded account of Puerto Vallarta." General Gan sat his glass down and lifted it again. "That may prove to be the wild card."

Zhang put the cigar between his teeth and spoke past it. "I provide the President and his cronies millions of dollars a year so that I may operate my business in anonymity. I can assure you that he does not want to damage our relationship. He will believe what I have provided him. Your job is to make him believe you. Just remember that your future is dependent on that."

General Gan sat back in the chair and looked at the blank screen where Zhang was just moments ago. He took sips of the Scotch and let them slide down his throat. A quick glance of his watch confirmed that several hours remained before they touched down in Beijing.

Two beautiful women came from a door near the rear of the plane and sat on either arm of General Gan's chair. "Master Ju has instructed us to relax you." They began undoing the buttons on his shirt. "The massage table is ready for you in the back of the plane."

General Gan finished his drink and rose, following the scant clothing dropped like bread crumbs leading the way to the back room of the plane. He walked through the door and watched as the two women rubbed massage oil over each other's bodies. Never letting his gaze wane, he took off his uniform and neatly laid it over a chair. "It would seem a happy ending is in my future."

One of the women patted the massage bed. "Why don't you hop up here and lay as flat as possible. We'll work out all your kinks."

General Gan walked to the edge of the bed and climbed on. Admiring his own erection, he placed a hand on each of the women. "Even age can't diminish desire when you are in the presence of two profoundly beautiful women."

One of them grabbed his penis rubbing it flat against his stomach. "Age doesn't matter when you have kept yourself in such good shape. Roll over to your stomach. I'll keep this out of your way."

The general obeyed, grunting as the woman continuously stroked his member against the position she'd placed it on his stomach. "I hope you two are around after I finish my business in Beijing."

The two women looked at each other with blank expressions and began to knead the general's shoulders. "We go wherever Master Ju instructs us to go."

General Gan moaned and rocked side-to-side as the women massaged his muscles. "Speaking of Ju, does he even like women?"

The women's gazes met and they both began to laugh. They moved further down the general's back and flipped their long hair over their heads allowing the strands to stream across his back. "Would you like us to show you what Master Ju likes during his massages?"

General Gan lifted his head and looked back at the laughing women. Glancing around the immediate area, he didn't see anything other than the women and their massage oil. He laid his head back down and closed his eyes. "Sure, if you're positive I'll enjoy it."

The women reached the general's lower back and rubbed each muscle. They then skipped to his feet and worked their way up his legs concentrating on the length of each muscle.

"This is wonderful." General Gan didn't try to, nor did he think he could, move. "Is this what Zhang Ju likes?"

"In a moment." One of them said. They reached the top of his thighs and moved to either side of the bed.

"It's not over is it?" General Gan asked but still didn't move.

One of the women took a bottle of massage oil from a water-bath where it was being heated. She held the bottle over the general's gluteus and squirted the warm oil over them. A large amount of the oil seeped between his gluteus then each of the women covered their hands with the oil.

They rubbed the general's gluteus until they could feel that no tension remained. The woman that stroked his penis earlier slid her hand beneath him and took him in her hand. She squeezed him and using long slow strokes, moved her hand up and down his length.

The other woman continued to rub his gluteus until she was sure that his attention was on his penis. Without a word, or missing a stroke, she inserted her finger between his gluteus instantly finding her mark.

General Gan tightened his gluteus. "Hey, what are you doing?"

The women pushed his shoulders down. "Relax— this is the Master Ju special. It's also called a prostate massage. Don't fight it and I promise you'll be rewarded."

General Gan remained still despite his reservations. In seconds, the woman's skillful fingers had reached the pelvic plexus, the nerves that supply the prostate.

Just as quickly, the other woman could feel his hardness grow in her hand. "You like the Master Ju special."

General Gan didn't attempt to respond. Instead, his breathing deepened. There was no fight left in him, he was along for the ride.

The woman stroking him used his breathing as her guide— the deep breathing received long slow strokes and tight grips. As his breathing became desperate and shallower, she stroked faster popping on and off of him.

Grunts formed in the back of the general's throat, but they reached every inch of his exterior. His muscles, which moments ago were rubbed free of tension now tensed beyond anything he could remember. A sound that could only be described as a growl released from his vocal cords. At the same time, the tension that crescendo spawned forth into a waiting towel.

The women's actions slowed until they could see that the general was spent. The woman at the back of the bed sat. "That is the first portion of your massage. During the second half, you will be expected to please us as well."

General Gan flopped to his back and smiled at the women. "I can't wait."

The women rolled a table of warm water to the side of the bed and pulled sponges from it to wipe the sweat from his body.

He reached for the women as they worked. "Does Zhang please you after you have provided him with such pleasure?"

They began laughing, finished their work and rolled the table from the side of the bed. They used towels to dry the general, re-oiled their hands and went to work on his chest.

Chapter
53

At a private landing strip at the Beijing airport, the President waited for Zhang's jet to land. Behind him the important members of the Party waited with the rest of the welcoming committee. The President turned to General Gan's second in command. "Is everything ready for his debriefing?"

He nodded succinctly. "The men are ready. They will do their duty. The general will not receive any preferential treatment."

The President shielded his eyes and looked to the sky. "They are here now. Prepare the music."

The plane taxied up to its mark and the President walked out to meet it. The band began playing China's national anthem, *March of the Volunteers* as soon as the door of the plane opened.

General Gan stepped from the plane holding the rails as his legs were still wobbly from joining the "mile high" club during his trip. He reached the tarmac and deeply bowed before the President. "It is good to be home."

The President slightly bowed and walked up, taking the general's arm. "We have much to discuss. We've missed you here." He turned and waved to the press, who he'd gathered to record the event. The event could be used as effective propaganda when he chose to confront the United States.

General Gan knew what awaited him if the least discrepancy was detected in his depiction of the events. If Zhang deviated in the least from what they'd practiced, the general would be in for a long evening. He chose to adopt a cocky, defiant stand. No matter what he did, he could not change the president's mind if he was determined to interrogate him. "I look forward to filling you in on the details of my abduction. The Americans will stop at nothing to forward their agenda and stop our progress."

The President released General Gan's arm and moved in front of the television cameras recording the event. "China owes a debt of gratitude to Comrade Zhang Ju for rescuing our top military General from the hands of a would-be aggressor. Our adversary has exhibited no shame violating all treaties signed with China and attempted to extract secrets from China's leading General, who refused to impart any of his wisdom. In the coming days, we will review our relationship with this conspirator to determine their future with China"

General Gan followed the President into a waiting limo. He fought to conceal his surprise— protocol dictated at least two soldiers trained in special interrogation be present in the waiting limo. He sat opposite the President. "Where would you like me to begin?"

The President sat in silence staring at the general. Thirty seconds later, the President raised a hand and stroked the side of his face. "Shouldn't you be asking why I have not followed protocol? Your very explicit instructions stipulate that we should be accompanied by your men."

"I will make no excuses for my men and will see to it that they are reprimanded." General Gan eased back in the seat and crossed his hands in his lap.

"You once told me that they would follow your orders regardless of who sought to override them. That appears to be a fallacy on your part." The President pulled his glasses off and took a cloth from the seat to clean them. Resting on the seat beneath the cloth was a G17C Glock. "How was your little junket to Mexico?"

General Gan couldn't hide the hard swallow that crossed his Adam's apple. He took an extra second to gather himself. "I went to Mexico to assess Zhang Ju's intent as it related to matters of the state. Premier Yi requested my presence at the meeting."

The President dropped the cloth next to the Glock and adjusted the position of the gun. "Don't you find it strange that Xie Yi didn't inform me of such an important meeting?"

General Gan regretted having mentioned Yi's name, yet he felt safe saying anything since Xie was dead. "He assured me that you had full knowledge of the meeting. He also suggested that it was of the highest priority and that no one else was to have any knowledge of the meeting."

"General Gan, neither of us has any illusions as to the state of Xie's character— cunning, deceitful, and self-serving." The President's hand fell to the Glock and his fingers danced across the handle. "Now that we both know that I was not informed, what was the nature of the meeting?"

General Gan's eyes jumped between the President's eyes and his hand on the gun. This was the one area that Zhang had not discussed; he decided truth was the best course. "Zhang Ju presented a plan to flood the United States with citizens from China and Mexico. He suggested that his people would provide each of the immigrants with documentation that placed them in the United States for five years. Under the U.S.'s new President, this would give each of the immigrants instant citizenship. In return, they were to receive the name of a hand-selected candidate that they were to vote into office. Zhang Ju assumed that in the course of three years, his people would be able to assume a majority of political power in the United States."

The President didn't speak right away, but his hand did move from the Glock. "Zhang Ju came up with this idea on his own?"

General Gan relaxed uncrossing his hands holding them with his palms facing the President. "Honestly, I have no idea. He was working with a Russian to secure ships to bring hundreds of thousands of our people to the U.S. He also employed several Mexican drug lords to shuttle our people along with the Mexicans across the border. If successful, his plan has merit."

"Indeed. This sounds an awful lot like a plan you yourself proposed...at least the end result." The President reached down and moved the cloth over the Glock. "I can see why your presence was requested. However, I am still concerned about the lack of contact with my office."

General Gan's confidence grew and he chose to take liberty with the facts. "There is a simple explanation. Zhang required all of us to deposit our cell phones as soon as we arrived. After the initial meeting, we were sent to our rooms to freshen up before dinner. It was then that a sleeping gas was released in the rooms. When we recovered, we were no longer at Zhang's complex."

The President rubbed the side of his face again. "Is this when the Americans took you into custody?"

"At the time, we did not know who had taken us. We were being held in isolation." The General realized that he'd spoken too quickly, which made his comment sound rehearsed. "Each time I was questioned, I demanded to know who had taken us and why—those questions were never answered."

The President crossed his arms over his chest. "Do you have any explanation to why Zhang Ju was not captured during the raid by the Americans?"

General Gan was ready for this question, but allowed a moment to pass before speaking. "He and his liaison, a giant of a man, took us into a secure bunker beneath the structure. They observed the strike team approaching and remained there witnessing the abduction via a closed-circuit broadcast. That was how he was able to forward the video to you."

"The Americans are not usually so sloppy. If they were planning a strike, they had intelligence and if their objective was to take everyone into custody, they would have waited until everyone was present to have a successful mission." The President's hand came to his chin. "Additionally, it seems implausible that Zhang would have been able to mount a successful rescue if the Americans were involved."

The General adjusted in his seat. "Zhang Ju's resources are vast. He pulled together a team to secure our freedom."

The President eyed the general sternly. "Is this when Xie Yi was lost?"

General Gan's mouth was dry, but he knew better than to ask for a drink of water. "Sadly, yes. Two other members of the group, Alejandro Javier and Armando Ramirez were also lost at this time. We were on a ship and they all were lost to the sea."

The President's hand rubbed across his chin and the intensity in his eyes grew. "The military's job is to provide protection to the citizens of China. High ranking members of our government should be protected at all cost. Why didn't you risk your life to save Xie?"

General Gan sat forward. "The scene was one of mayhem. Zhang's men were literally tossing us to a speedboat. Xie and Alejandro were the last two to be freed and our captors were now aware of the attempt to free us; there was nothing I could do."

The President's hand fell to his lap. "You should have contacted me the moment your freedom was secured."

General Gan was nearly on the edge of his seat. "Zhang did, sir."

The President's hand went back to the Glock. "Then, how is it that you and Premier Yi were seen at a fireworks company in Linyang?"

Zasha and Cole entered the hospital quarters of the ship. Alejandro was sitting up eating a small bowl of soup. He sat his spoon down and cleared his throat. "Pardon me for not standing, especially when such a lovely lady enters the room."

Zasha smiled warmly. "That is not necessary. How are you feeling today?"

"Much better than if you had not arrived when you did." Alejandro glanced quickly at the bowl of soup.

Cole motioned towards the bowl. "Please don't let us interrupt your lunch. If you would like additional food, I'll have some brought in."

Alejandro's head moved side-to-side. "After such an ordeal, it is best to begin slowly. Maybe by dinner I will be ready for additional food."

Zasha pulled a chair next to the bed and sat. "I spoke with Director Carson earlier. He is anxious to speak with you."

Alejandro dabbed the sides of his mouth with a napkin. "I was told each time I requested that I would have to speak with you to place a call to the Director. I must find out if he's heard from Marianna."

Zasha touched his shoulder. "Your daughter is fine. Cole and I picked her up at the airport in Ireland. She is safe in the States."

Alejandro choked back a lump growing in his throat. "Thank you. I have been very worried. When may I speak with her?"

Cole leaned against the bed. "If you're feeling up to it, we could be in Virginia by nightfall. We've got a plane topside, fueled and ready to launch."

Alejandro took note of the remaining soup in the bowl. "I will be dressed and prepared to leave in fifteen minutes— will that be too soon?"

Cole nodded. "I'll have some new clothing brought to you immediately." He turned to Zasha. "I'm going to assist in the preflight. You and Mr. Javier can come up as soon as he's ready."

Zasha watched Cole leave the room and turned her attention back to Alejandro. "How did you manage to get so far out in the ocean?"

Alejandro finished the last of his soup, wiped his mouth and placed both hands flat on the table. "Please pardon the indelicate nature of my question. You obviously work for Director Carson. What is your role with this operation?"

"You needn't apologize." Zasha sat forward in the chair. "My partner and I were the ones that intercepted Zhang Ju's meeting plans. We were also involved with the rescue attempt in Puerto Vallarta. After Zhang escaped the compound, I used satellite surveillance to track his yacht, which is now on its way to Africa."

Alejandro held up one hand. "Which is how we ended up in the ocean."

Zasha's hands went to her knees and she appeared ready to stand. "We monitored that yacht constantly. We never saw anyone leave the deck."

"Correct, we left via a hatch in the lower deck. Zhang had water sleds waiting below. He was taking us to a different location. I can't be certain how long we were in the water, or where we were headed, but we left from the coast of Rio. During our under-water trip, I could tell that something wasn't right. We encountered a large school of fish and I used the opportunity to break free from the group. From my hiding place, I witnessed someone in the group kill Xie and Armando. They sent one of the sleds to look for me and they nearly found me, but I managed to remain hidden. My guess is they planned to kill me as well."

Zasha folded her hands and sat even further forward. "Did you do anything to make them want to assassinate you?"

Alejandro was silent for some time. "There was an operative... CIA... the complex..."

Zasha pulled the name from memory. "Yes, Jesus Camarena."

Alejandro nodded. "He delivered a message to Marianna for me. I don't know why Zhang suspected him, but after we were moved, later, Zhang showed us a recording. We watched as someone shoved a knife into Jesus' chest. I don't recall divulging any emotion when we saw the tape…maybe he knew something. It was very painful to watch."

Zasha stood and touched Alejandro. "Jesus' death is not your fault."

There was a knock at the door and a corpsman walked in with clothing for Alejandro.

Zasha pointed to the bed. "Please place them on the foot of the bed and wait just outside the door." She waited for him to leave the room. "I'll be just outside to escort you to the plane. Do you need any assistance getting dressed?"

Alejandro shook his head. Zasha left the room to wait for him.

Chapter
55

General Gan opened his eyes for the first time in nearly an hour. He'd entered the tomb without protest even though he knew what he would be subjected to.

The President was standing at the foot of his bed and waited until the general held his eyes open. "Your story has remained fairly consistent; that's impressive. However, there is one issue that we have not dealt with. I hope it won't be necessary to repeat the process you have just undergone."

General Gan moved his tongue around the inside of his mouth in search of any moisture. It hurt when he tried to clear his throat, thus his voice was raspy when he spoke. "I have cooperated completely. What more would you like to know?"

The President signaled to one of the men conducting the inquiry. "Give him a drink of water; I want to hear him clearly." He waited while Gan drank. "The fireworks factory is of great concern to me. A worker saw both you and Xie there. This is not consistent with timing of your supposed rescue. How is this possible?"

General Gan was grateful for the water and swallowed trying to find his voice. "Xie was lost to the sea." His eyes shot to one of his men pulling a red-hot piece of metal from a fire. "It's true, just not when we first left the ship— as I stated earlier, it was several days after we returned from Linyang. Zhang was in possession of information that the United States was close to locating his yacht. We left the ship from the hull using a pressurized hatch. We were using water sleds to go to a new location. We encountered a couple of sharks feeding on a frenzied school of fish and Xie panicked. He swam away from the sled and we couldn't find him after the sharks passed. We searched for him until we were in danger of being under too long to sustain our trip."

The President looked to one of the men monitoring a lie detector. The man nodded and the President touched General Gan's leg. "Why did you lie to me earlier?"

General Gan swallowed hard happy to still have a small amount of moisture in his mouth. "Ultimately, it is the United States' fault; they should be made to pay. I knew that if you believed that they were directly involved their punishment would be much more severe. It was a mistake on my part, one that I will not repeat."

"Let's review your trip to Linyang." The President looked down to make sure that the general was still lucid. "Why is Zhang interested in a fireworks factory?"

General Gan worked hard to control his breathing. If the President knew that he was in Linyang, it was likely he knew why they were there. Zhang did not want the President to know Zhang's plan. Competition was the last thing he wanted. The general knew that his answers were tied to his life and his future with Zhang's organization. "Zhang wanted Xie Yi present so that he would have no difficulty purchasing the plant."

The President's hand went to his chin. He stroked it and looked at the general intently. "Zhang's investments have never been a secret to the state. To date, he has chosen to wisely place his money in the area of oil interests. What would possibly make him want to own a fireworks company?"

General Gan knew that his answer would be tricky, but if he didn't take a chance, there was no way to know just what the President really knew. "The company he purchased is a major supplier of fireworks to the United States. He never stated why that was important."

The President walked over to a table where one of the men handed him a file. General Gan struggled to hear them speaking.

The President opened the file. "Did Ling Cao ever divulge what Zhang spoke about at the factory?"

The officer who read the file shook his head. "There was never any mention of his reason. We have been to the factory; nothing is out of the ordinary there."

The President walked back to the side of the bed and tapped the folder in his hand. "What do you suppose that we have in this document? I'm disappointed General. Would you like to clarify your comments?"

General Gan fixed his eyes on the President and hoped that he'd read them correct. "If I knew anything else to offer, I would, but I was not included in Zhang's most intimate discussions. I believe my presence was more of a power play, nothing else. Zhang doesn't like anyone knowing much about what he does as far as I can tell. To counter his silence, he gives generously to anyone who could possibly hinder his progress."

The President closed the folder and handed it back to the officer at the desk and spoke loud enough for the general to hear him. "Take him through another round." The President pulled the officer outside the door. "I think he has been truthful, but we can't let him know that just yet. Scale back your efforts a bit; he won't be any good to us dead. We'll have to aid in the general's recovery and use him to have Zhang divulge his plans. Have the Secret Police keep an eye on the fireworks plant. If Zhang shows up take him into custody."

The officer walked back into the room and barked at the men in the room. "Shock him again and keep doing it until he speaks the truth." The President handed a written order to one of his men that indicated they should use a smaller dose of electricity.

General Gan rocked his head as best he could in the restraints. "No, no, I have told you the truth. Killing me won't change that truth."

Through the door, the President could hear General Gan scream each time the electrodes were placed on the general's genitals. He touched the door and spoke even though he knew the general couldn't hear him. "It will all be over soon my friend. Then we can get back to the business of running the country."

The CIA jet touched down on a private airstrip just behind headquarters. Alejandro looked through the window at the installation and he turned to Zasha. "Is Marianna here?"

Zasha nodded. "Director Carson brought her over about an hour ago. She's anxious to see you."

"As I am her." Alejandro held his hands out towards Zasha and Cole. "I would like to thank you again for all that you have done for me and my family."

Cole tilted his head towards Alejandro. "It's the least we could do for you. Director Carson thinks a lot of you and has good reasons for wanting you safe."

Alejandro's somberness intensified. "I'm certain that you have a lot of remaining questions; I know that I would, chief among them is why did I receive an invitation to Zhang's gathering?"

Zasha swung fully in Alejandro's direction. "The thought crossed my mind."

The jet pulled to a stop and one of the crew opened the door deploying the stairs. Director Carson appeared through the doorway and walked to Alejandro. He placed one arm around the man and pulled him close. "It is good to see you, my friend."

Alejandro returned the one-armed hug. "I'm pleased to be here. Your agents have taken very good care of me. I was just about to share with them how I came to be involved with Zhang. If I were in their place it is a question that would be burning in my brain."

Carson reached down and pressed a button on the chair swiveling it sideways. "Have a seat. We can deplane after you're finished."

Alejandro waited for everyone to sit and focused his attention on Zasha and Cole. "Jessie recruited me several years ago when the drug trade from my country intensified. The drug lords began tossing around vast sums of money to purchase political favors. I entered into an agreement with them in order to gain a handle on their operations. In turn, I funneled information to Jessie to aid both countries in fighting their trade."

Director Carson touched Alejandro's leg. "Alejandro is responsible for many of the arrests we've made fighting the illicit drug trade. As you know by now, three major traffickers, two from the drug trade and one in illegal immigrants spent the last few weeks with him. We have been on to them for years, but they're beyond cautious. The raid at Zhang's compound was an opportunity to bring them down and pick up a bonus, Zhang, who previously was only suspected of offenses against our country."

Alejandro nodded. "In the immediate presence of such evil it is difficult to maintain a conciliatory façade. Their trust in me was eroding by the minute, which is why I believe they targeted me when we left Zhang's yacht." He shook his head side-to-side. "Zhang offered Mexico, California and Texas if we helped implement his plan. He wants to flood the United States with immigrants from Mexico and China then provide them with instant citizenship in order to vote his hand-selected candidates into office...he wants your country for himself. Your new President has adopted a much more liberal policy towards immigration and citizenship— it would be difficult for you to combat Zhang's plan given such a policy."

Cole gripped the arms of his chair tightly. "Our new policy has made the United States one of the easiest countries in the world to immigrate to. This could come back to bite us in the ass."

Carson held one hand up ending Cole's retort. "Alejandro, were you privileged to other conversations where Zhang may have suggested deploying poison in order to thin our population making it easier to complete his plan?"

Alejandro's gaze fell to Carson and his eyebrows rose. "The benefit to being considered insignificant is people pay little attention to your presence. It is just this moment that I realize what Zhang must have shared with the top lieutenants in the group, his intention to eliminate some of us. Thus, there was no need to be cautious speaking around a dead man. Zhang left the ship one day with four of these men, Carlos Acosta, Rafael Calderon, Vladimir Nikitin and General Gan. When they returned, Carlos pulled a red, what looked like a seed, from his pocket and told Rafael that they would grind it and mix it with a rival's cocaine. He said that it would have their rival's customers dropping like flies sending people in search of a different supplier, namely them."

Director Carson slid forward in his seat anxious to continue his questioning. "Was this the only instance anyone talked about using, as you said, this red seed?"

Alejandro's brow knitted and the intensity of his stare grew. "This seems important; I'm sorry, but that was the only time I heard anyone mention it. What do you suspect he plans to use the red seed for?"

Carson folded his hands and placed his elbows on his knees. "That's just it, we don't have a clue. But, I can tell you whatever it is, it's not good."

Zasha's fingers moved rapidly across the keys on her iPhone. She raised a finger holding her place in line to speak. "If Zhang's plan is to build voting blocs by flooding the country with illegal immigrants and at the same time, eliminate the voting competition here, using cocaine doesn't make sense. According to the National Institute on Drug Abuse about three point six million people in the United States use cocaine; if you assume that the majority of these people use crack then you can further assume that most of them don't vote."

Cole drew back. "That sounds racist— surprising coming from someone like you."

Zasha shot Cole a stern look. "Not at all! Most people who use crack are only concerned with their next high. Politics is nowhere in the picture."

Director Carson jumped in the fray. "She's right, which means Zhang has another plan for the Abrin and we'd better find out what it is right away."

Chapter
57

Vladimir stood against a rail of Zhang's rented villa overlooking the ocean. He took a drink from his glass and turned to face Zhang, who was sitting on a chaise. "I'm giving serious consideration to settling down here. Buenos Aires seems to agree with me."

Zhang ignored the comment and redirected the conversation. "What's the latest on the shipments?"

A trade wind rippled Vladimir's gauze-like shirt across his taut frame. He walked to a table, refilled his glass and plopped down in a chair next to Zhang. "The ground Rosary Peas arrived at the factory without incident. The packets were surrounded by gunpowder. It's a good thing too. The Chinese Secret Police inspected several of the crates. They opened some from the top and others from the bottom. Can you believe I had to tell them to put out their cigarettes before opening the cases? Sons of bitches could have blown the whole place to hell."

Zhang lit a cigar and patiently blew smoke into the air. "What about the other shipment?"

"In three days, we will begin dropping off your people in the prearranged cities." Vladimir took a drink and set the glass on the table. "Has Pablo made the arrangements to get them to the U.S.?"

Zhang blew smoke in Vladimir's direction. "Everything is in order. When will the other ships begin arriving?"

Vladimir reached for his drink. "They are just days apart—that's three ships with nearly four thousand people aboard each. How will that number of people not raise the attention of the Americans?"

"In a month, the Americans won't matter. The shipments of fireworks will begin in a few weeks. Then, our people will sit on a ship waiting for their Independence Day celebration. A day or so later, millions of Americans' bodies will litter their cities." Zhang smiled past the cigar clinched between his teeth.

The serious expression on Vladimir's face seemed to convey contempt, which he quickly dispelled. "I've got to go back to Hong Kong."

The smile dropped from Zhang's face and he pulled the cigar from his mouth. "I don't need you taking unnecessary risks. What could you possibly do there that you can't here?"

"I've got to find Jenna." Vladimir drained his glass. "She would not have willingly left the city without telling me. Something has happened to her."

Zhang jabbed his cigar forward dropping ashes on Vladimir's leg. "You're being irrational. You said the people on the recording from the villa were her friends and we know that they are not who they claimed to be. You know as well as I do that they are with the U.S. government. They got to her and took her away."

Vladimir shook the ice in his glass and watched the ice cubes collide. "That may be the case— all the more reason I have to return. I'm going to find her. If she betrayed me, I'll kill her. If they took her against her will, I'll kill whoever was involved."

Zhang puffed several times on the cigar. "If you are determined to commit suicide over a piece of ass, I must insist that you wait until after we finish with the fireworks."

Vladimir grabbed the vodka bottle and tilted it towards the glass without pouring any. "That will defeat the purpose, don't you think?"

Zhang rolled the cigar between his fingers and looked blankly out over the ocean. "I can see that you're determined to proceed with this futile endeavor. Since I can't talk you out of it, at least allow me to send someone to investigate; I need you here."

Vladimir watched the vodka flow into the glass. "Just know that there is a limit to my patience. I want her found before July fourth. If she's going to die, it will be at my hands."

Zhang tapped the ashes from the end of the cigar. "If there's someone that you'd rather send, I can make the arrangements."

Vladimir looked back to the room where Borka and the Giant were talking. "Borka would be perfect, except, I may need him with me. I employed Jenna's neighbors to keep a watchful eye on her. Borka could find out what they know."

"Finding out what they know should be the least of your problems." Zhang blew a smoke ring into the air. "I have men at my disposal who are members of the Chinese Secret Police. They can extract the answers you need. No one in China would dare interfere with them. Their methods have been proven very effective, or deadly depending on one's perspective."

Vladimir tilted his glass in Zhang's direction. "How soon can you get them on the job?"

Zhang sat the cigar in a Baccarat crystal ashtray that appeared to have never seen a loose ash and then pulled his cell phone from his pocket. He punched a speed dial number and waited for the call to be answered. "I have a job for you. A young singer who used to perform at Felix disappeared from her home in Hong Kong about three weeks ago. I need to know who took her and where they took her. A close friend of hers suggests that her neighbors were paid to keep an eye on her. Find out what they know. I need answers right away. There's a million-yuan bonus in it for you if you can solve the mystery in twenty-four hours." He pressed a button disconnecting the call and lifted the cigar from the ashtray and flicked the loose ashes on the floor.

Vladimir sipped from his glass. "Greed is an excellent motivator. Let's see what it does for your associate."

Director Carson left the conference room and returned a few seconds later with Marianna. Her father's back was turned and she approached him quietly sliding her arms around his neck. "Papa, thank God you're safe."

Alejandro quickly turned to face her and couldn't hold back the tears that flowed freely down his face. "For a while, I thought I might never see you again."

Marianna kissed his cheeks and brushed away the tears. "Director Carson told me all about your ordeal." She turned her head to face Zasha. "I'm glad Agent Davis decided to intervene. She brought you safely back to me."

Director Carson stepped near the table and placed a hand on Javier's back. "Why don't you take some time to catch up? We'll leave you alone and when you're ready, I'll see to it that you are taken to comfortable quarters."

Javier nodded and pulled Marianna close to him hugging her tightly. "This should be over soon and then we will take some time to get away."

Director Carson signaled for his people to leave the room. He wiggled his finger at Zasha and Cole just as they cleared the door to the conference room. "We've had a hit at Miss Roulette's apartment in Hong Kong."

Zasha's mouth dropped open before she spoke. "What does that mean?"

Director Carson jerked his head to one side. "Let's go to my office. He walked in and waited for Zasha and Cole to enter before closing the door. "When we sent the Marines get Miss Roulette out, they also planted several devices in and around her apartment. One of the cameras picked up a man who came by asking questions about what happened." He reached for a remote and pressed a button playing the recording.

Zasha watched until she could see the man's face clearly. "Have you identified him?"

Director Carson nodded towards the playback. "Watch a minute longer. He flashes creds identifying himself as Chinese Secret Police. If you continue to listen, you will hear him mention Vladimir Nikitin."

Zasha listened to the man speaking Chinese and instantly translated it to English. "I knew he wouldn't let Jenna go without a fight. Despite his aloof behavior, I could tell that he was in love with her. Vladimir is a very dangerous man, if he can't find her. He'll come looking for her."

Director Carson nodded. "That may be, but he has a problem, only five of us know where she is. You set it up so that she would go to Xavier University in New Orleans. I assume Cole knows and that leaves Oscar, the pilot who took her there and of course, me. I don't see any of us being compromised."

Cole pointed to the screen. "Didn't we determine that the Chinese Secret Police have a large presence in New Orleans?"

Director Carson turned the recording off. "I believe the FBI has confirmed that to be the case. We don't know if this guy is acting in an official capacity. It's hard to believe that he is, so it doesn't matter how many of them are in New Orleans."

Zasha's brow was knitted tightly, pasting a look of pain across her face. "Jenna was my best friend at Georgetown. If Vladimir comes looking for her she'll be a sitting duck. I can't sit by and watch if she's in danger."

"That's just it; we have no way of knowing." Director Carson tossed the remote to his desk. "We don't know where Vladimir and Zhang are at this moment. Using the point where you rescued Alejandro, we have examined a wide grid of satellite photos and we haven't turned up a single lead. It's as if they've disappeared. I've got a group in China looking for the guy on the tape. If we can find him maybe we can get some idea of where the others are. Our main concern now is not Miss Roulette, but what Zhang has planned for the Rosary Peas. That has to be our concern."

Cole thought a minute pressing a finger to the side of his head. "Have we noticed any increase in activity at any of our borders?"

Carson shook his head. "Border security is stretched to the limit. There has been nothing unusual there. Even with the added vigilance, nearly one hundred thousand illegal Chinese cross our borders a year. If Zhang has increased that number, we haven't detected anyone. Customs is working overtime checking anything that comes into the U.S. from China, but even they can't examine everything. The quantity is far too great."

Cole moved to the edge of his seat. "What position has the President adopted with what we've provided him?"

The Director picked up a pen and began tapping it against the desk sliding it through his fingers. "This President is so pro-immigration that he seems to have chosen to ignore most of what we've said. He wants proof of the increased illegals. Before acting, he also wants to know Zhang's intentions with the damn Peas. My feeling is by the time we know, it will be too late to act."

Zasha's frown refused to ease. "We've got a lot of work to do. I'm going to New Orleans; I've got to keep an eye on Jenna. Since New Orleans is one of the country's largest shipping ports, Zhang may be using it to smuggle human cargo into the country. It only makes sense that we take precautions there."

Carson continued tapping the pen sliding it through his fingers. Abruptly, he brought it near his face. "You may have something there. If Zhang has a hold on the Chinese Secret Police, they could be assisting him in New Orleans. Maybe you both should head down there and see what you can find."

Chapter
59

The Chinese President sat in the middle of a garden tossing pieces of bread to the koi that anxiously pulsed their lips just above the surface of the water hoping to receive a morsel.

A very thin man wearing a traditional silk Tai Chi uniform and white gloves approached the President. Arriving next to the bench, he reached in his pocket and retrieved a wireless phone. "There is a call for you."

The President looked up from his fish, catching the man's eyes. "Were my instructions not clear? I do not want to be disturbed."

The man bowed. "Yes, but I believe this call may be of interest. It is Master Zhang Ju."

The President reached for the phone and waved the man away. When the man was a safe distance away, he pulled the phone to his ear. "Why are you calling me here?"

"Greetings to you as well." Zhang blew cigar smoke into the mouthpiece of the phone displaying his lack of respect. "I'm certain by now that you have subjected General Gan to the torturous methods of your tomb. Further, I expect that he has confirmed what I have already shared with you."

The President gripped the phone tightly. "Why was it necessary to subject him to such disdain?"

Zhang smiled realizing that the questioning was complete. "Because I had to be certain that he could be trusted. We're playing an extreme game whose ramifications reach far beyond ordinary. You have been more than adequately compensated for your efforts."

The President's face reddened. "Be cautious of your tone. I am still the leader of this country. I did what I did for China, nothing else."

"Save the sanctimony for someone else. Men in our positions of power don't need lectures." Zhang blew another round of smoke into the mouthpiece. "Your job now is to deal with the

Americans. They will begin to demand answers and will want your cooperation in locating me— make sure that they never get close."

The President tossed his last handful of bread to the fish. "How can you be sure that they don't already know of your plans to flood their borders with immigrants?"

Zhang took a long draw from his cigar and blew smoke rings into the air. "Because that is only part of the plan— no one else is privy to my master plan."

The President rose from the bench. "What does it have to do with the fireworks plant?"

Zhang flicked ashes to the floor. "Don't bother yourself with my investments. As a matter of fact, remove the Secret Police from the area. My investments are none of your concern."

The President turned and saw General Gan approaching. "If we are to trust each other, we'll have to be willing to share information."

Zhang pulled on the cigar. "I see you have company approaching; I'll let you go."

The President's head jerked from side to side looking for cameras. "How do you know that?"

Zhang laughed, pulled the phone from his ear and disconnected the call.

The President waived to General Gan to sit on the bench. "You're looking much better today. How are you feeling?"

General Gan wished he could subject the President to what he'd just been through so that he could understand just how absurd that question was. "I understand the necessity of your actions. I hope you agree that China's best interest is at the heart of any measures I have taken."

The President observed the general, but knew that he couldn't be transmitting anything to Zhang. He was released from the tomb. "Let's take a walk."

General Gan's face betrayed his sense of duty as he seemed shocked by the request. He stood making sure he didn't appear too steady. "Of course. We may have to move a bit slower than usual."

The President headed down a bamboo laden path. "Zhang has concerned us for some time. The Americans suggested his scheme to flood the U.S. with our people. We want to know more about his plan. This is also why Xie's death has troubled me so. Xie was working on something for us." He paused and looked at the general. "What is the most powerful word in the English language?"

General Gan Looked at him, puzzled. "I don't understand. What does that have to do with Xie?"

The President placed his hands behind his back. "The word is *free*. That is the most powerful word in the English, especially American English, language. People become intoxicated when they see free and no matter how insignificant the offer, Americans want whatever it is."

General Gan nodded. "They do seem overly interested in receiving something for nothing."

"Exactly, which is something Xie understood completely." The President looked around again and began walking down the path. "Xie developed a plan using technology items we ship to the United States. What could be more irrelevant than a digital picture frame, or an MP3 player? They're used for entertainment correct? How about a DVD, a DVD recorder, or a jump drive, or even smart refrigerators, or smart speakers? The secret is offering something free in conjunction with these products. Of course, the user would have to go online to retrieve the free item using a program imbedded in the products. Going online activates a stealth program within our products, which searches the user's computer hard drive and imbeds itself in the e-mail program collecting all their personal data. We have developed the program so that it remains hidden to anti-spyware and anti-virus detectors."

General Gan Smiled. "You're mining computers Chinese style— ingenious."

The President relaxed and offered additional information. "Another thing that Americans are fools for are what they call friendship questionnaires. After it implants itself in the e-mail program of a device, these questionnaires are sent out to their entire list. Once opened, the program imbeds itself in the recipient's device as well."

General Gan raised a hand for a chance to speak. "Within days, this program has spread to millions and is sending China information on these people."

The President smiled for the first time since he and the general reunited. "We get everything, their passwords, credit card information, banking information, online accounts, doctor's information, anything that's on their system."

General Gan nearly stumbled. "I can see why you would be worried about Zhang. If he somehow came upon this mining system, he could provide hundreds of thousands of our people with documentation proving that they're American citizens. The only thing he would need to do is kill the American with the data and have one of our people take his place."

Zhang watched the broadcast from General Gan. One of Gan's men also worked for Zhang and attached a button on Gan's uniform that allowed the signal to transmit. It was risky, but a risk that Zhang was willing to take. If General Gan was discovered, someone else close to the President would eventually have to take his place.

Zhang nearly danced around the chaise. Xie gave him a program telling him that it would be a powerful tool when the time was right. He killed Xie before finding out how to access the information, yet that was of little consequence. Now that he knew what the program did, finding someone to unlock its potential was inconsequential. Money would fill any void and techno-geeks were a dime a dozen in China. He knew he would have the information by nightfall.

Zhang walked into the villa and found the Giant and Borka watching a video filled with naked natives from Buenos Aires involved in all manner of sex acts. He signaled for the Giant to follow and walked back to the deck. "We need to find someone to break the code of a program the sniveling weasel gave me before we killed him. It is the key to our success with the plan."

The Giant scratched his head thinking of who would serve them best. "Rajiv Nair is in Hong Kong. He's Indian not Chinese, but he's usually the most efficient in these matters. Do you have any particular instructions?"

Zhang puffed on his cigar. "Attach a tracker on the program and tell him not to copy or test his findings. I simply want the password. If he fails to follow my instructions, make sure he doesn't live to share what he has found."

The Giant held out his hand for the jump drive and plugged it into Zhang's laptop. A few keystrokes later a program was synced to the Chinese government program Xie gave to Zhang. He flipped open his cell phone and punched in Rajiv's number.

Waiting for it to ring, he looked up at Zhang. "What should I tell him the job is worth?"

Zhang blew a stream of smoke from his mouth. "Tell him one million American will be transferred as soon as we have the password. Give him half up front if he balks."

The Giant turned his attention to the phone. "Rajiv, I've got a job for you. I need a password for a program I have. Rajiv, I only want the password, no testing it or copying the program. This is a high-priority mission. Can you handle it?"

Rajiv looked over his bank of computers. "I can get on it right away. Can you send it to me?"

The Giant typed in Rajiv's e-mail address and held his finger over the *send* button. "We understand each other, no copies or testing."

"I would have no business if I violated my client's confidence." Rajiv cleared his throat. "There is one other matter. I'm certain that you had a value attached to the job."

The Giant slid his finger across the button. "I've been instructed to wire you one million American as soon as you provide the password."

Rajiv eyes widened to their full circumference, unable to contain his surprise or delight at the figure. "You will receive my full attention. Depending on the complexity of the code, I should be able to have something back to you within the hour."

The Giant nodded and pressed the send button. "It's on the way. Call me the second you have it."

A chime playing, *"We're In the Money"* indicated the e-mail arrived. "I have it now. Let me get to work."

The Giant could hear Rajiv's keystrokes moving rapidly across his computer. "I can hear that you're busy; I'll expect a call within the hour." He looked up at Zhang. "We'll know something soon."

Zhang filled a glass with Balvenie 'Port Wood Scotch and puffed on his cigar. "Contact the fireworks company and get a list of our clients and prospects in the United States. They are approaching the two hundred and forty fifth celebration of their independence. We are going to send a letter offering a two-for-one deal of our premium fireworks as a build-up to their two hundred and forty third anniversary. The grandness of this year's show will serve as a prelude to what they will experience in a couple of years. Tell them that this should serve as China's commitment to our friends and partners in the United States."

Director Carson, Zasha and Cole sat at a conference table while Oscar projected an image on the screen and pointed to it with a laser pointer. "We've had Agent Hu and her team hold-up at a monastery here in Tibet. Recent chatter we've picked up suggests that someone may have compromised their position." He nodded towards the director. "We have decided to send you two in to get them."

Director Carson clicked the mouse bringing another picture to the screen. "We have gotten clearance from India to have you land in Nepal. The monks are going to be leading our team into the mountains." He pointed to Cole. "You're going to have to fly a chopper in without attracting the attention of the Chinese Air Force, get them, and get the hell out of China."

Cole raised one eyebrow. "Are we going to have any cover?"

Carson began tapping his pen through his fingers and his eyes locked on Cole's. "I'm hoping to avoid an international incident. However, India has insisted that they be allowed to scramble a squadron of fighters just in case. Even though India says they have taken measures to improve relations with China, I think they would love to have a reason to start some shit. Get in and out, understood?"

Cole nodded. "I'll need a fully loaded Sea Hawk just in case. I'm sure the Indians realize that things are tense as hell between the Chinese government and the Buddhists in Tibet. If they would be kind enough not to spark the Chinese, I'd appreciate it. I don't want to have to use the missiles on the Sea Hawk."

A red light on the intercom in the middle of the table lit up followed by a voice. "Director Carson, I have the Director of the NSA on the line. He said he needs to speak with you immediately."

"Patch him in." Carson waited for the call to go through. "Director Jimmerson, I'm in a briefing with Deputy Director

Fenton, Agent Zasha Davis and Agent Cole Peterson. They are the extraction team I'm sending to Tibet."

Director Jimmerson paused briefly. "What is the clearance level of your agents?"

Carson inched a bit closer to the speaker. "They're both SCI. Is your call involving China?"

Director Jimerson's voice both lowered and quieted. "Jessie, this information not only involves China, its implications may prove devastating for the United States."

Carson was literally on the edge of his seat pounding the pen between his fingers. "Let's hear what you have."

Director Jimmerson sighed deeply. "You recall some time ago this office informed corporations nationwide that their computer systems were at risk from a subversive stealth program the Chinese deployed in products coming from China? Well, it's worse than we thought."

Carson rose from his chair and leaned on the side of the table. "What are we talking about?"

Director Jimmerson gazed at a profile in his hands. "I have an Indian national operative in Hong Kong, Rajiv Nair. He's an I.T. specialist, who works as a hacker for hire supplying information to the highest bidder. His client list includes all types, governments, corporations and underworld figures. One of his biggest clients is Zhang Ju..."

Carson's face reddened and he could feel his blood pressure rise. "The same Zhang Ju we've been investigating for weeks?"

"One and the same." Director Jimmerson sat the profile down. "He received a call from Zhang's top lieutenant earlier to decipher a password from a program. Rajiv was instructed not to copy the program or test the password once he had it. Like most hackers, he didn't listen. He detected a tracking program Zhang attached to the job. He disarmed it and made a copy using equipment provided by the NSA."

Carson couldn't hold his impatience. "What does the program do?"

Director Jimmerson slid a hand across his face. "The program is attached to millions of products coming from China, such as digital picture frames, jump drives refrigerators and even smart speakers made there. They are all I.T. connected. Once a person activates the stealth program via the internet, it mines into their computers and collects all personal data, passwords, accounts, everything that can divulge who the person is and it doesn't stop there. The program sends e-mails to everyone on the person's list. It uses a stupid 'how well do you know your friend' questionnaire. As soon as anyone opens the questionnaire the stealth program attaches to their computer and repeats the process obtaining their information as well. Rajiv says Zhang now holds all the personal information of millions of American citizens."

Carson's head fell between his shoulders. "Oh, shit!"

Director Jimmerson closed his eyes and rubbed his temples. "That's an understatement. Do you have any idea why he would want this information?"

Carson slowly raised his head. "You've heard the briefings at the White House. This idiot plans on flooding the U. S. with Chinese citizens. Possessing this type of information, he could use it to drain the wealth of our citizens giving it to the illegals, or much worse."

Director Jimmerson stood and placed several items into a satchel. "I'm leaving Fort Meade in ten minutes for the White House. I've sent a team to torch Rajiv's place and bring him to Washington. If Zhang finds out he's been double crossed, Rajiv wouldn't be alive five minutes. Rajiv wants our protection. I've transmitted you what he sent to us. Make a copy and put it in a safe place."

Carson pulled a jump drive from his pocket, looked at it to make sure it hadn't been made in China and sat in front of the computer to downloaded the information. "I'll meet you at the White House." He disconnected the speaker and turned to Oscar sliding the computer to him. "Make another copy of this and keep it on you at all times. Until we know what we're dealing with keep it under wraps."

Zasha was straining to absorb the gravity of Director Jimerson's call. She reached towards Carson. "What do you want us to do once we have Julie?"

Carson slid the jump drive into his pocket. "Get back here as soon as you can."

Chapter
62

The NSA extraction team arrived at Rajiv's site and entered, collecting all pertinent computer equipment without speaking a single word. Once everything was safely locked in an armored vehicle, the team leader sat beside an empty desk with computer wires strewn across it. "Is this place wired?" He watched Rajiv nod and held his hand out. Give me the detonator."

Rajiv handed him the small device and sat next to him pulling out his cell phone. "They're expecting a call."

The team leader pulled an electronic wand from the side of his pants leg and waved it over the phone before handing it back to Rajiv. "Make it quick."

Rajiv took the phone and opened his laptop. He noticed the stern look coming from the NSA team leader. "I've got to confirm the wire has been sent."

The team leader pointed the wand in Rajiv's direction. "You've got one minute. Then we're out of here."

Rajiv dialed the Giant's number and waited for him to answer. "Was the password to your satisfaction?"

The Giant looked over to Zhang, who'd just received the password and was giddy retrieving the information the password revealed. He nodded towards Zhang. "Is it clean?"

Zhang's face never left the computer. "It's perfect."

The Giant put the phone against the side of his face. "Everything is satisfactory."

Rajiv cleared his throat. "You have additional information for me?"

The Giant pulled a slip of paper from his pocket and read Rajiv the ten-digit Swiss bank account code. "I'll hold while you confirm the funds."

Rajiv stroked the keys of his computer finding the funds and instantly moved them to a different account. "It was a pleasure doing business with you. Call me anytime."

The team leader waited for Rajiv to close his cell phone then took it from him and removed the battery. "That was one hell of a payday."

Rajiv quickly shut his laptop. "My funds are not part of this deal. I made that clear to your director."

The team leader dropped his feet to the floor and stood. "Then, I suggest we get the hell out of here before you never have a chance to spend a penny of it. What's the delay time on this thing?" He held the detonator out.

Sweat covered Rajiv's face and he swallowed hard. "Fifteen seconds."

The team leader put Rajiv in the back of the armored truck with the rest of the team and walked to the passenger's seat. He stepped in, held the detonator out, and pushed the button. With a wry smile he turned to the driver. "Haul ass!"

The driver gunned the accelerator and the truck lurched forward. "How much time..." The words barely left his mouth before the warehouse they'd just left exploded in orange flames. The percussion was so intense that he had to work to maintain control over the truck.

The team leader rocked back and forth partly from the blast and partly from the driver's maneuvers. "Damn, I do so enjoy a devastating explosion!"

The driver gained control over the truck and slowed his speed. He maintained a direct route to a waiting C130. When his nerves calmed, he looked at the team leader. "You're a sick motherfucker."

The team leader laughed and nestled into his seat. "Just keep it steady. We should be on the plane in twenty minutes." He looked in the truck's mirror and could only see the glow of the fire he'd caused. Through the vents, he could hear the sound of sirens blaring. By the time the police arrived and began asking questions, they would be in the air.

Twenty minutes on the dot, the truck rolled into the waiting belly of a C130. The turbo props of the plane were spinning at full speed and the cargo gate closed as the plane moved down the runway. The wheels left the runway and the C130 pulled skyward.

The team leader retrieved a satellite phone from the seat of the armored truck and dialed Director Jimmerson. "The package is on board. We should be over international waters in a few minutes."

"That's one load off my mind. Call me when you reach California." Director Jimmerson closed the phone and stepped from a helicopter onto the White House grounds.

Zhang sat in the back of a rented white Rolls Royce with Vladimir and Borka. "How long before the ship arrives in Hong Kong?"

Vladimir brushed Zhang's stray ashes from his pants. "It will be there when we land."

Zhang nodded and sat his cigar in an ashtray. "The trucks are loaded and en route to the Hong Kong shipping port. I don't want the shipment to sit for long. We have managed to get the Secret Police off our trail, so you won't have a problem loading the shipment. Since making the offer to double orders at no additional cost, the Americans have purchased the entire inventory."

Vladimir glanced at his empty glass and decided not to refill it. "When are they expecting delivery? We wouldn't want people testing the product beforehand, so too early is not good."

Zhang shrugged his shoulders and lifted the cigar. "Even if they did it wouldn't matter. They wouldn't be able to trace the problem to the fireworks before July fourth. But if it makes you feel better deliver them on June fifteenth."

Vladimir brushed at his pants again even though no additional ashes were on them. "That will give me nineteen days to find Jenna. Have you found out anything yet?"

Zhang put the cigar between his teeth. "We know that she was abducted; they weren't Chinese. Only one of her neighbors saw anything. She described the scene as a well-coordinated effort. The men were not dressed in uniforms but, they were white; probably American. Jenna was not fighting these men. The witness said that she fully cooperated with them. They did have guns, which could be a logical reason why she went willingly."

Vladimir's hand fell to the vodka bottle, which he fingered for several seconds before pulling it away without refilling his glass. "The fact that they went in plain-clothes meant they didn't want to be identified as military, which they surely were."

"There's no chance that we'll find these men still in China. They would have to disappear so that the trail ends." Zhang puffed on the cigar. "Even the Americans are required to log flight plans. I know someone who can tell us where they flew the day she left. Chances are, she's not in the same location, but it will give us a lead."

Vladimir eyed the vodka bottle and rubbed his hand across the stubble around his mouth. "Your people need to work quickly. In just a few weeks, I'll have to make delivery."

Zhang nodded. "Don't trouble yourself, we'll find her. Have you established a port to deliver the shipment?"

"I have an abundance of time to be at sea so I'll take the ship through the Panama Canal and drop the shipment at Norfolk, Virginia." Vladimir relented and poured a small amount of vodka into his glass and drank it in one swallow. "I'll have trucking containers pre-loaded so that they can be immediately transferred to trucks. It'll reduce any down time."

Zhang reached for the Balvenie Scotch and joined Vladimir in a drink. "That was good thinking. You were definitely the right man for the job. In less than ninety days, we will have everything we could possibility want."

Vladimir poured yet another drink. "Jenna is included in the things that I want. Then I think we'll come back here. I've grown fond of this place in the short time that we've been here."

Zhang pushed a button and the Giant and Borka got out of the front of the car and opened the back doors. Zhang stepped out and waited for the others to join him on his side of the car. "The plane is ready for you two. I've notified your contact at the factory. He will see to it that everything goes smoothly."

Vladimir and Borka walked towards Zhang's waiting jet. Once out of earshot, Vladimir leaned close to Borka. "I don't trust that son of a bitch."

Borka nodded. "That's a wise stance to take with him. His agenda is the only one he's concerned with. Do you expect that he'll honor his commitments to us?"

"He doesn't have a choice. We'll have his weapons on the ship." Vladimir glanced over his shoulder at the two men behind them. "We hold the key to his grand plan. He'll make good or his precious cargo will never make it to the United States."

Zhang watched the two men board the jet and turned to the Giant. "Get in touch with our people. I want the girl found before that idiot fucks up my plans."

Zasha, Cole, a flight crew and a ten-man Delta Force team waited in a black Sea Hawk helicopter waiting to begin the extraction in Tibet. They would not take to the air until Julie contacted them giving her location.

Zasha was obviously anxious shifting her position several times every couple of minutes. "Waiting is nerve racking. When we spoke to Julie earlier, she said they would be in place already."

Cole glanced at his watch. "They're traveling difficult terrain. Dharamsala is heavily fortified by the Indian military. Most Tibetans who arrive there are arrested, so they have to go into the hills as close to the border as possible. We don't want to encounter either side even though India knows that we're coming. Soldiers on the ground can sometimes be a bit overzealous and unpredictable."

Zasha's iPhone lit up and she nearly jumped from her seat. Without looking to see who was calling, she connected the call and placed the phone to her ear. "What's the location?"

Oscar eased to his elbows and leaned close to the speaker on his desk. "Take it easy tiger; they just arrived. I'm patching you in and sending you their signal."

Zasha fastened her seatbelt and made a whirling motion with her finger for Cole to start the helicopter. She watched a red dot light up on the on-board screen. She pointed to it. "There they are, let's get moving."

Cole triangulated the distance to the blinking dot and pulled the night-vision shield on his helmet down. "Estimated flight time in and out is about forty minutes. That's a lot of time for things to go wrong. If Julie notices anything on the ground, have her notify us immediately."

Zasha ignored Oscar and began speaking to Julie. "The Cavalry is on the way. Keep us apprised of anything happening on the ground. We'll be there in twenty."

Julie kept her voice low and her head turned looking around the area. "I don't know what's going on here, but the animals we've passed have been acting weird. Get here as soon as you can."

Zasha turned her attention back to Oscar. "Have you received any unusual weather warning of the type that would unsettle animals?"

"There's not even fog expected in the area tonight, which is unusual for them." Oscar stroked the keys of his computer searching for anything he might have missed earlier. "Julie, what kind of behavior have you witnessed?"

Julie scanned the area again. "I thought it was weird when we left Tibet earlier; water buffalo that were tied to posts were bellowing and straining against their restraints. While hiking up the mountain we passed a group of monkeys squawking and jumping from tree to tree as if a predator was pursuing them. Now the birds here are acting like they've lost their minds. It's creeping me out. I'm ready to come home."

The blades of the chopper were ripping through the air pulling the team skyward. Cole spoke into the mike on his helmet. "Hang on, Julie; we'll be there in a few minutes."

Oscar gave up looking for reports and moved his attention to the speaker. "Cole, you've got cover if needed. You're patched into a Hawkeye monitoring the area just in case."

A member of the Hawkeye crew broke in speaking to Cole and his crew. "Puddle Jumper, this is Eagle Eye, you've got clear sailing to the target."

"Roger, Eagle Eye. We're on the way." Cole climbed the helicopter to a cruising altitude to clear the mountains.

Zasha sat her phone in her lap and looked at the rescue team, who all were sitting in complete silence. They all seemed on edge although their demeanor could be explained as concentration on the task at hand.

Julie kept an eye on the sky constantly since disconnecting the call from Oscar. Hearing the unmistakable sound of blades beating against the air caused her to focus her monocular in the direction of the sound. She pointed in the direction of the approaching helicopter. "They're here!"

A member of her team popped a flare and waved it back and forth in a small clearing. An infrared light came on beneath the chopper and Cole guided it to a clearing on the ground. The Delta Force Team jumped from the helicopter the second it touched down and ushered Julie and her team past the opened door.

Zasha helped them in and hugged Julie as soon as she entered. "You're safe. Now let's get the hell out of here."

In the royal palace in Beijing a large bronze urn with eight dragon heads gazing outward in eight directions sat in the middle of a room lit by a single light. Each dragon held a ball in its mouth and around the base of the urn, under each dragon, sat a frog with his mouth open. The urn was designed by Chang Heng, who was an astronomer to the royal Han Dynasty in AD 132. It is also the first known seismograph. The simple design was comprised of an inverted pendulum. The slightest seismic ripple swung the pendulum causing it to strike a ball in the dragon's mouth which dislodged the ball making it fall into the frog's mouth below. The loud clang the ball made announced an impending earthquake. The frog that caught the ball indicated the direction of the earthquake. The frog pointing southwest of Beijing was holding the dragon's dislodged ball.

The last Delta Force Team member jumped in and closed the door. Cole looked back making sure everyone was there, then engaged the gears lifting the helicopter from the ground.

They reached ten feet and a loud explosion rocked the fleeing chopper. Cole's head jerked side-to-side. "What the hell was that? Eagle Eye, are we taking fire."

The engineer on the Hawkeye looked closer at his screen. "Negative, there's nothing even in your area. What are you experiencing?"

Cole kept the helicopter climbing and turned the infrared light on to look below them. He could see the monks below scrambling to avoid large rocks that were falling down the mountains. "Eagle Eye, find out what's going on down here. This is crazy!"

Oscar watched Cole's course moving in the wrong direction and immediately acted to correct it. "Cole, you're flying into China; adjust your course."

Cole was looking at things on the ground and took a second to respond. "It's okay, Oscar; I'm just trying to see what's going on."

"Change your direction now!" Oscar turned to a computer screen that was beeping indicating important information. "The U.S. Geological Survey just announced a huge motherfucking earthquake in China. Get the hell out of there."

Cole adjusted his course and headed over the mountains to the safety of India. He tilted his head and spoke over his shoulder. "They just had a big fucking earthquake down there. We got out just in time. We're headed home."

Zasha, Julie and Cole walked into the conference room at Langley fresh from their flight from India. Seated at the table, Director Carson and Oscar Fenton watched the devastation in China unfolding on the screen. Countless numbers of people wandered amidst the rubble crying and looking around as if they had just been dropped in a foreign land.

Director Carson's fingers collapsed from their steeple into a folded nearly prayer-like position. He spoke without moving his eyes from the screen. "Not to sound callous, but opportunity is born of chaos. A disaster of this magnitude has not touched the shores of China in decades. The world has already mobilized to provide aid for the people."

Zasha slid into a chair with her eyes locked on the scene. "How bad was the earthquake?"

Oscar slid a paper to her. "The U.S. Geological Survey estimates it as a seven point nine. The aftershocks are nearly as bad. China said that at least twenty thousand people are confirmed dead and it's just a day after the quake. We believe it's going to get much worse."

Cole leaned back in his chair watching bodies being piled together on the ground. "What's the President had to say about what to do next?"

Director Carson turned his chair facing the table. "As you might expect, he has offered aid to assist the Chinese government. They haven't agreed yet to let teams of relief workers in. From the look of things there, they won't be able to deny that they need outside help."

Julie's elbows were on the table with her hands folded and her head resting against them. She didn't look at the pictures or the others in the room. "I want to go back to China."

Director Carson opened a folder and took a picture from it and slid it to Julie. "This is a wanted poster that went out from the

Chinese government. Your hair wasn't gray then but your likeness is unmistakable."

Julie moved her chin to her hands and gazed at the Director. "I'll use a disguise; it worked before."

Carson shook his head. "I don't think it's a good idea."

Julie sat back and let her hands fall into her lap. "Opportunity is born from chaos as you have said. They won't have time to be concerned about me, but I can use the confusion to get back to Linyang and sniff around. Cao was trying to send me a message before he was killed. I believe it had something to do with the fireworks company." She held her hands out as Cao had from the window of his house. "He held his Buddhist prayer beads made of Rosary Peas and said, 'This is what it's all about.' They have to be linked."

Oscar looked at a map in his file. "That area sustained heavy damage. The buildings weren't constructed with the best products. I doubt if much work is being done in that area."

Zasha tapped the table with her finger. "It doesn't hurt to check it out. I'll go along to help. Since the President has offered aid, I'm sure he's deployed a ship to the area. If we fly directly from the ship to Linyang, we can avoid any unnecessary complications."

Carson and Oscar looked at each other and the Director's pen began tapping the table moving through his fingers. "Those damn Peas have been a major source of headaches because we don't have a clue what Zhang plans to do with them. The U.S.D.A. has been inspecting food coming from China very closely ever since some of their products caused deaths here. We instructed them to begin looking for Abrin since learning of the Rosary Peas, but nothing has turned up."

Cole sat up to the table. "Then I guess we're going to Linyang."

Carson slid two additional pictures across the table. "You two are no safer. They want you as well."

Cole looked at the pictures and dismissed them dropping them back on the table. "If we can save lives here, it's worth the risk."

Director Carson gathered the pictures and placed them back into the file. "I've got a meeting at the White House in an hour. We can discuss it when I return."

They watched the Director leave the room. Zasha leaned towards Oscar. "This is the best chance for us to pick up a lead on Zhang. We've searched the satellite photos all around the area where we found Alejandro and we've turned up nothing. If they were escaping underwater then they came up completely concealed."

Cole chimed in. "He is the key to everything. Based on the border patrol records, they haven't seen any unusual groups of Chinese people attempting to enter the country. They may be arriving some other way. If it's right under our noses that could also be how Zhang is managing to bring the Abrin in. In which case, I would have extremely tight constraints on the nation's water supply— it's the most efficient way to affect a large number of people in a short period of time."

Oscar nodded. "I agree that Zhang is the key. To date whenever we bring him up to the Chinese government, they label him as a common criminal; whereabouts unknown. Our intel suggests that he is a major source of extracurricular funding for China's president. So, you can bet that they're not going to be any help."

"Which is precisely why we have to go in." Julie locked eyes with Oscar. "It's the only way. Look at that screen— that could be the United States absent the overwhelming devastation. Nevertheless, bodies will be littering the streets if we don't act."

Oscar put his hands up. "I'm convinced, but the President needs to sign on. His stand on immigration will make him a tough sell on the people coming here. Yet, I can't see him refusing to let teams go into China. The earthquake is the perfect opportunity to infiltrate China with religious influence and to stimulate the idea of democracy among their people. Well placed teams can subtlety implant ideas of a better life. China's economic success is issuing the country a middle class. Once you begin to gain financial wealth, you're not likely to want to see it go. These are the people that will be most open to political change. The poorer people will want to have what the others have, which makes them more open to revolution."

Zasha leaned back in her chair. "Before we begin a revolution in another country; let's save the one we're already in."

Chapter
66

Zhang observed the news reports coming from China with idle curiosity. His only concern was the shipment of fireworks. He signaled for the Giant. "Have we heard anything from Vladimir?"

"Nothing since before the earthquake hit." He pulled a phone from his pocket and held it out. "Would you like me to make contact?"

Zhang waved a hand. "Yes, we need to make sure that the shipment is safe."

It took the Giant several minutes to raise Vladimir. Hearing his voice, the Giant's response was immediate. "You drink too much."

"Mind your own fucking business." Vladimir sat his glass on a table next to his bed. "What do you want?"

"Master Zhang wishes to speak with you." The Giant walked to where Zhang was sitting and handed him the phone.

"Master Zhang…he better have information about Jenna." Vladimir grunted and sat up in the bed pushing a young Chinese woman to the side.

Zhang took the phone and walked to the deck before placing it to his ear. "You have neglected to remain in touch. I trust everything has gone as planned."

Vladimir dropped his feet to the floor and rubbed his hand across his face. "I have lived up to my portion of the deal. What have you done about Jenna?"

The woman in Vladimir's bed rolled over, placed her hand between his legs and urged him to come back to bed.

Zhang heard the plea and paused to see if Vladimir would respond. "Have the women I provided you not taken your mind off of Jenna?"

"My mind is never off of Jenna. I expect to have resolution before time to deliver this shipment to the port at Norfolk." Vladimir placed his hand on the back of the woman's head, which was now between his legs working up and down his length.

Zhang listened to the change in Vladimir's breathing and knew that he wouldn't be able to remain on the phone much longer. "I will have something soon. We flooded the U.S. with the latest album she recorded in Hong Kong. In conjunction with that, we established a contest. Purchasers of the CD are encouraged to have Jenna sign their copy. Everyone returning an authenticated signature will be entered in a drawing for fifty thousand dollars. The jazz stations in the U.S. have jumped all over the idea."

Vladimir grunted then took in a sharp breath. "I'll give you points for creativity. Call me back when you have something."

Zhang disconnected the phone and summoned the Giant. He handed him the phone and lit a cigar. "Never underestimate the power of a good dick suck."

The Giant allowed himself a slight grin. "Indeed."

Zasha, Cole and Julie drove to Billy Martin's in Georgetown for lunch. They wanted a change of venue and to discuss among themselves how they should proceed in China. They took a table outside under the awning and ordered a bottle of wine for the table. Cole knew the Hendry Barrel Fermented Chardonnay would be excellent, but chose to accept the initial pour for his approval. "Ladies, I think you should order something else— this bottle is mine."

Zasha looked up to the waiter. "Ignore him and fill our glasses."

Cole waited impatiently for more wine to flow into his glass. "After all we've been through, we deserve this."

The three of them sat enjoying the wine and conversation that, so far, had not drifted to the task that lay ahead of them.

With the noon hour just minutes away, the staff at Billy Martin's put music on to welcome customers joining them for lunch.

Sharing a hearty laugh, the agents reached for their glasses and touched them in the center of the table. As Zasha's glass came to her lips, she stalled and slowly pulled it away. The voice coming over the speakers began low and rich demonstrating an in-depth interpretation of the song, *Someone to Watch Over Me*. Zasha didn't need more than the first few words to identify the singer.

Julie noticed the distress on Zasha's face. "Is everything okay?"

Zasha sat her glass on the table. "It's the song."

Cole laughed nervously. "Don't tell me that you're the sentimental type. Does this song remind you of an old boyfriend?"

Zasha's head darted around looking for the waiter. "It's not so much the song as who's singing it— the voice you hear is Jenna's. This was her signature song all through college. Where's the waiter?"

Cole stood waving his hands to get the waiter's attention. "Why are you so worried about it? I think she'd be happy to have the air time."

Zasha's concerned look met Cole's. "Jenna never released an album in the United States. Vladimir was the person behind her recordings."

The waiter approached the table. "Is there something I can get you?"

Zasha looked up working to remain indifferent. "The song that's on now; is it a CD?"

The waiter smiled jubilantly. "Yes, I'm surprised you haven't heard about it. It's a new release by a singer that graduated from Georgetown about eight years ago. The record company is sponsoring a contest. If you get your copy of the CD signed by the artist, you have a chance to win fifty thousand dollars. I hope she comes in here. Do you know her?"

Zasha gave the waiter a slight smile. "May I see the CD jacket?"

"Sure, I'll be right back." The waiter turned to fetch the CD.

Zasha took the CD looking at the cover, *Jenna Roulette, Double Down*. Jenna was sitting at a Blackjack table with two aces lying face up and a mound of chips behind each of the cards. She slid the jacket from the case and read the inside cover describing the rules for the contest. She put it back together and handed it to the waiter. "Thank you."

Cole and Julie's focus was locked on Zasha. When the waiter was far enough from the table, Cole leaned forward. "What do you make of this?"

Zasha took a drink from her glass. "It has to be Vladimir. We're going to have to go get Jenna. If Vladimir finds out where she is, I know he'll come for her. I can't let that happen."

Cole reached for his phone. "I'll get somebody on her until we can get to New Orleans."

Zasha nodded and was already dialing her phone. "I'm calling Jenna. I want her to hang low until we get there."

On the ride back to Langley, Zasha repeatedly dialed Jenna's number without success. Exasperated, she turned to Cole. "You sent someone over, right?"

"Yeah, they said they would be there in a few minutes." Cole gripped the wheel tighter. "How did we miss this?"

Julie offered insight. "This seems extreme to me. Why would anyone go to these lengths to find someone who left him?"

Zasha turned to face Julie. "Vladimir is a heavy-drinking control freak. He's probably pissed that we got her out of the country without his knowledge, which makes him dangerous."

Cole turned into CIA headquarters. "Don't forget about Borka; he's no slouch either. As a matter of fact, he's probably more dangerous."

Zasha pressed the redial button again and heard the call go through. "It's about time!"

"Well hello to you too." Jenna walked into her office at Xavier University and closed the door."

Zasha pressed the phone close to her ear. "Where the hell have you been? I've been calling non-stop for the past hour."

Jenna sat behind her desk and leaned back in her chair. "It's been crazy around here all day. People from the staff and students have been coming up to me and calling all day asking me to sign a copy of a CD I don't completely recognize."

Zasha's brow furrowed. "What do you mean you don't recognize it? Your picture is on it and that was definitely your voice I heard? You have seen it haven't you?"

Jenna tossed her hair with her fingers. "Sure, I've seen it. I've been signing copies all day. I had to cancel my class to deal with the requests. But, the strange thing is the songs on it are a compilation of songs from the CDs Vladimir was responsible for."

Zasha blew a frustrated sigh. "Jenna, did anyone from a record company contact you before releasing the album? Have you signed any contracts?"

Jenna held a copy of the CD before her face. "Today was the first time that I've seen it. The picture was shot a couple years ago for another album, but we changed the name. I haven't had time to think about the company or contracts."

Zasha stepped from the car. "You never were one for details. Do you even recognize the name of the releasing company?"

Jenna flipped the cover over and read the name. "It must be a small company— it's not one of the big guys. You should be happy for me."

"You should be happy for yourself if you ever see a penny from the sales." Zasha's sigh this time was more compassionate. "Did you tell us everything you know about Vladimir when you were interviewed here at Langley?"

Jenna tossed the CD to her desk. "Of course, I did. What do you think I left out?"

Zasha shook her head. "I don't know, but don't you think it's strange that Vladimir would go to such lengths to find you?"

Jenna's face tightened. "What does that have to do with the CD?"

Zasha folded her arms as best she could with the phone up to her ear. "Think about it, Jenna. Why would a small, unknown record company release an album and offer a fifty-thousand-dollar reward to one person, who got your signature on it?"

"What?" Jenna sat straight up in her chair.

Zasha took a quick breath. "You don't know?"

Jenna grabbed the CD and looked at the sticker on the front, *contest inside*. She opened it and read the contest rules. "I hadn't seen this."

Zasha dropped her hands then slowly pulled the phone back to her ear. "Do you now understand that this is a problem? I want you to lay low. Cole put in a call to have someone keep an eye on you until we get there tomorrow."

A smile crossed Jenna's face. "You're coming to New Orleans tomorrow? Great, then you guys can see my show."

Zasha's face soured again. "What show?"

Jenna curled her hair around her finger. "I'm performing tomorrow night at the university. With all the hubbub about the CD, they're expecting a big crowd."

Zasha's free hand went to her hip. "Cancel it!"

Jenna cleared her throat. "I can't."

Zasha was furious. "Why not?"

Jenna shrugged her shoulders. "The Times Picayune ran a big ad in today's paper and I've already been paid. It's a fundraiser for Xavier."

Zasha growled and rolled her eyes. "If you don't get killed before we get there, I'm going to do it as soon as I see you."

Julie decided to make the trip with Zasha and Cole treating it as a mini vacation. This was her first trip to New Orleans and she hoped to have a bit of time to see some of the city.

During the ride from the airport, Julie was both moved and depressed by what she was seeing. Years after Katrina, signs of the aftermath were all but gone and yet, the people still wore the aftermath on their faces. "It's hard to believe that we didn't do more to help New Orleans right after it hit. The city is back, but from what I read last night it's the original residents, who received the smallest benefit."

Zasha shook her head. "No one seemed to believe these people were worth the effort. I heard one person suggest that it was God flushing the toilet to get the shit out of the city. It's a damn shame that a country with so much can be so callous, or decides to selectively rise to the occasion."

Julie's face went slack. "I hope they take a more proactive stance in China. I'm not so sure they will. The Chinese government places little value on their people. They probably view the earthquake as a population-thinning event."

Cole blew air through his teeth. "All the more reason to send people in to plant the seeds of change in their people's hearts."

They reached Xavier University and there was no doubt the magnitude of what they would be facing until they got Jenna out of the city. People were lined up snaking around several buildings on the campus.

Zasha had to raise her lower jaw before speaking. "This is going to be a nightmare. It appears to be thousands of people here and the concert doesn't begin for another eight hours."

Cole scanned the crowd as he drove by. "If Vladimir is responsible for this, he'll have the information he's looking for. We'd best contact the New Orleans police chief and get photos of Vladimir and Borka handed out. We're going to need all the help we can get."

Julie leaned towards the front seat. "What are the chances that Vladimir will show up here?"

Zasha shook her head keeping her eyes on the faces they were passing. "Even with a crowd this large, I don't think he would risk it. He has to know that there'll be a large police presence. He probably just wants to know where she is."

Cole sucked in a large amount of air. "You could be right, he is ex KGB. That may suggest that he'll be careful. But, let's not forget who he works with. Add that to the fact that we know there's a large presence of Chinese Secret Police here in New Orleans and we could be looking at something much more difficult to handle."

Julie's eyes darted building-to-building. "Where is Jenna now?"

Zasha pulled out a map of the campus. She pointed to one of the buildings. "She's supposed to be there. I hope like hell, she didn't get caught up in the moment and come out here to greet her fans. That would be a very Jenna thing to do."

Chapter
68

Jenna sat at a table covered in copies of her CD, which volunteers collected from the crowd lining the buildings on campus. Sitting on either side of her were the FBI agents Cole called in to keep an eye on her.

Zasha, Cole and Julie walked into the room and the FBI agents stood. Cole held out his creds. "Easy guys, I'm Agent Cole Peterson and these lovely ladies are Agents Zasha Davis and Julie Hu."

"Have you ever seen anything like this?" She put her hand out. "Special Agent Bernadette Justice, we've had two teams on Miss Roulette since you called. So, do you have anything more on the terrorists?"

Jenna sat her *Sharpie* down and looked up at the agents. "Why do you insist on calling Vladimir a terrorist? You people just don't understand."

Zasha put both hands on the table and leaned towards Jenna. "Set your misguided feelings of romance on the shelf and open your eyes. Vladimir is working with the largest Triad Boss in China and they've set their sights on the U.S. Do you think their intentions are laudable?"

Cole cleared the room of volunteers and closed the door. Walking back to the table, he grabbed a chair and sat in it backwards. "You've gotten mixed up with some very dangerous people. They've killed two members of their group and attempted to kill a third. Your welfare means nothing to them. The fact that they've gone to so much trouble to find you suggests that they think you know something that can hurt them. What haven't you told us?"

Jenna looked longingly to Zasha. "I told you guys everything. Vladimir never discussed his business with me. To tell the truth, I really didn't want to know. He made my life a lot easier after I met him in Hong Kong. If it wasn't for him, I never would have been able to release an album." She stood and pointed out the window at the crowd. "I would never have been able to perform for a group of fans this size if it wasn't for him. Artists would give anything for a moment like this."

"I missed the intros, Special Agent Earnest Pucci. What are we dealing with here?" His eyes panned the agents and locked on Zasha.

She eased into a chair and leaned back. She took a few minutes to explain Jenna's connection to Vladimir and his connection to Zhang Ju. "Our intel points to a planned terrorist attack against the U.S. Zhang has taken the time to cultivate a crop of Rosary Peas. The seeds of this plant contain a highly toxic poison, Abrin. If he has found a way to release it en masse it will make the Rison gas release in Japan look like child's play. Abrin is seventy-five times more potent than Rison and it doesn't have to be transmitted in gas form. Once ground, the dust will kill as efficiently as gas."

Bernadette and Earnest looked at each other intently. She lifted a CD from the table. "How does the Abrin tie the players to Miss Roulette?"

Zasha shook her head and lifted a copy of the CD. She considered the information Zhang gathered on the U.S. citizens, but decided to keep it to herself. "We don't believe there is a direct connection. I honestly believe, Vladimir is simply trying to locate Jenna."

Cole motioned to Julie and they walked to a quiet corner of the room away from the others. "Call Oscar and tell him to have a copy of this CD scanned for Zhang's mining program. With the numbers of copies hitting the street, they could be using it to gather additional information on our citizens."

Zasha looked over her shoulder and got Cole's attention. "I'll have Oscar build a profile for Special Agent Justice as a talent agent. Then get the information on this recording company. I've got an idea." She turned to Bernadette pointing at the record company's name on the CD. "As soon as Oscar has everything in place, I want you to contact the record company as Jenna's agent. We'll have to find out why Jenna hasn't been contacted or issued a contract. If Vladimir is behind this, they'll want to know where she is.

Bernadette pulled a laptop out and fired it up. "Spinning a web to catch a fly. I'll do a little research on talent agents to familiarize myself with the lingo. Meantime, what do we do about the concert?"

Zasha set the CD back on the table. "We're going to need a lot more coverage. If Vladimir and Borka aren't already here hopefully they won't have time to get here before the show. Next, we'll have to release a concert schedule. Let's take it to the DC area. Our resources there will enable us to control the situation. We need to apprehend Vladimir; he has the information we need on Zhang's plan."

Earnest pulled a phone from his pocket. "I'll call the SAC and get a group of agents to attend the concert. I'll have him upload pictures of Vladimir and Borka to the agent's phones."

Cole walked back to the table. "Have him upload the pictures of any known or suspected Chinese Secret Police operating in the area as well; they could be in Zhang's pocket and looking to make a quick score."

Zasha came to her feet. "Good idea. The sooner we catch those bastards the better I'll feel." She let a hand drop to Jenna's shoulder. "You're going to be okay. Right now, you'd better get back to signing those CDs."

Julie walked to the table and handed a slip of paper to Bernadette. "You're good to go, here's the info on the record company. They're based in New York. The web site says they've been in business for ten years, but Oscar couldn't find anything to confirm that."

Bernadette opened the site for Hot Tracz Records and read over the profile listing artists no one ever heard of. She deferred to Zasha. "Do you think we should send over a couple of agents to check them out?"

Zasha tapped a stack of CDs with her finger. "Have someone confirm that they're at this location, but don't go in just yet. We'll send someone in tomorrow after the concert with a signed copy of the CD to enter the contest and see how that goes. As a matter of fact, if the company does exist, have a team go in after hours and plant surveillance equipment. Make sure a federal judge signs off on it, we don't want to leave anything to chance."

Bernadette called in the orders. "They're sending an agent by the location right away. As soon as I have confirmation, I'll call the company."

Jenna sat the *Sharpie* down again and reached for Zasha. "Why is it my life always seems to be filled with complications? All I want to do is make music and enjoy a few simple pleasures."

Zasha rubbed Jenna's shoulders. "Since when have you ever done anything the easy way? You wouldn't be the Jenna I know if you did."

Jenna watched the agents working around the room. "I guess all this debunks your journalist assertion. Does Vladimir know that you're really CIA?"

Zasha shrugged. "He's former KGB I'm sure he has some idea that I'm not a reporter. Regardless, it's not me he's looking for."

Jenna patted Zasha's hands. "I refuse to believe that he'd try to hurt me. He was always gentle around me."

Zasha heard Bernadette's phone ring and turned in her direction. "We'll know soon enough."

Bernadette answered the phone and nodded as she received the information. She disconnected the call and set her phone on the table. "Hot Tracz Records has a high-dollar address on Avenue of the Americas. They appear legit; let's see what they have to say."

The agents gathered around the table as Bernadette dialed the number and pressed the speaker function of her phone.

"Hot Tracz Records." An overly excited voice answered.

"This is Bernie Shaw with the Shaw Talent Agency. We represent Jenna Roulette. There seems to be some confusion concerning her latest release."

The voice on the other end lost all enthusiasm. "Just a minute please, I'll transfer you to Mr. Goldberger,"

"Ms. Shaw, Warren Goldberger here. I'm pleased that you have located Miss Roulette. All of our attempts to reach her have been unsuccessful."

Bernadette pointed to the man's photo on her computer screen so that the others could see the amusing-looking man with the over-sized round glasses. "Mr. Goldberger, can you explain how you could release an album of my client's recordings without her permission?"

He cleared his throat forcefully as if something were blocking his voice. "As I've stated, we have attempted to reach Miss Roulette. However, nothing is out of the ordinary. I stumbled across her recordings on a trip to Hong Kong and was moved by her level of musical interpretation, so I contacted the owner of her label there and purchased her contract. It entitles us to re-release her music here in the United States. She's quite good don't you think?"

Bernadette didn't waste time reaching her next point. "Mr. Goldberger, you are well aware that U.S. law requires that you establish a contract with my client before proceeding with a release."

"And we would have gladly done so if we'd been able to locate her." He stroked several keys on his computer. "That's why we established the contest in conjunction with the album release. Mr. Nikitin suggested Miss Roulette was here in the States. She'll be pleased to know that the album is certified gold. She has a substantial check waiting as soon as you provide me with an address."

Bernadette's eyes darted to Jenna, who gave a slight squeak hearing about the check. "We haven't even worked out terms of her contract yet, how do you know what to pay her?"

Goldberger laughed. "Most of that stuff is standard, but I won't quibble. Offering fifty thousand dollars to a person lucky enough to get her autograph has made this album the number one seller for the past couple of weeks. We've already netted millions. She's well worth whatever we work out." He paused to let it sink in. "Now, how about that address?"

Zasha lifted Jenna's chin. "Do you have any further questions of who's behind this? The only information they wanted was your location."

Jenna shook her head and wiped away a tear. "He once told me that he would never let anyone take me from him. I knew that he was possessive— I can't believe he'd go to these lengths."

Earnest's phone beeped and he pressed a button bringing Vladimir's image up followed by Borka's. "These are some scary dudes. No telling what they're capable of."

Cole tapped Earnest's shoulder after seeing Jenna's expression. "Let's go check out tonight's venue. We're going to have to know what we're dealing with to best position our people."

Zasha held up a hand pausing their retreat. "Make sure we get cameras positioned to cover all angles of the room, backstage as well. If Vladimir shows up tonight, we want to know before he realizes we're here. Sync it with headquarters; we can use the extra eyes."

A small black bus arrived on campus containing forty plain-clothes FBI agents. They were driven to the back entrance of the auditorium and were whisked in with their equipment.

The doors were scheduled to open in an hour and they had to get everything in place before the Xavier University Jazz Band could warm up.

The high-resolution cameras were designed to blend in with their surroundings to remain hidden from unsuspecting concert goers. In a backstage room, they set up a central command lining it with LED screens that displayed each camera's viewpoint.

Agents positioned themselves throughout the auditorium and checked their ear pieces that were disguised to look like Bluetooth cell phone receivers.

Positioned on the tops of several buildings, FBI agents posing as news crews panned cameras across the crowd searching for Vladimir, Borka and any of the Chinese Secret Police that were known to them.

Zasha waited in the dressing room with Jenna helping her to get ready for the show. "This is what you've been waiting for. The house will be packed, there's barely going to be standing room."

Jenna opened a bottle of water and took a long drink. "This is the break I've been waiting for all my life. I hope things run smoothly."

Zasha folded her hands and dropped them in her lap. "We're not here to disrupt your show. We're here to make sure you get through it in one piece. You go out there and do what you do. Nothing can prevent your rise to stardom. We'll do what we do. Soon you'll be able to operate without fear."

The Giant scribbled notes on a pad and disconnected the call he was on. He took the paper to Zhang. "Your idea worked. The record company was contacted by Roulette's agent today. They've asked for a meeting in Washington, DC tomorrow afternoon."

Zhang blew a stream of smoke into the air. "I never doubted the plan for a moment. Put someone on the girl, but don't tell Vladimir until after the shipment has been delivered."

The Giant hesitated. "If it was the Americans who got the girl out of Hong Kong, shouldn't she be considered a liability? At the very least, she's Vladimir's Achilles heel."

Zhang looked up and smiled. "I'm counting on it. We've already got the ships we need from him. When he goes after the girl, we'll take care of them at the same time. I'm not pleased with the way Vladimir has conducted himself during this portion of the operation. No piece of ass is worth the unrealistic attention he's given her. They're all liabilities, Borka included."

The Giant's phone jiggled in his hand and he flipped it open. He listened without speaking and closed the phone a few seconds later. "That was Goldberger— he got a hit on Roulette's name. She's performing this evening in New Orleans. We won't have to wait to put a tail on her."

Zhang puffed his cigar. "I think I'll place a call to Vladimir. I want to see how he reacts when I tell him we have a strong lead on the girl."

The Giant held his phone out. "Would you like me to place the call?"

Zhang lifted his phone and dialed. "I've got it I want to talk to him myself." He began as soon as Vladimir answered. "Have you gotten over your cunt addiction yet?"

"What do you have, Zhang?" Vladimir reached for a bottle to fill his glass.

Zhang blew a hiss of smoke into the phone. "We've got a lead on the girl. We should be able to confirm her location about the same time you deliver the shipment."

Vladimir took a drink of vodka to clear his mouth. "You insist on testing my patience. The shipment won't get near the United States if I don't have confirmation of where she is. Fuck you and fuck your grand scheme!"

Zhang bit the end of his cigar mashing it between his teeth, something he never did. "Getting into a pissing contest doesn't serve either of us. I'll have your information as soon as you reach shore. If it makes you feel better, you'll be only a short distance from her."

Vladimir sensed the tension. "Listen Zhang, I just want Jenna. I've kept up my end of the bargain at every turn— I would expect no less from you."

Zhang tossed the mashed cigar over the deck's railing and reached for another. "Satisfy my curiosity, why is this girl so important to you?"

Vladimir tossed back the rest of his vodka and wiped his mouth with the back of his hand. He wasn't sure the truth would best serve him at this moment, but he had nothing else. "She's carrying my child."

Later that evening, Jenna took the stage at Xavier University. She poured herself into every note, occasionally moving some in the crowd to tears. The pain in her voice was real and she delivered every note as if it were a statement of her life.

As she began to sing, "Someone to Watch Over me," Zasha grabbed Cole's arm. She watched as tears leaked from Jenna's eyes. She leaned close to Cole. "We missed something here, Jenna is a good actor, but she's not faking this."

Director Carson and Oscar Fenton sat in a private meeting when they were interrupted by a voice over an intercom. "Director Carson, I have U. S. Border Patrol and the Coast Guard holding for a conference."

"I'm not expecting a call. Did they say what the nature of the call is?" Carson's pen was moving through his fingers at a slow pace.

"No, sir, they only said that it was urgent."

Carson tapped the pen even faster and looked at Oscar. "Okay, put them through."

The voice began immediately after being given the *go ahead*. "Director Carson, we have a bit of a situation on the beach just outside of Miami. There used to be a long-standing wet foot, dry foot rule when dealing with any Cubans who reach our shore."

Carson cut in. "That's not news. What's the problem?"

The voice stuttered trying to find the words. "Well sir, they all have Cuban papers but…they're all Chinese-looking except for the boat's captain."

"Shit!" Director Carson stopped tapping the pen and came to his feet. "Is there a Coast Guard Officer on the line with us?"

"Yes, sir." Another voice answered.

Carson's face was growing redder by the second. "Where are these people now?"

"We have them at a Coast Guard facility. They needed food and water."

"Of course." Carson shot a look at Oscar. "I want you to sit on them. Don't process them and keep any contact to a minimum. The FBI will be there shortly." He pointed to Oscar to call the FBI and had another thought. "Do any of these people speak Spanish?"

The Coast Guard officer took the question. "All of them, sir."

Carson's face knotted across every inch of every facial muscle. His next question was directed at Oscar, though everyone heard it. "What the fuck is going on?"

Oscar didn't attempt to answer, but the Coast Guard officer did. "Excuse me, sir."

Carson waved as if the man was standing right in front of him. "I'm sorry, it was rhetorical. Make sure you keep them on ice until the FBI arrives."

Oscar pointed to the phone. "You still want me to give the FBI a call?"

Carson hit the intercom button. "We'll do it from here."

"Yes, Director?" His assistant responded to the call.

"Get the NSA and FBI directors on the line. We've got something that requires all our attention."

A few minutes later, Carson described the situation in Miami. Director Jimmerson was the first to respond. "Jessie, this has to be linked to the data that Rajiv discovered."

Carson nodded. "George that is precisely the opinion I'm operating on. We need to ascertain if they are willing participants or pawns in Zhang's game."

James McGavin spread two items on his desk. "Jessie, in your initial report on Zhang Ju, you mentioned an inoculation that could be used to ward off the effects of Abrin poisoning."

"Yes, the CDC is working on it, but as of yet, there has been nothing conclusive." Director Carson's pen was tapping through his fingers at a more rapid pace.

Director McGavin jotted a note on one of the pages in front of him. "The way I see it is, Zhang wouldn't be sending these people here to die— it wouldn't fit with his plan."

"What are you saying?" Director Jimmerson inquired seeking a conclusion.

Director McGavin circled what he'd just written. "The Chinese, specifically Zhang, may have beaten us to it and come up with a working vaccine. If that's the case, and the people the Coast Guard is entertaining are Zhang's, they will have antibodies in their blood stream directly related to Abrin."

Carson's pen stopped abruptly. "That's one hell of a great conclusion. If you're correct, we'll have all we need to manufacture the vaccine. When your team picks them up, run the test."

"I intend to." Director McGavin pulled the other sheet of paper directly in front of him. "This brings me to the second matter. The pursuers of Miss Roulette. Our joint teams will have her safely in D.C. tomorrow morning. By now, Vladimir Nikitin is aware that she is here. To aid in bringing him out of the shadows, we have taken the liberty to set up a concert at the Ford Theater, which as you know, is directly across the street from FBI headquarters. We have to take him down alive if he's going to be any use to us in finding out where Zhang is and what he's up to."

Carson tensed a little, not sure what McGavin would say next. "Agreed, we'll have a strong presence at the concert to assist your men."

Director McGavin placed his middle finger and thumb against the side of his head. "I think we're better equipped to handle the situation, but we'll welcome the additional manpower."

Carson squeezed the pen between his fingers but didn't tap it. "This is a joint operation between all our agencies. We all will participate in the effort and the credit upon successful conclusion."

Director McGavin was silent only a second. "I didn't mean to imply otherwise. I'll get back to you with the results from the detainees. We'll also begin questioning them in small groups to find out what they know."

Chapter
71

Vladimir walked out to feel the wind on his face as his ship steamed to port in Norfolk, Virginia. All morning a hard-steady rain fell, which was perfect— Customs and the Port Authority wouldn't waste time with nitpicking inspections and the dogs would have a difficult time locking on a scent. If the authorities were alerted to closely inspect shipments from China, Vladimir and his crew would be in luck— the ship and its cargo all held markings from Russia. The only Chinese people on board were the women Zhang provided and they wouldn't leave Vladimir's quarters.

About a mile out, Vladimir pulled a cell phone from his pocket and dialed Zhang. "We have arrived and will proceed to port if you have my information."

Zhang selected a cigar from his humidor and cut the end. "Did you ever doubt that I would come through?" He lit the cigar giving Vladimir time to consider the question.

"This is an important day for you. Let's not complicate it unnecessarily. Where is Jenna?" Vladimir tried to ease the tension spreading across his body.

Zhang blew a stream of smoke into the phone punctuating the fact that he wouldn't be rushed. "As we speak, she is meeting with an associate of mine, who represents the company releasing her latest album. As expected, Jenna had a talent agent get in touch so that she could be paid. You won't have time to reach her during this meeting, but that is of no concern. She is performing Friday night at the Ford Theater in Washington, D.C."

Vladimir blew a grateful sigh of relief. "That is a perfect venue, lots of people and she will be isolated backstage. I can use the confusion after the concert to disappear into the crowd."

"Aren't you forgetting something?" Zhang grinned and smoke escaped from his teeth. "If the Americans took her out of Hong Kong, they could still be involved."

Vladimir grunted and walked to the door at the helm of his ship. "The Americans have never been able to match wits with the KGB. Borka and I will get Jenna. Just as easily, we will leave and never be heard from again."

Zhang's eyebrows rose. "I trust you will be completely successful. Let me know how to reach you. I can always use a man of your talents."

Zhang disconnected the phone and called the Giant over. "Make sure we have someone at Jenna Roulette's concert on Friday. We don't want any loose ends, especially if the Americans are involved."

☯

Vladimir's ship was met by customs and the Port Authority. Several of the men were tethered to dogs that would aid in inspecting the ship's cargo.

Vladimir handed the ship's manifesto to the officer in charge. "We are transporting fireworks for your Independence Day celebration. There are just over one hundred containers. The crew is prepared to systematically open them. Where would you like to begin?"

The officer read over the paperwork and constantly brushed away drenching rain from his face, as the intensity increased. "Give me a minute— none of us wants to be out here longer than we have to." He walked to the men holding the dogs and instructed them to examine a sampling of the crates.

They went to work opening crates and physically examining several packs of fireworks. The dogs used to detect explosives would get a hit at every crate, so they were sent to inspect other ships that were arriving. The others that were trained to detect drugs quickly moved container to container remaining silent at each one.

With the inspection completed, a crane moved to the ship to offload the containers onto waiting transfer trucks. The process would take several hours and require Vladimir's crew. This provided time for Vladimir and Borka to go ashore. When the ship left shore, they would be lost in the city using Zhang to rent a car—

D.C. was three hours north and they planned to be there before nightfall.

One-by-one, the loaded transfer trucks pulled from the port. Each had a predetermined destination. Within the next one hundred and twenty hours the top fifty cities and the top fifty military installations in the United States would be in possession of their shipments of Zhang's fireworks roughly three weeks later, people in these cities and military installations would fall victim to Zhang's attack.

By the evening of July fifth, bodies would be lining the streets. The hysteria would allow Carlos, Rafael and Pablo to move thousands of people into the U.S. undetected. They would also use this time to spread additional attacks of Abrin onto food supplies and water sources, quickly eliminating scores of additional unsuspecting U.S. citizens. Days later, Zhang, aided by the Chinese President and his army, would be free to enter the United States and claim the country as his own.

Earnest posing as Bernadette's assistant showed Warren Goldberger into the agency's conference room. Around the walls were various pictures of Bernadette with famous singers, actors and writers. Each of the pictures were expertly modified by FBI technicians inserting Bernadette beside the famous subjects.

Goldberger studied each of them carefully. "This is impressive. Is Ms. Shaw representing all of them?"

Earnest sidestepped a direct answer. "This is my first week here, I'll be happy to ask Ms. Shaw."

Warren shook his head. "That won't be necessary. I suppose she will be here in a minute. I can ask her myself."

Earnest opened the door to leave. "She's finishing a call. Can I get you anything while you're waiting?"

Warren retrieved his cell phone. "I'm fine, thank you."

Earnest closed the door and walked to Bernadette's office. "He's about to make a call."

Bernadette sat in front of a monitor broadcasting a picture of the conference room. "Everything's set; we'll be up as soon as the call goes through. Now, let's see who he's calling."

Warren kept a close eye on the door while waiting for the call to go through. "I'm here now— everything is legit. It looks as if she's got one hell of a client list; there're pictures all over the walls."

Zhang pulled up Bernadette's web site. "There are several artists listed here. Do these names match any of the pictures?" He read the names.

Warren moved picture-to-picture. "They're all here. I'd have to say, she's got clout. How do you want me to handle it?"

"You've got twenty five percent of sales, whatever she doesn't take is yours." Zhang poured a glass of Balvenie Scotch. "Give her what she asks for; just make sure we find out where the girl is."

Warren's eyes shot to the door. "Will do— looks like they're here now." He quickly ended the call and slipped the phone in his pocket.

The door handle moved and Bernadette stepped into the room alone. She carried a stack of papers in her hand, which she placed on the table before extending to shake. "Mr. Goldberger, it's a pleasure to meet you in person."

Warren took her hand and moved his head to see the door. "Likewise— is Miss Roulette joining us?"

Bernadette took her seat and slid on a pair of reading glasses. She pulled a sheet of paper from her stack and slid it to Warren. "She is unable to be here at the moment. This is a signed and notarized power of attorney giving me all negotiating rights on her behalf."

Warren lifted the paper and took his seat. "This is highly unusual. I prefer meeting our artists face-to-face."

Bernadette slid her glasses off and folded her hands in front of her face. "Considering the fact that you didn't bother contacting Miss Roulette before releasing the album, you should view this meeting as a gift. If it is not suitable, we could move our discussion to a courtroom."

Warren's face soured. "I didn't mean to imply any discontent— I'm simply used to having our artists present, especially when delivering such a large check."

Bernadette pointed to his briefcase. "Why don't you get comfortable and let's see what you have."

He slid back in the chair and reached for his briefcase. He pulled an envelope from it and handed it to Bernadette. "The check represents Miss Roulette's take from sales up to last Friday."

She opened the envelope and nonchalantly set it next to her stack of papers. She jotted something on the second sheet on her stack and tapped her pen against the page. "I hope you brought your checkbook."

Warren's face screwed as he pointed to the check. "That's a million-dollar check!"

Bernadette took another sheet of paper from the stack. "Sales to date are in excess of thirty million dollars. An artist of Jenna's caliber should receive thirteen percent— that puts my

Anthony P. Jones   263   Red States

figure around three point nine million, plus a four hundred-thousand-dollar bonus for not contacting us ahead of time—bringing the grand total to four point two million even."

Warren felt a portion of his fortune slipping away. He jumped forward in his seat leaning as far as he could. "She wouldn't have anything if we had not established the contest. You can't expect me to take a hit like that."

Bernadette stood and pulled a tri-folded blue piece of paper from her stack. "You've got sixty seconds to stroke a new check. If you refuse, I'll hand you this, which will take our next conversation to court." She tossed the paper to him. "Consider yourself served. I'll be back in fifty seconds…four point two million, not a penny less."

Warren watched her leave the room. "Goddamnit, she's costing me over two million dollars. That bitch better sell a ton of CDs." He jerked a checkbook from his briefcase and wrote a new check.

Bernadette returned as promised with Earnest in tow. She saw the new check sitting where the old one once sat. She lifted it and handed it to Earnest. "Verify the funds and have them transferred to the agency's escrow account."

Warren watched Earnest leave the room and fell back in his seat ripping up the subpoena. "I hope you enjoyed raping me."

Bernadette closed her file and rested her hands on top of it. "If you try to cheat Jenna Roulette out of one penny of what she is due, I'll see to it that your next album will be cut from a prison cell. Thirteen percent, no shaving, no discounting, no excuses— fuck with me and I'll fuck you up. Oh, and in case you were wondering, that's a promise not a threat!"

Earnest stuck his head in the doorway. "Everything is taken care of. The funds are in our account."

Bernadette stood and smiled at Warren. "On behalf of Miss Roulette, thank you." She handed him a last sheet of paper. "Sign here, we need a formal contract."

Warren took a pen and signed the form. He gathered contempt from his toes and sent the paper careening in Bernadette's direction. "Have a nice fucking day!"

Chapter
73

Vladimir and Borka arrived in Washington, D.C. just after dark. Logged into the navigation system in the car, the Ford Theater was just a few blocks away.

Vladimir parked the car so that they could walk the remaining few blocks and take in their surroundings. People milled around the area, nothing seemed out of the ordinary until he spotted the large building just across the street. "Borka, we'd better double back. That's the FBI headquarters just down the block. There's probably a hundred cameras recording everything that moves in that area."

Borka suggested a different path to the theater and changed directions. He took a pair of binoculars from a bag and looked for cameras hidden anywhere in the area. "We might want to consider a disguise when we show up to the concert. The theater has cameras in front as well."

Vladimir took the binoculars for a look. "My guess is this is no coincidence holding the concert across the street from the FBI. We'll have to operate as if we're hot."

Borka examined items in his bag pulling out a small rectangular device. "We're going to have to get into the building before the concert Friday. I'll plant this under the alarm pad, when the numbers are pressed, it will record them and the sequence as well."

Vladimir shoved his hands into his pockets. "Just like the old days. Sometimes I miss the work even though the pay is better now."

Borka watched to see if the cameras at the theater were stationary or motion activated. A couple passing beneath them aided his research. "From the curvature of the camera lens it would seem that they cover a wide viewpoint. That seems even more evident because they didn't move when those people passed. We're not going to have any dark spots."

Vladimir pulled a flask from his jacket pocket and took a drink before offering Borka one. "Everyone working there will recognize any supplier making a delivery. Our advantage is we know Jenna, so day after tomorrow we will drop by to design a set for her. That will give us access to the backstage area."

Borka pulled the flask down. "With a building full of workers chances are not all the cameras will be activated during the day. Hats and glasses should get us by the cameras. I'll add a limp to my gait and about thirty extra pounds. That should keep them off track long enough for us to do our work."

Vladimir reached for the flask. "It's not like Russia here in the states, the cameras are always on, they don't trust anyone. I'll come up with something tonight."

Early the next morning, Vladimir and Borka waited in an alley watching for arrivals at the Ford Theater. A young woman was the first to arrive.

Vladimir quickly followed with Borka at his side. He was wearing loud yellow skin-tight pants, pink *Crocs* and a floral top tied and knotted around his rock-hard abs. The top was unbuttoned nearly to the knot and a pink scarf tied to one side of his neck completed his flamboyant look.

Borka gained an extra thirty pounds curtesy of a 'fat suit.' His choice of colors was more muted and far less gaudy.

If their dress left any doubt of their portrayal, the overdone makeup and sashaying gait removed it. Vladimir leaned against the young woman's station, bent one hand down at the wrist and dropped his chin against the back of his hand. "Excuse me, sweetie." He said as high pitched as his voice allowed him to go. "We are here to see the stage and dressing areas. Everything must be perfect when Miss Roulette arrives. Francois and I are her personal designers."

The young woman looked up at Vladimir's gel-spiked hair resisting the urge to laugh. "I'm the only one here at the moment."

"No problem, honey. You just show us where to go, we can handle our business without any help." Vladimir turned and pursed his lipstick filled red lips to Borka.

The young woman gazed at a clock them back to Vladimir. "We don't usually have people arrive at this hour…what did you say your name was?"

Vladimir shot a glance at Borka. "Valentino, we should be on your schedule."

She opened the appointment book. "There must be a mistake, or someone forgot to tell me."

Vladimir cocked his hip to one side and slapped a hand against it. "Honey, as much as we're being paid an hour, if we have to come back, Miss Roulette's people are going to be looking to recover the cost." He made several snaps with a wave of his arms and ended with, "Cha-ching."

The young woman looked around. "That won't be necessary. The stage is through those doors and the dressing area is just behind them."

"Thank you honey this will save us all a lot of time." Vladimir waved a hand. "Come on Francois. We've got work to do."

While Vladimir kept the young woman's attention diverted, Borka attached the decoder to the alarm system. Their main objective now was to see if anyone else had been backstage to set up a central command that would allow them to monitor the theater. It would be the type of thing the FBI would do if they suspected uninvited guests.

Immediately the pair went backstage and began checking doors— one was locked. Borka reached into a leather bag slung over his shoulder and retrieved a small scope, which he slid under the door. Tables lined two opposite walls. They were bare, no wires or cables giving any indication of their possible use. "It's clean, but why is it locked?"

Vladimir took the four-inch monitor from Borka and played back the recording. "Those tables aren't there for show, which is why the doors are locked. I'm going to get in touch with Zhang. To make this look good, we'll have the record company deliver a set that ties in with the CD cover."

Vladimir placed the call and Borka snapped pictures of the stage and dressing area. He noticed several catwalks above the stage and suspected that they would be occupied during the concert with FBI agents. He found a possible area that should provide a safe haven. A storage room that was packed with props for the annual production of *The Nutcracker* would have to do.

Vladimir finished his call and walked over to inspect the storage room. "They're going to check this room and demand that it is locked during the performance. Make a key; we'll find a spot in the back under the boxes and costumes."

Borka pulled another device from his bag, inserted it into the key slot and pressed a button. Several seconds later, a perfectly formed key dropped out. He put it in the lock and turned it locking the door. "We've got everything we need."

Vladimir shook his head. "Not quite, let's shift the boxes around leaving a place where we can hide. We'll leave the guns there now. We don't know who might be here tomorrow when we return with the set."

They left the stage and waved to the young woman at the front desk. "See you tomorrow, honey. We'll be delivering the set for the stage around noon."

Chapter
74

The following day a large truck pulled to the back of the Ford Theater at noon. They were met by staff, who opened the doors giving the delivery workers access to the stage area. Several large boxes were rolled down a ramp. Each was marked with a logo, Hot Tracz Records. The crew unloading took the boxes to the stage and began unpacking the contents.

The staff member, who let the workers, in walked over. "I've got to finish some paperwork. If you're done before I return, come through the doors at the front entrance and someone will find me to lock up."

The crew nodded and continued unpacking. When the staff member was gone from the room, one of the men unlatched the largest crate and Vladimir and Borka stepped from it. Borka grabbed a duffle bag and used the key he'd made a day earlier to unlock the prop room.

Vladimir motioned to one of the crew. "Put this crate back on the truck and leave the others here for break-down after the show."

Two men hurried the largest crate back to the truck. Vladimir joined Borka in the prop room. "All we have to do now is wait for everyone to leave this evening."

Six hours later, a chirp on Borka's computer let him know the building's alarm was set. The code appeared on the screen and he quickly jotted it down. Initiating a program, he reentered the code and the box he'd left below the alarm's key pad electronically transmitted the code disarming the alarm. "We're good to go."

Vladimir unlocked the door. "Let's see if anything has changed with the locked dressing room."

They used the scope to look into the room finding it the same as before. Gathering food from the duffle bag, they went to the stage and ate before returning to the prop room for their long wait.

The following day the theater was abuzz with activity. The FBI arrived shortly after the staff and began setting up equipment on the tables in the locked dressing room.

In the theater area, they positioned cameras that would feed directly to the bank of computers in the dressing room.

At noon, a black van pulled up to the theater's front entrance. Cole stepped from the van followed by Bernadette, Earnest and Julie. They took careful note of the people moving about the area.

Cole opened the door of the van and popped his head in. "It's clear, let's get in."

Zasha touched Jenna's hand. "Time for your sound check."

"Is all of this necessary?" Jenna followed Zasha from the van. Her legs buckled and she nearly fell to the sidewalk.

Zasha grabbed Jenna's arm, saving her from falling. "Are you okay?"

Jenna regained her balance accepting Zasha's support and hurried into the theater. "I'm okay, I guess I need something to eat."

Zasha pulled out a chair. "Why don't you sit down until we can get you something?"

Jenna's face became ashen and sweat covered it. "I need to get to the bathroom."

The young woman at the front desk pointed the way. Zasha took Jenna's arm and helped her to the restroom. Jenna barely made it into the stall before she began throwing up.

Zasha grabbed several paper towels and ran cold water over them. "Are you alright?"

Jenna came from the stall and plopped in a chair near the door. She took the paper towels and placed one behind her neck and the others on her forehead. "I'll be fine, I just need a minute."

Zasha stooped in front of her. "Is this just nerves, or is something else going on?"

Jenna put her hand on the paper towels on her forehead and rotated them to the cool side. She sighed heavily. "I was going to tell you earlier."

Zasha took Jenna's free hand. "Tell me what?"

Jenna moved the paper towels and sat up catching Zasha's gaze. "You're going to be an aunt— I'm pregnant with Vladimir's baby."

Zasha stood looking off distantly. "And he knows?"

Jenna fell back in the seat reapplying the paper towels. "Oh yes, he's overjoyed."

"That explains a lot." Zasha rubbed her face. "Why didn't you tell me earlier?"

Jenna slightly shook her head. "Things were getting so complicated. I just didn't think that you needed to know right away. At least you can understand why I've been so protective."

"Jenna!" Zasha's tone was sharp. She took a deep breath and calmed. "I'll have to tell the others. This may make Vladimir more difficult to reason with."

"Give him credit, he wants to be an involved parent." Jenna used the paper towels to dab at her tears.

"We'll have to see about that. I'm going to find Cole. I'll be back in a few." Zasha started for the door.

Jenna sat up doing nothing about the flowing tears. "Aren't you going to say you're happy for me?"

Zasha stopped, holding the door open with one hand. "If this is what you want then I'm happy for you. Your best interest is always at the core of my thoughts."

Bernadette presided over the command center. The crowd was monitored all evening using face-recognition software yet, no one even resembling Vladimir or Borka was detected. "Keep scanning the people, Zasha is certain that they'll make an appearance."

Earnest reviewed footage and released a short grunt-like laugh at Bernadette's comment. "A lot of baby's daddies try to run from responsibility."

Bernadette pointed to the screen in front of Earnest. "Yeah well, this guy is a different bird. We need to get him before he has a chance to get Jenna. There's no telling how he might react— he's crazy enough to try to kill everyone here."

The concert drew to a close after a second encore. As instructed, the staff cleared the theater quickly. Backstage, the FBI loosened up relaxing for the first time all evening.

Jenna came out of the dressing room and sat in a chair to sign copies of her CD for the agents who'd looked after her.

Borka slid his scope under the door taking in the positions of the agents. "She's sitting in a chair about five feet from us. The short Black woman, Zasha is next to her. I'll take her and you get Jenna."

Vladimir nodded and readied his AK-47. "Shoot anyone who draws a weapon."

With cat-like quickness, they burst from the prop room and grabbed the two women. Vladimir pointed his gun at Cole, who had his gun out as did the other agents. "A lot of people are going to get hurt if we begin a gun battle. The lovely Zasha will be the first to go."

Cole held his hand up to steady the other agents. "Vladimir, no one's been hurt yet, let's keep it that way. You've got information we need. No one is interested in killing you."

A wicked smile crossed Vladimir's lips. "You want Zhang. I could care less about him, I'm here for Jenna. Can we still work something out?"

Cole holstered his Glock. "Jenna may not be willing to abide by your suggestion."

Vladimir pulled her closer. "What about it, is your friend correct?"

Jenna shook her head. "I'll go with you, just don't hurt these people, they're only doing their jobs."

"You see, she does not object." Vladimir moved his face close to hers, but kept the gun on Cole. "What do you want Peterson?"

Cole's eyes darted between Zasha and Vladimir. "For starters, have Borka move the gun from Zasha's head." He nodded. "Go ahead and tell him what I've said."

Borka looked Cole in the eye. "I don't need him to translate— my English is as fluent as yours."

Shock spread across Cole's face. "He's a good actor."

Vladimir stroked Jenna's hair. "It always helps to have an ace in the hole."

Cole redirected the course of the conversation. "Let's get back to Zhang. What is he planning?"

Vladimir slightly relaxed. "Why do you think I've come for Jenna? He's planning..."

A single shot rang out and Vladimir fell to the floor.

Zasha grabbed Borka's gun barrel and jammed the heel of her boot into his instep of his foot. In one smooth motion, she flipped the much bigger man dislodging his rifle.

The other agents dropped to a crouch and fired at movement on the backstage catwalk. The sniper's rifle fell, immediately followed by the assailant.

Cole and Zasha cuffed Borka and turned to Vladimir. Jenna was on the floor holding his hand. Blood was everywhere. Jenna was clearly in shock and oblivious to reality as she sat down cradling Vladimir's head. "It's going to be okay now. Zasha can help us."

Zasha used all her strength to move Jenna. She took her to the dressing room and wet a towel to clean the blood off the side of her face, even though nothing could be done about the blood on her clothing. "You're going to be just fine."

Through her tears, Jenna observed Zasha. "Is Vladimir going to be okay?"

Zasha bit her lip. "An ambulance is on the way. We'll do everything we can." She didn't tell Jenna that the ambulance was for her. Jenna was in shock and Vladimir was very dead.

The FBI agents reached the body that fell from the catwalk. Black covered the person from head to toe.

Bernadette reached down and uncovered the face. Long raven-colored hair fell from the head cover. She turned the head and looked into eyes that expressed the unmistakably cloudy look of death. "She's Chinese."

Julie walked over and looked at the woman. "She was sent here to silence Vladimir. It was a suicide mission; she knew we'd be here. If she was after us, there would be bodies lying all over. She had the upper hand."

Red and blue lights pulsed drawing unwanted attention to the Ford Theater. Jenna was rolled out on a stretcher and whisked away to a hospital— Zasha was at her side.

Several FBI agents and Cole rushed Borka into a waiting van, which promptly disappeared underground just across the street.

Later in the interrogation room at FBI headquarters, Borka was completely uncooperative refusing to speak English or any other language.

Julie and Cole arrived at the safe house where Zasha was keeping an eye on Jenna.

Julie got a mug and filled it with hot water and added a tea bag. She sat at the table next to Zasha. "China has agreed to accept aid teams from the U.S. Cole and I will be leaving later this afternoon. Director Carson wants us to look for any connection to Zhang near his fireworks factory. That area was hard-hit and that's where we'll be taking aid."

Zasha looked over her shoulder at Jenna, who was mindlessly watching television. "I'm going to have to stay here a while longer. Jenna hasn't dealt with Vladimir's death. Have we learned anything new about the shooter?"

Cole handed Zasha a folder. She was Chinese Secret Police. Director Carson is going nuts trying to uncover a relationship between Zhang and the Chinese government."

Zasha looked over the file. "Borka wasn't any help?"

Cole shook his head. "He hasn't cracked in the least. It's been nearly a week and he's not said ten words."

"Have there been any additional sightings of Chinese illegals?" Zasha handed the file back to Cole.

Julie took the question. "Our borders are unusually quiet. We've assigned extra manpower at all major border crossings. Even the desert around Texas and New Mexico has been quiet."

Cole sat forward. "We've had all the U.S. internet providers add filters to catch Zhang's data mining program and shut it down. The NSA paid close attention to any internet chatter coming out of China, but it's all related to the earthquake."

Zasha tapped the table with her index finger. "Anything new on what Zhang's up to?"

Julie finished the tea in her mug. "He's been as quiet as our borders. I think it's a bad sign— quiet before the storm. Something big is about to happen."

Zasha refilled her coffee. "That's what I'm afraid of. Vladimir said he was here to get Jenna out. If he didn't think she was safe, we're probably not either."

☯

Julie and Cole landed on the aircraft carrier anchored just off China's coast. After a quick shower and something to eat, a helicopter would take them to Linyang. Their plan was to land near the fireworks company and work with the people in the area.

From the air the damage was overwhelming. The fireworks company sustained considerable damage. No one was near the plant, so Cole had the helicopter set down near it. A team of ten exited the chopper.

Cole called Arturo to the building. "What do you think, is it safe enough to enter?"

Arturo looked around the building. "We'd better not take any unnecessary chances. Let's suit up in a couple of the containment suits. Have everybody wait out here just in case."

Inside the building things were tossed but fairly empty. Cole lifted a roll of paper used to wrap the fireworks— it was covered in Russian writing. An aftershock rumbled and the building shook and creaked.

Arturo reached for Cole's shoulder. "Let's get out of here."

The building's supports gave way and the building began collapsing. The two men darted from the building waving for the others to move back. A large explosion knocked the two men to the ground and fire engulfed the building. Cole got to his feet and pulled Arturo up and they made their way to the others.

The noise attracted people living in the area. Before long, several people appeared near the site.

Julie walked to the helicopter and pulled out a box of MRE's. She spoke to a lady nearest to the chopper. "Do you have provisions? There's plenty here for everyone."

The lady moved closer. "There's nothing here. The markets have been out of food since just after the earthquake."

Julie held out packets of the MRE's. "It's okay, we've come to help." The lady approached and the others followed. Julie handed her several packs and signaled for another team member to bring over a case of water. "So, you live near here?"

The woman pointed behind her shoulder. "My house was spared. I've done what I can for my neighbors. Most are afraid to stay in the houses."

Julie handed her a bottle of water. "You're not afraid your house will collapse?"

The woman took a drink from the water. "It doesn't matter to the earthquake where you are. It can swallow you anywhere you happen to be." She pointed to the factory. "Look at what it's done there. Now we have no place to work."

Julie looked at the burning building. "Did you work there?"

The woman opened the MRE, took a small bite and closed the package. "My husband and I worked there for the past ten years."

Julie handed her another MRE. "Eat as much as you like, there's plenty here. Where is your husband now?"

Tears filled the woman's eyes. "He went to the school to find our daughter. Neither of them has returned. I wanted to go look for them, but I had to stay home with our youngest."

Julie put her arm around the woman. "We'll help you find them."

Cole and Arturo took their suits off away from the group. Cole called for a testing pack, which was tossed to him from a distance. He handed the pack to Arturo. "Let's see if there are any traces of Abrin on our suits."

Arturo conducted the tests. "There's nothing here. Let me see that paper you brought out."

Cole handed him the paper. "Chances are it'll be negative as well."

"You're right. If Zhang used this factory for the Abrin either he's cleaned it well or we're on a snipe hunt." Arturo nodded towards Julie. "Let's see what she's found out."

Cole walked over to Julie. "Is everything okay here?"

Julie moved her arm from the woman. "She hasn't seen her husband or daughter since the earthquake. I told her we would try to help. Let's walk her home. She's been trying to take care of her neighbors. Let's take several boxes of MRE's and water to her house. She'll equitably distribute them— she didn't even eat a part of the first one I gave her earlier despite the fact that there's been no food available."

Cole gathered the team. "Let's unload the chopper here. Julie wants to set up near the lady's house just over there. We'll set up our tents and take the supplies with us." He went to the pilot. "These people haven't had anything to eat for days. Head back to the ship and bring another load of MRE's and water."

The local people came to help unload the chopper and followed the team to their camp. The whine of the helicopter blades announced it would be lifting off.

Arturo turned and looked between the two boxes on his shoulders. "Let's go do some good."

Late that evening, Julie looked at her watch. She was sitting at a table in the lady's house with Cole and Arturo. "Tomorrow in America, people will be out to see fireworks shows all over the country. I bet a lot of what they will see was made by you right here in Linyang."

The lady rose to get the tea kettle that was now spewing a steady stream of steam. Out of habit, when guests were present, she opened a cabinet in search of sugar. A single glass was on the shelf.

Cole watched the woman. "There's sugar over here." The glass on the shelf caught his attention and he pointed to it. "What's in that glass?"

Julie translated and held her hand out as the woman handed her the glass. "What are these?"

Cole's heart skipped a beat seeing the contents of the glass. He became very excited and grabbed Julie's arm. "Ask her where she got these."

Julie shook the glass. "Where did you get these?"

The woman looked at the glass. "We used them in the fireworks. My husband took a few because he said they would kill rats if we mixed them with bait."

Cole was nearly on the table waiting for Julie to translate. "What did she say?"

Julie relayed her comments and Cole pulled the paper he'd taken from the factory from his pocket. "Ask her if they wrapped the fireworks in this paper."

Julie translated once again and the lady responded affirmatively.

Cole ran from the house to his tent. He grabbed a radio pack, cranked it and began calling the ship frantically. "May Day, May Day, this is ground force Alpha Omega, come in."

The ship's Captain answered. "What's going on Commander Peterson?"

Cole was breathing to the point of hyperventilation. "Patch me into Langley right away. I know what Zhang's up to."

A few seconds later, Oscar was on the line. "Cole, what's so urgent?"

Cole dispensed with any niceties. "Oscar, get the Director and the President on here now— we've got to avoid a fucking catastrophe!" He fired up a generator and plugged in a computer and scanner. He placed the paper he'd taken from the factory on the bed of the scanner and uploaded the picture and transmitted it to Langley.

Director Carson came on the line. "Peterson, what the hell is going on?"

Cole put on a headset to keep his hands free. "Director, Carson, I've just transmitted an image to you. This is the wrapping from fireworks that were manufactured here in Linyang. Notice that the writing is in Russian. Check to see if any of these fireworks entered the U.S. They are laced with Abrin. A worker from the plant just confirmed this to Julie. You're going to have to cancel any fireworks shows scheduled for tomorrow night unless you want a disaster on your hands."

Director Carson pulled the image up on the computer in the conference room. "Holy shit! Something of this magnitude could potentially wipe out over fifty percent of our population! Do you know what time it is here? Reaching hundreds of thousands of planned shows for tonight's fireworks is going to be virtually impossible."

Cole neglected decorum. "Regardless, get them stopped or there's going to be bodies lining the streets of America!"

Director Carson contacted the directors of the FBI and NSA requesting them to meet him at the White House. He instructed Oscar to reach every law enforcement agency in every town and city in the United States along with every military instillation and have them cancel any fireworks shows planned for the evening. "Contact all the news agencies and have them broadcast an imminent threat nationwide. Have them warn the citizens to remain indoors and not to attend any fireworks shows. Have them pass along the word that any display of fireworks including bottle rockets will be considered a federal offense."

Oscar looked at the Director. "This is going to cause pandemonium across the country. It's going to overload the system."

"I don't give a shit! Just make sure no fireworks shows go off this evening. Deploy the National Guard if necessary, just get it done." Carson left the room for his waiting helicopter.

Oscar sent a wire to all the news agencies and made sure his staff followed up with calls.

At the White House, Director Carson explained the threat to the President. "Sir, you're going to have to go on the air and explain the threat and make the people understand that the situation is dire. We don't have time to search for the fireworks that entered the country from Zhang's plant."

The President looked around the room. "Does anyone else have anything to offer?"

Director Jimmerson was the first to speak. "Mr. President, I think Jessie's right. It's noon here on the East Coast and many celebrations are already underway. We've got to reach the people, cancel any shows tonight and examine any fireworks with these markings." He held out the picture Cole faxed.

The President deployed a team of agents to the Mall between the Washington Monument and the Lincoln Memorial. They pulled to a staging area for the fireworks and jumped from their vehicles. The team leader looked over the fireworks already positioned to launch for tonight's show. "Mr. President, the wrappings match what Agent Peterson transmitted earlier. We're going to take one into the mobile lab to dissect it for confirmation."

The President looked at his advisors in the room. "God, I hope this isn't what we suspect it is."

Dressed in containment suits, a team of agents took the rocket into the lab. They removed the wick and used a blade to cut the wrapping from it. Pealing the paper away, they noticed wadding separating the top half of the rocket from the pyrotechnic chemicals below. They carefully inserted a probe into the top portion of the rocket and sensors lit up and chirped. "Mr. President, we have a major problem. The top half of the rocket is loaded with Abrin. It's separated from the ignition system and chemicals with wadding like you would use in a model rocket. The wadding would prevent the explosion from damaging the Abrin, which would be blown into the air filling it with poisonous dust."

The President fell back in his chair. "Fuck me!" He pressed a button on the intercom. "Get in touch with all the networks including cable. I'm going on the air in ten minutes. Make sure that they understand that my address will preempt every single channel broadcast across our airwaves. Do the same for all radio stations. This is a national emergency. Everyone will comply, no exceptions!"

The President began his delivery by urging calm. At festivals across the country, the speech was broadcast over the loud speaker systems. "Ladies and gentlemen, our country is facing a threat from people who don't appreciate the freedom afforded by the sacrifices we have made to enjoy our way of life, which is the reason for today's celebration. We have uncovered a plot designed to inflict great harm to our way of life via the fireworks display that you were looking forward to seeing tonight. To avoid tragedy, we have canceled all shows nationwide. It is imperative that everyone avoid all fireworks including personal displays. The threat has been confirmed. Anyone possessing fireworks must turn them in to authorities immediately. Not doing so could cost you your life as well as the lives of anyone near any such display. The National Guard has been dispatched to aid in the recovery of all fireworks. Please afford them your complete cooperation.

Festivals around the country erupted in pandemonium. Parents grabbed children heading for cars, subways and any available means to return home safely. Chaos that the President hoped to avoid could not be contained. People fled the streets, neglecting any sense of compassion.

Other than the National Guard the only people standing their ground was news reporters hoping for a killer story. Without specifics of what the fireworks contained, they accepted the responsibility of uncovering the details and making it known to the people.

Zhang was tuned to the cable broadcast of MSNBC when the President broke in. He cursed loudly and began throwing things around the room. "How the fuck did they find out?"

The Giant stood in the doorway away from Zhang's projectile range. "Master Zhang, we still have an alternative. It may not be what we'd hoped for, but we still can inflict damage."

Zhang stopped his tirade long enough to pour a tall glass of Scotch and grab a fresh cigar. "What are you talking about?"

The Giant entered the room. "I had our contacts within the Secret Police positioned in several cities in the U.S. deliver extra fireworks. As soon as you give the go-ahead, they will launch their stash in New York, Los Angeles, Chicago, Philadelphia, Houston, San Diego, Washington, D.C., Atlanta, Miami and Nashville. We may not strike the blow we'd hoped to, but we can cause significant damage."

Zhang lit his cigar and took several puffs before speaking. "Wait until it's dark across the U.S. and set them off. Contact Carlos, Rafael and Pablo and have them bring the people across the borders dumping their poison on crops and into the water supplies. I want hundreds of thousands of Americans dead in two days."

The Giant left Zhang to his obsessing and went to place calls to his soldiers waiting for orders.

At twelve midnight Eastern time, fireworks in the cities where the Chinese Secret Police were positioned took to the sky.

Carlos, Rafael and Pablo appeared from tunnels leading to the United States with thousands of illegals, who dumped packets of Abrin across fields of plants and water supplies near where they emerged.

People in the cities where the fireworks took to the air watched from the protection of their homes and called police to report the pyrotechnics displays.

The President went ballistic hearing about the fireworks going off after he'd explicitly forbade such displays in the U.S.

The Directors of the CIA, NSA and FBI were with him as they headed to an underground bunker at the Greenbrier, a spot that most Americans thought was debunked years earlier. "What the fuck is going on?"

Director Carson took the question. "We have to assume at this point that Zhang Ju had a backup plan. Hospitals in the areas where the fireworks went off need to be prepared for casualties. We need the CDC to contact administrators with the correct procedure to counter the Abrin. Deploying military units to set up MASH units wouldn't be a bad idea either."

The President pointed to Jessie. "Call it in. We've got to get the jump on these bastards."

Director Jimmerson leaned towards the President. "We can't assume Zhang would stop there. This would be an opportune time for him to strike our borders. That was on his agenda in Puerto Vallarta."

The President nodded towards Director Jimmerson. "Have the military deployed to our borders. Tell them to shoot to kill anyone trying to cross them. Scramble squadrons to fly around the borders. Tell them they have free reign to obliterate anyone near them. We have to stop this attack at all costs."

Military aircrafts took to the skies honing in on the cities under attack. Apache gunships concentrated on areas launching fireworks. Detecting heat signatures from the makeshift bunkers, pilots locked on and deployed rockets destroying all the firework's launching pads.

Planes patrolled the borders firing warnings and then mowing down anyone who insisted on crossing into the United States.

Cole, Julie and Arturo left China as soon as they uncovered the plot and a helicopter could retrieve them and get them back to the aircraft carrier. They were in the air when rockets rained down on positions launching fireworks. Hearing the news, Cole rose. "We've got to get back to D.C. as soon as possible."

The Pilot flying the Greyhound called for Cole. "Commander Peterson, can you come to the cockpit for a second?"

Cole made his way to the cockpit. "What's up?"

The flight engineer pointed to a radar screen. "We've been monitoring these ships for a while now. They appear to be an attack fleet— Chinese, they're headed in the direction of our coast. We've called it in."

Cole took a headset. "This is Commander Cole Peterson; patch me in to the White House."

A few seconds later, he heard a response. "This is Marine One, Commander Peterson. Please hold for the President."

The President placed the call on speaker so that the Directors flying with him could hear. "Peterson, what do you have?"

Cole sat in a free seat in the cockpit. "Mr. President, we've picked up a Chinese attack fleet heading in the direction of our shores— it has to be linked to everything else that's going on."

The flight engineer excitedly tapped the screen. "They've just launched fighters. They know we're here."

The President grabbed another headset contacting the Joint Chief of Staff. "Unfriendly aircraft have entered the air near American Samoa. Scramble a squadron of F-18s. If the Chinese planes refuse to back off, splash them. Nothing is to harm that Greyhound. Make sure we send up additional planes to cover the Pacific border. Then send a fleet of subs— I want the Chinese fleet turned back. If they ignore our warnings, put them on the floor of the ocean."

Cole addressed Director Carson. "Sir, we've heard that fireworks were still launched in several cities. Is there any casualty count?"

Director Carson slowed the tapping pen. "We've dispatched MASH units. They're equipped to handle the situation as long as exposure was kept to a minimum. God knows how bad it'll be if people ignored the warnings."

The President took another call, which came in while working to handle the Chinese attack fleet. "Sir, there are reports of thousands of people emerging from tunnels at several border locations. Border Patrol said the ground broke open and people began spilling forth."

The President slammed his hand down hard. "My orders were clear; if they don't surrender use whatever means to stop them. This is a direct attack on the U.S. by an adversary intending harm— this is war; eliminate the threat!"

Apache gunships diverted to the border areas and their 30 mm M230 Chain guns spewed rounds liberally in front of the encroaching illegals failing to deter the advancing group.

At one Texas border, Pablo Juarez removed a burlap covering from a surface-to-air missile and positioned it to lock on one of the Apaches.

The pilot heard the unmistakable beep indicating a lock on his position and he fired a barrage of missiles from his helicopter. A red flare screeched towards the Apache just as his missiles bombarded the ground killing Pablo and everyone in the general area.

The Apache pilot took evasive measures, launching chaff to deter the approaching missile, but the explosion damaged the helicopter and it spun out of control towards the ground. There was no stopping its descent. The helicopter slammed hard against the desert floor. The pilot was stunned, yet directed his guns to the rapidly approaching crowd and released a hail of gunfire mowing down scores of the people.

The Battle was completely one-sided and ended with bodies covering the border area. The crew of the downed helicopter emerged fully armed and cut down anyone who refused to stop.

Several double-bladed Chinooks arrived carrying troops, who deployed to take the living people into custody. At more than one site, the illegals tossed finely ground Abrin towards the troops. But, like the illegals, the troops had received a vaccine against the powder and they proceeded without fear.

This scene was repeated at border crossings along the Southern border of the United States. Bodies littered these areas. At the conclusion, Carlos Acosta and Rafael Calderone were among the dead. Hundreds of Chinese and Mexican illegals were in custody and the U.S. military watched, stunned by a blatant unconventional attack of their borders.

The President landed at the Greenbrier and was immediately ushered to the underground bunker by a host of military officers.

"Get the Chinese President on the phone. He's got to answer for this unprovoked attack. He's lucky if we don't blow them off the face of the earth!"

Zhang paced back and forth across the floor of his South American villa. He'd thrown everything within reach and resigned to endless puffing of cigar after cigar with a constant grimace on his face. He stopped in the middle of the floor and looked at the Giant. "We're going to the United States."

The Giant shot a distressed look in Zhang's direction. "They're a bit on edge right now. Do you think that's a good idea?"

Zhang looked for something to throw. Finding nothing, he plopped into a chair. "We have passports listing us as citizens of Buenos Aries. We will not be a threat. Make sure Goldberger has a line on the girl. I can assure you that she won't come alone."

The Giant's eyebrows rose. "What do you have in mind?"

Zhang blew several smoke rings into the air. "If we take her, the people who have disarmed our plan will be exposed. I want to watch all of them suffer before they die."

The Giant poured Zhang a glass of Scotch after retrieving the bottle from the floor. "That may be possible as long as we're careful. We don't need to take any unnecessary risks."

Zhang snatched the glass. "Just make it happen. This isn't over! Once we're there, we will come up with a new way to take their country. We'll leave for New York as soon as they're dealt with. There, we can blend in, just two ordinary citizens in Chinatown."

The Giant left the room to solidify their trip.

Warren Goldberger took the Giant's call and wasted no time reaching his point. "What was that shit in the desert all about?"

The Giant brushed off the question. "Stick to matters that concern you. Do you know where the girl is?"

Goldberger shook his head. "She's somewhere in the D.C. area. Her agent isn't very forthcoming with information."

The Giant poured himself a rare glass of Scotch. "Find out where she is Master Zhang would like to meet with her."

Warren lifted the morning paper and scanned the story about the mayhem at several U.S. borders. "I'll place a call to her agent and see what I can do."

The Giant swallowed a large gulp of Scotch. "Make it happen!"

Goldberger called the Shaw Talent Agency and was informed that Ms. Shaw wasn't available until later in the day. "Make sure you have her call me— the boss is coming to town and would like to meet with her and Miss Roulette."

A playback of the call was immediately routed to Bernadette. She listened to the recording intently and put her phone on speaker so that Earnest could hear as well. "Who do you think he's referring to?"

He hunched his shoulders. "There's one way to find out— call him."

Bernadette moved to an untraceable phone and placed the call. "Mr. Goldberger, I understand your boss would like to meet with my client and me. Are you speaking of Mr. Nikitin?"

"Yes, of course." Warren answered much too quickly.

Bernadette's eyebrows shot up. The FBI had not released any information about the shootout at the Ford Theater, which was contained backstage. With the shooter dead and Borka in custody, it was unlikely anyone possessed additional details of the event, especially Vladimir's death. "When do you expect him to be in town?"

Goldberger sat back in his chair. "Day after tomorrow should give us enough time. Will noon work for you?"

Bernadette jotted a note. "That will be fine. We can meet here in my office."

Goldberger examined his fingernails. "I'll see if that works. Let's assume it will. Oh, and Ms. Shaw, do make absolutely certain that you client is present— nothing else is acceptable." He didn't wait for a response and placed the phone receiver in its cradle.

Bernadette called Zasha and filled her in on the call. "We'll have a team together ready to handle any surprises."

Zasha looked over to Jenna. "This has to go smoothly. I'm not sure Jenna can handle much more excitement."

Bernadette's face tightened. "We'll take care of her."

Zasha brushed the hair on her arm down. "I'm going to have Julie and Cole join us, Jenna is comfortable around them."

Goldberger waited until eleven the day of the meeting to call Bernadette's office as instructed. Once she answered, he went into action. "Ms. Shaw, I'm afraid that we have several appointments today, which requires me to ask you to join us instead of meeting in your office."

Bernadette slid her glasses off setting them on her desk. "You have no regard for my schedule. I don't find this convenient."

Goldberger sidestepped the complaint. "We have the Presidential suite in the Willard Hotel. A car is on its way to your office. You've already blocked the time on your calendar— there should be no objections."

"You assume a great deal. My time is not cheap, not to mention the fact that you're inconveniencing three additional people." She shot a glance towards Zasha, who nodded her approval.

Goldberger remained unrelenting. "Bring everyone you deem necessary, I'll see to a generous compensation for their time. The car is pulling up to your building as we speak. If Miss Roulette is not with your party, the driver will leave."

Bernadette snapped her fingers putting Zasha in motion. "Everyone is here. Have your driver call when he is out front. With the change of venue, we may need a few additional minutes to prepare."

Goldberger watched a GPS locater program on his computer screen. "He is in front of your building now. I'll let him know you need a few additional minutes."

Zasha waited for the call to disconnect. "Bernie, we can't take the team of agents that have assembled here. Cole called a few seconds ago, he, and Julie are trapped in traffic. There was a bad accident on I-395. The two of us are going to have to handle this one."

Bernadette called one of her agents into the room. "Call the SAC, we're going to need to get a back-up team to the Willard. Make it look good, we don't want them to know that an additional team has arrived."

Zasha stepped into the conversation. "We can probably stall our leaving about fifteen minutes. It's a tight window, but you'll have to make it fit." She turned facing Bernadette, who'd just walked over. "Ladies' night out; this could be what we've waited for."

An FBI hostage rescue team arrived at the Willard and drove to the delivery area that ducked beneath the back of the hotel. Delivery drivers and hotel staff in the area were detained until after the operation. The FBI didn't want the possibility of a leak causing them complications or compromising their efforts.

A white Rolls Royce sat in front of the Shaw agency waiting to take the ladies to their meeting. Bernadette was the first to see the car. She turned holding her hand up to stop the group. "This is a problem. Zhang Ju's signature is a white Rolls Royce."

Zasha pulled her iPhone out and dialed. "This meeting just got a lot more interesting." She turned her attention to the phone. "Oscar, if our ride to this meeting is any indication of what's about to happen, we're about to meet Zhang Ju face-to-face."

"Oh, fuck me!" Oscar was on his feet moving towards the Director's office. "How in the hell did he get into the country?"

Zasha turned her back to the door checking her purse for additional clips for her Glock. "The man has moved like a ghost for weeks. Make sure the FBI knows who we expect to encounter."

Director Carson's voice broke in. "Agent Davis, I want Zhang Ju alive. His attempt to wipe us off the map had to be coordinated with the assistance of the Chinese government. My experience with leeches is that they won't cling to a dying body— he'll give us what we need to deal with the Chinese."

"I'll make sure our group understands. It might be wise if you let the hostage rescue team know." Zasha ended the call and silenced her cell phone.

Chapter
79

Cole and Julie arrived and she jumped out of the car seeing Zhang's signature car. She leaned inside. "I'm going in, you can park and catchup in a few."

The white Rolls Royce pulled up to the front door of the Willard drawing attention of anyone in the area curious to see who would step from the car. The ladies exited and walked directly towards the elevators. The hostage rescue team leader dressed in casual clothing tugged on the end of his nose after making eye contact with Bernadette. It was a signal that they were ready to move.

Goldberger was having coffee in the lounge when he saw the ladies enter. He hit a speed-dial number on his cell phone. "They're here, Jenna, Ms. Shaw and two other women." He closed the phone and went to greet them. "Ladies, I'm so pleased you could join us. Let me get the elevator."

Bernadette viewed Warren coldly. "Do you have an agenda for this meeting?"

Goldberger laughed holding the elevator doors open. He waved a key card over a reader allowing him to access the Presidential suite button. "The boss will take care of that. I have to wait here in the lobby for our next arrival."

Julie turned to Zasha just as they entered the elevator. "Sorry I'm late."

Zasha waited for the doors to close. "Bernadette, you go in first followed by Jenna. Julie and I will pull up the rear."

The elevator reached its destination and the doors opened releasing them into a vestibule area of the Presidential suite. A chime inside the room let the Giant know that the elevator arrived. He opened the door without a word and held his hand out for the women to enter.

Two accordion screens, often used as room separators, with brightly painted red dragons dancing across a black background ushered them toward the meeting area. The narrowness forced them to move single file. Zasha was the last to pass the screen. Her body tensed as a tight sound quietly escaped her vocal cords.

Before anyone could turn, the Giant slipped a piano wire around Julie's throat. What he didn't see was Julie tuck her chin to the chest when the sound came from Zasha. The Giant was nearly twice her size and lifted her from the floor tugging mightily at the wire.

Things were happening so quickly that there was very little time to react. Bernadette turned pushing Jenna to the floor and swinging her Glock towards their attackers.

Zhang never removed the cattle prod tazer from Zasha, who was convulsing on the floor. He was also a beat ahead of Bernadette, who received a blast to the center of her chest.

Jenna screamed and rolled on the floor next to Zasha.

In a simultaneous motion, Julie jammed both hands towards the Giant's eyes and brought both feet sharply to his groin. The Giant collapsed to his knees wanting to grab his eyes and testicles at the same time.

"Enough!" Zhang yelled loudly and swung the gun in Julie's direction.

Jenna's screaming stopped as she noticed the butt of Zasha's Glock peaking from her purse. She remained crouched on the floor, sliding the gun into her hand.

Zhang trained the gun on Julie, but hesitated when the Giant reached out taking hold of her long French braid. The Giant snatched hard at her hair. "I'm going to drop this bitch from the balcony."

Zhang lowered his gun. "Be my guest, we have the two we came for."

With her head down, but straining her eyes to see the two men, Jenna saw Zhang take a step towards her. Without thinking, she jerked the gun upwards and fired several shots.

Julie spun as if her braid was an axis swinging the butt of her hand with all her force. Her blow caught the Giant squarely under his nose breaking the bone slamming it into his brain. His grip on her braid released and he fell like a redwood just being cut from its base— slow crashing hard to the floor.

The front doors of the suite crashed open. Red lasers cut the air in all directions settling on Zhang, the Giant and Jenna, who was still holding the gun.

Julie moved quickly to her side. "It's okay; you can put the gun down now." She took the gun and sat Jenna on the floor.

The hostage rescue team leader radioed to his men in the delivery area to bring three stretchers and a body bag. His men were attending to Zasha, Bernadette and Zhang, who was bleeding profusely from his groin area, which was the only spot Jenna hit.

A sharp breath followed by a painful groan crossed Bernadette's lips. "It feels like I was just hit by a train."

"Relax." One of the agents said, and kept her down. "It's going to hurt like hell, but you'll be home by tonight thanks to that vest."

Julie and Jenna eased Zasha to a slightly elevated position and Jenna held her head in her arms stroking her hair. "I'm sorry I'm so, so sorry."

Zasha was still feeling the effects from the shock but raised her eyes to see Jenna.

The look brought a flood of tears to Jenna even though she thought she had no tears left. "I fucked up, again didn't I?"

Zasha managed a slight shake of her head.

Cole and Earnest burst through the doors right behind the stretchers. "What the fuck?"

Zhang woke up to find himself in a hospital bed surrounded on all sides with metal bars. He looked around taking in his situation. Shifting one leg, the pain brought back the memory of Jenna's well-placed shot. He thought better of moving and settled back in the bed. The throbbing between his legs forced him to call out. "Hey somebody, give me something for this pain. Where the hell am I anyway?"

A voice from the shadows responded. "You are the guest of Homeland Security. We'll be happy to provide you with relief from your pain. But first, I need you to answer a few questions."

"I don't have shit to say." Zhang wasn't sure which side to turn to in order to avoid the voice, so he stared at a spot on the ceiling.

"Suit yourself— the pain will get a lot worse before you get anything for it. Even then, it will take a while to work." The voice fell back into the darkness.

Zhang lasted nearly five minutes and once again called to the voice. "I haven't broken any laws— you can't keep me here."

The voice moved closer. "You consider killing a United States' citizen an innocent act?"

Zhang turned his head toward the voice. "That was General Gan and his buddy the President of China. I've done nothing wrong."

"We both know that is a lie. We have evidence linking you to the Abrin fields in Brazil and your fireworks company in Linyang. In addition, we have sworn testimony from a witness tying you directly to the murder of a CIA agent. You'll be lucky if we don't let you rot in here."

A sharp pain radiated across Zhang's body causing him to dry heave several times. He caught his breath. "What do you want, money? I can see to it that you're a wealthy man."

The man switched on a bright light causing Zhang to thrash side to side to avoid it. After a few seconds the light went out. "We put drops in your eyes that makes light extremely painful. If you lie to me again, I'll put the light back on for a longer period of time. How were you and your plan involved with the Chinese government?"

Zhang opened his eyes and tears streamed from them as if they could wash away the pain. "China's population needs additional land to fulfill our destiny. The United States stands in the way of China annexing valuable land needed to guarantee our place in history. General Gan sought to offer a peaceful solution by bringing millions of our people to the United States. But my President would have none of it. He wanted to thin the herd here in the US first making it easy to enact his plan. I thought we should have initially tested the Abrin on Japan— everyone hates those bastards. But the President wanted a one-shot deal. He even said that he didn't care if it caused the mutual destructions of both countries, or the world."

Blue lights, which had a more cooling effect, came on around the perimeter of Zhang's cell. He shut his eyes tightly and Cole stepped from the shadows. "This doesn't make a lot of sense. Why would the Chinese government continue pumping billions of dollars into our economy if they were planning on wiping out our country?"

Zhang attempted a smile. "You Americans are so stupid. For the same reason a business man like me would continue to let a gambler spend way past his means— sooner or later you'll need a favor and since you've got him by the balls, he won't be able to refuse. Your government was being pimped and too stupid to realize that you're a whore." He coughed and cringed at the pain it caused. "Your economy eroded before and it will again. People in the U.S. lost their homes in record numbers, but that's nothing compared to how it will be this time. Do you know who owns forty percent of those loans…the Chinese government— instant housing for our people."

Cole watched for any physical signs that would indicate Zhang was lying. He would have expected him to shut his eyes tightly anticipating the harsh light if he were lying, but it didn't happen. "Why would you get involved with a plot like this. You're surely not a patriot? Hell, you even killed one of the highest-ranking members of your government."

Zhang turned towards Cole. "The son of a bitch owed me money and had the nerve to demand more for his involvement in this endeavor. I'm a businessman; I do what I do because of profits. And now that you have me, you expect that this is over. This was just a dry run...we'll be back."

Cole pressed a button on a remote releasing pain killer into Zhang's IV and watched as he drifted off.

CDC teams dispatched to the cities where fireworks deployed and struggled with the local hospitals and MASH units to test people for Abrin contamination. The majority of people tested were found to be negative. Those who tested positive were put on ventilation and given an intravenous cocktail to clean their bodies of the Abrin.

Neighboring cities and states were receiving overflow patients, yet even with the massive effort to save lives; five hundred people succumbed to the poison. Abrin disproportionately affects the young and elderly, who comprised the largest portion of the dead.

Cities and town where the mass exodus of illegals escaped, began experiencing Abrin related illness. Packs of the white powder carried by people crossing the border was blown into the air by gunfire in attempts to harm the troops.

Several of the illegals slipped past the military net set up to prevent them from entering the country. As agreed, they spread the Abrin on fields of plants waiting to be harvested and, in any water, supply they could find.

Heightened awareness to the symptoms of Abrin poisoning, enabled doctors in the border areas to catch most cases. But death had a head start. Migrant workers, who missed the news about the poison, were lying down in tomato and pepper fields succumbing to a painful demise at the hands of an unseen foe.

Reports about Abrin poisoning flooded the CDC and White House. The news revelation concerning the border areas being afflicted with Abrin raised the death toll past two thousand.

The President sat in a meeting directing his first question to the Director of the CDC. "What is the status of the Abrin vaccine?"

The Director pulled a report from his file and handed a copy to the President. "It's been successful in our preliminary testing, but we haven't conducted human testing yet."

The President sat the paper down. He looked at the Director without sharing the fact that the troops responding to the borders, were already given the vaccine. "What level of confidence do you have in this vaccine?"

He cocked his head to one side and tapped the report with one finger. "I'd say about ninety percent. It performed quite well in test given the circumstances."

The President pointed to the Director. "Your conviction is about to be put to the test." His attention turned to the Joint Chief of Staff. "I want military teams deployed everywhere we've received reports of infection. They need to set up additional MASH units to treat these people. Get the people vaccinated and put a halt to this shit. If we don't act quickly, the death toll we saw during nine eleven will pale in comparison. Additionally, I want teams to test the all exposed areas— isolate the Abrin source whether it be food, water or just the goddamn air. Get the word out so that the people can be vaccinated. We have to let the people know that we are working to protect them."

Director Carson lifted a hand. "Sir, sooner or later word's going to get out that the illegals, who attempted to cross our borders were responsible for spreading the Abrin. When that happens, Minutemen groups will go on rampages. Everyone saw the pictures in the papers of dead Chinese and Mexicans littering the border areas. People always overreact; anyone who looks like the dead will be at risk."

Director McGavin took over for Jessie. "Mr. President, this is the perfect time to address the immigration problem. None of us here would choose to deny the contributions immigrants have made to this country. However, most immigrants have chosen to follow procedure to settle here legally. Many second-generation Latinos and Asians have moved into the power structure of our country…"

The President cut him off. "All of whom have called to protest the treatment of the people, who tried to cross our borders the night of the fourth. Until we are no longer the most powerful free nation on Earth, outsiders will risk everything to come here. Embracing this inevitability was one of the cornerstones of my campaign. Attempting to reverse my stance because of an ill-conceived plot won't change the outcome— people will still come. Some may even seek to improve upon Zhang's attempt. God knows, there're plenty of crazy people out there. We will maintain our course."

Director Carson pulled his iPhone from his pocket to receive an incoming text. "Mr. President, Agent Peterson has managed a breakthrough questioning Zhang Ju. Now may be an excellent time to hear what he has."

The President pointed to the phone. "Put him on speaker."

Cole explained his findings to the group gathered at the White House. Hesitation surfaced numerous times during his presentation. "Mr. President, I've read over General Gan's manifesto multiple times. It did suggest China should wipe out the population of the U.S., but only if we rejected an offer to surrender half of the country to China. This ultimatum has never been suggested by anyone from China's power base."

The Secretary of State sat forward getting the President's attention. "Sir, we need to compile all our evidence and present it to the United Nations. After Iraq, they will only listen to concrete reasoning. We're going to need them if we have to go up against China."

"What a pile of shit!" The President ran his hand across his mouth. "I once heard Billy Ray Cyrus say, "The more you stomp around in a pile of shit, the worse it stinks." We're facing complete chaos in nine of the largest cities in this country and along our Southern border. If Abrin found its way into the food supply, chances are our problems are about to compound. I've got to address the Chinese government with the strongest warning possible. We've got to cease the madness and try not to piss them off, lest they slam their purse shut and devastate our economy. At the same time, I have to convince the United Nations that the threat from China is real and will affect the entire world, not just us. And let's not forget, I have to keep the people here calm— what should I tell them, this was the act of a few deranged individuals? Somebody tell me, which way to step out of the shit pile to stop the stink."

Within an hour after the President's address to the nation, Minute Men enhanced their website soliciting and receiving donations to be used as reward money for anyone who turned in employers hiring illegal workers in the U.S. Membership in their organization was growing exponentially. Men and women in trucks, cars and even minivans rolled up in parade fashion to known illegal border crossings.

The President of the organization found himself in front of a bank of cameras and microphones speaking to all the major news networks. "Finally, you understand what we've been saying about the illegal immigrant situation. If you leave a wound untreated, it will fester. That is exactly what has happened here. The President of these United States is willing to let people cross our borders willy-nilly and this time they came armed to kill us. We ain't gon' let that happen. The President said that the government was lacking in manpower." He pointed over his shoulder. "Just take a look out there— we got plenty of manpower. We're willing to do what it takes to stop anybody from running across our borders. We ain't afraid to call this what it is— war."

Newscasters replayed footage of the dead after the breech of the U.S. borders then switched to people hospitalized struggling to cling to life after being exposed to Abrin. They ended by showing crying parents clutching pictures of children, who had succumbed to the Abrin attack.

The link to China did not escape the attention of the Minute Men, who also chose to provide coverage in China Towns across the U.S., which also became the object of the news cameras, attention.

The President and the Attorney General watched the news coverage. The President sat back and folded his arms. "You're going to have to take a turn in front of the cameras and make absolutely certain that the people know that we will vigorously prosecute anyone acting outside the law."

The AG nodded. "Yes sir, Mr. President. With the coverage this thing is getting, it's going to be a tough sell to the American people; they're already siding with the Minute Men."

"The American people are the ones that put us in office largely based on immigration reform. It should not be difficult to convince them that we are acting in their best interests." The President's head made a sharp turn toward the television with the announcement of breaking news.

The Chinese President was on the screen expressing his outrage at having uncovered a plot by the Silent Dragon Triad boss, Zhang Ju and his top general, Wen Gan. While he spoke a video of General Gan facing a firing squad appeared. "The Chinese people are saddened by the acts of two of our citizens. The United States and China have been firm allies and such acts will not be tolerated." To punctuate his statement, the rifles fired and the covered head of General Gan bowed as the bullets tore through the medals on his chest.

The Chinese President continued. "The United States was the first country to offer aid during our devastating earthquake. In a gesture of good will, we would like to offer any assistance to bring relief to the tragedy they have suffered at the hands of our misguided citizens."

At Langley, Director Carson, Oscar, Zasha, Cole and Julie watched the report. Zasha tossed a pen on the table. "A million to one, that son of a bitch is lying. I'll bet you Gan isn't even under that hood."

"He neglected to mention the fleet of ships he dispatched in the Pacific." Cole slid his chair to the table. "I'd have to agree with Zasha on this one. This was all a show."

Julie observed the group with more than a tinge of sadness. "These events are going to bring a world of unjust persecution to my people living here working hard to make America a better place. My parents have already called about negative treatment. We have to endeavor to place the blame where it should rightly fall."

Director Carson folded his hands in front of his face. "Then I suggest we get to work. China is going to have a force field up against us, but we can't let that stop us. We're going to have to find a way into their inner sanctum to build our case."

Oscar closed his folder and stood. "I'll see who we have on the ground and check with NSA as well."

Director Carson dismissed the group and went to his office to call Director Jimmerson. "George, we've got to look into what's really going on in China."

Director Jimmerson rose and walked over to close his door. "I've already got boots on the ground. You're probably not surprised to learn that General Gan is alive and well. They've moved him to an undisclosed location. I hope to have a lock on his position in the next few days."

"I would have expected nothing less." Carson's pen began tapping and sliding through his fingers. "Once you find him, let's keep an eye on him. We need to let things settle a while before taking action."

"Then, you're going to love this." Director Jimmerson lifted a report. "The Chinese President has scheduled a trip to Havana in December. What do you want to bet that that son of a bitch didn't think to get an inoculation against Abrin poisoning?"

Carson's tapping stopped. "What do you have in mind?"

On December twentieth, the Chinese President arrived in Havana. His affinity for Cuban coffee was mentioned at nearly every stopping point in Havana.

Alejandro Javier saw to it that one of the people assigned to the Chinese President's quarters was employed by him, including his daughter, Marianna.

The Chinese President returned from a tour of Havana and requested a Café Cubano. Marianna brought the coffee into the President's quarters and prepared it in front of him. She loaded two heaping teaspoons of sugar in the demitasse cup and stirred.

The Chinese President watched and ran his hand up and down Marianna's thigh. "Take the first sip to make sure you have prepared the coffee just the way I like it."

Although, she knew the sugar was laced with Abrin, she didn't hesitate complying with his orders. Getting out of the room was her only concern. She was headed home, where she could be attended to by a medical team. "It's perfect, sir."

"As are you." He took the coffee downing most of the contents in one swallow.

"Will there be anything else?" She took the empty cup and placed it on a tray.

The President resumed stroking her thigh. "You can stay with me."

Marianna stepped aside and held her breath before speaking. "I'll send someone to attend to your needs."

The President removed his hand. "Very well; are you sure you won't reconsider?"

Marianna left the room and proceeded to a waiting car, which drove her to a dock. There, she climbed aboard a boat and retrieved a cell phone. Her call was answered promptly. "Feliz Navidad, Papa."

Alejandro breathed a sigh of relief. "I'll see you at home. Don't be alarmed, the vaccine has protected you. Thank you, Marianna."

A house sat alone on a hill in Ningxia, China. Even after plastic surgery, the man walking the small dog was recognized as General Gan. The person watching him at a distance put the monocular in his pocket and pulled a knife with a seven-inch blade from his side.

When he was a few feet from General Gan the little dog turned and barked aggressively. He approached the general without fear. "General Gan, Comrade President sent me to find you." He grabbed the General behind his head and slammed the knife into his chest. "You and Zhang Ju are responsible for my sister's death. She was killed in the desert trying to make it to America."

General Gan's eyes widened and his lips parted as he fell to the ground.

The man who stabbed him proceeded to cut out his heart and tossed it to the dog after tying his leash to the General's leg. "You tore out my heart; now we're even."

The White House Christmas party was in full gear the night of December twenty second. Director Carson's iPhone chimed and he pulled it from his pocket. A breaking news video came on the screen. He rushed to the President's side. "Sir, you need to see this."

The President took the iPhone watching the video. *While touring coffee plantations in Cuba today, the Chinese President's breathing became labored. Doctors traveling with the group attended to the Head of State. Their efforts were unsuccessful and at seven this evening, he died. An autopsy later revealed that the President suffered from a lung ailment.*

Director Carson took the iPhone after the President stopped the feed. He leaned close to the President and whispered in his ear. "Merry Christmas, Mr. President."

Made in the USA
Middletown, DE
18 October 2022

12997035R00189